INDIAN LAW

James Tindall

Look for the following novels from this author:

Jagged Grass (Book I, Seminole Trilogy)

The Transparency (Book II, Seminole Trilogy)

Sun God's Treasure (Book I, Sun God series)

Alas Omega (Book II, Sun God series)

Authors Note:

This is Book III of the Seminole Trilogy.

INDIAN LAW

Book III

Seminole Trilogy

James Tindall

Library of Congress Cataloging-in-Publication Data

Tindall, James

Indian Law/James Tindall

p. 329

ISBN: 978-1-7372476-6-1

Published by DTP Publishing, Denver, Colorado

Printed in the United States of America

10 9 8 7 6 5 4 3 2 1

ISBN: 978-1-7372476-6-1

DEDICATION

To the Seminole Indians of the

Seminole Tribe of Florida.

The fiercest of all warriors,

keepers of the Glades,

and,

to my friends in the intelligence community,

and,

Felisha, Ilasiea, and Patrick.

James Tindall

Disclaimer:

The locations mentioned herein are real. While the many other geographic settings mentioned are also real, any description or likeness of characters that resemble persons living or dead is entirely coincidental.

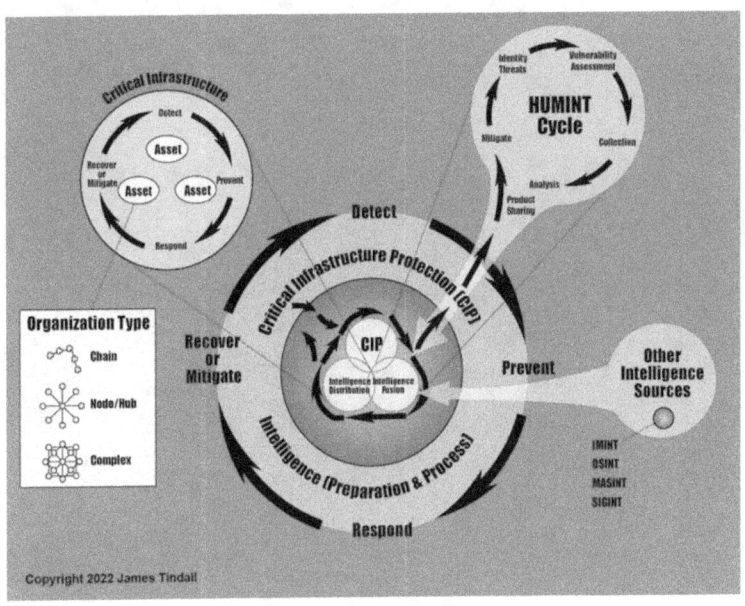

Copyright 2022 James Tindall

CHAPTER 1

Li's heart was beating faster than he had ever known as he fled his pursuers. His uncle had talked him into joining the army so he could build a foundation for the future. Although he had never felt good about it, he had followed his uncle's advice and joined the military. They promised him lots of travel within the country, but directly after basic training he was stationed at a remote army post northeast of Hong Kong near the coast in Guangdong Province; he was never allowed to leave. It was so secret that only those stationed at it knew of its existence. Li could hear the men behind him slowly getting closer as he ran through the mangrove swamp, trying to reach the coast before they overtook him.

A month before, he had blackmailed a fellow soldier who kept a cell phone hidden outside the post perimeter and was able to call his fiancé. After describing the computer system he guarded, she instructed him how to wire it so he could call her. Once a week they talked, keeping conversations short and never mentioning names for fear of being caught. Like any good journalist, his fiancé had begun pursuing a story about his post. Because its name and location were secret, eyebrows were quickly raised. There were rumors of a journalist digging for answers in Hong Kong, but so far, she had eluded the MSS. They didn't know who she was but knew that she had to be getting information from someone inside the post. Suspecting that the officers had somehow found out, Li slowly prepared his escape by getting his hands on enough bamboo to build a small raft, which he kept hidden in the forest near the shoreline. Growing up in a fishing family, he was an expert raft builder.

The chain-link fence around the post had small gullies here and there, washed out by heavy rains. He had searched until he found one that was covered with undergrowth and unnoticed. Continually patrolling the perimeter, it was the one perk he was able to give himself. He had become more nervous each passing day because his inner self kept telling him something was very wrong. So, on a hot sunny day, a few weeks earlier, he had begun sneaking out of his bunk and hurrying to the coast, just over a mile away. Working for two hours each time, about three times per week, he had completed his small raft and hidden it away, covering it with reeds and grasses. For the past two weeks, he had smuggled food and water to it.

The bombshell had come the evening before while he was standing guard. He overheard a technician listening to a recording on the computer and immediately recognized his fiancé's voice.

"What the hell?" he thought. "How could this be?"

It was the conversation they had about no soldier at the post making it home. Somehow, he had connected the wires improperly; the recording would be his death warrant. When Li saw the colonel heading down into the computer bunker just prior to his shift, an ominous foreboding fell upon him. It was time to go.

Dusk had settled; that time of day where you could see well enough to recognize objects, people, and animals, but too dark to see very far ahead. Li was running fast as he could.

"Zhàn"

Li froze in his tracks, looking about for the source of the voice. He quickly recognized the silhouette, his lieutenant, who had leveled his Type 92, 9 mm pistol directly at Li's chest.

"Come now," Lieutenant Guo said. "You didn't think you would go alone, did you?"

"You knew?" Li asked.

"Yes. I have been watching you. The commander was going to arrest you during chow. I was hoping that you would make a run for it before he did."

"That means you know why I am going," Li stated.

"Certainly," Guo said. "Why do you think I have been here so long. Everyone who leaves is killed. This post is far too secret to end up on a CIA watch list."

"I've wondered what all the computers are for, even though they do not look like computers," Li replied. "They look like a framework from a construction site."

"They are for hacking," Guo replied, holstering his pistol. "Do you have room enough on your raft for both of us?"

"Yes lieutenant," Li said. "With a second person, we can make better speed."

"Good, let's go," Guo said. "Judging from the sound we have maybe thirty minutes before they catch up to us."

The two raced toward the coast. There was just enough moonlight to cast small shadows, but not enough to keep from getting smacked in the face from bamboo, mangrove limbs, and shrubs that grew densely along their path. They reached the hidden raft about ten minutes later and slid it into the water.

"See that small island a few hundred yards away?" Li asked, pointing.

"Yes, I see it," Guo said.

"We must push toward it as fast as we can and circle around to the back side," Li exclaimed.

"Let's not wait."

Li had made two makeshift paddles and cut a couple of longer, slim bamboo poles to push with. He quickly moved to the front of the raft, poling on his left, and Guo to the rear, poling on the right. Poling together, the lightweight bamboo raft sped across the calm water, reaching the small island, built by sand and alluvium coming off the slopes. Breathing heavily by the time they reached it, they circled behind a mangrove thicket, pulling the raft close while they continued to watch the shoreline. It had become fully dark; they could barely distinguish a few taller trees along the edge of the water. A few minutes later they saw flashlights on the narrow beach. They had barely escaped.

"We need to hide," Guo said.

"Why?" Li asked.

"Patrol boats will be coming shortly," Guo replied.

"I hadn't thought of that," Li replied. "Let's pull the boat into the inner part of this thicket, there's an open patch of water inside and the mangroves are too thick for lights to penetrate."

"Good idea," Guo said.

A few minutes later the two were inside the small island. It was then they heard the roar of boat engines. They could see the glow of lights along the shore as the boats provided better illumination for the search. High tide had washed their tracks and drag marks from the raft away leaving no evidence of them entering the water.

"Hopefully they will think we went along the shoreline," Guo said. "That will give us more time to slip away. What was your strategy for escaping?"

"I guessed patrol boats would eventually come," Li said. "So, I figured I would hide out in this place for several days until they assumed I had made a clean getaway in the forest."

"Not a bad idea," Guo said. "How long did you anticipate for food and water?"

"One week," Li said. "Guess we will just have meager rations

4

for about four days with two of us."

"That will work," Guo said. "Let's get some sleep and come morning, we'll develop a new strategy."

The weather was as hot and muggy in Miami as it was in Guangdong Province. When Genesis and Li Na pulled up to the small hotel, it was literally ringed with security. The average person wouldn't notice, but they weren't average. They had been in the security and spook business too long.

"Obviously we are not meeting just the Director of DOE," Genesis said. "He doesn't travel with this much protection. There is a big fish here."

"Who do you think it is?" Li Na asked. "You don't think . . ."

"Yes, I do," Genesis replied. "The Director CIA."

"Have we ruffled too many feathers?" Li Na asked. "What would he be doing here?"

"I'm guessing he wants a favor; a big favor," Genesis replied. "He's not here for a suntan. Obviously, someone or some group in your triads may have something of great value that he wants."

"What could it be?" Li Na asked.

"We're about to find out," Genesis replied.

No sooner had he pulled the car to the curb than an agent opened each of their doors, quickly ushering them inside. Genesis had identified eight men directly around the hotel, several more across the street, three on the roof, and entering the lobby, another seven. The group had taken over the entire hotel. No staff were present, only two well-dressed men in business suits sitting in lounge chairs in the middle of the lobby. Behind them were three more agents, all armed with automatic weapons. Genesis and Li Na became apprehensive, but they could only wait and listen to find out what was so important.

"Have a seat Genesis," Jonas Rothman, Director DOE said, gesturing with his hand. "You too miss."

As they took the seats offered them, Li Na felt the eyes of the two men on her."

"We will get directly to the point," Jonas said. "We need something and you two are going to get it for us."

"And if we refuse?" Li Na asked.

"You will not! Let me introduce myself. I am Phillip Ross, Director of the CIA."

"You don't know much about me," Li Na said. "What makes you think I would cooperate."

"I know all about you Li Na Liu," Phil said. "You'll cooperate because you'll get what you want and so will we."

You could cut the air with a knife. The meeting had gone from cordial to high tension in an instant — the two sat glaring at each other.

"Bring us some lemonade," Phil said. "Let's unsnarl the tiger here. Genesis, you've known me for a long time and have run many missions for us under your alias JB, which you will now begin using again — immediately. It is a necessity for security and intelligence reasons; Jonas will fill you in later. It is critically important. I would not be meeting you here and discussing this with you if it were not for Jonas who brought it to our attention that both of you performed very well on your latest operation."

"What are you referring to?" JB asked.

"Your recent activities," Jonas replied. "You see, you have uncovered a deep cover plot for an attack on our energy resources."

"You mean the power grid?" Li Na asked. "What do the triads have to do with that?"

"It is not the triads themselves," DCIA said, tossing a large photo on the table between them. "It is the single man that controls them. The man in that photo."

Li Na glared at it, instantly recognizing her enemy, the man that had given the order to kill her family. Despite the years gone by, she would recognize him anywhere.

"That is Ye Bocheng," Li Na gasped. "How did you get this?" "Resources," Jonas said. "Our combined resources are far superior to yours."

"That is correct," DCIA said. "Tell me what you know about him and then, I'll tell you what we know."

"Very well," Li Na said. "He works with the Hong Kong triads and from what I know, is my boss's boss and works out of Beijing. I found out he was the one who killed my parents and gave the order to kill Genesis, I mean JB's fiancé. We have been studying him and how to find him. When we do, I'm going to chop his head off."

As she spoke, the passion and anger in her voice increased. Her hands began quivering as she sipped the lemonade that had been placed before her. She was staring menacingly into the eyes of the CIA Director. He stared back, realizing that more than anything, she wanted this man dead. His spy sense knew they could make a deal that would be acceptable.

"Now, I'll tell you what we know," Phil said calmly. "The man before you is General Ye Bocheng of the People's Liberation Army Ground Force operating out of a small, secret military base somewhere in southeast China. He is also leader of several triads, and it was through them that he got his hands on a countermand device that can decapacitate nuclear energy plants. Combined with computer hacking that from the post he has been able to keep us from finding, this man is very dangerous to us and our allied countries. He can hack into a power grid with his computers and devastate a nuclear plant with the countermand device."

"Why don't you just send in a cruise missile to take him out?" JB asked. "It would save us all a lot of trouble."

"We considered it if we could find him," Jonas replied. "Even the CIA has been hampered since the Chinese took over Hong Kong and we had to move Hong Kong Station elsewhere, not to mention the course of action you suggest would lead to war."

"That's correct," Phil said. "So, what we are offering is combining our resources. Because both of you are private citizens, you can work as our operatives. The advantage is that Chinese intelligence has no record of you. We will give you full support, whatever you need and of course, pay you well."

"What do you want in return?" JB asked.

"First, we need the countermand device," Jonas said. Then, we need to find out what kind of computer system he has and either destroy it or plant a virus in it."

"However," Phil began. "We need to find out where this secret base is so that you can complete the mission. We are working on that, but you may be able to help us through your triad connections Li Na. We either find the base or find him and tail him to it. All our resources are at your disposal."

"As are ours," Jonas replied.

"I just want him dead!" Li Na exclaimed.

"Once we get what we need, I don't care if you cut his nuts off and feed them to him," Phil responded. "This is far larger than a vendetta. Thousands of lives could be at stake, perhaps millions. General Bocheng may start with the United States, but it won't stop there. What do you say? Deal? Our resources for your help?

Li Na eyed JB, who nodded slightly. She looked around the room at the agents and back to the two directors. Watching each one carefully, as if she were a predator.

"Deal," she said. "We will need your resources on call. We will work with your people to come up with another strategy to find Bocheng and get what we all want."

"One more thing," JB said. "I've worked with you before. We do not want anyone knowing us or what we are up to. Only those with need to know."

The two directors looked back and forth from Li Na to JB. They had gotten what they came for and were delighted as they stood to leave, shaking the hands of their new agents.

"What we need is for you to give a good dose of Indian Law to him," Jonas said.

"What's that?" Li Na asked.

"It's right or wrong Miss," Jonas replied. "They don't believe in getting the authorities involved in something they can solve themselves. They become judge, jury, and executioner. So, solve it JB and you, Li Na."

"I look forward to working with both of you," Phil said. "It promises to be interesting. And JB, it's good to have you back in the fold."

Li Na stood watching them as they walked out the door, their agents tailing them. Within two minutes, they were gone. The staff re-entered the room as the two of them sat silently in thought, sipping lemonade.

The office of Congressman Blaine Childress from New Mexico looked posh to the average eye, but to Childress, it was a mere means to an end for stealing the taxpayer's money. When he couldn't steal it, he was looking for new opportunities for additional revenue streams. Serving on and connected with most of the Congress and Senate energy committees, there was an endless line of people, countries, and companies continually attempting to convince him of their position and needs. Always doing favors, he was quite savvy at developing relationships in which he was on the receiving end of large payoffs. Like many congress critters, he also was on the Chinese payroll, constantly doing favors. Tragically for him, he didn't realize he was in the third stage of spy recruitment — developing. It was the stage where intelligence officers didn't lead off by asking potential sources to secretly betray their country or even their employer. Instead, it is the stage in which recruiters begin to ask for trivial favors to establish rapport and trust. Because such favors are generally small, it is the most dangerous phase of the five phases of spy recruitment because it is the phase where the recruit unknowingly crosses the line into espionage. The phase where the recruit begins a treasonous path. Blaine was on that path; he had been blinded by the money, graduating to the handling phase without realizing it. However, there would be no forgiveness for the information he was selling to the Chinese. It was treason at its highest level.

"Your two o'clock is here sir," the intercom crackled.

"Send him in."

The door opened and closed softly as the man turned to face Blaine from across the room.

"Clint, so nice to see you again. Do you have what I asked for?"

"Yes congressman," Clint replied, placing the large manilla envelope on his desk.

"Be seated while I go over this," Congressman Blaine said as he began to study the contents. "Very good Clint. This is an excellent start."

"What do you mean a start?" Clint asked. "I gave you everything you requested for the southeast grid and that's most of what you wanted for the western grid."

"I need all the facilities and their capabilities," Blaine said. "You're in too deep to get out. After all, you're getting forty percent of the take. I couldn't do it without you and if they link us to what is likely going to happen, death will be a welcome relief."

"I never wanted this," Clint hissed. "You pushed it on me."

"No, it was the money you wanted; just like me," Blaine replied, glaring.

Clint stood without saying anything, his eyes narrowing as he looked at the congressman. He knew the man was right. Sadly, there was nowhere to turn. The desire for money outweighed his common sense.

"You mentioned deep," Clint said. "How deep?"

"Too deep," Blaine replied. "You'll find out soon enough. I need the rest of the western grid information within a few hours."

"I'll go back to the hotel and work it up for you," Clint replied.

That will make us even."

"Yes," Blaine replied. "We will have each done our part. I'll meet you near the Lincoln Memorial in three hours."

General Ye Bocheng of the People's Liberation Army Ground Force arrived at the docks on an Army Patrol Boat. For the most part, the dock looked abandoned. Baren earth where the road led from the beginning of the dock to its end made it look seldom used. The road was invisible to those who traversed the river, as well as from the air. He stood on the dock momentarily, watching downriver as if he expected someone was following him, an old habit in the intelligence world. He was a slim man with a hawkish face and penetrating stare. On the post and within the triads, no one dared disobey him if they wished to live. The sun had just set as he turned to get into his vehicle, his driver opening the door.

There was commotion on the post, officers and men scurrying about when the general arrived. His second in command came running up, out of breath as Ye got out.

"What is wrong Colonel Wu?" Ye asked.

"General," Wu said. "Two men are missing, Lieutenant Guo and private Li. We were going to arrest Li at chow as you commanded, but he didn't show up."

"How long have they been gone?" Ye asked, looking across the post.

"Since just before sunset as nearly as we can tell," Wu said. "We picked up the trail of at least one of them going toward the coast. I dispatched a squad to follow the trail and gunboats down the river. So far, they have found nothing, no signs at all."

"Did you assume they would head for the coast, or did you find a trail?" Ye asked.

"We found a definite trail," Wu replied. "The sentry's discovered a small gully under the fence beneath undergrowth and tracked it from there. Apparently, it has been frequently used."

"Hmmmm," Ye mused. "A planned escape. That's a first. It was bound to happen at some point."

"I will order the men to keep searching," Wu said. "I will also order the gunboats to coordinate with them."

"No," Ye replied. "It's dark. You're not going to find them until daylight. Post two guards by the shore and recall the rest. Muster again at dawn. Tell the gun boats to maintain their search."

"Yes General," Wu said as he trotted away shouting orders.

"That journalist was the cause of this," Ye thought. "Her stories had reached the ears of men on post and created fear that they would not survive after leaving. They still would not, it was time to muffle this annoying journalist and her friends."

Engine sounds reverberated across the water from three patrol boats posted offshore.

"Those boats could not have gotten here so quickly," Guo said.

"They are from the river. You know the dock area where they land supplies for the post?"

"I have seen it only once when I arrived," Li replied. "But those boats look like the ones I saw there."

"They are LX-12x border patrol boats armed with heavy machine guns and typically an eight-to-ten-man crew. They will not give up the search until they are certain they will not find us."

"They are only looking for me," Li said. "They do not know you are here."

"Not yet perhaps," Guo said. "But when I don't show up to my post, which was an hour ago, they will presume we both made a run for . . . ."

Guo was interrupted by the staccato sounds of machine gun fire. Crawling through the mango roots, he could see that the patrol boats were firing into shrubs along the beach and into the small islands like the one they were on. If anyone were hiding in them, they'd be killed or follow human nature and make a run for it.

"They are firing into islands like this one," Guo said. "We have nowhere to hide."

"Not true," Li said. "Once we determine where the boat is going to fire from, we can turn the raft on its side and duck into the water behind it."

"Good idea," Guo responded. "The raft will take some of the energy out of the bullets and the water is at least six feet deep."

"Let's tie a rope to the bottom of the mango roots and we can pull and hold ourselves below the water," Li said. "It is the best protection we are going to get."

While the two prepared, they could hear machine gun fire from several different directions. The boats had separated and were firing sporadically at each small island they came to. Only a few minutes passed before one of the patrol boats headed directly toward them. Before its spotlights were close enough to illuminate the mangroves, the two had turned the raft on its side and made ready to pull themselves under the water. The first bullets ripped through the leaves above them while they pulled themselves down.

Li could hear the bullets striking the raft and shrubs above. He could also feel the concussion from the bullets as they impacted the water. A couple of times he could feel the energy of the water trail hit him when a bullet passed close by. The thirty seconds the bullets were firing seemed like an eternity. Suddenly they stopped, and he could feel the vibrations of the boat's engines pulling away toward another target. He let go of the rope and surfaced, trying to regain his breath as he breathed heavily. His eyes adjusted quickly to his surroundings; he found Guo lying face down in the water. He put the raft back on its bottom and struggled to get Guo aboard then, began pumping Guo's chest and gave him mouth to mouth. In a few seconds, Guo began sputtering salt water and regained consciousness. The small amount of moonlight revealed a darker splotch than water on Guo's shirt. He had taken a bullet to his left shoulder above the armpit. Li helped him sit up while he checked his back. The bullet had passed through without striking bone. Lacking medical supplies, Li took off his shirt and then, removed his tee shirt to use it for a bandage. Doing the best he could, he dressed the wound and laid Guo back down.

"You need to keep pressure on the wound to stop the bleeding," Li said. "I will also immobilize it with a makeshift sling."

"Sorry to put a monkey wrench in our strategy," Guo said, grimacing. "It wasn't my intent."

"The best laid plans seldom work as intended," Li said. "The problem we have now is that we cannot wait in hiding. We will need to move in darkness to get medical help before infection sets in."

"That doesn't sound promising," Guo replied, feeling the pain come alive around his wound."

"I agree," Li replied. "We have two options. The first is to head toward Taiwan and hope we run into someone friendly."

"Hmmmm, we are more likely to run into our navy than a friendly. What's your other option?"

"My fiancé and I have a friend in the outskirts of Shantou about twenty-five miles from here," Li said. "I grew up on the ocean. My father was a fisherman. All my life I have paddled rafts because that is all we could afford. I figure I can get us to Shantou in about seven hours. My friend will hide us, and we will figure out what to do after we get you patched up."

"Are you sure you can get us there that quickly?" Guo asked.

"Positive."

"It sounds like the patrol boats have gone back upriver," Guo said. "Looks like that's our safer option. Let's head for your friend's place. I'd rather die quickly from a bullet than a slow infection."

Within a few minutes, Li had managed to get Guo and the raft to open water. Looking carefully about, he began paddling the raft toward their destination. It was so light, being constructed from bamboo, that is slid across the calm water effortlessly. As Li had promised, they made Shantou long before daylight.

Director DOE and DCIA had boarded their private jet in Miami and were on the way back to Washington DC. Jonas was staring out the window deep in thought.

"What's troubling you?" Phil asked.

"If we do not find this post and the countermand device, we're in big trouble," Jonas responded. "Our entire country will be at risk of going back to 1830 in the blink of an eye."

"Quite correct," Phil replied. "Our military defenses will be strained to the utmost and our country would be open to attack from any major power."

"Our entire critical infrastructure system will fail," Jonas said. "Without power our water distribution, communications, banking, emergency services, and other critical infrastructures will become inoperable. Millions will die within two weeks."

"I have worked with JB before," Phil said. "He is the best. Tell me. How good is this, Li Na?"

"I have worked with him too," Jonas replied. "I agree. Ah, she is very cunning and intelligent. She has her own spy network and has worked in intelligence and counterintelligence with the Chinese for years. I would put her right up there with JB. They are our best hope of pulling this off."

"Good," Phil said. "I would hate to know the fate of our nation rested on two novices."

"We need to give them our full support," Jonas said. "As long as they have the needed resources, they will make it happen. I also need to agree with JB. The fewer who know about this the better. What are your thoughts?"

"I agree totally," Phil said. "I'll re-activate JB under his former ops name so that none of my people will suspect anything. Based on the location, the only person who needs to know besides us is our Chief of Station Taiwan and Albert Pike."

"Why there?" Jonas asked.

"After the Chinese took over Hong Kong, it was too risky to maintain Hong Kong Station," Phil said. "We had to adjust in Taiwan to accommodate various personnel, including a Mandarin speaking COS, and resources. Besides, we are certain that General Bocheng is somewhere in southeast China."

"Li Na is an expert in that area," Jonas said. "I am sure they will find him. If you don't mind my asking, what was JB's ops name?"

"That's extremely classified," Phil said. "However, under the circumstances I will tell you and you will tell no one else. Agreed?"

"Agreed."

Phil picked up a small pad and wrote the name down, revealing it to Jonas. Afterward, he crumbled the piece of paper and put it into his half-empty champagne glass. The ink began to immediately dissolve.

"You would need to know anyway in case you get a call from our COS," Phil said. "This thing could get as hairy as they come and very political. You need to be prepared for every scenario you can."

"I understand."

Li Na and JB had flown to a secret training camp in Virginia to hone their skills with electronics, pistol, and knife. Communications were a key element for their success. It had been a while since JB had used satellite communications equipment. In the past it had been rather bulky and heavy, which would not be suitable for this mission. He was hoping the equipment had improved and was easier to use. When he and Li Na walked into the building, along with one of her men, the instructor was waiting behind a table that had only two pieces of equipment on it. A small radio and a larger radio with an antenna that looked like a spiderweb.

"I am instructor Cook. Please sit down and we will begin. My commander has informed me that time is of the essence. I was briefed a little bit on your backgrounds."

Cook picked up the small radio showing it to them so they could see it clearly. A sergeant walked up and handed each of them one as Cook explained how it worked.

"This radio is what we call the 171. It weighs just over a pound and is very versatile, compact, and easy to use. It's what we call a multi-mission solution. Its basic benefits compared to past equipment is that it has robust voice and data for missions that move quickly, it's resilient in both contested and congested environments, it also has a simplified operation along with versatile operational modes including MANET and legacy LOS. From what the commander told me of the potential terrain you will be operating in, this should serve you well. Any questions?"

"What's the range?" JB asked.

"Up to 10 miles on flat terrain," Cook said. "If you're in steep mountainous terrain, maybe three miles give or take a mile. All radios still have communication problems in tunnels, concrete buildings, steep terrain, and similar conditions. If you are aware of equipment shortcomings, you should find this radio sufficient to maintain communications within your group. Any other questions?"

There were no other questions about the radio, so the instructor moved to the next piece of equipment on the table.

"This is what we call the Falcon," Cook said. "You will find that it will expand mission effectiveness with wideband, SATCOM, and legacy narrowband. At twelve pounds, it is much smaller and lighter than similar radios you may be familiar with. It has MUOS-ready hardware and NINE Suite B encryption for secure voice and data up to Top Secret. I'll demonstrate its use later. This spider web looking apparatus is a portable UHF, SATCOM antenna. It is light weight and easy to set up. Both these radios should allow you to communicate with your team as you complete your mission."

"I have a question," Li Na said. "Is there a radio we can use to communicate to our group and also to satellite?"

"There is," Cook said. "However, it's a tactical SATCOM radio, like a secure walkie talkie. It utilizes the Distributed Tactical Communications System provided by the Enhanced Mobile Satellite Services Program Office within the Commercial Satellite Communications Office of the U.S. Space Force. It is light weight and works well but since yours is a very clandestine mission I would hesitate to use it due to its powerful signal."

"In other words, the target could probably fix our location," JB said.

"Precisely," Cook replied. "So, opt for a little more weight, especially if you have more to your force than the three of you. Let's take a short break and then, get started on how to efficiently operate the equipment."

The three spent the next five days learning in various combat-type environments how to operate the equipment without fail. Li Na's colleague, Xin Cao, would be the primary operator and he would also teach the remaining members of Li Na's team how to operate the devices.

Lieutenant Guo and Li had reached the large harbor of Shantou, often called Swatow. A prefecture-level city on the eastern coast of Guangdong Province with over five million in population in city proper, but like any metro area around the globe, the total population was over twelve million. In effect, it was a megacity — a city with ten million or more. In the 19th century it had been a city of some significance being one of the treaty ports that had been established for Western trade and contact. It was one of the original special economic zones of China established in the 1980s. Although it had not fared as well as other such cities, it had positioned itself as eastern Guangdong's economic center and was home to Shantou University. The harbor was filled with sampans, ferry's, fishing boats, and large commercial vessels. The small raft was one of many in the bay allowing the two men to easily blend with the mix of other boats and ships.

Li had been here multiple times to visit their friend with his fiancé and knew the harbor well enough to find a place to put their raft, away from curious and prying eyes. He had paddled it to the west end of a container storage yard at Longhugou and slipped it down a short tributary offshoot of the harbor. Conveniently, a small group of trees overhung the water creating a perfect place to hide it. Once hid away, he helped Guo up the small bank and they began walking along the end of the storage yard, west through a construction area. They had about two hours of darkness before they needed to be off the street.

"What does your friend do?" Guo asked as they walked along Haibin Road.

"She and her husband are journalists," Li replied. "They had to go into hiding and are very careful about what they write and how they put it out after the military moved into Hong Kong."

"They are anti-government then?" Guo asked.

"Not so anti-government as pro Hong Kong," Li replied. "They don't push the PRC agenda. And, like all governments, those who don't push the current agenda are considered enemies, except in China, where it can get you shot."

"I'm not so pro government myself anymore," Guo said. "It's all about control and power and they can never get enough."

"That's right," Li said. "Everyone sees it, but there is little they can do about it."

"How far do we need to go?" Guo asked, the pain from his

wound beginning to hamper his pace and movement.

"They live in the Shipaotai Residential District," Li said. "Luckily for us it is in the northeastern quarter. It's about a mile from here, maybe twenty-five minutes."

"Let's hurry," Guo said. "We must not be seen."

The two walked as quickly as they could, east along Haibin Road and then, walked north on Dongxia S Road then, back west across several streets until they reached Linghai Road.

"My friends live on this street," Li said. "That high-rise apartment there, nodding in the direction."

"Will they be home?" Guo asked.

"Yes," Li said. "The husband will leave for work in about an hour, but the wife works on her computer. Don't worry, it's set up so the government and police cannot track her. She's adept at electronic intelligence."

A few minutes later, they were at the door. Li knocked three times, followed by two more knocks and finally four knocks in a row.

"That's a signal?" Guo asked. "Yes, so they know we are friends."

A shadow at the peephole indicated they were being watched. The door cracked open revealing a slim woman who quickly drew them inside. She looked furtively left and right down the hallway before closing and locking the door.

"You look horrible," Pei said. "Come, sit."

"It is good to see you again," Li said "I won't beat around the bush. We're in trouble and need help."

"Kang," Pei called out, raising her voice a little. "Come."

Her husband Kang appeared from the bedroom, a long wooden club in his hand. A smile broke out on his face; he leaned the club against the wall.

"Li, it is so nice to see you again," Kang said. "I heard a little bit about what you were talking about. How can we help?"

"We need to patch up Guo first and then, we need to find a way out of China," Li said.

"That will be difficult," Kang replied. "But there may be a way."

"Tell us what happened," Pei said.

Li and Guo rehearsed the events that had got them here and the escape in detail, leaving nothing out. It was the only way to gain their trust and assistance. As they told their story, Pei and Kang watched them carefully, glancing knowingly at each other. The two men were facing hardships that had become common place in China. They needed to move quickly.

"We may have a way to help you," Pei said. "The problem will be getting you out of country."

"What do you think is best way? Li asked.

"It's not the best way," Kang interjected. "It is the only way with our limited resources."

"Your fiancé Lan developed some contact resources from the U.S. government," Pei said. "She was in contact with a couple of people she and others believed were from Hong Kong Station."

"You mean CIA?" Guo queried. "That's what I heard they were, but when the PRC took over, they vanished."

"Yes," Pei said. "I believe they were, but they would not say. Anyway, she made a deal with them that if she obtained any intelligence of interest, she would send them a message and would receive payment for it."

"So, she is their asset in Hong Kong," Li said, smiling. "That doesn't surprise me."

"But it should concern you," Kang said. "If the authorities find out, she and all her acquaintances, including you, will be executed."

"It's too late for us on that account," Guo said. "If we're caught, we'll be shot immediately."

"What are you saying?" Li asked. "Lan can help us get out?"

"In a way," Pei said. "She has a way to get a coded message to them and they can decide if they will answer it."

"How will they answer?" Li asked

"Either by message, action, or both," Kang said. "She contacts them with simple communication and codes, though she will not reveal how. For example, one code is SMB, which means secret military base. They've been looking for one for some time, but no one knows why."

"We do," Guo said. "That's where we are from. The base has a massive computer array underground and is camouflaged from the air, so satellites are unable to detect it."

"Because that is the case, I'm certain they'll work with you," Pei said. "You have what they want, and they have the resources to help you."

"How can we make it happen?" Guo asked.

"You cannot, but we can," Kang responded. "All you need to know about us is our first names. How we get it done, we will not tell you."

"We will make the contact secretively," Pei said. "I will contact Lan and she will make the arrangements. We know she is on the PLA watch list; thus, all communication is clandestine."

"Please let her know I'm okay," Li said. "What do you want us to do while you're making the arrangements?"

"Kang will help you bind his wound," Pei said. "We don't have access to a doctor which is what he needs, but we have a decent medical kit with pain killers, sutures, and antibiotics."

Journalists are always busy; today was no exception. Lan was sitting at her desk in the South China Morning Post offices, putting the finishing touches on her article about the housing outlook for the new year. It promised to be a real ball buster for the real estate industry. Since the Chinese government had taken over, she had to become a jack of all trades. One day she was working on a story about economics, the next street crime, the next real estate, and on it went. Her favorite time was preparing crossword puzzles in Pinyin for the paper. As she sat contemplating a new one, her phone rang. She instantly recognized the voice on the other end and realized the message would be important. No names would be mentioned, and great care would be exercised not to divulge critical information.

"Good morning," Pei said. "We are going to a badminton game tonight with a friend who just arrived?"

Lan's attention was immediately focused because she knew the caller meant Li.

"I hope the friend had a safe trip," Lan replied.

"He did, the ride was a little bumpy," Pei said. "He said to say hello."

"We were hoping you could come with us and after the game maybe you could give us a ride?"

"I may be able to arrange that."

"You should, because my friend tells me he knows a good place to eat that SMB you're so fond of," Pei said. "Not a bad trade the SMB dish for a taxi ride, neh?"

Pei had her full attention now. The SMB was worth a lot of extra money to her. Knowing that her fiancé was no longer at the secret base, gave her a feeling of relief. She had always suspected that's where he had gone since there was no contact allowed from inside or outside until he had the good fortune of borrowing a fellow soldiers secret phone. Knowing that Li could identify the location, which he had refused to do when they talked, her mind raced. She needed to arrange transportation, which would be difficult on such short notice. She would edit the mornings crossword puzzle online and get immediate action from Taiwan Station.

"I'm swamped with work, but could attend the game," Lan said.

"Oh, something I forgot, we may bring another friend along if that's okay?"

"Sure, no problem," Lan replied. "There's always room for one more. It'll be fun."

If the authorities had been listening in, all they heard was a conversation of two friends talking about a badminton game,

James Tindall

one of the most popular sports in Hong Kong.

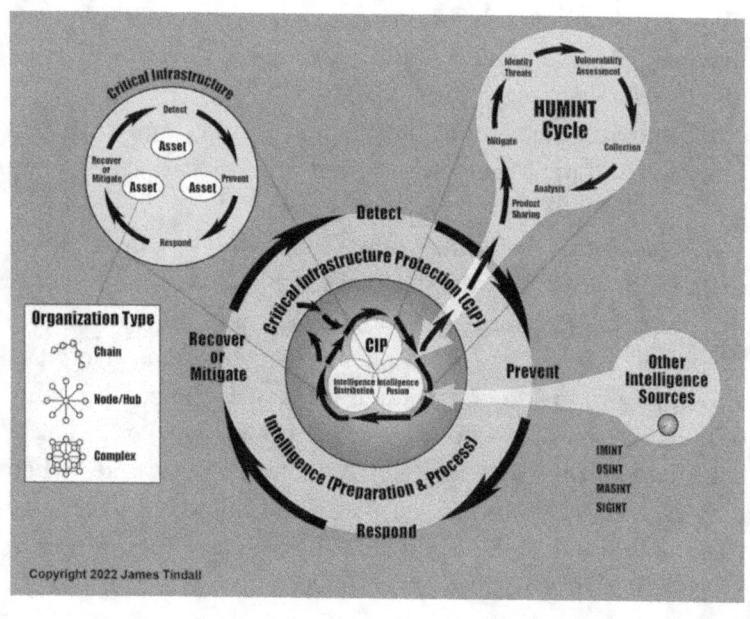

CHAPTER 2

The park for their clandestine meeting was near empty as JB hurried along the sidewalk to meet with Jonas. As he got closer, he saw someone on a bench who seemed familiar. "Damn!" he thought. "Dakota, what are you doing here?"
"Having my lunch," Dakota replied, smiling as he turned and stood to greet his friend. "What brings you out this way?"
"A private meeting with Jonas," JB said. "What a surprise to find you here."
"This place keeps my insanity at bay. I see Jonas coming now so, I'll leave you to it. Let's catch up when you have time."
"Roger that," JB replied. "Give my regards to Mabel. I hope she is enjoying DC."
"It ain't home," Dakota grinned, "But it's tolerable."
    He waved as he departed. From habit, Jonas had arrived with his standard contingent of personal security that had spread out across the area, waiting patiently, observing, while Jonas conducted his private meeting.
"Good afternoon," Jonas said, sitting down. "How's training?"
"We got through it pretty well," JB said. "There won't be any hiccups on that end. We are now working with pistol, rifle, and knife combat techniques. I'd like to refresh our hand-to-hand

combat skills, but do not know if we have time. Any luck on finding the location?"

"We have a little chatter out of Hong Kong that seems promising," Jonas replied. "We will know by tomorrow. Keep training as much as you can for now."

"Anything else?

"You may get your wish to train hand-to-hand," Jonas replied. "We have arranged for Lunadi to meet you, Li Na, and your team in Miami. Train as much as you can before you leave."

"About that, what are you anticipating?" JB asked.

"As Phil said, once you depart, you'll use your old operative name," Jonas said. "The plan is to travel from Miami to Taiwan Station on the outskirts of Taipei. The COS there will help you finalize your strategy, but she has been told that you have final say. There's too much riding on this for bureaucracy to get in the way."

"I agree," JB said. "Who is she?"

"Pamela Nguyen," Jonas replied. "Many consider her a real ball buster; she speaks fluent Mandarin, Vietnamese, and English, without accents. She has 15 years of intelligence operations experience including five in the field. She's not as good in the field, not even close as you are. However, she is an excellent strategist and if you don't hit it off on the wrong foot, I think you will make a good team. The question is Li Na."

"What about her?"

"Her goal is to kill this guy, but we need the intel first," Jonas replied. "You need to keep her on track and please don't let two strong willed women go at it. This mission is crippled if you do."

"I'll handle it."

"Good luck," Jonas said, shaking hands. "I'll let you know if anything develops."

When Jonas walked away, JB watched him carefully while his security detail trailed behind.

General Bocheng was concerned. No one had ever left the post and lived to talk about it. It was so secret even the bureaucrats in Beijing didn't know about it. He motioned to his sergeant standing outside by the outer door.

"Find Colonel Wu, now!"

The general was scrutinizing a large map of the area that hung on his office wall.

"You wanted to see me general?"

"Yes," Bocheng said. "How is the search going?"

"We trailed one person's tracks to the shoreline," Wu replied. "About halfway there, another set of tracks joined him. We presume the second set belonged to the lieutenant."

"Nothing other than that?"

"We found an area close to the water that looks like it was used for the construction of a small bamboo raft."

"And the gunboats found nothing?"

"No general. No sign of them anywhere."

"Hmmmm," Bocheng mused. "There is no way they could have escaped our detection is there?"

"I believe they constructed a raft and are hiding along the shore somewhere, maybe in the marsh area where soil from the mountains have formed small islands. We put a helicopter up; no sightings so far."

"Let's look at what we know," Bocheng said. "They didn't leave by vehicle and air travel is out of the question, which leaves either travel by foot or raft. Did the dogs pick up their scent?"

"No general," Wu replied. "That is what's strange. They had good scent trailing them to the shore; that is where it ended. They lost the scent."

"So, they either walked in the water offshore to throw off the dogs or they escaped by raft. How far do you think they could have gotten on foot?"

"They have a twelve-hour head start and likely no packs," Wu said. "My estimate is one mile per hour, which would give them a fourteen-mile lead."

"Alright," Bocheng said. "Let's assume they made it twenty miles. Take the helicopters and deploy four men and a dog here, and here, pointing at the map. Converge back to the point where you lost track of them on the shore."

"Yes general," Wu replied. "I suggest we deploy the gunboats again and search the small marsh islands."

"Yes, do that," Bocheng said. "Have them look for broken branches in the mangroves, depressions, and so forth. Tell them to be methodical. That will tell us if they escaped by raft. In case they did, how far do you think they could have traveled?"

"The sea was calm all night sir. My estimate is about eighteen miles, more if they know what they're doing."

A corporal knocked at the door.

"Come in," Bocheng said. "What do you have for me?"

"I checked personnel records sir. The lieutenant came from a farming background and Li came from a very poor fishing background. Other than that, nothing extraordinary."

"Thank you, corporal," Bocheng said. "That is all."

"Because Li was poor, he will have experience with small rafts," Wu said. "Lots of it."

"We need to enlarge the search radius for them," Bocheng said.

"Yes, considerably," Wu said. "I change my estimate to twenty-eight miles."

"That far?" Bocheng asked.

"Yes," Wu said. "The raft is lightweight bamboo. Whether they hug the shore and pole or paddle in deeper water, they can travel a long distance during a night, more than you may realize."

"That would put them as far as Shantou to the southwest and Dongshan Harbor to the northeast. Deploy three additional gunboats in each direction. Coordinate with air support. I will contact MSS and help develop a strategy of their possible contacts."

"I'll get on it immediately general."

The general watched his Colonel walk out the door; he sat down and made a call on his sat phone.

Li Na and JB, along with her men had arrived at an abandoned factory on the outskirts of Miami. It was owned by the Federal government and served various purposes as needs demanded. Recently used as a short-term safe house, it was now going to be utilized for hand-to-hand combat training. The three vans pulled into the open roll-down doors and the team got out. In front of them stood four men, two flanking each side of a long table that had various sharp-edged weapons, clubs, pistols, and AK-47 rifles. Directly in front of the table were ten chairs. Scattered around the room in a square formation were eight training mats.

"Please take a seat," one of the men by the table said.

"It looks like we're in for some serious training," Li Na said. "However, my men are already well trained. Do you really think these guys can help us improve?"

"Maybe not," JB replied. "But he can."

Lunadi appeared holding a Katana, which he laid on the table.

"I remember him from the presentation he gave on infrastructure," Li Na said. "He is a fighter too?"

"One of the very best," JB replied.

"Good morning to all of you," Lunadi said. "I was contacted by DCIA and Director DOE. They asked me to do what I could to help prepare you in H2HC for an upcoming mission. I will do what I can in the short time we have. I have been sent your records and know somewhat of your skills. None of you are novices. Before we begin, do you have any questions?"

"My men are all well trained in combat arts," Li Na said. "What makes you think you can improve their skills?"

Lunadi eyed her for a moment. His eyes narrowing as he stared at her. Since she wanted to be such a smart ass, he would return the favor.

"Because I am better than all of you," he said flatly, challenge answered, as he picked up the katana, he had laid on the table. The men on either side, feeling something was about to happen, stepped away from him.

"Who is your best fighter, Li Na?" Lunadi asked.

"I am," she said defiantly.

"Don't....," JB began to say, his voice trailing off.

No sooner had she responded than the long sword was thrown through the air, which she grabbed deftly, removing the blade from the scabbard. There was about ten feet between the table and the first row of chairs where she now stood facing Lunadi. "Is this man insane?" Li Na thought to herself. "I can carve him like a ham."

"You are the sword expert," Lunadi said. "Come get me. If you best me, you can get back into your vans and leave."

Her indignation aroused, she accepted the challenge without a word as she sliced at him from a one handed high-ready position, the tip just missing his chest as he sidestepped. Li Na's slice reverted to a figure eight as the blade sliced outward, followed by a strike with her left hand that held the scabbard toward Lunadi's head. In an instant, Lunadi executed a left, front crossover leap grabbing her left wrist with his left hand and wrenching the scabbard away with his right, slamming her in the face with his right elbow while he pulled and raised the scabbard slightly above his shoulder, crashing it against her right wrist. The blow knocked the sword from her grasp as he hooked the back of her left knee with a right inward heel kick that immediately reverted to a right, side kick to her hip. Li Na sailed a dozen feet across the room, crumpling to a heap on the edge of a mat. Before she had hit the ground, Lunadi had re-sheathed the sword and laid it back on the table. Two of his men helped Li Na to her feet and back to her chair, blood trickling down her chin from a bloody lip.

Her men were in awe of Lunadi's skill; JB looked on in admiration because he knew none of them could best Lunadi on his worst day. A soft, rare smile, came to his lips as he thought, "Indian Power."

Li Na was still trying to catch her breath because the kick had slid from her hips into her lower abdomen. Her men looked on wondering how she had been beaten so easily. In less than three seconds the challenge had ended. They kept looking from her to Lunadi and back, appreciating what they had just witnessed.

"Allow me," Lunadi said as he knelt in front of her. "Sit up straight please.

When she did so, he pressed firmly on her stomach, slowing her breathing, and relieving the pain.

"Are you alright?" he asked, compassion filling his eyes.

She nodded slightly, understanding he had meant her no harm.

"I am glad," Lunadi said, stepping away. "This brings me to a question for all of you. How did I best her so fast, despite the added range of the weapon?"

"You recognized her body motion," JB said.

"That's a big part of it," Lunadi replied.

"The rhythm she used was off," another said.

"That too is part of it," Lunadi said.

"You anticipated her timing, ahead of her stroke," another chimed in.

"Very good," Lunadi said. "I can tell that you are all excellent fighters. The key concept is that I fought her, not the weapon. Even skilled fighters often fight the weapon held in the opponent's hand. While any weapon, edged, blunt, or a firearm gives the opponent extended range, you must remember one key principle; you are fighting the opponent, not the weapon they hold. Never forget that. You must also be able to accurately read body motion."

"So, my body motion gave me away?" Li Na asked.

"In a way," Lunadi said. "Remember that if you are in a particular stance, your movements become restricted to what you can do from that position."

"I could have kicked or attempted a knee strike instead of using the sword?" Li Na asked.

"Exactly," Lunadi replied. "Unfortunately, those who are accustomed to using a weapon to gain an upper hand have a feeling of power and invincibility and thus, generally rely on the weapon far too much. It was immediately evident in your challenge. Sorry, but I took advantage of it."

Li Na was shocked. She had remembered when she saw him at the presentation, she had thought he was a true warrior. Now, she realized just how right she had been.

"What are you going to teach us?" Li Na asked.

"We have only a short time," Lunadi said. "Because of that, I am going to teach you ten fighting principles that hopefully will help keep you alive on your mission. It's my version of the old 'kill or be killed' that was taught to soldiers during WWII."

"Will it be against armed opponents?" one of the men asked.

"Yes, both armed and unarmed," Lunadi responded. "The principles work against both. I am not fond of nomenclature, but let's go over two of them. Often you hear the term close quarters battle or CQB, which generally refers to armed versus armed opponents. Still others refer to close quarters combat or CQC, which can refer to combat against unarmed opponents, even though a great many still consider CQC as combat against armed opponents. I prefer hand-to-hand combat or H2HC, which refers to either because it doesn't matter whether the opponent is armed or not; you are fighting the opponent, not the weapon."

"But don't we need to be concerned about the weapon?" one of the men asked.

"Precisely," Lunadi replied. You need to be aware of what the weapon can do, especially its range, but not at the expense of the opponent."

While Lunadi responded to questions from her men, she marveled at the simplicity of his explanations and his style of fighting. She now understood why JB had fought so well in various situations. He had trained with this man. The dots were beginning to connect.

"Why did you start to say don't to me?" Li Na asked.

"Because I knew what the outcome would be," JB explained. "Student's usually do not question the master lest they get put in their place."

"You knew he would best me?" Li Na said.

"I have not seen anyone beat him," JB said. "I trained with him for a long time."

"When he gave the presentation," Li Na began, "I knew he was a warrior, but thought he was more of a brain."

"Lunadi is one of those rare men that can use both sides of his brain," JB said. "He is as equally creative as he is analytical."

"I no longer doubt that."

"Tell me, how long did it take you to learn the sword?"

"I spent hours practicing and three to four evenings during the week in the dojo working with the instructor."

"Lunadi has spent over 18,000 hours instructing students, not including his day job."

He watched the light of understanding come to her eyes.

"Now you have some understanding of his skill sets," JB smiled. "Beware that to him, all things are connected."

"I wished you had warned me ahead of time," Li Na said smiling, rubbing her jaw, which was red and swelling.

The two men had met several more times because the congressman's handler required more information. Walking along the south side of the reflecting pool as they approached the Lincoln Memorial, Clint obscurely slipped the congressman a flash drive that contained all the previous information and the most recent that had been requested. Blaine pulled out his Android phone and inserted the end of the flash drive into it. Having the latest version of a file explorer, the information popped up instantly.

"This will do," Blaine said. "I'll call you if I need more. Thank you. We should have payment shortly. I'll tell you where to meet to split it."

"It will be 60:40 as agreed, correct?" Clint asked.

"Yes."

Clint paused and stooped down, acting like he was tying his shoe. The congressman continued walking. Standing up, he walked the opposite direction not noticing he was being watched. Blaine continued walking slowly, still studying the information. Turning right at the end of the reflecting pool, the sidewalk began to bend left in a semi-oval shape, heading toward the Vietnam Memorial. The congressman took the sidewalk to the right toward a group of benches just past a large ornate lamp post. Taking a seat on the third bench, the prearranged dead drop, he pulled a piece of duct tape he had brought and placed it horizontally across the flash drive. Looking about, he deftly pressed it beneath the bench. He lit a cigarette and smoked it until the burning tobacco reached the filter. Deciding he had been casual enough, he left. The agent who had watched Clint, continued observing the congressman, remaining behind so he could determine who would pick up the flash drive. It would be in his next report to his boss.

Pamela Nguyen had been named Taiwan Chief of Station (COS) a month after the Chinese took over Hong Kong. Personnel from both stations had been reassigned. Fortunately for her, she had gained the favor of DCIA who thought highly of her skills and, which allowed her to hand pick most of the people at the station. Although she often didn't agree with them, everyone was good at their jobs.

She was a slim woman with long black hair to mid back: athletic and agile. Her gaze was penetrating and unnerving.

She exercised daily and remained constantly alert. Having been a field operative, she was adept at various forms of physical combat and an excellent shot with a pistol. Because of her field work, her colleagues respected her since she wasn't the typical bureaucratic type that Langley assigned to such posts. They understood that although she was a risk taker by nature, she didn't take unnecessary risks without the benefits outweighing the costs. Pamela was sitting behind the large desk across from her deputy chief, Albert Pike who, like her, had spent over a decade as a field op. He glanced at his watch.

"It's about that time," Al said.

"Yes indeed," Pamela replied as they arose and walked across the room to the conference table at the back and again began to quickly peruse the papers and photographs in front of them. They were intelligence dossiers on the people that were going to be inserted into Chinese territory and their backgrounds. The mission intrigued both to the utmost. At the same time, they knew if it failed their careers in the agency would be on the line at the least or completely over.

"You know, this makes me wish I was back in the field again," Al said, as he stared across at his boss.

"Me too," Pamela responded. "Until I have to jump out of that airplane or stand in a downpour watching my target."

They both laughed at the thought but vividly remembered how adrenaline had flowed through their veins while on mission. The two continued to peruse the intelligence they had been given, anxiously awaiting the call from two colleagues, now their bosses, who they had served with in the field. For once, Langley may be able to get something right, a mission that would be led by their best former operative and four authority figures who had first-hand experience in field operations. The large high-definition screen at the back of the room changed from black to blue and then to pictures of the participants involved in the meeting. All other personnel were excluded.

"Good morning," Phil said. "We are joined by Jonas. I see you have been going through the intelligence packets."

"Yes director," Pamela said. "Looks like an interesting mission."

"Cut the director crap! We are all on a first name basis here. I cannot count how many times we have pulled each other's asses out of the fire."

Flash backs of past missions immediately entered their thoughts. They seemed like only yesterday.

"Got it," Pamela replied, smiling. "If you do not mind me saying so, there is not a lot here other than the personnel records."

"That is correct," Jonas said. "Phil and I wanted to fill you in personally. This is eyes only for the two of you."

"No other personnel are to be involved in oversight of the mission, except perhaps your counterintelligence chief," Phil said. "I'll leave that to you."

"Field agents are only to be told what they need to know," Jonas said. "If we screw this up, well."

"What's the skinny?" Al asked.

"This is what we are attempting to find out," Phil said. "You are both aware that we have been looking for a secret army base somewhere in southeast China. We have narrowed it down and hope to locate it soon. The mission will not begin until we do."

"What's so important about this base?" Pamela asked.

"Fill them in Jonas," Phil replied.

"This base has a computer network of very large scale and capacity," Jonas said. "With it they have been hacking and probing the U.S. power grid. There are two problems. First, if they succeed, they will decapitate the grid, telecommunications, water distribution and treatment, defense systems to an extent, emergency services and commodity supply lines as well, not to mention others."

"Why that would kill millions," Al burst out.

"Exactly," Jonas replied. "With the power grid down and the resulting chaos, death would be widespread within ten days."

"As if this is not horrific enough," Pamela began, "what's the second item?"

"This system is most likely underground and surrounded by a giant faraday cage, which means even if we knew where the base was, a tactical strike with a nuke wouldn't completely disable it."

"That is where you come in Pamela and Al," Phil broke in. "We must find this base. And, when we do, the operatives in your intelligence packets will be inserted and hopefully end the threat."

"But none of them are qualified field agents," Pamela interjected. "Without experience the mission has a high likelihood of failure."

"Ah, but we have saved the best for last," Jonas said as he posted a picture on the screen.

"That's Jack..." Al began, quickly interrupted.

"Shhhh," Phil said. "You are only to know his name, not say it, ever. He will be leading the mission."

"That's a relief," Pamela said. "He's saved my ass more than once, as well as the rest of yours. You may not know it, but he is required study at FSB, GRU, and MSS. They still cannot figure out how he did some of the things he did, despite the fact they have duplicated several of his missions. As a matter of fact, I cannot either."

"That gives me some measure of confidence," Al said. "At least we have one ringer in the basket."

"This may give you more relief," Jonas said. "The entire team has been training with him, including combat training by Lunadi. They will be ready once we find the base. The woman, Li Na, has considerable intelligence experience including several years with the Chinese military. She and her men are excellent fighters and recently pulled off a successful mission with JB, almost as difficult as this one. They were simply outstanding."

"That's comforting," Pamela said. "What happens when we find the base?"

"You two and the team leader will develop an entry strategy," Phil replied.

"Once that is done," Jonas interrupted, "you'll provide all necessary logistics."

The group was interrupted by a knock at the door.

"Come in," Pamela directed.

"Excuse me for interrupting, but you'll want to see this immediately,"

"Al, I think you know Steve," Pamela said, eyeing the report she had been handed. "Our head of counterintelligence. Thank you. This is most helpful."

She waited until Steve had left the room.

"Hold the presses folks," Pamela said. "Looks like we just got a break. An asset in Hong Kong contacted one of our agents. There was brief mention of two men that want out of country who escaped from an SMB."

"What's an SMB?" Phil asked.

"It's our code for secret military base," Pamela said. "If we can get them here safely, you'll have enough information to do what is needed by mission personnel."

"Time is critical, which I'm sure you're aware of," Jonas said. "Do you have a timeframe for exfil?

"It will happen this evening, after nightfall," Pamela replied.

"Amazing," Phil said. "It's not often we catch a break like this."

"It may not be so easy," Al said. "There are always hiccups."

"Well, don't stand around," Phil said. "Get to it."

The monitor went blank. Pamela and Al stared across at each other, the silence growing. They were in disbelief that the intelligence had dropped in their lap at such an opportune moment. Suddenly, they burst out laughing, relieving the tension.

"That news was impeccably timed," Al said.

"Yes, it was," Pamela remarked. "The timing could not have been more crucial. It gave them the impression we are good at what we do."

"We are," Al said.

"Yes, we are," Pamela replied. "Do you know the asset the communique refers to in Hong Kong?"

"Yes," Al replied. "She's a reporter and good. She hates the Chinese government with a passion. She's one of the good guys as it were."

"What course of action do you suggest?"

"Let's have a chat with her handler," Al said. "Then, give him all the support he needs to get those two men here. If they are defectors from the base, they will know everything necessary for our success."

"Hmmmm," Pamela said. "Assuming we succeed, we will both have our choice of future assignments."

Lan was excited. Despite occasional contact with her fiancé, she did not know where the base was. The online crossword puzzle was quick to change. Pre-keyed, it had been quickly interpreted by her contact who had cut out certain squares for letters and words to interpret it. He had told her to standby while he made the necessary arrangements. What bothered her was that the Chinese government intelligence network was very active and now, would be particularly active since these two men had escaped from a secret base. It would not take long for them to track her down. Time was becoming more critical by the second. The MSS agents would likely be watching her by the end of day.

She excused herself to take a lunch break. Today she would walk five blocks from her office in a meandering route. Instead of taking the elevator, she took the stairs and exited the side of her office building rather than the front. Traversing a short delivery alley, she walked to the next street over. Ever so watchful as her handler had taught her, she made certain she was not followed. She walked down one-half block and turned right into another delivery alley that was several buildings from her own. Like most of the newer buildings in Hong Kong, it was made of steel and glass. Lan walked into the lobby and sat down on a sofa for a moment, observing her surroundings and watching the street through the plate glass windows. Making certain no one was tailing her, she exited the building turning left and walked two blocks to another office building then, down a long hallway and out the back side. She stood outside the exit for five minutes, smoking a cigarette. There was no activity, so she walked another block along the sidewalk, stopping here and there, looking into the glass of the buildings that reflected the street scene behind and around her like mirrors. She looked for the ever-present signs of someone following her. Cutting down a back alley, she entered a smaller office building and made her way to the front where there was a small café. Taking a seat at a corner table against the wall, she waited and watched for signs of MSS agents.

She waited fifteen minutes before her handler arrived and sat to her immediate left with his back against the opposing wall, ever watchful of eyes on them. She had worked with him for several years and didn't even know his name, just his initials CS. He had told her that was all she needed to know.

"Are you sure you weren't followed?" CS asked in whispered tones.

"I was careful and followed your training," Lan said, whispering. "I'm sure we're alone."

"Good," CS said, as he ate his vegetable rice bowl, which Lan had ordered for them. "This is what you need to do. You need to get your friends on a small boat and go straight out for twenty miles, to this point."

The agent had sketched a small map, leaving out many geographic details so that if someone found it, they would have no clue it was of value.

"They need to be there by 2030 hours," CS said.

"What if they are not?" Lan asked.

"We may not be able to wait for or help them," CS said. "As you know, the Chinese patrol coastal waters and the Taiwan Straits constantly. We know their schedules and need to avoid detection. We will be waiting to pick them up. That's all you need to know."

"There are two things I want," Lan said. "First, there is a friend who will use his boat to take them there, but he will need to be paid. Second, I'd like to know more because one of the men is my fiancé," Lan replied. "Anything would be helpful."

"Tell your friend we will pay him five times his normal rate for the transportation," CS said. "As for the second matter, it's for your own safety that you know only what we have discussed. We will have people waiting at that location for exfil. You need have no knowledge other than that."

"What else do you need?" Lan asked.

"Nothing," CS responded. "Get them to those coordinates on schedule. We will take care of the rest. As soon as we can, we will have your fiancé make contact. I don't have to remind you that you may be in jeopardy once night falls. Make one last call on your burner and replace it."

"I understand," Lan replied. "Have you made arrangements for my departure?"

"Yes. It's being taken care of."

The two fell silent as they ate, continuing to observe their surroundings to make certain no one was watching. Lan finished, nodded, looked about, and departed the way she had come. She wandered down several backstreets, through a couple of office buildings, and circled back around so that she entered her office building's front entrance. Careful as always, she didn't detect anyone tailing her and was back at her desk about an hour later. Her co-workers hadn't noticed she had been gone.

Lan pulled a burner cell out of her purse and made a quick call to finalize her transportation out of country, relaying her instructions in code as usual. She called Pei being cautious not to use names of people or locations.

"I worked out the math problem that stymied you," Lan said. "Your answers should have been 230156 and 1165757, in that order. I will meet you at 8:00 pm for the tutoring lesson. Don't be late; I am pressed for time."

"How will you get here?" Pei asked.

"Our friend with the ferry service," Lan said. "He has agreed to five times as long as he can keep the schedule."

"That's great news," Pei said. "I'm looking forward to our session."

Lan made her way to the next floor's bathroom and removed the battery from the burner phone, tossing it into the trash receptacle. She next went to two more bathrooms on separate floors discarding the remaining phone parts that she had broken in two. There was a vendor down the street where she would purchase another burner directly after work — only two hours away. Making it back to her desk and sitting down, she was suddenly gripped by fear. Her heart began pounding; she had goose bumps all over her arms. It was as if an icy chill encompassed her. Looking about furtively, she inwardly wondered if she was being watched. Like many field agents about to make a major move, paranoia had crept in, but it would keep her alert for potential danger. She would miss her job as a journalist, but it was too dangerous to stay. Capture meant certain death.

Pei knew exactly what the numbers were. The first was north latitude and the second east longitude. She retrieved a hidden map to check the coordinates. The location was about twenty miles offshore. She instinctively knew that her friend would not want to go that far with his ferry boat, a modernized sampan. Such vessels were not meant for the open sea but given the current winds of about three knots and sea temperatures of 60° to 70° F, the waters would stay calm out and back and one could survive for quite some time if thrown overboard. After all, it wasn't as if they were in the artic in a blizzard. The lieutenant was resting on the sofa, asleep from the wound trauma. Li was watching the sunset across the ocean as the sun sunk low in the western sky, casting a broad luster, engulfing the water in a golden sheen. He turned to look at her, a distant gaze in his eyes.

"Good news?" he asked.

"Yes," Pei said. "Pickup tonight at 1800 hours. I need to call my friend and arrange transport. It will take us at least an hour to get to the boat."

"It's not that far away," Li said.

"Correct," Pei replied. "But we must be very careful to avoid detection from MSS agents. I'm guessing anytime now they will be in full operation looking behind every blade of grass and every apartment brick. They are quite good and because most people are afraid of the government, they will cooperate to save their own skin."

"When do we need to leave?" Li asked.

"In about forty minutes," Pei responded. "Look, we must be more careful than ever before. I've laid out some clothes in the bedroom for you to change into. Luckily both of you and Kang are all the same size. Beside the clothes is a garbage bag. Place all your old clothes into it, everything. I must get rid of them in case the MSS visits my apartment, which is almost a certainty but hopefully after we have gone. None of us will be returning."

"And if they come before you leave, how will you do that?" Li asked.

"By telling them basic truths mixed with just enough lies," Pei said. "After all, I'm a journalist working from home and Kang has been at work all day. That stack of papers over there is a story I wrote ahead of time. It will convince them that I've been working all day as well. After all, there is no way I could help two fugitives and get that done too."

"What if they don't believe you?" Li asked.

"They will," Pei said. "They'll check cell phone records and all of that. I'll make one more call on this burner and will dispose of it. Trust us. We have done this more than a few times for which the CIA pays us well. Our biggest problem is not to get lax. Those who become distracted against the control and power of the MSS go to an early grave. Wake your friend and change. Do so quickly."

While Li and the lieutenant were changing, Pei made her final call to the ferry captain.

"We have a tutoring session at 2000 hours," Pei said. "We need to be there on time."

"How far?" the captain asked.

"Further than you would like," Pei said. "Just under two hours at five times normal."

"Hmmmm," the captain replied. "Okay, everything is calm enough. I don't anticipate any problems. Be here by 1730 hours if you want to make it to the game in time after the tutoring lesson."

"See you soon," Pei said.

As soon as the 30-second conversation was over, Pei removed the battery from the burner then, twisted the phone into two parts, breaking the hinge. She put one part into the kitchen trash. Just in time, the two men walked out with the bag of old clothes.

"Where do you want this?" Li asked.

"Just set it down there and put this in it." Pei said, tossing part of the burner phone to him. "Wipe your fingerprints off it before tossing it in with the clothes. We must hurry. Check every corner of the apartment where we have been, wipe it down."

The three collected the bloody bandages from suturing the lieutenants wound and placed them in a garbage bag from the bathroom, along with the third part of the burner phone. Pei looked cautiously around each room including where the men had changed to make sure she hadn't missed anything, not even a spec of blood. Satisfied, she took the three small trash bags.

"Wait here," she said. "I'll be back in about five minutes."

Pei walked up the stairs to the next floor and dropped one of the bags down the trash chute. She then walked down to the next two floors beneath hers and put one bag in each trash chute on each floor. She hoped that others would drop trash down the chutes so that the three bags wouldn't be noticed in case of a search. After all, from the account of the escape, the soldiers didn't know they had wounded anyone. She quickly ran back up the stairs. Taking one last look around, she was satisfied. She would miss her apartment.

"Come, we must hurry."

Steve was hovering over the conference table in Pamela's office along with DCOS Albert Pike.

"We have everything set to go," Steve said. "I began putting the operation in motion when I received the communique this morning. Thanks for including me in this."

"What are your plans?" Pamela asked.

"That's what I wanted to run by both of you," Steve replied. "We will meet them at these coordinates, 23°01'56 N latitude and 116°57'57 E longitude. The question is the best way to exfil them. We can either do so via Sikorsky helicopter and fast boat, submarine and fast boat, or freighter and fast boat. I've ruled out the latter since Chinese ships in the area would pick it up on radar."

"Hmmmm," Al mused. "The helicopter would be faster but potentially expose it to radar. The submarine would be stealthier but would require re-tasking through the Navy. It would also likely be followed by a Chinese sub. Too much activity could cause an international incident. At this juncture, we cannot afford it."

"I agree," Pamela said. "Are you thinking of using the Sikorsky CH-53G we outfitted with stealth skin and transporting the fast boat with it?"

"Exactly," Steve replied. "The pilots have nerves of steel and can fly fifty to one hundred feet above the water and drop us off fifty miles from the extraction site. It would then take us about an hour to reach the target and an hour back to rendezvous with the chopper again, at which time we would attach the fast boat and head back on the return leg."

"That means the chopper would need to go about 165 miles each way then, return to pick you up where it initially dropped you off."

"Correct," Steve said.

"It could work well," Pamela said. "The chopper would take about fifty minutes out and the same back, which means to pick you up at the same point, it would need to leave about the same time you pick up the targets."

"Yes," Steve said. "The chopper is currently at Kaohsiung City awaiting orders, along with the fast boat and four-man ops team. It would begin its extraction leg ten minutes after us."

"That's a tight schedule," Pamela said. "Are you sure you can do it?"

"Fairly certain," Steve said. "What are your thoughts?"

"Let me get this straight," Al said. "The chopper flies you to this point, drops you, then your boat motors to the extraction rendezvous. While you're doing that, the chopper returns, refuels, and about the time you pick up the targets, the chopper begins its extraction leg to your original drop point?"

"Correct."

"I agree with Pamela," Al said. "That's a tight schedule."

"Let's do this," Pamela interjected. "On your return leg, let's delay the chopper about ten to fifteen minutes, just in case. Additionally, let's place a backup boat here, half-way on the return leg."

"Get me Colonel Diets of the 1st Special Forces Group," Pamela said, speaking loudly as she depressed the speaker button to her assistant.

"We will get him to provide one of his interceptor boats for this," Pamela said. "He's been itching for it."

"Pamela," Diets said. "I hope all is well at Taiwan Station. What do you need?"

"You've been longing for it for a long time," Pamela said. "We have an extraction we need support with. It can potentially get very hot. Would you have a problem with that?"

"It's what we train for and beats training other nations troops," Diets said. "How soon do you need it?"

"In a few hours out of Kaohsiung City area," Pamela replied.

"We have a couple of those boats about an hour away now," Diets replied. "How about we use both of them?"

"The more backup the better," Al chimed in. "By the way colonel, when Pamela said potentially hot, if it goes that way, you better be armed to the teeth."

"Roger that," Diets replied. "I'll get both boats ready. Shoot me the meeting place so we can coordinate with the other party."

"Will do," Steve said. "I'll get it to you shortly."

"That went well," Al said.

"Indeed," Pamela replied. "I hope the rest of this extraction goes the same."

James Tindall

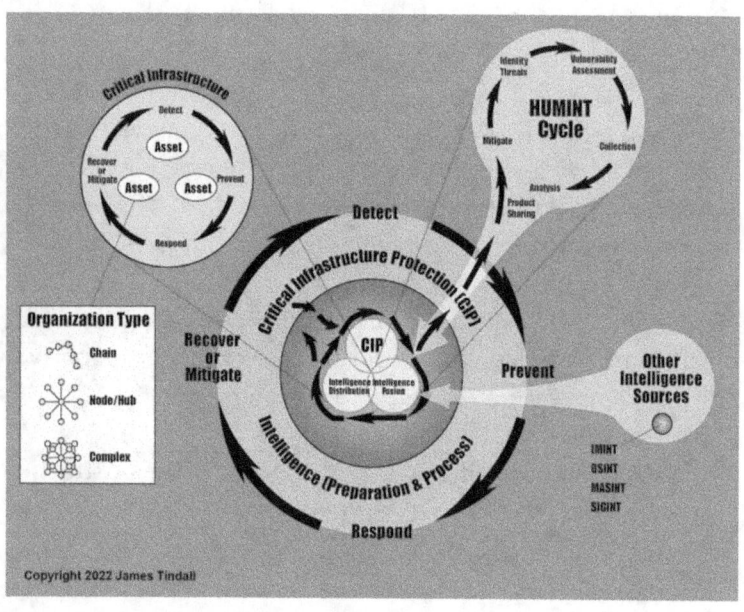

CHAPTER 3

The group of men Li Na had brought to Miami were having a great time learning hand-to-hand combat from a master. Already they had learned several key techniques they had not known before. They were looking forward toward the day's training. They had separated into five teams of two, each on a mat to protect themselves from falling on the concrete and were ready when Lunadi, smiling, walked in.

"I must be getting soft in my old age," he said. "In the old days you wouldn't have the luxury of protective mats. You'd get your bruises on the concrete floor."

Everyone laughed.

"Today, we're going to teach you a knife technique," Lunadi said. "It's relatively simple and can be done against an overhead attack or thrusting attack. We will utilize the first since it is simpler. You should know that ninety percent of people are right-handed. We'll begin with that premise. I will work with JB and Li Na; my colleagues will work with the rest of you."

"Is this one of the principles I have done before?" JB asked.

"In a manner of speaking," Lunadi said. "But, like the others you have learned this week, this is a kill technique, but not for self-defense. I do not imagine you're on a mercy mission."

Li Na grinned. "Certainly not!"

"Okay, both of you face me and I'll walk you through it. I'm coming at you with an overhead knife attack. What do you do first?"

"Side-step to avoid the weapon," JB replied.

"Correct, but not much," Lunadi said. "Let's use the clock principle again so, glide with your left foot to about 11 o'clock as you do a left inward parry so that your left-hand glides from the attackers left arm, just above his or her elbow, sliding down to the wrist. Next, take your right, guarding hand and place it atop your left hand and the opponent's wrist as the arm moves downward."

"Do we try to stop the motion?" Li Na asked.

"No," Lunadi replied. "Once your right hand syncs with your left and the opponents overhead attack, keep the motion going and guide the blade downward and into the opponent's thigh."

"So, we're in a left neutral bow to 11 o'clock still?" JB queried.

"Basically," Lunadi replied. "From the thigh stab, keep your right hand atop the opponent's wrist and knife. Rapidly slide your left hand into an inverted pincher grab to the opponent's throat and neck, like this, as you step forward with your right foot to 12 o'clock through and behind, pulling the attacker down across your right leg as you pivot into a right neutral bow, sinking down. The moment you marry gravity, strike the opponent with a downward right-hand sword to the throat, ending life."

"Are there alternative moves?" Li Na asked.

"Yes," Lunadi replied. "There are several depending on how lethal you wish to be."

"This isn't lethal enough?" JB asked, with a small laugh.

"Yes, but you can be quicker about it," Lunadi said. "The first option is to remove the knife from the thigh without losing continuity of motion and the right overhand strike, when you pull him down and against your thigh, becomes a knife stab to the attacker's chest."

"And the other scenarios?" Li Na asked.

"There are three more," Lunadi replied. "The second is with the left-hand parry, guide it down and strike to the opponents throat with a leopards paw strike."

"That's with the fingers curled in and striking with the middle knuckles of the hand?" JB asked.

"Yes," Lunadi replied. "The third alternative is to utilize the same motion and employ a right-hand finger poke to the opponent's eyes. It is not initially lethal, so you'll need a quick follow up for the kill. Snapping the neck will do. Choose what suits you from your own experiences or from what you've learned here. Your moves must be second nature."

"You said there was a fourth alternative," Li Na said.

"Yes, the most lethal of all if you already have it in your hand," Lunadi said. "It is the left-hand parry with a right-hand knife thrust to the opponent's throat. Make sure to slide your left hand over his mouth to muffle the sounds."

"I especially like the last one," Li Na said. "It's quick and easy."

"Yes," Lunadi replied. "The snakes fang."

Both directors were sitting on the park bench, security ever present. They could not afford to meet in an office around others who were too political; most of them a bunch of ass kissers on their way to the top. Their plans would be overheard and divulged to those not needing to know.

"What do you make of the call from COS Taiwan?" Phil asked.

"I think we are finally going to find the base," Jonas replied. "If Pamela and her team can make this happen, our agent and his crew are ready for immediate mission execution."

"There's a lot riding on this," Phil said. "I assume the crew knows they are expendable?"

"Yes," Jonas replied. "JB knows the risks. As for Li Na, she has such a lust to kill this man for murdering her parents that she'd gladly go to hell with him for the opportunity. Her team is so loyal to her they'll follow her to their death, like Ronin avenging their master. Their expendability has been explained to them. If they fail, JB is just another mercenary out for a thrill ride."

"Good," Phil said. "The country cannot afford this coming back on us. Pamela and her group have come up with several options for the extraction. She will update us in a few hours."

"I assume we do not want this beamed into our offices?" Jonas queried.

"Certainly not," Phil replied, handing him a scrap of paper. "Meet here at that time. She will fill us in; we will have live feed as much as possible. I've given her carte blanche on what to do."

"See you then," Jonas said, rising.

The two men went their separate ways as inconspicuously as possible.

General Bocheng was apprehensive. He had always assumed if the location of his secret army post were revealed that the Americans or perhaps Britain would launch an attack to destroy it. "No, he thought. It would be too risky if it was discovered they were the ones. War would be inevitable and as much as both sides postured and threatened, neither wanted it."

He needed to act now. Picking up his sat phone, he called his long-time friend, one of only a few who knew what he was doing. Since 1983, when it was first formed and they worked together, Jeng Po had worked his way to the top of Guojia Anquan Bu, the Ministry of State Security, the Chinese Government's intelligence arm, responsible for foreign and counterintelligence operations. Jeng was Deputy Minister of Operations and had ties to the People's Liberation Army whose General Staff's Second and Third Departments also engaged in military and counterintelligence. Reflecting the structure of Russia's FSB, formerly the KGB, the MSS is responsible to the premier and state council. The Chinese Communist Party-Political Science and Law Commission oversees ministry activities, but like the Americans, Britain's, and their allies, not all things are divulged to those at the top unless absolutely necessary. It is just the nature of spy business.

"How are you, old friend?" Jeng asked.

"Well, and you?" Bocheng asked.

"I have no complaints."

"I assume you need my help?"

"Yes. I have two men missing," Bocheng said. "They escaped and we are not sure where they may be, but as you know, it is essential no one learn about this base and what we do."

"I understand clearly."

The general described all that had happened. As he listened Jeng reflected to their beginning, when both had worked intelligence and he had become part of the MSS when it formed in 1983 as one of its youngest field agents while Bocheng had joined the PLA. Both had done very well for themselves and were in positions, where, despite successes, were required to perform without waiver or mistake. Either could cost their life.

"Where do you think they could have gone?" Jeng asked.

"I know they would like to make it to Taiwan," Bocheng said. "With the small raft they constructed that would risk discovery by one of our vessels and likely would not be possible. They could not have made it to Hong Kong either so, my best guess is Shantou where they would attempt to reach the island or Hong Kong."

"I am thinking similarly," Jeng said. "I'll get field agents on it right away, concentrating on Shantou. We have a list of dissidents there we can shake down. What can you tell me about the two men?"

"The lieutenant has been here almost since the beginning," Bocheng said. "I believe he found out that if he left, he would meet the same fate of those now departed. Li is from a poor fishing family. He had a fiancé in Hong Kong who was a journalist. We are not sure who it was since after he was posted here no contact was allowed to the outside. However, we did find a communications link from the computers to call out and suspected it was him. We were going to arrest him, but he was one step ahead. The link was disabled. Li had mentioned to one of his friends that she worked for a news outlet but didn't say who."

"Does the name Lan, mean anything to you?" Jeng asked.

"I'm not familiar with it," Bocheng said. "Hold one moment, I'll find out."

General Bocheng wrote a quick note and handed it to his sergeant. It was to ask Li's friend if he ever mentioned the name Lan. The sergeant left and returned several minutes later.

"He said that Lan is Li's fiancé."

"Thank you."

"Jeng, yes, Lan is Li's fiancé," Bocheng said. "Why is that important?"

"She works for the China Morning Post," Jeng said. "We have suspected her of being an asset for the CIA but have no proof. We have her under surveillance when our suspicions are raised. I must admit I was lax, but we were hoping to discover her network. If anyone in Hong Kong could help your men disappear, it would be her. Talk to no one else about this. I will get my people on it right away. Oh, you can have our triad connections look for them too. We will need lots of eyes and ears to find them assuming they didn't drown on the raft."

The first call on Jeng's list was the director of 1st Bureau for Domestic Affairs and the 5th Bureau for Provincial and local offices. The latter directed intelligence operations for Guangdong Province. He also merged in 3rd Bureau from Hong Kong, Macao, and Taiwan, as well at 4th Bureau and 11th Bureau for technical and computer support. Jeng was sitting at the conference table in his office. He greeted all the directors as they joined the video conference. The first thing he did was hold up pictures of the two men that General Bocheng had sent.

"We need to find these two men immediately," Jeng said. "I will not tell you why other than it is an urgent matter of state security."

"Do you have a general location of where they were last seen?" 1st Bureau Director asked.

Jeng could not let these people know about the base, none of them were cleared. "The last best estimate is Shantou."

"Any contacts we should concentrate on?" 4th Bureau Director asked.

"All of you are aware of Lan Tau who works for the China Morning Post," Jeng said. "I believe she could be involved. You also are aware that she is high on our watch list. Get into her phone logs at work and her cell phone records. Let's see who she has been talking to. Also, monitor phone records from any unknown phone around her area to Shantou."

"Are you thinking there is a connection?" 4th Bureau Director asked.

"We know she has a small, trusted network," Jeng said. "She could not have survived this long without it. Perhaps this will expose them."

"I'll get all my agents in Shantou on this immediately," 5th Bureau Director said. "We have a large network there."

"Very well," Jeng replied. "I expect the same eagerness from the rest of you. The pictures of the two men and background has already been sent. You may want to enlist the local police as well for apprehension. Make up a story that they are suspected of murdering a state official, as well as a police officer. Dusk is upon us, so time is of the essence. You all know it is hard to find people in the dark."

The group chuckled because as former intelligence operatives themselves they had all failed to find targets in the dark at one time or another.

"Begin at once," Jeng directed.

J onas was sitting in his office, getting nervous about the entire operation. If they could not find the base, he was certain a full-scale hack of the entire U.S. power grid was imminent. He suspected the countermand device was for something else. From the last mission JB had done with Li Na in Florida, it was almost certain the device was for nuclear targets, at least that would be his story if required to explain it. Never-the-less, he cautiously put all grid owners and operators on notice. It wouldn't matter that 85 percent of the power grid was owned by the private sector. It was up to the DOE, DHS, and other federal agencies to protect it. His heart jumped into his throat when the phone began ringing.

"Damn phone," Jonas muttered. "Scared the hell out of me. Rothman here."

"The lead we have looks more and more promising," Phil said. "I think it's time to get the team ready. Be discreet."

"Understood," Jonas replied, hanging up the phone.

His agency was responsible for the operation. Since it involved the U.S. power grid, the CIA could only appear to be working on the international part. But hell, everyone knew the CIA operated on U.S. soil. He never understood the big secret about it, only that the congress critters on Capitol Hill always needed to cover their asses at the expense of lower-level personnel that did the heavy lifting. Funny how they always took the credit for the work of those below them and were always ready to throw the same to the dogs if things didn't go as well as planned. A bunch of plausible deniability BS that covered the entirety of actors of state within the beltway. It made him want to throw up every day.

L unadi could tell that JB and Li Na were enjoying the training, especially since they got to throw each other around. Secretly lovers, no one knew of their intimate relationship, however, the sharp eyes of Lunadi were not fooled by the pretense. He hoped that JB knew what he was doing. As an instructor he had observed the nature of too many students not to be able to recognize the closeness of those he trained. His job was only to train them further in H2HC. He did not know what mission they were going on because it was need-to-know, but he did know that if JB was involved, it was hyper critical. The fact that all of Li Na's team were not affiliated with the U.S. Government was also a tell-tale sign. It meant they were all expendable if the operation blew up in their face. It sometimes happened but Lunadi knew that guts would take over where their knowledge and skills ended. It was why training was so important. Everything needed to be second nature.

The group had trained well and Lunadi was hoping he could have another week with them for fine tuning their newly learned skills. Whether or not he would, might mean the difference in life or death for some of them. He took great pride in watching his men train them and the additional skills they were learning in defense of the country. His thoughts were interrupted by an incoming call, giving him a feeling of apprehension.

"JB," a colleague said. "Call for you sir."

"Hello," JB answered.

"JB," Jonas said. "We have an exfil about to take place. Ready your team."

"You found it," JB asked.

"Both of these men escaped from there," Jonas replied. "We are certain if we can get them to Taiwan Station that they will give us the details we need."

"Any special instructions sir?" JB asked.

"Arm for the unexpected," Jonas said. "And friend, I do not need to reiterate, but will. If you or your team members get caught, we will disavow all knowledge."

"We knew that going in sir," JB said, looking at Li Na with a slight nod.

"Special Operations Command South has a C-17A fueled and ready at Homestead Air Reserve Base," Jonas said. "Get there as quickly as you can. It's a long flight to Taiwan."

"Roger that sir," JB replied.

The activity in the training area had stopped, all eyes on JB. Operatives had an uncanny intuition for news that would activate them. This group was no different. They knew, without JB telling them that the time had come, and they would soon be on their way.

"What's up," one of the men asked.

"Mount up immediately," JB said. "We have a long flight ahead and will lift off as soon as we get to the airport."

"Where is departure?" a team member asked.

"Homestead," JB replied. "About thirty minutes ride."

The men began packing their gear bags, mostly clothes and training equipment. The bulk of their gear, including weapons and communications equipment remained in the vans they had arrived in. Lunadi, JB, and Li Na heard the men talking and laughing; chattering like school children as they packed. It was obvious the time had been well spent and enjoyed. They wanted to return and continue training if opportunity presented itself and they had developed a new-found respect for Lunadi. He had left a mark on them they would not forget. They quickly gathered around for last minute remarks.

"I have a few words of advice for you," Lunadi said. "Remember you are fighting the person, not the weapon they hold. Also, read the body language and motion. Pay strict attention to situational awareness. Use your own weapons as extensions of yourself, especially your pistols; you won't miss that way. Finally, in the words of my past instructor, remember that he, or she, who hesitates, meditates in a horizontal position. I am not privy to your mission but know that you'll be going in harm's way. Watch out for each other and work as a unified team. Good luck to you all."

The men came up to shake Lunadi's hand and his instructors. They had built a comradery that would be a lasting one. Combat situations had a way of doing that. Last goodbyes said, the men piled into the vans, talking, and laughing about their experience.

"Well, you two," Lunadi said. "It's been great working with you. I'll say it again. Watch out for each other and good luck."

"We'll do that," JB said, his eyes moistening, shaking hands.

"Thank you," Li Na said. "I learned much more than I expected and will treasure the time spent here."

The ride to the airport was brief. Cleared through security, the team grabbed their gear and headed out onto the tarmac. As soon as they had arrived, the pilots were notified and the four Pratt and Whitney turbofan engines that powered the aircraft roared to life. The smell of jet fuel was everywhere when the team walked up the ramp into the rear of the aircraft. A SOG captain met them at the back of the plane, yelling over the sound of the jet engines.

"Sir," the captain said. "We've set up a communications pod and rest area forward of the helicopter. We have partitioned it off to kill some of the sound and make it as comfortable for you as we could on such short notice. There is also storage for your gear inside it."

"Thank you, captain," JB said, shaking hands.

"Roger that. Good luck."

He motioned the team forward past the helicopter, which JB noticed was a modified stealth version. By the time the team had entered the partitioned area, the rear ramp was closing. They had barely sat down when the aircraft started a slow taxi to the runway. Within a few minutes the aircraft turned and stopped.

"We are cleared for takeoff on runway 24," the pilots voice said from the intercom. "Buckle up, we've got a long flight with two mid-air refuels."

Unlike commercial planes a transport had no windows. JB knew the plane could take off on runways as short as 3,500 feet. In this case, the pilot would conserve fuel and use a larger portion of the runways' 11,200 feet. The aircraft was so heavy that the swaying motion was small and before realizing it, they were airborne.

Kang hurried from work across the Shantou Queshi Bridge to a small pier east of him where he disappeared into the crowd and slowly made his way to the boat. The boat owner was tidying up under the upside down, 'U' shaped cover where his ferry passengers sat. The ferry wasn't made for open water, but the forecast called for calm seas for the next twenty-four hours. Its best feature was that it was constructed entirely of wood and unless another boat or ship was within a short distance, it would be undetectable.

"How was your day?" Kang asked, climbing aboard.

"It was busy," Ning replied. "Did I understand correctly that I will be paid five times my normal rate for this run?"

"You did," Kang said. "Two men to the specified location. They should be here shortly."

"Are they hot?" Ning asked, knowing if they were, it would be harder to slip by potential patrol boats.

"I do not think so from what I know," Kang replied. "At least not yet. However, they likely will be within the next couple of hours."

"Hmmmm," Ning mused. "We need to get them on board as quickly as we can. It will take about two hours to the rendezvous point."

"It will be dark in a few moments," Kang replied. "I'll go keep watch for them and for any police or field agents. Standby to cast off."

Kang disembarked and moved toward the darkening shadows along the docks. There was quite a bit of boat traffic along the walkway past the docks. A few people had sat down at some of the outside eateries and were enjoying themselves. He kept his eyes peeled for any sign of danger. There was nothing unusual that he could discern, having been trained to spot field agents, tails, and anything out of the ordinary. Thanks to Pei, he had become adept at it.

Pei had gotten caps, sunglasses, and masks for Li and the lieutenant. The masks were dark navy blue. In China it was common for most people to wear masks due to coal use for cooking and heating, which served as the major energy source. With the recent pandemic, even more people wore them. Along with the caps and sunglasses, the two men would be unrecognizable to anyone that did not know them personally.

She negotiated the route, being careful to look before exposing themselves as they furtively crossed streets and crept stealthily down back alleys. Leaving long before Kang got off work, it would take all her skills to reach the dock on time. Several times, she thought she saw someone following them, but it turned out to be people returning home from errands or work. They finally made it to a taxi stand near the north end of the bridge. She double checked to make certain the lieutenants wound was still bound well and not bleeding. No sign of blood, she gave them their instructions.

"Tonight is a soccer match," Pei said. "We will be going to it with some friends who we will meet at some apartments across the bridge. That is our cover. You must pretend to be excited and laughing about the good time you're looking forward to having. Also, keep your heads slightly down in the taxi so the bill of your hat obscures your face. Do you both understand?" They nodded affirmatively as Pei waved for a taxi.

The three climbed in, smiling and laughing as if they hadn't a care in the world.

"Where to?" the driver asked. He seemed a jovial man, all smiles.

"Just across the bridge," Pei said. "We're meeting some friends to go to the soccer match."

"It promises to be a good one," the driver said. "Who is your favorite team?"

"We don't care who wins," Li replied. "We're just happy to go see them play. It's nice to get out of the house with this pandemic stuff."

"I understand," the driver said. "It's put a damper on everything."

"Pull up there and let us out," Pei said.

"I can take you the rest of the way," the driver responded.

"Oh, thank you, but our friends are going to meet us here," Pei replied.

"Okay, maybe I'll catch you when you return," the driver said.

"Yes, we will be coming back to this same spot," Pei said. "It would be nice to ride with you again."

When the taxi pulled away, the group began walking north toward the large apartment buildings. Pei noticed the driver glancing back at them through his rear-view mirror. About a half block later, the three darted down a small street to the left and circled back east of the bridge, heading toward the docks. The sun had set, it made Pei feel safer. If the authorities questioned the taxi driver, he would point them in the opposite direction. She was aware of MSS and army intelligence field operations. Her father had served with both and had trained her from childhood to be a field operative. A wise man, he felt certain that someday she would need such skills to survive. He wasn't wrong. When she had married Kang, she had trained him as well. Nearing the docks, it was time to slow down and be extra cautious. They made their way to Haipang Road then, cut through Haibin Park and Shantou Gang north toward the harbor. Finally reaching the docks where the boat was moored, they came to a stop, loitering near a small vendor whose cart was deeply shadowed. Looking about, they slowly walked along. Pei's heart leapt when she spotted Kang. One by one, they made it to the ferry and climbed aboard. As soon as he saw them, Ning cranked his engine and retrieved his mooring lines.

Darkness had fallen completely; there were many small boats in the harbor allowing them to easily blend in — they remained unnoticed. The group was quiet, all serving as lookouts for potential danger. Ning kept the boat about half of its 25-knot speed so that he didn't appear in a hurry as he negotiated the harbor, which had larger container ships moving in and out. Within ten minutes, they were passing beneath Shantou Bay Bridge. Reaching the mouth of the harbor just under three miles later, he hugged a mile off the shoreline, passing the Haojiang District. After another six miles they passed about a mile northeast of Biao Corner into open seas. They were just under twenty miles from the rendezvous point. He turned off his running lights and opened the throttle to about eighty percent. They were obscured by the dim light from a waning crescent moon that filtered through low cumulous clouds, gently moving eastward across a velvet dark sky. The further the boat traveled from shore, the more stars they could see. Ning had given each of them a small pair of binoculars to watch for patrol boats, posting them on the bow, stern, and both sides of the boat.

"If all went well," Ning thought to himself, "he would be much richer in a few hours. All of you, pan about ten degrees across the water and sky before moving to the next section you'll observe. This will give us the best chance of detecting anyone coming toward us."

Colonel Diets had gotten two of his WP-18 interceptor boats prepared, including a small patrol boat stationed about three-quarter out on the route to refuel, once the second boat reached station. With a range of four hundred nautical miles, they would easily have enough fuel to return to base, even if they had a skirmish with the enemy. He joined a conference call with Pamela and the Directors.

"We are ready on my end," Diets said.

"Tell us what you have," Pamela demanded.

"As per our discussion," Diets said. "I have stationed two WP-18's; interceptor 1 here at location A and interceptor 2 here, at location B, pointing to the map on screen."

"Do you have enough firepower if you need to engage?" Jonas asked.

"Certainly," Diets said. "Any standard patrol boat or plane can be destroyed with our weapons on board. Our primary system is a Venom 30 mm, gas operated, electrically primed revolver gun with an effective range of 1.2 miles and maximum range of 1.9 miles. In addition to that, we have both surface to air and surface to surface missiles in the bows. We have also retrofitted both crafts with two fifty caliber machine guns using the M20 API-T round, which should do the most damage to boats and aircraft. Short of a destroyer, we can hold our own."

"How fast are your boats?" Pamela asked?

"We have a max speed of 75 miles per hour," Diets said. "If we cannot outgun them, we should be able to outrun them. I might also add that both are mission specific, meaning they are composite stealth type. Highly classified. The enemy will not detect us."

"Outstanding!" Jonas exclaimed.

"I do not need to remind you that you are expendable if captured or killed," Phil said. "And, you should know that the lives of millions of Americans ride on this."

"My men and I understand sir," Diets replied somberly.

"If you should happen to run into one of their gun boats, what is your top priority with it?" Pamela asked.

"We will use our fifty's and 30 mm to take out it's communications," Diets said. "Our techs have installed a software that will automatically detect it and let our 30 mm cannon home in on the signal. The fifty calibers will focus on the entire bridge where the boat captain will be. It is unlikely they will be able to contact their commanders."

"Hold on one moment," Pamela interrupted as her assistant began to whisper in her ear. "Alright, Sky One has just picked up the fast boat and attached it via its under-fuselage hooks. They are enroute to the primary rendezvous point. When will interceptor 2 be on station at point B?" Pamela asked.

"It is enroute and will arrive on station in approximately thirty minutes," Diets replied. "We have planned per your strategy to be on station at least one hour prior to needs. The interceptor at point A has been on station the last half hour."

"Good," Phil said. "Remain in readiness until this operation is completed. Maintain radio silence with your crews until visual siting upon return."

Steve Watson watched the horizon from his fast boat attached to the Sikorsky above. It was not the most pleasant ride he ever had, but he knew from mission status and discussions with Pamela, DCIA, and DDOE that this was likely one of the most crucial missions any operative or soldier had ever been a part of. Failure could be catastrophic for the country. Typically, the mission would have been assigned to Navy Seals, but none were in theatre at present and the mission had been too sudden. He had barely been able to get himself and three other operatives ready. Taking his eyes from his binoculars and looking down, they were so close to the water below that he felt he could reach out and touch it, although he instinctively knew it was at least twenty feet away. From what he had been told the helicopter had been modified for stealth and even if it hadn't it couldn't be flying more than one hundred feet above the water. These pilots were good. He made a note to send a recommendation to Colonel Diets for them. Despite the warm air, Steve was beginning to get a chill from the wind in front and the rotor wash above. They had been going a little over an hour when the comm in his ear crackled as the chopper slowed to a hover, lowering the boat to the surface where the crew quickly detached it.

"On station," Steve said.

"Roger," the pilot replied.

The chopper was swiftly on its way back to base where it would refuel, wait for about a half hour and return for pickup. The fast boat was already enroute to the rendezvous an hour away. The sea was as calm as Steve had ever seen it. The craft bounced across the water at over fifty miles per hour. It was not the ship to shore rubber hulled fast boat, but a riverine special operations craft; called SOC-R by special forces. They were armed to the teeth with pistols and M4's and the boat had two M2, fifty calibers, as well as a 7.62 mini gun attached. For avionics they had GPS navigation, Furuno radar, forward looking infrared, and a secure satcom.

"Omega to Coyote," Steve spoke into the satcom. "Enroute to point Charlie."

"Roger that," Pamela replied, the directors watching the entire operation from a van in a secluded area near the Whitehouse.

"How long?" Phil asked.

"They should arrive at point alpha in about forty minutes," Pamela said.

"Do you have satellite feed of that area?" Phil asked.

"It's not as stable as we would like," Pamela replied. "However, we haven't detected any other vessels or aircraft. Our primary focus is point Charlie and the mouth of Shantou Harbor for faster vessels that may be headed our way."

"I'll keep my fingers crossed," Jonas said, wiping his forehead.

"This is the most critical time," Pamela responded. "If we can pick up on time without waiting, it boosts the chance of a successful mission enormously."

"True," Phil said. "But let's not underestimate the enemy. They have a knack for staying a step ahead."

"That's right," Al said. "But in this case, the only ones who know about this are the four of us, Steve Watson, and Colonel Diets. The men used in the operation thought it was a training exercise until they were on station."

"Hopefully that will alleviate any moles in our groups," Jonas said.

"You think we have a mole?" Pamela asked.

"I can only tell you that the director and I have performed several missions with other teams," Jonas replied. "Each one failed because the enemy was a step ahead. If one had failed that may be acceptable, we might have slated it to chance, but all three failed. It is not a coincidence, which I don't believe in. The enemy had to have inside information."

"That's news to me," Pamela said. "If you are correct, the next phase of the operation could be in serious jeopardy."

"Remain alert and cautious," Phil said. "No unnecessary communications and eyes only."

"We will not involve any other personnel or groups," Al said. "That should help us. I'll contact JB and his team who are enroute and tell him to maintain permanent blackout."

"That will help," Jonas said. "Let's get this phase completed successfully then, we'll have some time to go over the strategy for phase two."

The aircraft encountered heavy turbulence across the Pacific directly after its first refueling, making for a bumpy ride. Notwithstanding the ups and downs, the men were having a great time practicing what they had learned from Lunadi and generally fooling around. No one said anything; it was a way of relieving tension that mounted the closer they got to operational theatre. Thinking about home, JB realized how his life had totally changed after Mary Jane had been killed. He had left the CIA because of her. It was why he had moved back to the reservation. His thoughts were pleasant seeing her face and constant smile; ah, memories. They would have probably had a son or daughter by now. He sighed. It was all water under the bridge. Li Na was as much of a warrior as himself and he pondered whether meeting her was a stroke of luck or was part of the grand scheme of things. Sitting next to him, she could see him out of the corner of her eye. His face was calmer than she could recall, and she too wondered about their relationship.

"A penny for your thoughts," she said softly.

"I was just thinking of the past on the reservation," JB replied.

"You mean about your fiancé?" Li Na asked. "Do you miss her?"

"Yes, to both," JB said. "It's funny how you have plans for your future and then, without warning, the plans go up in smoke. Not because of you or anything you did, but because of someone you had no knowledge of."

Li Na thought about what he said. It was true. Her family had been killed in similar manner, by someone she as a child had no knowledge of. It was uncanny how incidents linked together in a way that a person one didn't know, could have influence over them.

"I feel the same," she said. "Do you think it is strange that our paths crossed?"

"Curious," JB replied. "I was just thinking the same thing. Do you think it was by chance or is it part of life's grand theatre?"

"I do not believe in chance," Li Na said. "Chance is coincidence, which doesn't exist in the Asian mind. Our meeting was not accidental. It is part of the grand scheme, fate if you will."

He sat staring at her, a small grin on his face. She was more beautiful than he believed he was worth as a man but the two had a strong union, both body and soul. They thought much alike, were strong of character, and spoke the truth boldly. They were not killers by choice but by the choices they had made and those they worked for, each believing strongly that what they were doing would bring more justice to the world. He wouldn't say so, at least not now and neither would she, but their love for each other, though they struggled to hide it, was evident to those who had the gift of discernment. The crackling of the sat phone brought both to the present.

"Roadrunner," JB responded.

"JB, Coyote," Deputy Chief of Station Albert Pike said. "We may have a problem."

"How can I help?"

"There is the possibility of a mole within our groups," Al said. "We need to go total communications blackout so if there is one, we can control the damage he or she may do."

"What do you suggest?" JB asked.

"Collect all cell phones so there are no communications to the outside until this is over," Al replied. "No communication other than by your teams sat phone."

"Understood sir," JB replied. "I'll get right on it, out."

He looked at Li Na then, around the group. Everyone was looking back, wondering if there was news of the mission. Whatever it was, they knew that they would be part of it and there would be no complaints.

"Word from Coyote," JB said. "It is time to go communications silent. There's too much at stake. I need everyone's cell phone. Please place them in this case, which Li Na will retain the key for. Until the operation is over, no more phones."

While he spoke, both he and Li Na observed the group. Not one of them seemed bothered by the process. They had probably anticipated it because secret, clandestine missions, almost unquestioned, required communications blackouts. The ease of pinging a specific cell number had long made it prerequisite. Once all the phones were collected, Li Na locked the case. The banter and joking resumed as if nothing had happened.

"Welcome to the world of secrets," JB said.

"I wouldn't expect it any other way," Li Na said, grinning. "Now, back to our conversation."

"I too feel our meeting was not by chance," JB said. "We have far too much in common compared to most people and probably more than we should. It is almost as if we are like peas in a pod, not to mention the enjoyment we have being around each other."

"Yes," Li Na said, with a softness in her eyes as she stared at him. "And don't forget our love."

"You knew," JB stammered.

"Of course; I knew when we first met, and it goes both ways."

"You are more astute than I imagined."

"Don't worry, we will not speak of it again until after this is over."

She sat down next to him, her hand brushing his.

General Bocheng was more than worried. It was dark and there still was no word from any of his intelligence network. It was as if the targets had disappeared. There was no way the intelligence groups were that poor in their methods. However, he had to remind himself that the targets had more than a twelve-hour head start; all MSS agents were playing catch up. If they were still in China by tomorrow, they would be caught, if not — his mind began to wander.

"Colonel Wu," Bocheng called.

"Yes sir," Wu said, rushing in from the outer office.

"I want you to triple the guard," Bocheng said.

"You think they got away?" Wu asked.

"We have not found them yet," Bocheng said. "It is a possibility; we should not let our guard down."

"Tripling the guard will require more men sir," Wu said.

"Hmmmm," Bocheng mused, looking out his office window at the compound. "Okay, get the extra men, but they are to guard the outside of the post only. I do not want them inside the post around the other men. It is imperative that they do not discover what we are doing as a unit."

"Understood sir," Wu said. "I'll attend to it immediately."

The general's sat phone began to ring. He stared at it not wanting to answer for fear something else was going wrong. Finally, extending a trembling hand, he picked it up.

"Bocheng," he said, his voice faintly quivering.

"My friend," Jeng said. "Do not be discouraged. I have some news. One of our agents questioned a taxi driver who picked up two men and a woman who appears to fit the description of your men. We are uncertain who the girl might be."

"It wouldn't be Li's fiancé," Bocheng said. "She is in Hong Kong. The lieutenant is from Beijing so, I don't believe he knows anyone in Shantou."

"Still, I believe these are they," Jeng said. "The taxi driver said one of the men was favoring his shoulder and winced when he got in and out. Did you shoot at them?"

"Yes," Bocheng said. "The gun boats shot the trees along the shore area and also the small islands nearby hoping to drive them out if they were there."

"I think you may have succeeded," Jeng replied. "My agents will follow up and canvas the entire area with the local police to get more eyes on the street. I'll update you as soon as I know more."

"As I recall, you have several Z-10 attack helicopters," Jeng said.

"Yes," Bocheng replied. "Two are fully operational, one is down for maintenance."

"What armaments do they have?" Jeng asked.

"They are armed with 30-mm automatic canon as their primary weapon," Bocheng said. "They also have anti-tank guided missiles, the HJ-10, as well as air-to-air missiles. The primary role is to protect the base if we are discovered. Why do you ask."

"It occurs to me that we should look at who would benefit if these two men escaped," Jeng said.

"The Americans," Bocheng stated flatly.

"If you were going to smuggle them out, how would you do

it?" Jeng asked.

"Air would be the quickest way," Bocheng said. "Water would also work but doing so would leave them exposed and a sitting duck if they are discovered. Land would be too risky without a good intelligence network."

"I agree," Jeng said. "But what if one of their submarines picked them up."

"That would be a mission of stealth," Bocheng said. "The Americans would follow international law and pick them up outside of the 12-mile limit under the UN Convention. My men have already checked Shantou port, only a few container ships have departed."

"They wouldn't need a container ship, only a boat with enough range to get to the 12-mile limit or a little further," Jeng replied. "I suggest you get your patrol boats to do a grid search of the area out to at least the limit. What range do your helicopters have?"

"They could fly to Taiwan and back, if necessary," Bocheng said. "But if we're talking about a grid search, we will need to observe combat radius, which is only 25 to 30 percent of the maximum range. It's the only way to give them enough time over the search area to ensure any kind of success finding them. But all of this is speculation since we do not know where they are or where they are going."

"Set up your search grid and strategy just in case," Jeng said. "Start near the limit and work outward. I'll get back to you."

Pamela was following extraction progress along with the directors and Al. Steve and his crew were minutes away from the rendezvous point.

"The team is almost there," Pamela said. "Our satellite coverage, which will last only a few more moments, shows them about five miles out. We can see their convergence."

"Remind me again," Jonas said. "What's the objective?"

"Steve will pick them up and return to the original drop off point with Sky One," Al said. "They'll attach again under the fuselage and head back. Colonel Diets and his two interceptor boats are stationed along the route in thirds. With their speed, if trouble arises, they should be able to respond quickly enough to make sure we get these two men to station safely."

"How long until JB and his crew arrive?" Phil asked.

"They should be here about three hours after we have the targets to the safe house," Pamela said. "They will be able to watch and perhaps aide in the questioning."

Steve was peering through his binoculars. Salt spray cascading over his face and upper body as the fast boat cut through the water. The droplets on his face cooled his nervousness. This was usually the most critical part of an extraction mission — when initial contact was made. There was always an uncertainty how people would respond, as well as potential threats from the enemies who wanted to spoil the operation.

"There, sir," one of the men said. "About two thousand yards."

Steve trained his binoculars in the direction. A small, covered sampan sat dead in the water, lights out. It was barely discernable in the dim light. It didn't show up on the boats radar. "That was good," Steve thought, as they steered the boat toward it.

Lan had slipped quietly away from her desk and down the street, crossing several more streets to throw off any followers. She picked up another burner phone and called her CIA contact.

"I'm out," she said.

"Good," CS replied. "Go to the small café where we had lunch. Beneath the table we sat at is a small envelope taped to the underside. It has a key in it; go quickly and retrieve it then, make sure you're several blocks away and contact me again.

Fear gripped Lan's stomach as she made her way to the

spot. "Things were moving too fast," she thought. Once inside the building she became even more cautious. No one was seated at the table they had used. She walked around other tables with purpose as she made her way to it, casually taking a seat.

"I would like a tea," she told the waitress. "Please make it to go. My friend is supposed to meet me, but I may be too late."

Lan's eyes darted sideways, all around, and toward the upper floor which overlooked the café. Certain no one was watching, she felt slowly and carefully for the envelope and deftly removed it. Pressing her fingers and thumbs firmly against it, she could feel the key through the paper. As she shoved it into her small pack, her heart almost stopped. She noticed a man near the door who appeared to glance her way and then speak into a microphone on the lapel of his jacket. She paid the waitress for the tea and slowly walked through the café and out the furthest exit onto a crowded side street. She noticed the man slowly walk the same direction, gradually picking up his pace. It was dark outside and difficult to see things clearly. She quickly removed her coat. About fifty yards down the street, she saw the man exit the building, so she cut in a diagonal direction toward the far side of the street then, turned back in the opposite direction.

Walking next to the buildings, she placed other people between the man and herself. He was heading down the initial direction she had turned, obviously looking for her. He had started to jog to catch her, but the long sleeved, light green blouse blended in well with the colors others around her were wearing. It practically made her invisible to anyone expecting to see the small black windbreaker she had rolled beneath her arm. It was obvious the man was an MSS agent as she watched him go in the direction she had initially headed. Lan, glancing quickly about, took the second small street to her right and began a meandering route toward the harbor.

She had gone several blocks, walking directly with, behind,

or in the largest groups of people she could. Her apprehension would not go away; anxiety increased with each step. She remembered back to her surveillance training from CS who had taught her to make sure she always maintained situational awareness no matter what. She calmed herself while she called.

"I have it," she said.

"Remember the place we first met?" CS asked.

"Yes,"

"Go there and open box 17. In it you will find an envelope for you. Meet me at the predetermined location."

Lan was grateful for this man. She did not know him well, but as long as he was her handler, he would take care of her. She was too valuable an asset to throw to the wolves. And, whether in Hong Kong or some other Mandarin speaking location, she had skills most did not and would continue to be an asset. At least there would be security moving forward. The apprehension and fear she felt quickly changed to situational awareness as she rehearsed the surveillance lessons she had been taught and reflected on her training. It was perceiving and understanding all the factors and conditions within the fundamental risk elements such as path, self, vehicles, other people, physical environment, and type of operation, that comprised any given mission. Her safety before, during and after the mission depended on it. She remembered that maintaining situational awareness required an understanding of the relative significance of all operational related factors and their impact on her escape — present and future. Thinking about it brought a calmness because it helped her focus completely on the mission. Her enemies were not just opposing agents, but more importantly, stress, fatigue, anxiety, and finally perceptions — acuity, discernment, and observation that would not be accurate because they could cause her to fixate on a singly identified important task or item, which would reduce her overall situational awareness. At that point, things could become deadly.

The place they had first met was the apartment building of an old man she had been helping. The building had five entrances with the mailboxes directly across the lobby from the ground floor elevators. She surveilled the building for about a half hour. It was busy being directly after work with many coming home before beginning another day tomorrow much like the one today. Walking with a small group, she neared the elevators and mailboxes. Along with several others checking their mail and a small crowd waiting for the next elevator, she dexterously slipped the key into the mailbox and pulled out the single envelope. Sliding it into her pocket, she pretended to wait on the elevator with the rest. Acting exasperated at the wait, she calmly walked around the corner and out the exit, once again, slipping along side streets finding the nearest taxi.

The taxi headed to the airport as directed. She took out the envelope and discreetly removed the contents. It had a passport, several hundred dollars that she could convert at the airport, a flight reservation to Taipei, and a burner phone. The new phone was a signal to get rid of the one she had. She stuffed the passport and money into her small pack and put the burner phone in her pocket. Immediately, she took the battery out of the other phone and quietly broke it in half, letting one piece drop to the floor, she slowly slid it under the driver's seat with her foot. It was now dead. No amount of pinging from a cell tower would locate it. Before she knew it, they had arrived. Paying the driver, she thanked him and proceeded to check-in. On the way she found a restroom where she entered a stall. She hung her backpack on a small hook and took out the passport, which showed an issue date four years prior. Not being new, it likely wouldn't arouse suspicion. It identified her as a British National named Chloe Ruan; an unusual name that demonstrated a mix of English and Chinese origin since Ruan was the name of a common Chinese musical instrument, which she was quite familiar with, having learned to play it. Essentially a four-stringed lute with a fretted finger board, a Ruan is a classical cultural instrument in China having been developed in the second century by workers on the Great Wall of China. A smile crossed her lips as she thought about the pleasing, very recognizable sounds she had created with one. Placing everything back into her pack, she carefully opened the door to the stall, just a crack. The restroom was empty. She dropped the other half of the burner phone in the trash then, quickly washed her hands and headed to the ticketing counter.

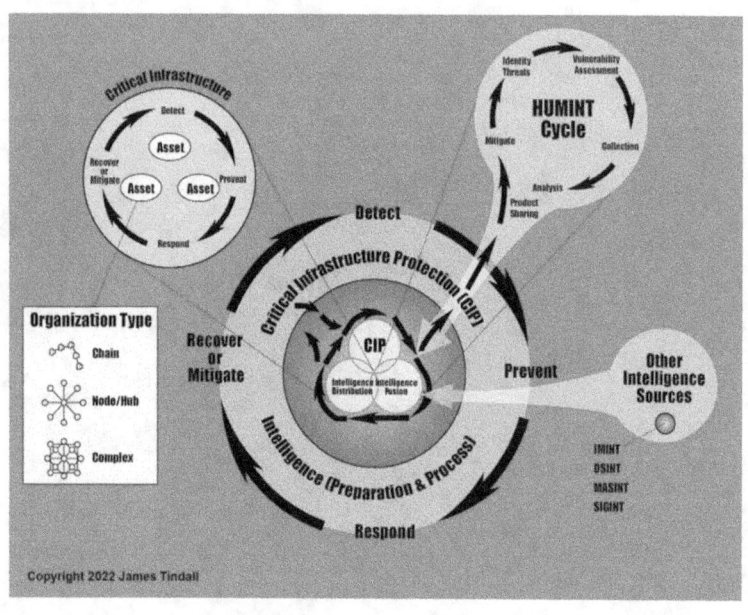

CHAPTER 4

The fast boat slowed to one-third speed about a thousand yards out. Steve ordered the men to station. The three took position behind the mini-gun and two fifty calibers; this was no time to take chances. The slight breeze blowing toward them would help isolate the sound of their engines until they were within firing range if needed.

"Any vessels or planes on radar?" Steve asked the helmsman.

"Negative sir."

"Good. Everyone keep their eyes peeled."

Steve kept his eye on the other boat, scrutinizing it while moving closer. Nothing seemed out of the ordinary considering the situation.

The group on the sampan had reached the rendezvous point. Unlike those coming to extract them, they did not have the luxury of high-tech radar equipment and were unable to know if they were being followed. Their only luxury was GPS. At least they knew they were in the specified location. Pei and Kang sat near the bow watching toward the front, scanning the sea for their rescue party because that's how they thought of them. Li was watching aft. The lieutenant had succumbed to a fever due to his wound and, while doing what he could with his binoculars, he was sweating so much that his shirt was drenched. Ning had seen similar conditions before. If they didn't get the lieutenant medical treatment soon, shock would set in, perhaps death.

Pei and Kang were apprehensive. While they looked forward to being out of China, sitting and waiting was getting on their nerves. They knew if they were captured that there would be no mercy and, in the end, both would be shot or worse. A knot of fear gripped Pei's stomach while she watched through her binoculars. Several times she thought she saw someone approaching but after rubbing her eyes and looking again, there was nothing. Now, it was happening again.

Look there!" Pei exclaimed. "A boat. Is that them?"

"I believe so," Ning said. "Kang, send the signal."

Steve saw the signal immediately; three slow red flashes were visible, which was repeated three times.

"That's them," he smiled, relieved.

Often on a mission, meeting at a rendezvous could be the most difficult and dangerous part, especially in vast, open spaces, whether land or sea. The boat sped up to close the distance and pulled alongside the sampan. Steve's men, being untrusting agents, kept their guns trained on the boat and occupants until they were certain the situation was safe.

"Helmsman," Steve said. "Glue your eyes to the scope. Watch for anything suspicious."

The crew's initial fear vanished when they were sure those on the sampan were not Chinese agents.

"I'm Steve; we're here to extract you. Please identify yourselves."

Pei introduced everyone quickly, by name only and then pointed to the lieutenant.

"He's been wounded and has a fever," Pei said. "We have done all we can to help him but do not have the needed medicines."

"Bobby," Steve yelled. "Help the lieutenant; he has a shoulder wound."

The two boats had been lashed together at bow and stern. The fast boat engines idling at low throttle, a throaty roaring sound cascading over them. Bobby helped the lieutenant aboard the fast boat and sat him down behind the helmsman to begin treating his wound. He remembered some years ago he would have given the lieutenant morphine, which didn't work nearly as well as war movies portrayed. Thanks to the Tactical Combat Casualty Care unit and the U.S. Army's 75th Ranger Regiment, the new painkiller for severe wounds was ketamine.

"This is going to hurt," Bobby said, as he jabbed a large needle into the lieutenant's left humerus. Bobby was using intraosseous infusion or IO as the medics called it. Rather than morphine into intramuscular tissue, IO injected medications, fluids, or blood products directly into bone marrow, the bone providing a non-collapsible entry point into the systemic venous system. Best of all the injured remained relatively lucid.

Pei, Kang, and Li were quickly put aboard the fast boat.

"Do you speak English?" Steve asked Ning.

Ning nodded his head and shrugged his shoulders.

"I can translate," Pei offered stepping back aboard the sampan.

"Tell him to return using a different route than you came out on," Steve said. "It is most important. Also, he'll want this."

Steve pulled an envelope from a pocket of his black BDU's, handing it to Pei who passed it to Ning. It was the agreed upon payment. Ning quickly opened it and thumbed through the bills, a smile creasing his lips as he listened to what Pei was saying.

"Wǒ míng bái," Ning replied. "Xiè Xiè."

"He said he understands and thank you," Pei said.

Steve gave Ning a saluting wave as he and Pei jumped aboard the fast boat, unlashed it from the sampan and both boats were underway. The rendezvous had taken just under seven minutes.

"Full throttle," Steve yelled over the roar of the engines. The four new passengers began to relax. They had not realized it, but their muscles had tightened and constricted because of the stress of the escape from Shantou. They were just now aware of it. They could feel their muscles relax as the boat sped across the water to the next rendezvous point at fifty knots. It was time to call the boss.

"Coyote, Omega" Steve yelled over the roar of the engines. "We have the two packages along with assets. Exfil smooth so far; nothing on radar. Heading to Point B."

"Understood," Pamela replied. "We have sketchy satellite images but see no threats at the moment."

"Omega," Phil interrupted. "Having discussed the matter with Coyote, it is imperative that you get as much information as you can right now. We can ill afford losing it should threats arise."

"Agreed," Steve replied. "I anticipated that and have brought maps and have translators aboard. I will pursue and relay the information ASAP."

"Your man knows what he's doing," Jonas said.

"That's why he is head of counterintelligence," Al replied, smiling. "He'll get the job done. We should have a map incoming shortly."

"Why would you say that?" Jonas asked.

"Because if they all got killed ten minutes from now, we would know the location of the base and then, we have JB's team to send in. The map will give us the location, we can take it from there."

"Good idea," Jonas replied. "It's been a long time since I was in the field. Makes perfect sense. Kudos to you and your station."

Pei and Steve hovered around the two men and unfolded a map, illuminating it with a red light.

"Would you show me the location of the post?" Steve asked.

"It is there," Li said, placing his finger on the map location.

"Go up this river to about here," the lieutenant grimaced. "There is a small dock almost unnoticeable. From there a road twists and turns through the forest and undergrowth to the post, about two miles northeast. We tested the road with the helicopters. It is virtually invisible from the air unless you know exactly where it is; the forest obscures most of it."

"The post is fenced with chain link and razor wire on top," Li said. "It is well guarded with a platoon on duty every shift."

Steve marked the locations the two men had identified, circling each with a large marker with a dot in the middle.

"Give me a moment," Steve said. "Pei please hold the map open so I can get a good picture."

Within a couple of minutes, the picture was on the way. Pamela, Al, and the directors were studying it on the monitor.

"Coyote, Omega," Steve said. "Do you have the picture?"

"Yes, we're looking at it now and comparing it to a recent satellite image. Overlaying it, we can see exactly where the post is."

"Good," Steve said. "This is what they told me."

Steve relayed all the information he had at the time.

"I'll question them for additional details and relay new information immediately."

"Keep at it," Al said. "Let's get every piece of information we can. Once you get back, we'll question them at the safe house."

Jeng's MSS agents had begun reporting in. The lead on the taxi driver had paid off. It was time to initiate a response. He picked up his phone.

"Ye, my friend," Jeng said. "Do you remember the taxi driver I mentioned?"

"Yes," Bocheng said. "What about it?"

"The information was valuable," Jeng said. "Using our agents and the local police, the group of three were tracked to the docks. It appears they left on a small ferry. It shouldn't be able to make more than twenty knots or more."

"How long ago was this?" Bocheng asked.

"Apparently, they left at dark," Jeng said. "Four hours at most."

"Hmmmm," Bocheng mused. "Let's say they could do thirty knots, that could put them as far away as 136 miles. That's an awfully large area."

"I do not think they would go that far initially," Jeng said. "The ferry wouldn't want to be too far out on open seas, despite calm weather. They are not built for that."

"Right," Bocheng mused. "From our earlier conversation, we're thinking a stealth mission. That means they are meeting another boat."

"I agree," Jeng said. "And it would need to be a small vessel to stay off our radars."

"Okay," Bocheng said. "I already have a dozen gun boats near Shantou Harbor. I'll have them begin a search grid to thirty miles out and have them work with the helicopters."

"Are you sure?" Jeng asked. "Seems a little far to me."

"Yes," Bocheng said. "The boats are likely rendezvousing anytime or have already. I don't care about the boat coming in, we need to stop the one or more going out because that's where the traitors will be."

"I see your strategy," Jeng said, smiling. "Maybe you should have my job."

"You can keep it," Bocheng laughed. "I get to play with guns every day and don't have to sneak around."

The two had a great laugh and while they had been talking, Bocheng had written short orders to Colonel Wu as a flurry of activity started in the compound.

"What are you authorizing me to do?" Bocheng asked.

"Whatever it takes," Jeng replied. "Leave any bad news stories to me. Get your helicopters and gun boats on the move. You know as well as I do the importance of Operation Guillotine.

Phase I was a great success thanks to you and your men and our agents in America. Hopefully Phase II will follow suit. We can ill afford these men giving critical information to the enemy."

"Understood," Bocheng said. "But I have one small problem. The anti-tank missiles on the helicopters may not be accurate enough to stop a fast-moving small boat and there is no time to swap them out for air to surface missiles."

"A minor annoyance," Jeng said. "You can fly much faster than any boat. Use your 30 mm canon to take them out. Whether you believe friendly or not, eliminate as a precaution."

"Agreed."

The airport was crowded; Lan instinctively knew the flight would be full. After all, it was Friday evening. The weekend flights were always busy, especially from Hong Kong to Taoyuan International in Taipei. She had made it through security and customs checks with her passport then, picked up her tickets while the agent checked her passport again. So far, so good. Not far from the counter, she noticed CS; they made eye contact briefly to acknowledge each other. Once away from ticketing, she would go through a second security check. Her handler merged in behind her as a precaution. When she presented her passport to the agent, he looked at her, scrutinizing her face carefully. She became apprehensive.

"What is your purpose for visiting Taipei?" the agent asked.

"I have family there," Lan replied, looking directly at the agent. "It's my grandparents and some cousins."

"Don't we all," the agent responded, handing her passport back. "Have a good weekend."

Lan felt relieved when she passed through the X-ray machine for one final check before entering the terminal. CS was in the next row over, taking off his shoes and removing his belt and electronics. It reminded her how simple air travel had been in the past. As she walked down the terminal, there was a men's restroom to her left. It was at that moment she noticed a slim man in his late forties wearing a black leather jacket. For some reason he stood out, seeming more official than other people she passed, too professional. She stepped onto a horizontal escalator attempting to be as nonchalant as she could. Because it was dark, the glass on each side of the terminal was like mirrors. The man had gotten on the escalator directly behind them. Her handler was about fifteen feet away, pretending to read the economics section of the newspaper he held. The agent walked up quickly behind her, assuming CS was just another passenger, he slipped between the two. She knew something was up; fear gripped her throat. She had to remain calm.

Lan glanced out the corner of her eye, at the large windows on the far side of the terminal to her right. The escalator was ending next to the seating area for gate 21. The man got so close to her that she could feel his breath on the back of the neck. The moment she stepped off the escalator, the man grabbed her by her right arm, leading her to an authorized airport personnel door just past the seating area.

"Do not make a fuss Lan Lau," the agent said.

So intent was he on his mission he did not notice CS slip right up behind him. Any observer would think the three were together. The man pushed the door open with his right hand.

"We have you now traitor," the man said. "Did you really think your new passport would throw us ...."

He was cut off in mid-sentence; CS had slipped up directly behind him and snapped his neck. As he started to fall to the floor, CS caught him.

"We must move quickly," CS said. "If there is one of these men, there are more, especially given the circumstances."

Laying the agent down, CS searched his jacket pockets. Finding a wallet, he pulled it out.

"As I suspected," CS said, unfolding the wallet. "An MSS

agent. Remove the battery from his cell phone. Make sure you wipe it down and throw it into that bin. Cover it so it is not on top."

Lan did as she was instructed. Despite having covered violent issues as a journalist, she was appalled at how deftly and how indifferent CS was at ending the man's life. She finished her task, turning back to the dead agent on the floor and CS to find him looking about the small room and the two doors that led into it, one from either side. Against the wall was a short row of lockers for employee clothing and a maintenance door covering electrical wiring, terminal communications, and other equipment. He opened the door to discover just enough room to push the body into a narrow space in front of the electrical panels. The two hurriedly shoved the body into the small space, turned the inside lock on the handle, and closed the door. Lan watched CS as he looked carefully around the room to make sure there was no sign of a struggle, that nothing was out of place.

"We're done here," CS said. "I don't think these lockers will be used until the next shift. By then we will be in Taipei."

He opened the door just enough see into the small alcove that led from the terminal walkway. "You go first; I'll be right behind you. Go to the boarding area and act naturally."

Catching an opening in foot traffic between the people walking by CS gently nudged her out the door. Like traffic on a highway, groups of people passed in waves. When the next space between groups arrived, CS merged into the walkway toward the departure gate. Boarding had already begun. Each took their assigned seats, which were several rows apart, CS behind her. Lan was trying to control her emotions as she thought back over the events of the day and particularly the dead agent. "Better him than me," she thought. Suddenly, there was a slight jerk; the aircraft was backing onto the tarmac. A few minutes later, it was in the air, and she finally felt relieved.

In mere moments they would be out of Chinese airspace, Taipei about two hours away.

Two helicopters were in the air. General Bocheng's men had managed to switch out the antitank missiles on one of the choppers and replace them with eight semi-active laser-guided, air to air missiles. Coupled with almost a dozen gun boats Bocheng had managed to find, he hoped that would be enough. A few of the boats were Chinese Coast Guard. Adding to his own and three from Harbor Police, it was quite a sizeable force. They were already on station and searching. This mission was a simple one; it was pure search and destroy. Any vessel or aircraft, small in nature, would be destroyed. The helicopters had begun their search about five miles from shore and would work primarily eastward. The gun boats wouldn't be able to keep up with them but would be close by.

The fast boat was nearing rendezvous with Sky One. Within the next twenty minutes, they would be suspended beneath the helicopter and on their way back. Steve had gotten all the information he could from the two men as the boat sped across the water. He knew they would be interviewed again at the safe house. Either way, there was enough for JB's group to insert and eliminate the base. He remembered JB from about five years before. He was so good that both Russian and Chinese intelligence groups used examples of his missions to train their own personnel. As the Chinese said, he was deadly. Steve wondered what had happened to him because one day he was just gone and no one at Pakistan Station mentioned him anymore, nor did the Navy Seals he had worked with. Now, apparently, he was back. He also wondered why he was not supposed to mention the name, only the initials and why he was leading a group that were not American. It was unlike JB because he typically operated alone and preferred it that way. "I guess the answers will be forthcoming soon enough," he mumbled to himself.

"Boss," the Helmsman interrupted his thoughts. "The bird will be here in five minutes. He pointed to the radar screen.

"Good," Steve replied. "I'll be glad to get this exfil behind us."

With all the Sabre rattling and posturing from China, the U.S., Taiwan, and Japan, the boat was in a hotly contested area, with each side claiming the territory or rights to travel freely through it. The Chinese Navy had already sunk a few boats that the cowardly leaders of the other countries had let go unpunished. That certainly didn't bode well for them. If they were seen on the open water by the Chinese, it was a forgone conclusion that no help would be coming from their own forces. He was glad that Pamela and Al had the foresight to work with Colonel Diets and position two interceptor boats along route. He reckoned that interceptor 2 was beginning to head east toward Kaohsiung City to stay close to Sky One, which would overtake them within a few minutes. The goal was for the interceptor boats to protect Sky One and the occupants in the fast boat suspended from it from enemy vessels and aircraft. Not realizing it, Steve was gripping the support rail next to the helmsman so hard his knuckles were white.

"You okay sir?" the Helmsman asked, pointing to his hand.

"Oh," Steve said. "Just wanting to get this done."

"I have visual," a team member said, pointing.

"Stop the boat," Steve ordered. "Keep it idling until the harness is attached. "Okay everyone, it's time to hook up to Sky One. We cannot waste a moment. Once we hook up, it'll be a bumpy ride so, keep your heads down."

Sky One was immediately overhead and descended far enough for the crew to guide the multiple single-point hook ups to the four points of attachment on the boat. With a manual release lever, the helicopter could lower to near water surface and the crew could instantly release the boat if necessary. Within five minutes, Sky One was heading eastward on its route. Once again, Steve was impressed with the pilots' skills. As before, the chopper was flying a hundred feet above water surface. Being directly beneath the fuselage, the crew and passengers could feel the main rotor wash; it was noisy and for the uninitiated, scary.

"Let's keep the speed to around sixty or seventy knots," Steve radioed the pilot. "If you pick up anything on radar, speed up. Worst case scenario we put the boat back in the water and you haul ass home. We will do whatever we need to avoid the enemy."

"Roger sir," the pilot replied. "We have electronic jamming and chaff for anti-missile defense. Also, we'll pass over interceptor 2 in about twenty minutes."

"Let's hope we don't need it," Steve responded, settling down to avoid as much wind as he could.

The crew was on edge because this was critical part of the mission. The helicopter could not maneuver as quickly as their fast boat; they felt exposed, like sitting ducks.

Crews aboard the interceptor boats were bored. It's like they were forced to babysit a helicopter like a fledgling bird as it returned to the nest. They had no idea things were about to change drastically.

General Bocheng was at their military communications console, along with Colonel Wu and several support staff.

"We found something sir," a chopper pilot called in. "It looks like a helicopter. It flew out and hovered at a point then, it returned from the direction it came. The detection is sporadic, but it's a helicopter given the speed."

"How far are you from it?" Bocheng asked excitedly.

"They are going about half our speed sir," the pilot replied. "If they maintain it, we will be within firing range in approximately thirty minutes."

"Can you push faster?"

"Yes sir," the pilot replied, but we will exceed our combat

radius and may need to ditch off the coast."

"Then do it," Bocheng stated coldly.

"Roger sir," the pilot replied. "What are your orders for engagement?"

"Destroy that aircraft as soon as you are in range," Bocheng said.

"Understood."

"Colonel," Bocheng ordered. "Direct all gun boats to the coordinates given by the pilot. Have them assist in any way they can. We must not let these two men fall into the American's hands."

"Yes sir," Wu replied. "Do you think it feasible we should begin moving to an alternate location?"

"Not quite yet," Bocheng responded. "Let's await the outcome of this engagement."

Pamela, along with Al and the directors were monitoring the mission live, pleased with the progress.

"It looks like we may just pull this off," Al said.

"Don't count your chickens before the eggs hatch," Jonas responded. "However, I must say things look promising."

"I want to commend you on the operation so far Pamela and Al," Phil said. "The station has done a commendable job. Makes me think the agency did something right for a change in appointing you both as station leaders."

"Thank you, sir," Pamela said.

"Ma'am," her assistant barged in. "Excuse the interruption, but you need to see this."

"Give me a live feed of this," Pamela told her as the aide rushed out the door.

"Gentlemen," Pamela said. "We have activity coming across the water."

The live feed appeared on screen as the group attempted to quickly assess what was happening.

"Where's this feed from?" Phil asked.

"Our Predator drone," Al replied. "It's flying at its maximum altitude; 50,000 feet. The satellite imagery was too sketchy, so we put it up."

"Does it have enough fuel to stay aloft until we recover our people?" Jonas asked. "And is it armed?"

"Yes, to both," Al replied. "It's carrying four R9X, laser guided, 1,000 mile-per-hour, kinetic-energy based missiles. They're a variant of the Hellfire for less armored targets. If you recall it is the type that took out the Iranian terrorist leader, a few years ago. They can take out the helicopters or boats if we decide to engage."

"Good, but let's hope we don't need it," Phil said, wiping his brow. He knew instinctively that things were about to become problematic to say the least.

"If I am not mistaken," Pamela began, "Those are two helicopters and behind them about a dozen gun boats. We better notify Steve and the interceptor crews. I don't want them getting a giant surprise. Al, notify Colonel Diets of the situation."

"Exactly," Jonas said. "Put it on conference."

"Omega, Coyote" Pamela said.

"I read you," Steve replied.

"We have activity behind you," Pamela said. "It looks like two helicopters and about a dozen gun boats. It's the helicopters you need to worry about."

"How far?" Steve asked.

"About fifty miles," Pamela said. "If they are armed with the weapons we suspect, they will be within firing range in less than thirty minutes."

"I understand," Steve replied. "Let me work out a strategy and get back to you."

"Major," Steve said, contacting the pilot.

"Yes sir," the major said.

"According to intelligence, we have two helicopters approaching and will be close enough to fire in about a half hour," Steve said. "Do you have them on scope yet?"

"No sir," the Major replied. "At our current altitude, we won't likely pick them up for another ten minutes. We'd need to climb a couple of hundred feet to see them."

"Maintain altitude and speed," Steve said. "We're going to be the cheese in the mouse trap. If things go wrong, we will lower to surface and detach."

Steve looked around at the crew. They knew something was up. Like most operatives and soldiers, a little action was more welcome than boredom. They eagerly awaited his orders.

"Men," Steve said. "We have bogies approaching about a half hour out. Looks like two helicopters. Man, your guns. Take care not to shoot the fuselage above. If things get too bad, we'll detach."

The men were excited that something was happening and obeyed the orders given. All were now scanning the sky for the enemy — on edge, alert, adrenaline pumping.

"Interceptors 1 and 2," Steve yelled into his mic.

"Receiving loud and clear," the helmsman of each responded.

"Can you see the bogies on your radar?

"Yes," they responded in unison. "They are 30 miles out and closing fast."

"This is what I want you to do," Steve began.

Genesis and Li Na had received the transmission from Taiwan Station. They also had received satellite images of the base and were scrutinizing them, comparing them to their detailed topographic maps of the area. They began marking the locations of the dock, road, compound, and close ups of the buildings, which were few. Their operatives had gathered around a square cargo box that served as a makeshift table in the enclosed area.

"The compound looks deserted," one of the men said.

"I believe that's the basic idea," Li Na replied. "It's difficult to make out and appears to be nothing but a couple of huts from the eye in the sky. That's why the satellites have not been able to pick it out."

"I agree," JB said. "Approaching up the river and down the road is out. They know we may have information about the post by now, so the likely approach is from the same location the two men escaped, along the shoreline."

"That's quite exposed," Xin Cao said. "Is a boat approach feasible?"

"Ordinarily I would say yes," JB replied. "But given the almost certain heightened security, there will be gun boats patrolling the area, as well as two-man teams with dogs."

"What are you thinking?" Li Na asked.

"Halo jump," JB replied, grinning.

"Into the unknown?" Xin Cao asked incredulously.

"He's right," Li Na said. "It's the only way."

"One of us needs to go in a day before," JB replied. "Since none of you are qualified, it will be me."

"A solo halo jump?" Xin Cao asked.

"No," JB said. "A specialized wing suit, which I'm experienced with."

"You won't be able to carry much equipment," Xin Cao said.

"You're right. But all I need is a radio, pistol, knife, and I'll be taking my little Black Hornet."

"What's that?" Li Na asked.

"Essentially, it's a squad level personal reconnaissance system that will give us immediate covert situational awareness. It has electro optical and infrared imaging sensors."

He pulled out the case that had a pair of the Black Hornets inside and demonstrated its operation to the men and Li Na.

"To the uninitiated among you, the technology of this little thing bridges the gap between aerial and ground-based sensors. It has the same situational awareness of a larger UAV, as well as the threat location capabilities of unmanned ground vehicles. It's very light weighing only 33 grams, quiet, almost silent in fact, and has a flight time of twenty-five minutes. I used them in the Middle East."

"How fast can it go?" Li Na asked. "Thirteen miles per hour or for you guys, about 22 kilometers per hour. It's not about speed, but stealth."

"That's an awesome piece of technology," Xin Cao said, his eyebrows raising. "I'd like to get my hands on one."

"They only cost $195,000 each," JB responded laughing. "And only defense contractors or military can buy them."

"Then I'll need to pass until I make my first million," Xin Cao replied, all the men laughing.

"What is your intent?" Li Na asked.

"I'll do a night jump using a wing suit," JB replied. "Once on the ground I'll survey the compound and the surrounding area and defenses. They won't even know I'm there. The next night all of you halo in. In case communications have issues, land a hundred yards in from the shore to avoid any boats in the area."

"What if communications fail?" Xin Cao asked.

"I'll flash my moonbeam in sequence of three once every ten seconds."

"Get some rest crew," Li Na said. "You'll need it. Once we land, things will get frantic."

The men went back to their jovial banter and kicked back, trying to get as much rest as they could. They knew the pace would be non-stop; they would hit the ground running.

"You never told me you knew how to use wing suits," Li Na said.

"It never came up," JB responded. "I used them in Afghanistan to infiltrate enemy held territory to collect information for station. I'd drop out of a black hawk and was on my own for a week or more at a time."

"Like a regular ninja," Li Na joked.

"Sort of," JB said. "But the goal was more like Green Berets operations, to work behind the lines without being detected while gathering intelligence."

"What kind of equipment did you use?" Li Na asked.

"The very basics," JB replied. "A satcom phone, pistol, knife, and some MRE's. Most people think of high-tech, James Bond films when they think about spy work, but you know as well as I do that it's the person on the ground using basic equipment that gets the job done."

"You must have nerves of steel," Li Na said. "I never realized that about you."

"I'll take that as a compliment. It's just that I'm not allowed to talk about past missions or agency work. I gave them my word."

Li Na nudged up next to him and squeezed his hand, a feeling of contentment washing over both. One of her men passed by and kissed at them several times.

"You don't need to keep it a secret," he said with a grin. "Everyone knows."

She seemed embarrassed, but knew such relationships were difficult to hide.

"Tell me about JB," Li Na said. "Why all the secrecy? And why won't you divulge the name for the initials?"

"Secrecy," JB said. "It's all about secrets. I'll tell you only; do not divulge it to any other (he leaned over and whispered the name in her ear). You see, I worked for the CIA for some time; all over the world. Too many spy agencies know that name. Because this mission is so critical, they didn't want it divulged and floating around. Many in the CIA know it, especially before I left."

"Because of Mary Jane?" Li Na asked.

"Yes. She was the reason. Life in the agency was not conducive with marriage so I left for her. Once she was killed, everything changed. All I could think of, like you, was getting the person behind it. Oh, I got the one that did it, but I wanted the man up the chain, giving the orders. Since we have been on this quest, I keep thinking about previous missions and honestly, this one is not unlike them. What I never realized was that the Chinese were hooked into Mexican cartels and thus into the mafia."

"I assume they've asked you to come back?" Li Na asked.

"Oh yes," JB replied. "The DCIA himself, whom you've met, Phil Ross, has asked me personally as has Jonas, DDOE. I've worked with both men, saved their lives, but they've also saved mine. It is difficult to say no for something one has such a passion for. I'm guessing all the foreign spies think I'm dead hence the use of my initials only until I'm formerly reinstated. That won't occur until after this mission."

"You know," Li Na said, compassion in her eyes. "It would be nice to work on something constructive rather than on revenge. We could hire on with them as subcontractors, sort of a free-lance hit team. What do you think?"

"You would do that with me?" JB asked.

"Yes. I would. I believe in us."

He slid his hand down, squeezing her thigh. She could feel the longing building up inside her. He was lucky they were in mixed company, or she would pounce on him like a tiger on its prey. Instead, she was satisfied to stare into his eyes.

Interceptor 2 had begun approaching Sky One. Doing 75 mile per hour, they passed beneath the chopper a couple of minutes later. The crew had manned their guns and were watching behind as the blips on the radar screen drew closer; the interceptor was heading full speed along the westward route to help intercept the bogies. Adrenaline flowed as the boat sped through the water; despite the calm seas, it bounced up and down, throwing spray high in the air, leaving a long white wake behind. Colonel Diets' voice began to echo out of the speakers on both boats.

"This is a critical situation men," Diets said. "We cannot afford to lose the cargo on that bird. Go hot. Once they come into range, take them down by any means necessary. Out!"

The pilots in the helicopters called into headquarters to update General Bocheng.

"Sir, we are within five minutes of firing range," the pilot said. "Do your orders remain the same?"

"Yes, captains," Bocheng screamed into the mic. "Eliminate them immediately."

"Yes sir."

Interceptor 2 sped toward the helicopters, arming their surface-to-air missiles. At almost the same instant, Sky One passed directly over interceptor 1, which was also speeding toward the bogies to join interceptor 2. The crews on both boats were no longer in a state of boredom because hell was coming to breakfast.

About a mile apart, the helicopters 30 mm auto cannon began firing on the approaching boats. Immediately the boats began evasive action as they returned fire. Within a few seconds, several 30 mm projectiles ripped across the bow of interceptor 2, who returned fire with its fifty caliber and Venom 30 mm cannon. The cannon ripped through the tail boom and lower fuselage of the helicopter. Almost immediately, the helicopter cannon returning fire, strafed interceptor 2 and put the boat out of commission. Interceptor one launched one of its surface-to-air missiles; the helicopter exploded in midair a few seconds later. The remaining helicopter's cannon strafed the cabin and aft section of interceptor 1, knocking it out of commission as it sped onward at maximum speed toward Sky One. Interceptor 1 managed to launch one of its SAM's. The pilot yawed right and pitched nose down avoiding a direct hit, the missile nicking the chopper at the juncture of the tail boom and fuselage. There was a small fire, but the helicopter sped toward Sky One.

Steve was listening to chatter over the radio when the team saw the first helicopter explode. Both boats were crippled. Now, it was up to Steve's crew. They manned the fifty calibers and minigun, waiting for the helicopter to move within range. A mile away, the helicopter launched its first missile. The men saw the tail fire and began shooting. Just when they thought they were goners, the bullets connected, and the missile exploded. Steve knew the explosion would initially be assumed by the pilot of the helicopter as a hit, until his radar displayed otherwise. The real question was would he come closer before launching the next missile or fire again from where he was? His question was answered in an instant when they observed another missile approaching at a frightening speed. Once again, they fired with everything they had, the missile exploding below the tail rotor system close to the airframe, fragments wounding Pei and Kang. Sky One pitched forward and downward for an instant before recovering. The crew knew that chances of destroying a third missile were slim at best. Steve realized that with two misses, the pilot of the Chinese helicopter would close the distance before firing its next missile and likely, he would fire two missiles at once. There had been no time to detach the boat and there wasn't now.

Looking around the boat Steve saw fear in the eyes of all aboard. Everyone, get close to the side. When I give you the word, jump; it is the only way to survive. Steve picked up his binoculars and could just make out the Chinese helicopter as it closed the distance. He was just about to yell jump when it exploded. Everyone aboard began yelling in joy.

"A direct hit ma'am," the remote pilot said. "Both birds are down. The two interceptor boats are stalled in the water Sky One is making maximum speed toward Kaohsiung City."

"Thank you," Pamela said. "Return your bird to base."

"Did I hear that correctly?" Phil asked.

"Yes," Pamela said.

"We had no options remaining," Al said. "It was the correct call."

"Yeah," Phil said. "Until the Chinese come calling."

"They won't," Pamela said. "The predator descended to two

hundred feet before firing. It won't show up on their radar and currently their satellite is not above scene."

"That's a relief," Jonas said. "Where do we stand now?"

"Interceptor 1 has power back and is making about thirty knots returning to base with interceptor 2 in tow," Al replied. "They lost four men. Sky One is making maximum speed to Kaohsiung City where the two defectors and rest of the exfil team will be taken to a safe house for debriefing and further questioning."

"What about our asset in Hong Kong?" Phil asked.

"Our agent has her enroute as we speak," Pamela responded. "They will be landing at Taoyuan International Airport in about thirty minutes. They will also be taken to the safe house and debriefed."

"Where is JB and his team?" Jonas asked. "They are the final lynchpin on whether we can make this operation a success."

"Landing later today sir," Al said. "Pamela and I sent them everything that Steve had gotten from the men they extracted. They've been developing a strategy for the last few hours. From last report to station, they had everything well in hand."

"Yes," Pamela interjected. "Before you ask, they also will be taken to the safe house."

"Very well," Phil said. "Excellent job so far. Keep us apprised."

CHAPTER 5

The monster of a plane skidded onto the runway of Chiayi Air Base in southwestern Taiwan, rubber burning briefly from its tires as it slowed and took a taxiway to a far hangar at the corner of the airport. The ramp lowered quickly, revealing a sergeant major at the bottom to greet them. Typical for a military air base.

"Please follow me," he said. "Your people are waiting for you."

The sergeant walked swiftly into the hangar, directly towards a door to his right. Two men were standing casually outside entry. One of them had a huge grin on his face as the group walked up.

"JB," Steve said. "It's so good to see you again. It's been a long time. This is David who will help me brief you."

"Steve, you old war horse," JB said. "What the hell are you doing here?"

"I'm head of CI for the station. And who is this lovely woman?"

"This is my colleague Li Na," JB said.

"Pleased to meet you," Steve said. "Come inside; everything is set up with the station."

The team had looked closely when Steve had called him JB, wondering if it was a code name of some sort. They shrugged it off as they filed into the room and took seats facing a large, monitor.

"We were informed that the extraction went well and that you had two defectors in custody," Li Na said.

"That's correct," David replied. "We lost four men on the interceptor boats. It was dicey for a short time, but we got the job done. Given the nature of the operation, we thought it would be safer to brief you here rather than have all operators at the safe house, not far away."

"Yes, indeed," Steve interjected. "The two men we extracted are at the safe house now. We should have live feet shortly of the interrogation. I'll fill you in on what we know so far, which you're probably already familiar with."

On the left wall next to the monitor, was a large map of the area of the Chinese post. It was a small-scale topographic with elevation relief, roads, streams, and vegetation. Steve pointed to it as he turned on a projector hooked up to a small laptop so that the team could see the entire map without crowding each other around the one on the wall.

"As you know," Steve said, pointing. "This is the location of the post. And this is a satellite view taken a few hours ago."

"What are we looking at?" JB asked. "There's nothing to see."

"Correct," David said. "That's why we have never been able to locate it. Zooming in gives a bit more detail. There."

An enlarged view of the central compound of the post revealed a couple of small buildings, barely seen through the canopy of the trees surrounding them. Near the northeast quadrant was what looked like a small set of stairs surrounded by a short wooden barricade with two guards next to it.

"We believe these stairs lead down to the central computer banks," Steve said. "At least from what the lieutenant said. The other defector, Li, has never had access to the area."

"So, the computers they use to hack the grid are in an underground shelter?" JB asked.

"That is correct," David replied. "According to the lieutenant, it is over 20,000 square feet in size with four guards posted within. And from what we can determine, the entire underground complex is a giant faraday cage."

"Destroying it will not be easy," Steve said. "That's your job. You will need to determine a way to succeed."

"How do they get the signal in from the outside?" JB asked. "They need some kind of receiving dish to send and receive from the hacking, don't they?"

"I agree," Steve said. "That is something I failed to ask the lieutenant. Once the interrogation begins, we can forward any questions you have to the station, and they will ask them."

"That's a good question," David said. "I had wondered the same thing myself, and so looked at the area literally with a magnifying glass. I came up empty."

"Like you," Steve enjoined. "We know it has to be there and it's critical we find it."

"What is this?" Xin Cao asked, pointing to a sliver of what appeared to be a circular object.

"Hmmmm," Li Na said. "Looks like it could be associated with the post, but it's quite a distance from it."

The group was staring intently at the object that Xin had noticed when the monitor came to life, revealing the directors, Pamela, and Al.

"Good morning, everyone," Pamela said. "It's been a long night so let's get to it."

"Let's skip the introductions," Phil said. "Time is short."

"Roger that," Al said. "Team, we have been questioning the two men Steve and his crew extracted. From what Steve told us immediately after, the men have not varied from their initial information. That of itself is good news."

"Now for key information," Pamela said. "Is there anything specific that you want us to ask them?"

"Without doubt," JB said. "We need them to describe the compound and how it is laid out."

"We can do that," Al said. "Hold on a minute."

The monitor blinked as the picture changed revealing the directors, people at the station and two more live feeds of the men who had been extracted. They were in separate rooms being questioned by different agents.

"Okay," Pamela said. "Can you see the two men?"

"Clearly," Steve said. "What we need is for you to give them a map. Let them point out the location again then, have each of them sketch the compound and explain what is located on it and how to access it."

"Hold on," Al said.

The group could see the doors opening into each room. An individual appeared carrying a large map and sketching material, placing it on the table in front of each of the men.

"First question please," Al said. "It will be piped directly to the interrogator."

"Show us on the large map where the post is located," Steve said.

Both men pointed to the same location and then showed how the boats came upriver to supply it.

"That's what they told me before," Steve said. "So far so good. Where is the communications dish or network that they receive their signal from and use for satellite uplink to hack systems with?"

Without hesitation, both men pointed to a location several hundred yards away from the main compound. It was the sliver that Xin had identified. When they pointed to it, Xin smiled as he stood up, mockingly beating his chest, and blowing on his fingers as he next rubbed them on his shoulder. The rest of the men grinned.

"One of our men identified it earlier," Steve said. "It looks like it is not covered with trees, just painted in a camouflage pattern to make it look like it is."

"That is what they are telling the interrogators," Al said. "Next question?"

"Tell them to sketch the compound," Steve said. "How large is it?"

The two men quickly sketched the compound, making a notation of length and width. The rough measurements were two hundred by three hundred yards. As the two men being interrogated sketched the outer dimensions, Xin was tracing the compound on the satellite map the team used.

"Where are the generators or power source for the compound?" JB asked.

The men marked a spot about fifty yards from the northeast corner. Each time they identified a location, Xin marked it on the team's satellite map. He had deftly traced the fence line around the entire compound, along with the one gate that led into it. The questions continued.

"Where are the general's quarters?"

"How many men are in the compound?"

"Does the computers have a backup power source?"

"Where is it?"

"What type of armaments and weapons are present?"

"When do shifts change?"

"Where are sentries located for post?"

The questions seemed endless, some repeated more than once to ensure the answer was the same. Both had been hooked up to the box and were monitored the entire time using voice stress analyzation. The interrogators and the equipment indicated the men were telling the truth. After a few hours, making certain that they hadn't missed any specific points that could jeopardize the mission, questioning was over. Periodically during the session, the men had been given drinks and snacks then, they had been led quietly out of the rooms.

"What do you think?" Pamela asked the interrogators.

"Based on their body language, stress measurements, eye contact, and other parameters we measured, they told the truth," the interrogator replied.

"The information given coincides with what they told your operators before they arrived," the other interrogator added. "It is our estimation that they were not hiding anything and were truthful.

"Excellent," Pamela said. "Thank you for your efforts gentlemen."

"What do you think JB?" Phil asked. "Is this enough for your team?"

"Everything they said corroborates with what we received from you earlier. Answers to our questions filled in the remaining gaps. We have enough to proceed."

"Great," Phil said. "We will leave you to it to make final preparations. Get some rest. Insertion scheduled for the team tomorrow night. JB will be going in tonight."

The two directors vanished from the screen, leaving only Pamela and Al.

"Okay, JB," Pamela said. "What do you need from us?"

"I'll need more later," JB replied, "But here's the list. The first few items I will need before I leave tonight. The others need to be available so the team can deliver them on insertion."

"Alright," Al said. "I'll get right on it. They'll be delivered to you right away. Let's convene about sundown and go over the strategy."

Congressman Blaine Childress of New Mexico had driven his sedan to a small Chinese restaurant about a mile north of the Whitehouse near the junction of Adams Mill Road and Florida Avenue. He pulled into the small dimly lit parking lot. It seemed darker than usual; the heavy rain seemed to snuff out the light. He exited his car and turned to go into the restaurant, rain drenching him in an instant. Two men stood in front of him blocking his path, appearing from nowhere. They had advanced so quickly it scared the hell out of him. The congressman had a pistol trained on him.

"Open trunk please."

Blaine opened the trunk as ordered then, the second man deposited two leather duffle bags and closed it.

"Payment as agreed."

Before the congressman could respond, the two men had disappeared into the darkness. It took a moment for his heart to stop racing then, the elation of the money kicked in. Not being able to contain himself, he couldn't resist the impulse as he unzipped the duffle bags revealing a mix of twenties, fifties, and hundred-dollar bills. Quickly zipping the bags shut, elation swept over him as he hurried into the restaurant to escape the rain and seated himself at a corner table, a big smile on his face. After he finished his meal, he quickly made it back to his car and climbed behind the wheel.

"I have it," he said. "I'll call you soon for a time to meet at my place.

General Bocheng had lost contact with his helicopters. Instinctively he knew they were down. The gun boats were patrolling off the coast and working their way out further toward the potential extraction point. They would find the wreckage and any potential survivors if he was correct in his assumptions. The real question was should he move the post to the secondary location miles away or, should all the men and equipment remain where they were. Any attack on the post would come from a select handful of men. It would be almost certain suicide for them to attack a superior, well-armed force.

"Colonel Wu."

"Yes, General."

"Get me Lieutenant General Teng."

"Right away sir."

It was not something that General Bocheng wanted to do, but he had no choice. It would be better than making an immediate move to the secondary location. They were in a critical phase of an operation and needed to finish it before moving equipment. His phone began ringing.

"General Teng sir," Wu said.

"General Teng," Bocheng said. "It has been a while."

"Yes," Teng replied. "Longer than it should have been."

Lieutenant General Shing Teng was a person to be reckoned with. There was no one that was more pro party or pro-China than this man. He was previously chief of staff of the Armed Police Force in Xinjiang. Purportedly, the city was where the UN and the U.S., as well as others implied that China had detained at least one million people from the Uighur ethnic minority. Now, he was head of Hong Kong Garrison, which kept a very low profile. Teng was as brutal as they came and would resolutely defend national sovereignty and security interests. At this moment, he was exactly the kind of man Bocheng could trust.

"How can I help you old friend?" Teng asked.

"You are one of the few people I can trust," Bocheng said. "You also know what our post does. I need some men, mostly as a precaution?"

"What for?" Teng asked.

Bocheng had thought carefully about what questions Teng would ask him, and he was prepared for this one.

"Two of my men appear to have deserted," Bocheng said. "I need more men to help search the area. As you know, we cannot leave this facility unprotected, neither can we afford its discovery."

"I see," Teng responded casually. "No, we cannot. How many are you requesting?"

"I believe that two platoons would be sufficient," Bocheng said.

"Your station is critical to our national security," Teng responded. "I will have three platoons sent immediately. Given your distance, they should arrive in approximately four hours."

"Thank you, sir," Bocheng said.

"No problem," Teng replied. "Make sure you find them then, eliminate after questioning."

"Yes sir," Bocheng said.

He knew the general was not pleased. He also knew the general was aware of the importance of the facility and mission of he and his men. With the additional men, Bocheng saw no immediate reason to move to the secondary location. If an attack came, it would not from missiles and bombs from aircraft outside Chinese territorial waters. The additional men should prove more than adequate for a defense.

The base facilities were not the best, but the men were making the most of them. They had all gotten showers and spent the day checking equipment and their weapons, readying themselves for deployment. Li Na and JB were in cramped quarters with a twin bunk. Both had showered and refreshed themselves. Their playfulness while showering together had led to a deep intimacy that spent them completely. The kind that only those who didn't know if they would live through tomorrow could appreciate. Dusk was approaching quickly; JB had a lot to do to get ready for his jump.

"This is going to be a dangerous mission, isn't it?" Li Na asked.

"You're not a stranger to danger," JB replied.

"No," Li Na said. "But my dangers have been one on one, and I have always been in control. I've never been on a mission like this. It's scary. We will be jumping into a pitch-black night and no backup except for us."

"Isn't that what you have done before?" JB asked.

"Yes, but not to this level of complexity. Doesn't it scare you?"

"Certainly, but fear keeps you alert and alive," JB replied. "I won't lie to you though; this will be different."

"In what way?" Li Na asked.

"They'll be waiting for us," JB said. "They know they lost two helicopters and that loss means the two men escaped."

"This facility is very valuable to them, isn't it?"

"Yes, and then some," JB replied. "If they are hacking the grid, a shutdown in power could affect the lives of thousands or millions depending on where the hack is. That is their goal."

"You're assuming they'll be successful," Li Na said flatly.

"Without a doubt," JB said. "Let me tell you a story. In 2013 there was an attack on the Metcalf transmission substation in Coyote, California, which is near San Jose. It was initially reported as vandalism, but many in the know believed it to be far more. The gunmen damaged seventeen electrical transformers during what the media termed a 'sniper attack' to hype it up, although the power company and Department of Homeland Security wanted the incident to stay low on the radar."

"You don't believe it was vandals?" Li Na asked.

"No," JB said. "I do not. Prior to the attack, a series of fiber-optic telecommunication cables were severed. Following the attack, investigators found small piles of rock from where the shots had been fired. It was the type of formations that are used to scout sniper firing positions. That alone proves it was not the act of a typical vandal. They directly targeted transformers which leaked over 50,000 gallons of oil and overheated and sent an equipment failure alarm to the power company. During the investigation, more than one hundred AK-47 cartridge casings were found. Military experts indicated that the assault appeared to be a professional job. I was working with colleagues at the Naval Postgraduate School in Monterey at the time, with the Center for Homeland Defense and Security. Most of us believed the same thing — a pro had done it, not a vandal. The casings of the expended rounds were checked; there was not one fingerprint or partial on any of them. The Federal Energy Regulatory Commission, as well as the FBI believed it to be domestic terrorism, but they did not say that to the press. The bottom line is that it was a sophisticated attack. One has not occurred since."

"What do you think they did it for?" Li Na asked.

"I think it was a preplanned attack to determine how we would respond and how fast," JB said. "Whoever did it was looking at our weaknesses and what a small level attack would do to the immediate infrastructure."

"I'm thinking you do not believe that attack was the end of it?"

"Absolutely not," JB said. "It was too well planned; I believe it was a precursor to another much larger attack. It's been almost a decade and nothing like it has happened again. Truth be known, I think it was the same ones we're going after now."

"Why do you suspect them?" Li Na asked.

"The weapons for one thing." JB replied. "And if you couple a physical attack with computer hacking, you can affect a vast area and millions of people."

"I never thought of it like that," Li Na said. "Everything is connected to our power supply."

"Exactly," JB said. "And if that supply is cut off, we'll be back to the 1850's in the blink of an eye, using candles for light. Just imagine not being able to use a television, smartphone, or any electrical device, or turn on your tap and get water. Every industry would crumble overnight. No banking, no communications, nothing."

"That's a bleak picture," Li Na replied softly. "I guess we better treasure the moments we have."

"Yes," JB said, grabbing her buttocks and pulling her closer as the two had a long kiss that aroused them deeply. It was time to go; he grabbed his duffle and was out the door.

The extra men had arrived at the post; Colonel Wu had issued them their orders per the general's instructions. "Only a fool would try to attack us at such a stage of readiness," he thought. With the new reinforcements, it would be nearly impossible for any small group to succeed in taking over the post. He was glad though, because of what was currently about to happen thousands of miles away. Governments would want to retaliate.

"Everything is set," Colonel Wu said. "When do you want to begin?"

"Now," Bocheng replied. "The time for waiting is over."

The two men walked across the compound to a small square barricade, about chest height that was built around the entrance to the banks of computers below. Colonel Wu didn't care much for the personnel allowed in the area, thinking they were just a bunch of nerds. But they could work magic with keyboards and so, he tolerated them. They descended the stairs and walked down a well-lit hallway for about twenty feet. It suddenly turned right into an alcove where two guards stood at attention, their AK-47s at the ready. The two soldiers inspected the identification of each of the men, despite the fact they knew exactly who they were. The officers were allowed to pass through the doors where two more guards stood watch.

Once past the guards there were about a dozen men and women in white lab coats sitting at several stations in front of a vast array of server racks and monitors. Standing seven feet tall, each server rack held twenty-four rack servers; each one the equivalent of a large hard drive for the largest computer most people could imagine. Colonel Wu never fully understood what they were for, but he had estimated about 10,000 of them in the large open room. There were columns on a regular basis supporting the reinforced concrete ceiling overhead. The walls and ceiling were wired with a lattice of copper that would protect them from an EMP or large solar flare. The room was in fact, a giant faraday cage.

"Are you ready to begin," Bocheng asked.

"At your command general," the technician replied.

"Commence now," Bocheng ordered.

"We will take down the RPC," the tech said. "It's part of their Eastern Interconnection of the grid."

"That should give DC a taste of their own medicine for once," Bocheng grinned. "Are your ground teams in place?"

"Yes sir," the tech said. "They have already recoded the older legacy systems. Our hack will attack the larger, upgraded main stations. We awaited your specific instructions to initiate."

"How many people will it affect?" Bocheng asked.

"Our rough estimate is 92 million," the tech said.

"Outstanding."

The MSS agents had been embedded in the U.S. for almost a decade. During that time, they had researched the energy grid of the country to the smallest detail. They knew as much about the grid as the people who managed it, especially its vulnerabilities. Unlike gas or water, electricity in the grid cannot be stored in large quantities. It needs to be generated the moment it is used. For their mission, this meant that supplies must be kept in constant balance with demand. Electricity flows simultaneously through all transmission lines in an interconnected system in inverse proportion to the electrical resistance of the lines. This means that electricity generally is not able to be routed over specific lines and that both generation and transmission operations in the U.S. and Canada, must be monitored and controlled in real time on a 24/7 basis. Otherwise, a reliable and continuous supply of electricity to users is not possible.

For the MSS agents this was a perfect scenario because providing the supply requires the cooperation and coordination of hundreds of electricity industry participants. The entire U.S. grid has over 200,000 miles of high-voltage transmission lines and serves over 330 million people. They were about to disrupt a third of it. Just like the 2003 New York City blackout, blamed on a fallen tree, their work would be the monkey wrench that would cause the same rerouting problem, initiating an electrical surge through substations incapable of handling the load, taking them offline, especially the lower voltage distribution lines for residential and commercial customers. The transformers at the generating stations would not be able to step up the electrical voltage for efficient transport and then, step down the voltage at substations to deliver power. Their operation would trigger the entire system under the RFC to collapse, almost immediately. The two main functions of adequacy and operating reliability that assured the dependability of the grid would fail. The agent smiled.

"What are you smiling about?" his colleague asked.

"This system is unreliable," the agent said. "The entire premise is that it can withstand sudden disturbances such as short circuiting and loss of system elements to avoid uncontrolled cascading blackouts or damage to equipment, especially large transformers."

"I don't see the humor," his colleague said.

"You must," the agent said. "We proved them wrong in the New York City blackout and in our attack on the Metcalf substation. Don't you see? The system operators will not be able to take controlled actions to maintain the balance between supply and demand within a controlling region. When we execute the strategy, there will be no voltage reductions or rotating blackouts because there will be no power to furnish the distribution feeders."

"Oh, I get it now," the colleague said. "It's what our handlers told us about cascading blackouts when an interruption cannot be restrained from sequentially spreading beyond and are predetermined by studies. In our case, most of the southeastern part of the U.S."

"Precisely," the agent said. "It occurred in 1965 and again in 2003 in the Northeast and in 2011 in the Southwest. The government was able to disguise and twist the narrative then. This time they will be unable to do so."

Computer hackers under General Bocheng's command began their job at the post. Brightly lit, the underground computer and server array, connected to the giant satellite dishes began sending commands and lines of hidden code to major electrical hubs and substations of the corporation that controlled the southeastern portion of the U.S. power grid. The MSS agents had used a keypad to access SCADA (Supervisory Control and Data Acquisition) of some of the older legacy systems. Counterparts in various control rooms throughout the grid had done the same thing, but via computer access. Theoretically, SCADA, a system of software and hardware, allowed control of industrial processes locally and at remote locations, monitored and gathered real-time data, and directly interacted with sensors, valves, pumps, motors and more through a human-machine interface. The MSS agents had taken control of the system through rekeying older valves and controls with their keypads while hackers in China did the rest. Both logic controllers and remote terminal units (microcomputers) that communicated with an array of objects that the flow of electricity relied on, were temporarily under control of a foreign power. And, briefly, the SCADA software could no longer help operators and other employees analyze the data and make management decisions. Loss of power could not be prevented.

Jonas Rothman, Director of the Department of Energy, was finishing a long day and just heading out the door when the lights went out. Having learned hard lessons during operations in the Middle East, he pulled his trusty small, red-lensed flashlight from his briefcase and began walking down the stairs to meet his security team. "Damn power," he thought. "It's becoming more unreliable by the day."
When he found his detail, they were looking around, apprehensively.
"Something wrong?" he asked.
"Sir," the lights are out everywhere," the agent said. "My sister lives in southern Virginia. She says her whole neighborhood is

dark."

"Get our command van," Jonas said. "Make sure it's powered up."

No sooner had he gotten the words out of his mouth than the president called.

"What the hell is going on?" the President asked.

"I'm not sure sir," Jonas replied. "It appears we have a widespread power outage."

"Find out and get back to me," the President said. "We're on auxiliary power here, which increases security threats. Find out how large the outage is and report back."

"Yes Mr. President," Jonas replied, murmuring to himself. "This is going to be one giant headache."

His phone began ringing from multiple callers. He decided to answer the most important one. The Director of NERC, Cynthia Hanson.

"How bad is it, Cynthia?"

"Reports are still coming in," Cynthia said. "From the reports and satellite photos, it looks like most of the southeast U.S. Do you think this could be an accident?"

"No! It's too widespread. What do you think the damage will be?"

"Catastrophic Jonas," Cynthia replied. "The administration has now put us in a real bind. Pushing vaccinations and deliberately disrupting our supply lines to push their agenda of power, control, and money; it is going to hurt us badly."

"I understand," Jonas replied. "The last time I checked, the larger transformers needed for replacement were scarce."

"We have only two in New York State," Cynthia said. "Reports so far say that eight are out; I'm guessing there will be more. This is scary Jonas. Replacing those we do not have could take up to eighteen months."

"We will need to replace the ones that power the capitol first," Jonas said.

"Right," Cynthia replied sarcastically. "Power the incompetent so they can make things even worse."

"Now, now," Jonas laughed. "Don't let them hear you say that."

"At this point, it doesn't matter," Cynthia responded. "They should have listened to us. We told them this was coming."

"Yes," Jonas said wryly. "But you cannot teach old dogs and full-fledged narcissists and traitor's new tricks. Update as soon as you can."

"I'll do that," Cynthia said. "Stay safe out there."

His command van pulled to the curb with its three-man staff, along with two lead and two follow vehicles with his security.

"Can we access the Internet?" Jonas asked, sitting down.

"Yes sir," the tech replied. "As long as we have power, we can access it via satellite from sources in unaffected areas."

"Is New York still online?" Jonas asked.

"Yes sir,"

"Contact the telecom hotel and tell them what we need," Jonas said, passing him a small piece of paper. "This is the authorization code."

"I need to speak to the director. This is DDOE Jonas Rothman."

"Jonas," Jeff said. "I figured you'd be calling."

Jeff Stiles was the Secretary of the Department of Homeland Security. Like Jonas, he had served in the field in combat and as a special operative and had developed a keen sense of politics — navigating in what he termed a bureaucracy of fools.

"This was no accident." Jonas said. "What can you tell me?"

"We have been monitoring a few suspected MSS agents," Jeff replied. "Along with the FBI. We suspected they were up to something, but they recently eluded us. We have dispatched teams to track them down. I'll let you know if we catch them. Also, the Chief of our Cybersecurity and Infrastructure Management Agency discovered the hack as it was in progress. They were too late to stop it."

"Did you determine the origination?" Jonas asked.

"It was quite sophisticated," Jeff replied. "It bounced off servers all around the globe at random. We do not know the origin, but we suspect the Chinese. We've been looking for the source but haven't located it."

"We have," Jonas responded curtly. "Between us only, there is an operation in place as we speak to take it out. I'll let you know if we succeed."

"You had better hurry," Jeff said. "It's difficult to know if they have sabotaged other areas or not. Even if they didn't, the sophisticated computer attack along with their men in the field could be duplicated rather quickly."

"How quickly?"

"It is evident that they know our system," Jeff replied. "Potentially another attack could come within three to seven days. All they need to do is gain the access like they did for this one. I know you realize this, but the grid is not well protected and its old and weak, despite what the media and administration tell us."

"Understood," Jonas responded, sighing. "I'll let you know if we have success so you can monitor the infrastructure and make certain we destroyed the hacking location."

"Very well," Jeff replied. "I'll wait for your call. Meanwhile, we will maintain our search for the operatives and monitor the infrastructure systems."

Jonas feverishly took phone calls and made others. The command van had gone to the highest location close to the capitol and parked. The security details surrounded it with an envelope of high-powered automatic weapons. They knew what was happening and prepared for the worst since MSS operatives could be anywhere with a variety of assignments for each team. Similar in operation and capability to the CIA, they were not to be underestimated.

The CV-22B Osprey awaited JB on the tarmac, the rear ramp lowered to the asphalt. He stood in the door of the hangar, with Li Na and his team. He walked in front, obscuring her slightly as he reached behind and gently squeezed her hands. It was the only display of affection he could give at the moment.

"Men," JB said. "The time is upon us. I'll drop in tonight, about 0200, to scout the location. You'll follow tomorrow night. Make sure to triple check your gear. We can afford no mistakes."

"Do you think they'll be waiting for us?" Xin asked.

"They know their choppers were destroyed and the two men are gone," JB said. "It's a safe bet. Count on it so you are not surprised. You know the culture better than I do. My guess is that they have called in reinforcements. Be prepared for it."

"Agreed," Xin Cao said, the rest of the men nodding affirmatively.

"I'll catch you later," JB whispered to Li Na, as he walked to the Osprey and up the ramp. The two Rolls-Royce turboprop engines roared to life and the ramp quickly closed, the team watching it from the hangar door. Within a few minutes they were airborne. He had barely sat down when his sat phone rang. It was the directors on a joint call.

"Gentlemen," JB said. "How can I help you?"

"You need to destroy that base immediately," Jonas said, as he described what happened.

"When will you make your approach?" Phil asked. "It's imperative to get this done."

"My insertion will be in about two hours," JB replied. "I will scout the area, get a count of the opposition, and double check locations of all targets. That will take me the rest of tonight and tomorrow. Tomorrow night, the rest of the team will insert."

"How long to completion?" Jonas asked.

"My estimate is three days max," JB said. "We're only going to get one chance at this. If we don't do it right, you can bring some body bags."

"Do you have absolutely everything you need?" Phil asked. "We will spare no expense."

"Yes," JB said. "I have the small drones with me and others coming tomorrow. I won't lie to you. This is a mission of stealth against a likely overwhelming number of the enemy."

"Understood," Jonas replied.

"I agree," Phil said. "It's difficult to wait, but we know the ramifications. Proceed as quickly as you can."

"We cannot afford another strike like this one," Jonas replied. "Take that bastard out!"

"I'll do my best sir," JB replied. "What did they do?"

"They took out the entire southeast grid," Jonas replied.

"Damn!" JB exclaimed. "I best get moving. We will succeed sirs, out."

Steve had been waiting in the background, sitting in one of the thirty-two seats aboard. This was going to be interesting.

"Time to save the world JB," Steve said. "We've got something new for you. Now, you've flown the delta wing version we used before. This one is electric; I'll let Sergeant Major Dickson explain it. Get your wingsuit on."

He donned his wingsuit like he had many times before. Like most, it consisted of cloth webbing between the legs and underneath the armpits. The electric impellers, for extra thrust were attached to the chest with a quick-release harness.

"Now listen up," Dickson said. "We must stay out of Chinese territorial airspace. We've made runs like this many times so, they won't be suspicious when they see our blip on their radar."

"Basically, you're telling me the jump will be high and out to sea?" JB queried.

"Exactly," Dickson said. "Now pay attention. This is a lightweight carbon fiber jetpack with electric impellers. It weighs about twenty-five pounds, including its 50-volt lithium battery. By the way it has a 15-kW output. Are you familiar with most standard wingsuit jumps?"

"Certainly," JB replied. "We typically jump from a 3:1 ratio of length to height, which gives us the ability to glide just beyond four miles when dropping from 12,000 feet."

"That's right," Dickson said. "But how far are international boundaries?"

"Twelve miles," JB began, "but that means . . ." His voice trailing off.

"Exactly," Dickson said. "You get the picture. We need to get you a minimum of twelve miles, but due to our added buffer so that we are not considered in their airspace by the Chinese, you need to get to your target from about eighteen miles out."

"How the hell am I supposed to do that?" JB asked, tension in his voice. "Typically, we glide about four miles maybe a little more."

"That's where this electric jetpack comes in," Dickson said. "When you have flown delta wing versions with fueled jet packs, you've always kept them on through landing, this one will be jettisoned."

"Why?" JB asked. "Not wanting to hear the answer he knew was coming."

"The maximum altitude you can still breathe oxygen is around 20,000 feet," Dickson said. "To get you to your target, we need to climb to that altitude and drop you. The second you're away from the plane, ignite the impellers and slowly drop to 12,000 feet, once at that altitude, jettison the jetpack by pulling on these quick release handles; just like on a parachute."

"Let me get this straight," JB said. "You want me to gradually drop, getting the maximum distance from the pack?"

"Precisely," Dickson said. "You'll get exactly five minutes of thrust from the pack, which should put you about four miles from shore."

As he was talking, JB was doing the math in his head.

"That's means I need to maintain a glide path of about twenty-three degrees for fifteen miles," JB said. "You sure this thing can do it?"

"Look, you'll be reaching a speed of 180 miles per hour for five minutes. The rig will get you there if you maintain altitude along the proper glide path."

"That's a big if," JB said. "If I screw up, I'll be swimming the last mile to the shore."

"That's right," Dickson said. "So don't muck it up."

"You drive a hard bargain, Sergeant Major," JB grinned. "I'll make it work."

"I wish I were going with you," Steve said. "This is going to be one interesting and dangerous mission."

"Yes," JB said. "But this is one where I'm better off alone so I can get everything prepared for the team. Tell me, do you think those two men told us the truth?"

"Yes," Steve said. "Voice stress analysis works very well. Besides, everything they told us about the post, at least the physical structures and dimensions were verified. Why do you ask?"

"This is a difficult mission," JB replied, his lips tight. "The last thing we need is misinformation to trip us up."

"That's what you're about to find out," Steve said. "Good luck. They know you're coming."

JB tipped his fingers in mock salute as he turned and walked to the lowered ramp behind him. The roar of the airplane was extremely loud as he waited for the green jump light.

"Remember," Dickson yelled, pointing. "The shore is eighteen miles on your right."

He gave him a thumbs up just as the jump light went from red to green. JB stepped off into the darkness, swinging to his right at a ninety-degree angle and pressed the on switch for the electric impellers. What a rush. It was incredible. He was a man flying like a bird, but so much faster. Almost since the dawn of time, men and women had long dreamed to fly. He remembered watching brown eagles when he was a kid and thought that one day, he would fly like them. Thanks to technology, it was now a reality. The twists, turns, and dives in a wingsuit were not yet up to par with eagles, but perhaps soon.

The moon dimly lit a cloudless sky as he sped through the air, keeping an eye on his altimeter. Like all technologies, the use of wingsuits for extreme sports had quickly made their way into special operations groups in the military. They were a perfect way to stealthily insert operatives behind enemy lines or into specific target areas. And as usual, the military had vastly improved the technology far beyond what extreme sports enthusiasts were accustomed to.

"You better watch out Iron Man, JB is here."

Right on que, five minutes later JB reached the 12,000-foot level and jettisoned the jetpack. In a way it was a relief because he felt more mobile and freer. He could barely make out the water below, a slight glimmer here and there. The feeling of freedom in a wing suit was unlike he felt anywhere else. All alone, diving like a water turkey at home, he relished the speed as he dove to his target. Ahead of him he could make out a few lights here and there. To his left was the glow of Shantou, over thirty miles away. Around the world, one could make their way in the dark to any city because the glow from their lights was like a welcoming beacon. Using the cascading light of the moon, he could barely see the shoreline as he sped through the cool night air. Deciding to play it safe, he decided to open his chute just a little early to glide in. When he pulled the cord, it didn't open.

"Damn," JB thought, his heart racing. "That's just great."

He quickly tried to open the chute again; it failed. He would need to execute a water landing; it was his only option. Instructors had talked about it when he had gone through jump school and spent hours and lots of dives in wingsuits at Ft. Bragg. The agents had seen several videos of extreme sports enthusiasts landing in the water, but the instructors would not permit them to practice it although they taught the operatives the principle of how to implement one. His heart pounded uncontrollably as the freedom he had felt seconds before vanished, turning into a life-or-death situation. He remembered the video of a wing-suited extremist landing on a lake in Italy. Angling along the shore instead of straight in, he had mimicked the flight of a jetliner, nose up as the wheels touched down. Mimicking the maneuver, JB kept his glide path was a shallow as he could. His body arched with chest and head up, he hit the water, his knees touching the surface first, rapidly dragging the rest of his body beneath the water. Managing to keep his head up, he rapidly slowed and within a few seconds, had stopped, the water shallow enough to stand.

"It beats landing on rocks," he thought.

He remained standing in the water for a few moments, looking carefully about. Slowly wading to shore, he took cover among a thicket of bamboo trees. About two minutes later, he heard voices then, saw the faint glow of a cigarette from two soldiers that passed within a few yards of him. Had his parachute not malfunctioned, he would have landed right on top of them. Adrenaline began to flow through his body as he pulled his suppressed .22 from inside of his suit. It was for protection only, just in case. If he killed any soldiers now, the element of surprise would be gone, and he and his team would face certain death.

The post was quiet; the new troops had been given their assignments and were efficiently carrying them out. Colonel Wu was grateful for their presence. More importantly, he was ecstatic about their mission in the U.S.

"What's the status of the mission," Bocheng asked.

"So far, about twenty crucial transformers are down, sir," the tech said. "It will take over a year for many of the areas to achieve normal operating status."

"Good," Bocheng stated flatly. "And Washington?"

"Their primary transformers are down," the tech said. "All major agencies are operating on secondary power sources, mostly generators."

"How long can they operate that way?" Bocheng asked.
"Much like us sir. If they have the fuel, they can continue, but I doubt they have enough power to operate more than critical systems."
"What do you mean?" Bocheng asked, puzzled.
"Well sir," the tech replied. "We have a small post and must conserve except for critical components. So, they will put most of the backup energy into communications and critical unit operations. Power for agency buildings and so forth will not be available. In a real sense, only critical, or as they term it, essential personnel will be working."
"Very well," Bocheng stated. "I suppose that Washington will get the spare transformers first. How long before they would be up to full power again once replacements arrive?"
"You don't just put in a large transformer and flip a switch," the tech said. "Once you replace it, the transformer must be slowly regulated before bringing to full power. That could take from a couple of weeks to over a month for each one."
"Excellent," Bocheng said. "Well done. You deserve a promotion. We need to hit them while they are crippled. How long before we can execute the second phase of the mission for strike two?"
"Rushing it, we could do it in about four days," the tech replied. "But we want to be sure, correct? To be certain, we need a week before executing this one."
"The impulse in me says rush it," Bocheng said. "But the strategist in me says to wait. Alright, initiate all protocols to execute phase two in one week. It's not like they'll get the power back on by then?"

The general and the group of technicians laughed. They had created havoc and they knew it. More importantly, the next strike would shut down two major power grids and leave the U.S. dark for more than two years. Because some of the major components for the transformers were made in China, there would of course be a delay in manufacture and shipment.

America had become weak and impotent under the past administration, which would become the world's laughingstock before they were done.

"General," an aid called, rushing up. "You'll want to see this."

"It's just the same old plane doing its same routine trip," Bocheng said. "It's staying just out of our airspace. Surely, they don't think we're bothered by it. Still, keep an eye on radar to make sure they don't drop anything out of the plane."

"Yes sir," the aide said. "We're doing that. It just appears to be flying up the coast normally and is currently turning back to Taipei. We just thought you should be informed."

"Thank you," Bocheng said, a slight smile crossing his lips. "Soon we will not need to worry about them because Taiwan will be ours once again. Alert the patrols to be on heightened surveillance for the next two hours."

Pamela was on the phone with Al and Steve. So far, the mission was going as planned.

"Insertion was a success," Steve said. "I just received a coded message from JB."

"Is the rest of the team ready?" Al asked. "No time for slip ups."

"Yes," Steve said. "They will leave early tomorrow morning for Hong Kong and our friend will escort them to the target area. I do not foresee any problems, but we are triple checking everything."

"Make certain there are no mistakes," Pamela said. "In case you're unaware, the entire southeastern power grid is down."

"I was told by JB, after the directors called him for a pep talk," Steve said. "How the hell did that happen?"

"It wasn't an accident," Pamela said. "Our friends at DOE and DHS suspect an MSS team on the ground combined with hacking from this site."

"Correct," Al said. "They could not pin it down to this exact location, but based on our intelligence, this has to be the group that did it."

"What are we looking at?" Steve asked.

"Most of the emergency and other services will be on auxiliary power," Pamela said. "This could last for months. The average American will need to fend for themselves. There will be chaos and death. Millions could starve, it is inevitable."

"Is it that bad?" Steve asked, perplexed.

"And then some," Pamela retorted. "Hold on, the directors want to chat."

The large monitor in Pamela's office came to life as pictures of the directors popped up on the screen.

"I assume you've heard the latest," Phil said.

"Yes sir," Pamela replied. "We were just talking about it. How bad is it?"

"It's very bad," Jonas replied. "We are still getting reports, but the government here is in disarray and panic. We are all on auxiliary power."

"For how long?" Al asked.

"We don't know," Jonas replied. "But it's going to be catastrophic. You are all aware that modernized infrastructure runs on electricity. Without it, we're dead in the water. The average person in this area will have no access to news, phone, social media, food, or gas. Transportation will halt and goods will halt with it. With 95 percent of all goods being transported by truck, it will be a fiasco. Currently, DHS and FEMA are working on a plan to place supply stations in certain areas that trucks can reach with the gas they have in their tanks. These will be at large box stores, which are being barricaded as we speak. It will take time to set up."

"Meanwhile, people will be starving," Phil interjected. "Where are we with the team?"

"JB made insertion a few hours ago," Steve replied. "I was with him on the plane. Contact was confirmed and he is surveilling the enemy."

"The rest of the team will be inserted tomorrow night," Pamela said. "Al and Steve have been heading that up."

"DHS and FBI, as well as Langley are expecting a second operation or second phase of what just happened," Phil said. "I don't need to tell you how critical it is to destroy that facility."

"We will do our best sir," Al said. "The team is ready, and we are giving them all the support they need."

"Do you still have that Chinese cruise missile we captured?" Phil asked.

"Yes," Pamela replied.

"Can it be used in this operation if the team fails or as a backup?" Phil asked.

"We may be able to use it," Pamela said. "But we would need to be able to launch it from a location outside of Taiwan. I'm not even sure if we can make it work given the time frame."

"Get on it anyhow," Phil said.

"Whatever we can do to prevent a second attack is a requirement of greatest importance," Jonas interjected. "We're running out of time."

"Understood sir," Pamela said, the conference at an end. "Al, investigate the cruise missile status, will you? I don't have much hope, but it may be another option. It could force us into war with China. This whole mission is looking grim."

"I'll get right on it," Al replied.

"Steve," Pamela said. "Make sure the team and JB have all the help they need. Whatever it takes."

"No worries," Steve replied. "I'm on it and will give you hourly updates."

Pamela sat back in her chair, examining the bleak prospects of the mission. She knew JB was their best; he had never failed to accomplish the task at hand. She also realized they were desperate but using the Chinese cruise missile against a Chinese military base was at most unwise and potentially catastrophic. However, given the high stakes, it could be the only salvation for the remainder of the U.S. power grid. It was ironic that all the cold war strategies were playing themselves out in a high-tech face off. She had to make sure the missile was worth the risk. Looking through her office window to the cubicles in the station, everyone was hard at work, oblivious to the dangers back home. She needed to talk to Jeremy, a former explosives structural engineer turned CIA support staff. She walked out her door directly to him.

"Jeremy," Pamela said. "How familiar are you with cruise missiles and their explosives capabilities?"

"I stay up on them," Jeremy said. "What's up?"

"I want to know the effects of a Chinese cruise missile if it hit above a target that is below ground?"

"You mean you would like to know if it could penetrate to a target below the surface?" Jeremy asked.

"Exactly."

"It depends on how far below the surface the target is," Phil responded. "The missile will create a crater, but only five to eight feet deep. It is not like a bunker buster type bomb that will penetrate and blow up after penetration into a hollow area."

"That's not very deep," Pamela said.

"No, it's not," Jeremy replied. "However, the newer versions of our cruise missiles can be deployed against stationary targets such as hardened bunkers or strategic installations using a blast or more accurately, penetration warhead. The warhead is essentially a 1,000-pound explosive."

"How does it work?" Pamela asked.

"It is multi-stage and can cut through armor or concrete, which allows the second stage main warhead to penetrate inside to the target. This is how it allows for hard-target penetration."

"Now for the sixty-four-dollar question," Pamela said. "Will the Chinese cruise missile do that?"

"I'm assuming you are talking about the one we captured," Jeremy replied. "Unfortunately, no. It still uses the older, original technology as do even many of our own cruise missiles. It was designed to attack above ground targets such as buildings, ships, and other structures."

"How deep is this facility that you are describing?" Jeremy asked.

"It's thirty to fifty feet beneath the surface," Pamela stated flatly.

"Well, I hate to break it to you," Jeremy replied. "At that depth, even the newer technologies would not penetrate. You would either need to hit the entrance dead on and force the explosion through the facility or use a bunker buster."

"Thanks," Pamela said, as she walked away. "You've been a big help."

"So, even if they used the Chinese cruise missile," she thought. "It would merely scratch the surface. God what a pun. This was going to be all about boots on the ground — JB and his team. He would make it work; he had to. After all, he had a new girlfriend and wanted to come home to enjoy her."

CHAPTER 6

The two directors were sitting in their command van near the capitol mall. It was the safest place given the circumstances. Power was out in almost the entire southeastern U.S. as well as in DC and at the White House. The government was running on auxiliary generators and back-up power. All non-essential personnel had been sent home. It would not take long before tragic circumstances affected almost ninety million people in the southwest, but there would be cascading effects around the entire country.

"Take a walk with me," Phil said, as they climbed out of the van, their security detail fanning out in front and behind them. "I didn't want to say it in front of the men, but I want to know what we're up against here. You're the expert. Let's have it."

"It could be worse than we ever imagined," Jonas said. "I do not even know where to begin."

"At the beginning," Phil replied. "Walk me through it so I can understand it. I'm a spy man, not a resource or infrastructure expert."

"Alright," Jonas replied. "I'll give you the short version. As you know we have lost twenty-two major transformers. Essentially, we are dead in the water. Mostly, only the White

House, other secure locations, hospitals, and emergency personnel have back-up power. Most grocery stores, gas stations, pharmacies and the like have none. Because of that, things will go sideways quickly. First, because of the outages, stores will close due to hygiene conditions — a public health policy since most policies do not allow stores to be open if toilets and the like will not work. But that's not the half of it. Gas stations will not be able to pump gas. Most cell phone communications will fail within twenty-four hours as their batteries drain from use, and emergency services will be affected on a large scale. Then, the worst begins to set in."

"What could be worse?" Phil asked. "No gas, no communications, no water, what?"

"No food," Jonas asked. "Without water a person can live generally three to four days and without food, seven to ten days. It's a generalization, but that's the gist of it. But that's only the beginning."

"You're thinking of riots and demonstrations," Phil said. "Right?"

"Worse," Jonas said. "Roving mobs with a kill mentality. Once people figure out what is happening, they can easily be whipped into a frenzy because now, life has become about personal survival."

"So, what you're really saying is we are sitting on a powder keg," Phil responded.

"Absolutely," Jonas said. "We need to get ahead of this thing at once. It's something that FEMA and DHS have not really prepared for. And, given the traitorous house and senate the president inherited, we could be in for one hell of a shock."

"What are you suggesting?" Phil asked.

"The storm has already hit," Jonas said. "We need to begin setting up staging areas around the perimeter of the southeast and within each state. The big box stores have long been set up for this scenario. They need to be activated immediately. Food and water will be delivered to them, and the National Guard will serve as security. Get on the emergency broadcast system and begin telling people not to panic and that as a precautionary measure, actions are being taken to provide food and water. Specific gas stations can be fitted with temporary generators and when the gas is gone, move on to the next one. That's within the perimeter. On the edges of it, place more aid stations or staging areas. Each needs to have stockpiles of food and water brought from areas with no electrical outages."

"That's a tall order," Phil replied. "I'm not sure we can do it."

"If you cannot," Jonas replied. "Then, you need to get ready for the death of millions and the big reset. The people will take control and the southeast will be a no-man's land. The remainder of the country will be filled with riots and massive demonstrations, the likes of which you have never seen. A revolution will begin. We need to make this about the affected people, not a free for all."

"You mean like 9/11," Phil said. "Everyone in the country rallied around those affected and New York City."

"Exactly," Jonas replied. "Do you remember what happened when the hurricane struck Texas a few years back?"

"Not really," Phil replied.

"The people knew the government couldn't solve the problem alone," Jonas said. "Katrina showed them that. So, individuals from all over the country drove in with pickups, small trailers, box vans, and cars with blankets, water, food, and all kinds of items, as well as for emotional support. We need that same spirit here. Get the people involved and they'll feel good about helping others. It will quale most of the riot types and get them actively engaged helping others and lessening the burden on the government. We cannot handle it by ourselves anyway. I'm telling you that we need to do this immediately, as well as get every cargo plane and semi-tractor rolling or we'll be buried in an onslaught of despair and violence."

"You paint a bleak picture," Phil said. "We can try one thing, which we've experienced here and there in localized disasters, and it has worked well."

"You're referring to crowdsourcing?" Jonas asked.

"Yes," Phil said. "If we can implement it properly, it could be the answer to saving the country."

"I agree," Jonas said. "Let's get on the horn to the President, DHS, and DoD. We may just be able to pull our butts out of the fire."

After a harrying drop into the water, JB was sitting in the dark, listening for sounds of other patrols, adrenaline racing through his body, sweat oozing from every pore. He had worked his way along the shore for several hundred yards in each direction, stopping here and there to listen and observe. The only sounds were from buzzing mosquitos, frogs, and collared scops owls that seemed to be abundant in the area. Next, he moved inland about two hundred yards and searched along a route heading northeast then, moving toward the shore one hundred yards, he backtracked southeast. His face had scratches all over it, as well as his hands from creeping through the undergrowth. Every scratch burned from the salt in his sweat as it slowly flowed over the open tissue. He took out a bandana and tied it around his forehead to keep the sweat from dripping into his eyes.

He was surrounded by broken forest and shrubs. Near the northeast end of the area he had scouted, he found a small clearing about eighty feet across; it would serve as their base. Looking at his map he was just under a quarter mile from the post. It was time to deploy the Black Hornet drone. He could fly it out about one and one-quarter miles and still be connected, which wouldn't be necessary being merely a quarter mile away from his target. At max speed it could be hovering over the post in barely more than a minute. Even though the mini drone was very quiet, he calculated half speed would be better and so, set the drone to fly at one hundred fifty feet and six miles per hour. Using the FLIR camera, he would be able to detect anything with a heat source, especially sentries. He did a couple of quick calculations and determined two minutes to target and two minutes back. Giving the drone a reserve of five minutes of its twenty-five-minute flight time, it could hover over the area above and around the post for a little over fifteen minutes, which should be adequate.

He prepared the drone and set up his ground control station that consisted of a base station, controller, and display. Opening it, he pulled one of the mini drones from within, along with the one-handed controller. The base station would enable all necessary functions to plan, execute, and analyze the mission. With its own internal batteries, he would be able to fly more than a dozen missions with the drone before the rest of his team arrived tomorrow night. Putting on his night vision goggles, he launched it into the dark night. It was whisper quiet as it rose above him and not more than twenty feet away, he could no longer hear it. He guided the drone to the target and began flying it in a polygon pattern from a couple of hundred yards outside the boundary of the post, beginning on the north end.

The intent was overall surveillance so he set a polygon waypoint that would be about a two-mile flight path, giving him overlapping views of the post and the area directly surrounding it. He was watching the screen carefully to get an idea of what was inside the fence and directly around it. With the camera pointing straight down, he could see perhaps fifty or more guards roaming all around the outside perimeter. There were another twenty within the compound. The few buildings that he could see were lit with red lights; he presumed so that night vision could be maintained. Here and there, a couple of guards stood talking, smoking cigarettes, the glow clearly visible each time they inhaled. Like JB, they swatted mosquitos on their face and neck frequently. He started the drone on its return route, climbing some in altitude and pointing the gimbal of the camera about twenty-five degrees down angle. Halfway back, he hovered for a moment as he yawed the camera in a 360-degree maneuver to get a better picture of the surrounding area. He could see several patrols as they along the trail surrounding the post; he was certain one of them was those he first encountered after ditching in the ocean. A smile creased his face as he brought the drone home and landed it next to him. He immediately replaced the battery for the next flight then, began carefully studying the video the drone had recorded. It was good resolution and very clear. While viewing it, he made a few marks on his map, which he would look at more carefully during daylight.

After analyzing the video, he crept back toward the shore, being careful not to make a sound. He watched the patrols through his night vision as they passed along the edge of the water, each time taking the same path and recording their interval of passing. It appeared there were three different patrols on the same route. He wondered if during the day the interval would be longer with fewer patrols since they would be able to see further. When the patrol passed, he noticed the moon glimmering faintly on the water. Suddenly, a gun boat appeared and began firing a machine gun into the woods. He hugged the ground, grains of sand sticking to the sweat on his face. The patrol that had just passed began yelling at the boat crew. His Mandarin wasn't what it should be, but he could make out the gist of the conversation and almost laughed aloud.

"What the hell are you doing?" a soldier screamed.

"We thought you were the enemy," the gunner yelled back.

"You almost killed us dumb ass," the other soldier screamed at the boat crew. "If we need you, we'll call, now get your butts out of here!"

The gun boat pulled away, the crew laughing and yelling back at the soldiers on shore as they stomped off. Within a few seconds, the sounds of nature once again pervaded the night. As an experienced operative, JB made a mental note to determine the gun boats patrol schedule as well then, decided to check in. Picking up his sat phone he pressed the on button, nothing happened. He discovered a bullet had passed clean through it, leaving a uniform round hole. "I guess the bullets came closer than I thought," he murmured. There was no other way to communicate; he hoped Coyote would not panic, having discussed such things before insertion.

Taiwan Station was buzzing with activity as the men and women who toiled away in their cubicles for little pay but had a great love of country, went about their assigned tasks. Half of them had been tasked to help with the mission at hand. So far there were no major wrinkles. Looking up, Pamela saw that Al had returned, hopefully with good news.

"I hope you have something promising for us," Pamela said.

"Yes," Al replied. "The missile is in working order and can be made ready in a few hours."

"That's more than I had hoped for," Pamela said. "However, we may not be able to use it. I've been informed by Jeremy that it'll just make a big bang on the surface but is not able to penetrate a bunker such as the underground computer network."

"That doesn't sound good," Al replied. "Should I ready it anyway?"

"Yes," Pamela said, a knock at the door. "Come in. It's at least an option."

"I hate to interrupt," Steve said. "But we have had no word from JB. He was supposed to check in about two hours ago."

"Damn it!" Pamela exclaimed. "It's starting to pour. Why do you suppose he did not?"

"I wouldn't be alarmed," Steve said. "This has happened before. He was wearing a wing suit, which doesn't afford a lot of protection when you hit the ground. His sat phone could have gotten damaged in any number of ways."

"Yes," Pamela retorted. "And he could have gotten captured."

"That's a possibility," Steve said. "But I believe unlikely. I'm going to move forward as planned. He and I had discussed such problems before insertion."

"I agree with him," Al said. "Let's not be intimidated by a lack of communication at this juncture."

"Where is the rest of his team?" Pamela asked.

"They're in crates in Hong Kong believe it or not," Steve grinned. "One of our trusted assets has a cargo plane going along the coast to Shantou and then on to Longhai City and several other coastal towns along his route. The target area is right along his path. The team will exit the crates out of Shantou, and he'll use a slow climb to 20,000 feet, which is when the jump will be made."

"There's no problem with all their gear?" Al asked.

"Negative," Steve replied. "Trust us. We've planned this from every angle. Our strategy is sound."

"Very well," Pamela said. "Make it happen. Things are getting nasty in the states. Everyone goes berserk when they can't see their favorite show or connect on social media."

Jonas had gone over all the reports and collaborated with FEMA, DHS, FBI, DOI, DOE, CIA, all the major intelligence agencies and many other federal agencies and first responders throughout the southeast. The number of transformers that had been damaged, essentially killed the entire power grid throughout the area except for some localized coal-fired generation plants that had managed to stay online. The staging areas and crowdsourcing had been implemented; it was time to announce it to the American people.

Jonas and Phil were at the White House to brief the President. The press room was complete mayhem; every reporter was screaming questions at the White House Press Secretary who answered as best she could. Phil hid himself in the background. When the press secretary noticed Jonas, she immediately directed the groups questions at him. It was time to be both elusive and political. The goal was not to create a panic. "Thanks Sally," he thought. "Mighty big of you."

"Let's calm down and I will answer your questions as best I can," Jonas said. "I'll start with an update of what we know for certain. The southeastern U.S. has suffered a major blackout. We continue assessing the damage. Several primary transformers and substations are down, which is causing rerouting of electricity and distribution problems."

The press corps began screaming questions. Jonas held his hands up, motioning downward with his palms to get them quiet and ordered.

"Alright, ladies and gentlemen," Jonas said. "It is not feasible to attempt to answer questions from thirty journalists at once. So, I'll point and the person I point at will ask his or her question. I'll do this until you're mostly satisfied."

"Sir," a reporter asked. "How long will the power be out?"

"That's difficult to answer," Jonas said. "We will know more later in the day and will update you."

"What caused the outage?" another reporter asked.

"Do you recall the New York City blackout?" Jonas asked. "Remember that the causes listed for it were a software glitch, a fallen limb on the power lines, a raccoon on the wires, and other potential causes. At this point, we simply don't know. There were waves of thunderstorms across much of the area so it could have been a lightning strike. When I know, you'll know."

"What can we do to prepare for the effects of the outage?" another reporter asked.

"Hurricane Katrina taught us a valuable lesson," Jonas said. "It proved to us and the nation that the federal government does not have the resources and logistical capacity to provide support for large areas and a great number of people. This is what I want you to get to your listeners. We need the help of every able bodied American to do what he or she can to help reduce the effects of this outage. In a few moments, the President of the United States will give a personal address. You will know more then."

The questions went on and Jonas did all he could to answer them in a manner to reduce potential panic.

"Do you think they bought it?" Phil asked.

"I hope so," Jonas replied. "The presidential address should quell their thirst for a while."

"Let's hope so," Phil said.

Reaching the Oval Office, the two were admitted inside to brief the President before giving his address. The camera crew and all others were ushered out.

"Let's have it," President Bill Armstrong ordered.

"The numbers you were given before have not changed," Jonas said. "We have a major catastrophe on our hands, but you need to convince the people you're on top of it and play down its severity."

"So, you think the plan FEMA and DHS gave me is the way to go? President Armstrong asked.

"We do sir," Phil responded. "It's our best option."

"Do you really believe crowdsourcing will help?" Vice President Vince Reisner asked.

"It worked perfectly in Colorado," Jonas replied. "One of the most disastrous fires they ever had was dealt with by the first responders while the people, all crowdsourced, brought food, clothes, water, blankets, and other things in greater abundance than anyone thought possible; much more than was needed. The real problem is getting the required items to the right places as fast and expeditiously as we can."

"Then, we really need FEMA and DHS to be on the money," President Armstrong said.

"Yes sir," Jonas replied.

"Do us a favor," the President said. "Look over this short speech and give us your thoughts."

Both men huddled over the speech and made a few comments, which the Vice President and President adjusted on another copy.

"There is one key point you need to make Mr. President," Jonas said. "This is about Americans helping Americans. One thing my mother always taught me was that people are happiest when they are helping others. That applies here. Play on their humanity and compassion. Everyone wants to help; they just don't know it yet and they don't know how; tell them."

"Excellent thoughts," the President said. "Both of you wait outside until this is over then, give me any updates you have. Vince and I will make minor adjustments to the speech. Jonas and Phil exited the Oval Office, already making calls to get a better grip on what real conditions were on the ground. It wasn't as bad yet as it was going to be.

The President and Vice President made final touches on the speech while the camera crew made ready. On que, the president began.

"My fellow countrymen and women. Today, we have had an unprecedented electrical outage in the southeastern part of the country. Reports are still coming in and while we do not yet know precisely how bad it is, I believe in preparing for the worst. Let me tell you a brief story. When I was in Afghanistan, one of my fellow soldiers was an atheist. However, when the bullets started flying around us, he was the first to begin praying. It was a testament to the adage that there are no atheists in foxholes and that in combat your teammates are your protectors. At this moment, it doesn't matter what your political or religious persuasion is, nor should it. I am calling on every American, every person listening to my voice, to do what you can to help other Americans in the affected area. You are their teammates. Currently most of the southeastern U.S. is in blackout. Like you, they have jobs, families, bills, and personal issues to deal with, and like you, they cope with them as best they can. There are times in life when the problems we confront is beyond the scope of the individual to solve it. This is one of those times. A time when you need to lean on others who are stronger and the stronger must help all they can. The outage could be far reaching and is beyond individual capabilities to solve. Through no fault of their own, those in the affected area have been thrown into the dark ages where they will read by candlelight and haul water from the nearest creek or pond by hand. They need all of us to help them. I can think of no greater service than to serve your fellow Americans. This is not something that you need to think about for a day or week, it is something you must do today, right now. Both myself and the Vice President ask for the help of every American during this crisis because the problem is too large for the government to fix in the time needed. Its solution is in your hands, the people, all the people. In a few moments, the emergency broadcasting system will activate. Depending on what area of the country you live in, you will be directed to specific locations to send or personally transport aid items. Please follow the directions as closely as you can. Your fellow Americans are depending on us. You, the American people, are the solution to this problem. We will update you as often as we can. God Bless you all."

The camera crew packed up and left the room, leaving the President, Vice President and two directors to carry on their discussion.

"Any news from the field," Bill asked.

"One insertion has been completed," Phil replied. "The rest of the team will be going in shortly."

"Both the VP and I believe they will make another strike," Bill said. "We cannot allow that."

"Looking at the scenario and strategy we have in place," Phil said. "We are convinced that the team will make sure that doesn't happen."

"What about that cruise missile you said we had?" Vince asked. "Will it work?"

"Yes," Phil replied. "We are keeping it as a backup right now; it is ready to be immediately deployed. However, I don't know that it will serve a great purpose since it cannot penetrate the underground bunker the hackers are in."

"Hmmmm," Bill mused. "If we are unable to prove the Chinese did this, we cannot just go to war with them. Vince and I are convinced that you need to capture one of their agents, no matter the cost. With one in hand, we can turn the tables and make them pay."

"But the first order of business," Vince interjected, "is to destroy that facility. How long before that can happen?"

"As you are aware sir, we need to make it look like it was anyone other than us," Phil said. "Our operative is JB who is leading a team of Hong Kong triad members loyal to their boss, Li Na. They are hell bent on killing this General Bocheng. We are giving them all possible help."

"What about this JB?" Vince asked. "I read your report. How good is he?"

"He is a master of death," Phil said. "Our very best. The team he's working with have great respect for him. If you want someone dead, send him!"

"I have great confidence in him," Bill said. "Do you? That's the big question."

"Indeed sir," Phil replied. "Both Jonas and I served with him. He saved our lives in circumstances that were worse than we could imagine. On one mission he served as overwatch and took out over a dozen insurgents hell bent on our demise. The enemy called him Shadow because that's where he would come from. They say you never hear the bullet that kills you. That's him. Those who die by his hands never hear him."

"It certainly sounds like he is the right weapon in this case," Vince said. "When this is over, I'd like to meet him."

"Yes sir," Phil said, looking askance at Jonas.

"If you need anything from this office," Bill said. "I'll make sure you get it. Go do your thing."

The President and VP watched the two men leave, not speaking until the door was closed behind them.

"Do you think we're doing the right thing?" Vince asked.

"Yes," Bill sighed. "If anyone can get things done under the radar and done right, those two men can. We can always conduct a military strike if necessary. I'm hoping it won't come to that. You know as well as I do if we take that route the future will be uncertain at best."

Having run more than a dozen sorties with the Black Hornet, something had caught JB's eye on the last drone pass. Once he had retrieved the drone, he decided to check it out. As he eased through the undergrowth, the plants and mosquitos seemed to attack him from everywhere. What seemed like hours but was only about thirty minutes found JB directly under a satellite receiving dish. There was not one, but four. "Damn it!" JB thought. "This facility is more capable of communications and therefore damage than we suspected."

Just at that moment, the sound of a patrol approached. He slipped back into the jungle, letting them pass.

The team was readying for the drop. They had not heard from JB since he inserted the night before. Li Na was worried. It was unlike him not to maintain scheduled contact. She shrugged the worry off as the team made their equipment ready. Within the crates there were two large brown bags that JB had instructed them to bring along. She wondered what was in them but didn't have time to look. The team had checked and rechecked their equipment to break the boredom of the day. They traveled light, mostly pistols, M4's, C-4 explosives, M15 and M24 grenades, and personal equipment such as knives, suppressors, and MRE's. Going over the strategy they had devised, they had planned on four days, but COS Taiwan was now telling them three days and no more. As they approached the drop point, they lined up near the cargo door, waiting for the jump signal. They were exiting the aircraft at 20,000 feet and would free fall to around 3,000 feet and open their parachutes. Suddenly the signal was given.

Li Na and the team jumped as quickly as they could. Free-falling through the air always exhilarated her. Despite the warmth on the ground, at 20,000 feet it was cold. Within a few seconds, they had reached terminal velocity of about 120 miles per hour and would free fall just over one hundred seconds before opening their chutes. As they fell, she and her team peered into the darkness below, wondering what awaited them. Clouds had obscured the moon and they could barely make out the difference between the water and shore. She wondered if JB was still alive. How would they carry out the mission if he were not?

The drone of the plane's engines above drifted down to JB's ears. It was the only one he had heard since the night before. There was no doubt it was Li Na and the rest of the team. They would be on the ground in about three minutes. Peering around to make sure he was alone, he pulled out his flashlight, checked to make sure it was working and began sending his signal; two flashes with a slight pause and then, three flashes into the night sky. The sound of the plane disappeared. A slight breeze was blowing from the shore, JB kept sending the signal hoping the team would see it. They couldn't afford to be spotted.

Li Na, peering into the darkness below, suddenly saw the signal — JB was alive. A jolt of ecstasy passed through her body quicker than she could blink. The thrill of plummeting through the air paled in comparison to what she was feeling. Her lover and companion was okay. She hoped beyond hope that when this was over, they could perhaps settle down, but at the same time didn't know if her passion for excitement would allow it. She was sure that JB knew how she felt, if not fully then, partially. She had committed to this path long ago. When the law didn't work, it was time for the people to take control. Live or die, this would end her years of seeking revenge. Once behind her, maybe she could move forward like a normal woman. Was there such a thing?

The night goggles allowed JB to easily detect enemy and friendly alike; he kept scanning the sky above and lower toward the horizon while persistently sending the signal. Abruptly, a few yards in front of him, he saw Xin Cao thud onto the ground. The team had remained near each other and then stacked to stay close after they opened their parachutes. Thanks to the MC-6 steerable chute, they were able to make a precise landing in the small clearing. Every team member was accounted for; no one had been injured, a frequent occurrence on such missions. They quickly bundled their chutes and hauled them along with their gear to where JB pointed.

Li Na was excited to see him. She was about to hug him but held back.

"Not in front of the men," she thought.

He gathered the entire team together. The group had already put on their night vision and were able to see well in the darkness.

"Why didn't we hear from you?" Li Na asked. "We were wondering if something happened."

"My sat phone was shot," JB said, holding up the damaged phone. "A gun boat came by and unloaded on two soldiers doing their patrol. It was quite comical really, but they sprayed the woods with bullets. Luckily, the soldiers didn't get killed. Let me borrow your sat phone and check in."

The team split up and took up watch position while JB checked in, Li Na remaining close by.

"Roadrunner, Coyote," JB said.

"Thank God," Steve replied. "What happened."

"Damaged device," JB replied. "The flock is in the nest."

"Understood," Steve replied. "COS requests start. You have 72 hours."

"Roger Coyote," JB replied. "Roadrunner and chicks on the move."

Pamela had been biting her fingernails. Missions were always fraught with inconsistencies and unknowns. Hearing JB check in was a relief. It meant the mission was going as planned.

"What are we looking at?" Pamela asked.

"He will have the job complete in 72 hours or sooner," Steve said.

"Quite right," Al chimed in. "He's a pro and has good men with sufficient equipment."

"So, you're saying he's on top of it already?" Pamela queried.

"He was on top of it since he got there," Al replied. "I am certain he has done the needed surveillance. Now his team will be given individual and two-man assignments and the mayhem will begin."

"You're awfully confident," Pamela replied with a grin.

"He's our best," Al said. "If you see him coming, it's not for you, for out of the shadows shall come death."

The phone on the conference room table began to ring, it was the directors. Al put it on speaker.

"Phil and Jonas," Al said. "You're on with me, Pamela, and Steve.

"We need an update," Phil said.

"Quell your fears," Pamela said. "Just heard from Roadrunner. Seems there was an equipment failure. Coyote is running the show with him; the chicks are in the nest. It's a go."

"Did you inform Roadrunner of the deadline?" Jonas asked.

"Yes," Steve said. "They are on the move now."

"I need something from you Pam," Phil said. "Roadrunner is

an expert at hunting people down. It appears that Li Na is as well. As soon as they complete this mission, I want the entire team brought to Andrews."

"May I ask what for?" Pamela asked.

"We want them to hunt down the MSS agents responsible for this disaster," Phil said.

"How will you handle that with the Chinese?" Al asked. "It could become very heated."

"If caught, they'll be listed as terrorists," Phil replied. "That way, we are not obligated to return them to their host country."

"Ah," Al said. "Very sly."

"Okay," Phil said. "You have your orders. Keep us updated on the hour of your progress."

The phone went dead.

General Bocheng was standing in the compound near the entrance to the computer bunker. Colonel Wu had joined him for a smoke. They could dimly hear the plane overhead as it passed. Colonel Wu looked at his watch then, tipped his head upward to blow circles of smoke into the air.

"What did you look at your watch for?" Bocheng asked.

"Just checking general," Wu replied. "The plane is on time, flying its same route every night to deliver cargo to the coastal cities."

"You don't think there is anything to worry about do you?" Bocheng asked.

"No. All is well in hand. I've thought about the Americans potentially sending in Navy Seals or some other Special Operations Team, but that would be foolish."

"I agree," Bocheng said. "We have more than enough men to repel an assault from a small group and satellite coverage provided by the MSS shows nothing amiss. Even Jeng, the Deputy Minister of Operations for MSS says there is no excessive chatter from the Americans or their allies."

"That's understandable," Wu said. "Given what the Americans are up against with the power outage, there's little time to focus on other matters."

Wu laughed aloud.

General Bocheng looked at the man through the smoke rising from his cigarette. He knew Wu to be very competent, which is why he had appointed him second in command. Wu was an educated man having earned a dual master's degree in engineering and business from Tsinghua University in Beijing. Considered one of the best universities in the world, he had been a top student. The man was a brilliant strategist and pro party. Bocheng doubted he could find a more loyal officer.

"Tell me something," Bocheng said. "Why didn't you seek assignment elsewhere?"

"General," Wu said. "This is where I want to be. My enjoyment is not in having rank. You know I could have been a general in my own right by now. I am here because it is where I can serve my country best, by creating chaos in the west. Don't you think?"

Bocheng hadn't realized the real desire Colonel Wu had just expressed. Now it all made sense why he had turned down two post commands that would elevate him to the rank of a general.

"Why do you hate the Americans so much?" Bocheng asked.

"When I was a young man growing up in Hong Kong my mother was on her death bed," Wu replied, a faraway look in his eyes as he remembered. "She had a severe heart problem and needed a transplant. The only way to get it was to go to San Francisco, but the U.S. State Department refused her visa. The refusal was a death warrant. I decided right then that someday, I would have my revenge. Now, I have it. They will learn that the treatment of one individual can affect the lives of millions. Can it not?"

"Yes, it can," Bocheng said. "We are now witnesses of that fact."

The two stood, as they smoked their cigarettes, watching their patrols and taking in the pungent night air. Talking was unnecessary; finishing, they walked away. The general returning to his office to go over the next attack strategy and schedule for the MSS agents in the U.S., while the Colonel made his rounds, checking on security in the bunker and the patrols around the perimeter of the compound.

General Bocheng unlocked the bottom right drawer of his desk and pulled out a box. Placing it on his desk he took out the countermand device. He had examined it quite a few times. It was the original. His engineers had reverse engineered it and made a dozen copies.

"Patience my little pet," Bocheng thought. "When this is over, you'll be attached to some of the west's nuclear plants. Perhaps we will begin with France, Belgium, and Germany."

Colonel Wu walked in, wondering what the device was that the general was looking at.

"Sergeant," Wu asked. "Have the patrols spotted anything out of the ordinary along the shore?"

"No sir," the sergeant replied. "A gun boat opened fire on two of them believing they were an enemy."

"None killed?"

"No sir. Just some terse words exchanged. I have warned the gun boats to identify who they shoot at next time before raining a hail of bullets."

"Very wise of you sergeant," Bocheng said. "Keep us abreast of anything out of the ordinary."

Both officers watched him leave and then, stared at the countermand device.

Jonas was in the PEOC (Presidents Emergency Operations Center), along with Phil and the VP. The final assessment of the damage was dismal indeed. The men were grim faced, as were the personnel manning the surveillance and communications equipment. Everyone realized it would take a miracle to salvage the country. Akin to pulling a rabbit out of a hat, the lust for power and control that had gotten them to this point, the ousted previous administration, would need to be swept away completely if they were to overcome this disaster and survive as a country. The president's speech had been rerun many times on all news networks. From what they could determine so far, there was a massive outpouring of compassion from the American people.

The news showed videos of households packing food goods, water, and blankets into cardboard boxes and giving them to anyone headed to the outage area. Other reports showed many households making sandwiches for truckers who passed through cities and towns enroute to help. While the four men monitored the newscasts, they felt a glimmer of hope. The Department of Homeland Security and FEMA had shut down most of the roads and instructed truckers and others bringing relief onto the major interstates traversing the southeast to specific areas to unload their cargo. Truckers and convoys of pickups and cars were pouring into aid stations set up along Interstates 10, 20, and 40 from Eastern Texas through Arkansas, Mississippi, Alabama, and Georgia, forking off onto I-75 down into Florida. They watched similar convoys moving in from Interstates 55, 65, and 75, north to south through Arkansas and Tennessee, as well as I-77 and I-95 through North Carolina. The DHS and National Guard had set up specific gas stations as fueling depots, providing them with generators to run their pumps, as well as resupplying stocks of supplies on their shelves. The lines were long, but it was working. More generators were coming into the area from all over the U.S. People in the southeast were giving thanks for the compassion they were shown.

"It's ironic," Bill said. "For the first time I can remember in the last twenty years, it's not about parties or politics, but about the people."

"Wouldn't it be great if all politicians took a lesson from what they're seeing?" Vince replied.

"We could always get that out on the air," Phil responded.

"Actually, it's not a bad idea. People first over parties. That's what's saving the U.S. The people, not the politicians, have always saved it."

"True," Vince replied. "In our darkest hours as a nation, the people have always stood up and succeeded."

"Get that out there Phil," Bill responded. "Start the narrative. It will help keep the people fired up."

"Yes," Jonas interjected. "And it will start sending some politicians into the shadows."

The men chuckled softly.

"I think you should address the nation again," Vince said. "Include some of this and show the compassion shown by the American people. Also, I believe we should make them understand that this could be a prolonged outage as we continue to assess the damage."

"Good idea," Bill said. "By the way, how is the operation going?"

It's underway and well in hand," Phil said.

"The team has a 72-hour deadline sir," Jonas replied. "When they are finished, they will return here to hunt down the MSS agents in the field. The FBI is attempting to find them now."

"That's good news," Bill said. "We may just get out of this without a war."

The Executive Assistant Director of the FBI for the National Security Branch, Sam Stromberg, was sitting in the conference room with the heads of the FBI's Counterterrorism Division, Counterintelligence Division, Directorate of Intelligence, and the Department of Homeland Security's Office of Intelligence and Analysis.

"Welcome gentlemen and lady," Sam said. "We have been tasked to find MSS agents believed to have sabotaged the southeastern power grid in coordination with Chinese hacking from abroad. Can any of you shed light on the potential whereabouts of these men and or the next target."

Each of the heads had worked long and hard to get where they were. Olive, the head of DHS Intelligence and Analysis was a shrewd woman with a good sense of political and business acumen. She never divulged her hand, keeping her information and opinions close to her chest. She would have made a good Native American because she never showed emotion. Her face was ever a blank canvas, as it was now.

"Jeff and I have been working on that connection," Olive said. "With all the intelligence we gathered, along with the rest of you, we picked up some extraneous chatter in Mandarin just before the blackout started."

"Can you get a lead on the MSS agents with it?" Sam asked.

"We believe so," Jeff replied. "One of the communications led us to a cell phone that we are investigating. We will know more in a little while."

Jeff was head of the Directorate of Intelligence. He had graduated from West Point and had worked in intelligence in the military followed by a five-year career in the CIA, then to the FBI where he had been exemplary. Everyone trusted his judgement.

"Any idea on the potential next target?" Sam asked.

"Several of us have been discussing that matter," Jack Donovan, replied.

Jack had spent seven years in 75th Ranger Regiment in the U.S. Army. He had been in almost every hell hole in Latin and South America involved in intelligence gathering for a variety of clandestine operations. He prided himself on the ability to read others and read situations that others could not. He was especially well suited for this task.

"What have you concluded?" Sam asked.

"Theoretically, the target could be anywhere," Jack said. "However, we know two things about these agents; at least we think we do. First, they want to do the most damage possible and second, they likely will not strike close to the last target, which gives them a greater chance to escape once they complete their mission."

"But there's no guarantee of that," Olive interjected. "Why not take out New York since they are already in the area?"

"Hey, it's New York," Jack said, grinning. "Who cares? Seriously, our analysis shows that another target would accomplish much more damage."

"Which one?" Sam demanded.

"The Western Interconnection," Jack responded. "It is vast in size, very vulnerable, and serves about 75 million people in fourteen western states, as well as one Mexican state and covers about two million square miles. More importantly, it affects the entire western seaboard and ports. These include Ports of Los Angeles, Long Beach, Seattle, and Oakland. The Port of Los Angeles alone handles forty percent of all imports from Asia."

"The power grid there is weak, isn't it?" Sam asked. "I mean it seems like it wouldn't take much to push over the edge."

"Correct," Jack responded. "We all know that California has insufficient power, especially at peak use times, which is why they have had rolling blackouts for years."

"But finding the MSS agents in such a large area is like hunting for a needle in a haystack," Olive blurted out.

"I won't argue the point," Jack replied. "But we have two things going for us. The first is the cell phone communication, which admittedly is weak. But the second is their language. There are large Chinatowns in San Francisco and Los Angeles, as well as many Mandarin speakers throughout the state. My gut tells me that's where they will be."

"Hmmmm," Olive mused. "Sir, I wouldn't rule out the possibility of a double strike, one in northern California and one in the south."

"That would devastate the U.S. and collapse the economy within ten days," Sam replied. "Not to mention drive us back into the stone age."

"That's correct," Sebastian Franks said. "As head of the Directorate of Intelligence, our data and analysis would concur with what Jack and Olive are implying. I suggest we concentrate efforts in that region and task all seventeen members of the U.S. intelligence community. We can ill afford a mistake on this one. We will need a request from the President."

Everyone nodded in agreement. This would be a tough, demanding task. Almost impossible.

"I will get the President to issue the request," Sam responded. One thing you should know is that Jonas Rothman, Director of the Department of Energy, is heading this operation up to an extent. His office will give us all necessary help to pinpoint the mostly likely targets. I've been on the phone with him; they will forward all the information to us shortly. Go home, grab some extra clothes, and come back. I'll have some strong coffee and sandwiches on hand. We will not leave this room until we have accomplished this task. Oh, and one more thing. The President is assigning a special team to capture these agents or kill them. We will give them full cooperation."

"We have teams that can get the job done," Jack replied. "Why bring in an outside team."

"Do you speak fluent Mandarin?" Sam asked.

The group stared at each other.

"Neither do I?" Sam said. "That's required in Chinatown where these agents are most likely to be. Also, the leader of the group, JB, was in Delta Force. He'll be working closely with us. This team is now in pursuit of the hackers."

"That means . . .," Jack began.

"Enough said," Sam stated. "We all know what that means."

"Again, I'd like to protest," Jack said.

"Protest noted," Sam replied. "This comes directly through the Director FBI from the President. We will help find them and JB's team will nab them. We will also provide backup SWAT teams at their request. I'll ask that we send a liaison along if you like."

"That would be fine," Jack replied. "I'd like to volunteer."

"Noted," Sam said. "It's going to be dangerous, but it would give us clout in organization with the groups. I'll make the request and send you along. That will allow you to collaborate directly with us. It will help the operation."

Dawn had come too quickly as the team prepared to perform recon all day. Gathering the group around, JB went over the drone footage from the night and day before, familiarizing everyone with the layout of the base and inner compound. Putting it together with the maps they had already gone over many times, each had a good feel for their surroundings and how they could move about to avoid detection.

"Let's avoid killing any guards for the moment," JB said. "If one comes up missing, they'll launch a manhunt to find us. Our mission relies on surprise. Let's keep it that way. While you're out scouting, I'll take more drone footage of the camp. Daylight will help us identify anything we may have missed during the night."

"But won't they hear or see the drone?" Xin Cao asked.

JB started the drone and flew it up about fifty feet and out at a forty-five-degree angle. Xin Cao's eyes opened wide in amazement.

"It's hard to see and I'm unable to hear it."

"Watch this," JB said as he took the drone up to three hundred feet.

"Incredible," Xin Cao said. "If we cannot hear it, they won't be able to either."

"Correct," JB responded. "I'll keep it at three hundred feet altitude to get a better overview of the compound. I can zoom in close to identify high-value targets. We will need confirmation that we have the general in our sights. Tonight,

I'll bring it down to one hundred feet and then, we will make final plans."

"Xin," Li Na said. "Take two of the men with you and recon the fence. Determine if there is an easy way in. If not, we will make one. The other men can shadow the foot patrols and reconfirm their schedule. I want one man down by the shore to monitor the schedule of the gun boats."

"Oh," JB said. "Check on the four satellite dishes outside the fence. Determine the best way to disable them."

"Will do," Xin Cao said, leaving.

"How difficult do you think this will be?" Li Na asked.

"It should not be too bad if we can keep the element of surprise," JB said. "If we do not, we will meet our fates."

"I'm much more accustomed to stealth against one target," Li Na said. "This many makes me apprehensive."

"It's okay," JB replied. "I feel the same. Besides, I have a surprise for all of you that will make our job easier."

"What is it?" Li Na asked.

"You'll see."

The day dragged on, getting hot. It was ninety degrees and climbing with matching humidity. The entire team was wet with sweat from every pore. As they shadowed the foot patrols, the schedule did not change. It was the same as they had kept since JB began monitoring them the night before. Xin Cao watched them carefully, including their mannerisms. It was a tactical mistake not to alter patrol schedules. But why would they? Inside their own country there was little to fear. The team's task would be made somewhat easier because they were so regimented. What bothered Xin Cao the most was the number of soldiers around the outside of the compound. This would have been a much easier mission if the general had not reinforced the guard.

Xin's men slipped around the edge of the compound locating several places underneath the fence where a person could crawl unobserved and enter. The primary goal was to kill or capture the general and to destroy the computers in the bunker, as well as the bunker itself. Looking at the small sketch he had made, the best approach would be from the area closest to the general's office and the bunker, which was in the center of the compound. The three-man team found a large gully located near a storage shed close to the fence that heavy rains in the area had washed out. It was easily large enough to crawl in. They took turns clearing the debris while two of them kept watch. An hour later, the gully was cleaned. One of the men slipped beneath the fence and covered the top with dead limbs, making sure no trace of human presence was noticeable. Once finished, they did the same on the outside of the fence then, moved back into the woods to wait and watch. The shade wasn't much respite against the high humidity and heat as they sat watching and sweating. The patrols inside the compound seemed lax compared to those that roved the shore and outer perimeter. Xin Cao and his men watched the patrols, continually timing them. They were on twenty-minute intervals, the same as the other patrols directly around the base. Waiting until dusk, they slowly made their way to the satellite dishes, studying them then, headed back to the clearing. By the time they arrived, the rest of the team was assembled. Li Na and JB had dug a large hole to bury their parachutes and other disposable gear, including their MRE packaging.

"Everything we don't use or will discard goes into the hole," JB said. "No trace can be left behind that will identify who did this. We will cover it before moving out."

"That's why we're disposable right?" Xin Cao asked as the others laughed softly.

"Got that right," JB responded. "I'd say if it looks like you'll get caught you should save the last bullet for yourself."

"I know the men haven't said anything," Xin Cao said. "But the odds seemed stacked against us; we are outnumbered ten to one. How are we going to get around that?"

"I have something for you to see," JB replied.

He arose and pulled two bags from those among the equipment. No one had opened them because they were his. From one he pulled a weather balloon with a payload attachment at the end of the cable that was attached to the bottom.

"This is our equalizer; a steerable weather balloon," JB said. "And this, pulling a small box from the other bag, is a collection of autonomous killer drones. Each one has a three-gram shaped charge in its frame."

"Let me guess," Li Na said. "You're going to drop them from the balloon."

"Correct," JB replied.

"I've heard about these," Xin Cao said. "How are you going to keep them from killing us?"

"They can be programmed for specifics such as age, sex, uniform, ethnicity, and other parameters. These have been programmed to identify and attack Chinese uniforms. I would have also programmed them for ethnicity but didn't want any mishaps."

"We appreciate that," Li Na said, smiling.

"Why do you need to launch them?" one of the men asked.

"They need a boost first to get them going," JB replied. "They will get that when they drop, and they'll fly for just over five minutes."

"How do they work?" Xin Cao asked.

"They detect your heat source and motion," JB replied. "Once they locate a target the artificial intelligence chip inside, will determine if friend or foe. The micro drone will then attack the forehead and set off its charge, which will penetrate the skull into the brain and lights out."

"Sounds gruesome," one of the men said.

"It is certain death," JB responded.

"Can't you just run from it or fight it off?" Xin Cao asked.

"No," JB said. "The reaction time of each drone is supposed to be one hundred times faster than a human and, you cannot outrun them."

"When will you drop them?" Xin Cao asked.

"Let me explain fully how it will work," JB said. "Once we are in position, cover yourselves with your space blankets just as a precaution. I will launch the balloon and use the Black Hornet to confirm its location. Once it is about five hundred feet above the middle of the compound, I will release the drones. Within a few seconds you will hear what will sound like mini pops or small firecrackers. Wait until they are infrequent then, we will move in."

"That simple huh?" Xin Cao mused.

"Yes and no," JB said. "We still need to gain access to the bunker. If they close it off, we will need to blow it. And unfortunately, we, especially Li Na, set off on this mission to get the general who was responsible for her fathers' death. There is a real possibility that one of these drones will get him first."

"I don't care," Li Na said. "I'm part of the mission that will see his end. That is satisfaction enough."

The men fell silent for a moment because they knew how much it meant to her to get the man who ordered the death of her family. She had recruited each of them through the years and whatever happened they were prepared for it.

"Very well," JB said. "I just wanted everyone to be aware of the issue. Now, down to business. I will send the Black Hornet up about fifteen minutes before the attack. We need to take care of the roving patrols along the outer perimeter during that time. And we will set timed charges on the satellite array, generator, and vehicles, including the helicopters. Next, we will launch the micro drones and enter the compound. Xin Cao, I, and Li Na will move to the general's office and take care of him. The rest of you will split off left and right around the inside of the compound, circle it to make certain everyone is down, then we will converge on the bunker. Let's get some rest for a couple of hours. We'll make final preparations then."

The team laid down in the shade, attempting to find refuge from the heat, unsuccessfully. No matter what they did, the sweat continued to ooze from their pores. It was unbearable, even to them and they had grown up with it.

"Would you mind if we kept surveillance with the drone?" Xin Cao asked.

"No," JB replied. "Locate the patrols positions and keep an eye on the compound. Remember that you only have a twenty-five-minute flight time."

Xin Cao was excited to fly the Black Hornet. He had been flying drones for a long time and this was an opportunity that he couldn't pass up. It would be a feather in his cap to brag about flying it. He took out the map he had sketched and sent up the drone, flying it around the perimeter and pinpointing the location of the roving patrols. Yawing it to the right near the shore, he got a visual of a gun boat in the distance, heading back south toward the river that led to the docks. They had brought a couple of larger batteries and a solar charger to keep the drones' batteries up to capacity. By the time he finished, combined with other surveillance information, Xin Cao could accurately estimate where each patrol would be at any time of day. The patrol schedule never varied. "Good for us," he thought.

"You make this mission sound mundane," Li Na whispered.

"In a very real way it is," JB whispered back. "Our men are well trained, so far we have the advantage of surprise, and we have a good strategy."

"You don't think anything will go wrong?" Li Na queried.

"Something can always go wrong," JB said. "But we are all well skilled and I believe what Lunadi always told us."

"What's that?"

"Guts take over where knowledge and skill ends."

"You are very pragmatic."

"Thank you. Although a mission is very dynamic, it has an ebb and flow motion. While we attempt to anticipate that motion, it can always be interrupted by the unexpected. It is then that reflexes and training take over."

"I can see that you really believe that," Li Na said.

"It is what it is," JB replied. "You just need to go with what you are given. Once the operation is interrupted, it becomes a crap shoot."

"You know," Li Na said. "I could kiss you right now."

"I can think of other things I'd like to do to you," JB smiled.

"What will happen to us?" Li Na asked.

"Assuming we get out of this alive, I'd like to be with you," JB responded. "I've been meaning to ask you about what you envision for our future, but well."

"I feel the same," Li Na whispered back. "The future can be bright for us. My problem is that I'm addicted to the hunt for the bad guys, no matter whose side they are on."

"You mentioned before you wouldn't mind working on contract for the CIA," JB said. "They want me to come back, but I didn't want to if it meant losing you."

"I will never try to change who you are," Li Na said. "I'm behind you; whatever it takes to be together. And if we can work as a team after this, I wouldn't mind that at all."

He sat, staring softly into her eyes, his hands touching hers. It didn't go unnoticed by a couple of the men. They had known Li Na for years and had never seen her fall for anyone. Most men in fact were afraid of her. She had such beauty and grace, but their remained the air of death about her, like that of a tiger watching its prey when it was about to leap. Except with Li Na, the characteristic was there all day, every day.

"JB," Xin Cao said. "You better have a look at this."

A helicopter was landing in the compound. Within seconds the rotors stopped turning and a man in civilian clothes stepped out, the door opened by a security detail that had come with him. It was obvious he was important given the deference the soldiers showed him, saluting him as he passed by. He was met by General Bocheng who gave the old Chinese greeting that denoted friendship and respect.

"Zoom in on him," JB commanded.

"Okay," Xin Cao said, bringing the drone down to two hundred feet.

The hornet had three cameras on it, one pointing straight ahead, one on a 45° down angle and one pointing straight down. Xin Cao zoomed in on the two men. Their faces as clear as if standing in front of them.

"I recognize him," JB said. "I don't remember from where, but believe he is one of their intelligence men."

"That's Jeng Po," Li Na said. "He is Deputy Minister of Operations for the MSS. I have seen him in Hong Kong with my boss. I have always wondered if he was involved in triad operations."

"He may not be involved in them," JB said. "But he is certainly involved in the hacking of the U.S. power grid. It makes perfect sense now. He is the one giving the orders to the general; he must be."

"Do you think he will be here tonight?" Xin Cao said. "Are we supposed to kill him too?"

"I need to call this in," JB replied. "Bring the drone back and put in a fresh battery."

Albert Pike, Deputy Chief of Station was sitting in his office with Steve, going over the strategy of the operation.

"Both of you get in here," Pamela shrieked, over the speaker phone.

They walked quickly to her office door, stepped inside, and closed it.

"What's up?" Al asked. "Not trouble, is it?"

"More like an opportunity," Pamela replied. "I have Phil and Jonas on speaker. Gentlemen, I have Al and Steve here with me."

"What's going on?" Phil asked.

"We have an opportunity sir," Pamela said. "The team has spotted Jeng Po on site. He just landed in a helicopter."

"We've been trying to get a bead on him for several years," Phil said. "Jonas and I was wondering where the generals' orders were coming from. What do you think?"

"I've worked with the Chinese a long time," Al said. "The general may be getting his orders from Jeng, but you can bet they come from the top."

"Agreed," Phil said. "All of you know as well as I do that it's a way for the leaders in Beijing to shift responsibility. It's no different than us using plausible deniability for the President."

"The question is do we take him out?" Jonas asked.

Without hesitation, the group said 'yes' in unison.

"I think that takes the doubt out of it," Phil said. "Do we have the means to do so without compromising the mission?"

"No sir," Steve replied. "Only if he stays for the night. If so, he will be a target like the rest of them."

"That's a big if," Phil said.

"Perhaps not," Al replied. "Pamela and I did quite a bit of research and intel collection on him. He may look at this as a break in his normal routine."

"I agree sir," Pamela said. "The two men are long-time friends. It is likely he will stay the night, especially since it's already late afternoon. Hold please, we have JB on the line."

"Did you get all of that?" Al asked.

"Yes," JB said. "My team members also think that Jeng will stay the night. What action do we take with him?"

"Eliminate him," Phil said. "Do you foresee any problems?"

"Only one sir," JB replied. "We can cover all our tracks except one. Once the show starts, we won't have much time to exfil. We must leave no evidence behind."

"Agreed," Jonas said. "They must never know it was an American led team. What's the problem?"

"The micro drones sir," JB replied. "It is unlikely we will be able to find the ones that do not execute the kill command."

"I see," Phil said. "Suggestions?"

"Sir," Al said. "If I may. It's a bit extreme, but we have outfitted a fishing trawler to launch the Chinese drone."

"Wait," Phil said. "Are you suggesting we launch the drone into the compound?"

"It's the best way to eliminate all traces of what happened," Al said.

"I concur," Pamela retorted. "The explosion from the drone will get rid of evidence left behind. It will also make it difficult to recognize who was present in the compound."

"Can we launch the missile without being detected by the Chinese military?" Phil asked.

"Yes," Al responded. "It's already deployed on the trawler, which is standing by off the coast of Fuzhou. It is roughly two hundred and fifty miles out. If we launch, the missile will strike the target twenty-seven minutes later."

"You've already done the math?" Phil queried.

"That's what you pay us for sir," Al replied. "Say the magic word and the post disappears."

"What about response time to the post from the Chinese?" Jonas asked. "Won't they investigate when the post is attacked."

"They will," Pamela said. "The average response time is thirty minutes."

"Keep that in mind on your launch," Phil said. "What about the team's schedule?"

"They move at midnight," Steve said. "They're on a fast track and 24 hours ahead of schedule.

"Keep us posted," Phil said, signing off.

"This could be risky," Pamela said. "If they catch that trawler after launch there will be proverbial hell to pay."

"Relax," Al said. "The boat has only three personnel. We've set charges to sink it as soon as the missile is away. Colonel Diets has two interceptor boats that will pick up the men."

"My oh my," Pamela said. "You're brimming with

confidence."

"We have planned this to the last detail," Steve said. "Once the team assaults, everything else will be set in motion. They need maintain only the element of surprise."

The general wasn't surprised to see Jeng. They met on and off to keep in touch when occasion allowed. He watched Jeng step from the helicopter, walking out to greet him.

"Jeng, my friend," Bocheng said. "What brings you out this way?"

"I just wanted to see an old friend," Jeng replied.

"Come this way," Bocheng said. "Let's share a drink in my office."

The rotors of the helicopter had stopped turning; for Jeng, the silence was stunning. He stopped at the two steps that led to the deck of the general's office and turned to look over the compound. Guards were positioned here and there, a slight breeze blowing inland from the South China Sea. He breathed deeply through his nose, sucking the fresh air into his lungs. A Light-vented Bulbul was sitting in the top of a nearby tree singing. Its white and black colored head and yellow wing tips standing out in stark contrast to the greenery of its surroundings. Jeng watched it for a moment. It didn't seem to have a care in the world.

"You do not know how lucky you are to be in the calm of nature," Jeng said.

"It's a welcome relief to the noise of buses and cars in Beijing," Bocheng said. "Yes, I am fortunate."

General Bocheng walked behind his desk and opened a small cabinet, pouring them both a thimble of baijiu, a Chinese wine typically 40-50 percent by volume alcohol. Despite looking clear like vodka, outsiders called it firewater because a single sip felt like a mouthful of flames. Bocheng passed a thimble, much like a shot glass to Jeng.

"Gānbēi," Jeng said, toasting.

They both downed the alcohol and then poured another, Jeng taking a seat across from the general.

"Any news?" Bocheng asked.

"None," Jeng said. "One of our patrol boats found what we think was wreckage from your helicopters. Everything is strangely quiet."

"Did you catch the people in Shantou?"

"No. Also, our target in Hong Kong vanished. We found the body of one of our men in a storage area at the airport, but no sign of the girl."

"You think someone helped her?" Bocheng asked.

"It wasn't her that killed our agent," Jeng said. "That would be impossible because she's like a shy mouse. She had help. It's a certainty."

"The CIA?" Bocheng asked.

"Most likely," Jeng responded.

"You don't think they will try anything here, do you?" Bocheng asked, his eyes arching.

"They would be a fool to attempt anything," Jeng said. "Even if they could get a team here, they would be seriously outnumbered. But it is wise of you to strengthen security."

"Whether they come or not," Bocheng said. "We will not relax our security for at least a week."

"Good," Jeng replied. "Better to stay cautious. Our intelligence analysts tell me you dealt a serious blow to the U.S."

"We did," Bocheng said. "It seems that we knocked out at least twenty major transformers and power is now erratic across the entire southeast region."

"Can they trace the hacking here?" Jeng asked.

"No!" Bocheng said emphatically. "They have no way of knowing it is us. They will probably presume it was and would be correct, but they cannot prove it. Even if the two that escaped lived to tell them, they're too cowardly to do anything about it anyway."

"Will the next attack occur as scheduled?" Jeng asked,

James Tindall

watching the general's reaction closely.

"Absolutely," Bocheng said. "The field agents are working on their end as we speak. My computer experts are ready on this end."

"Do you think it will be as devastating as the last attack?" Jeng asked. "I know we discussed this before still, I'd like your opinion based on real-time results."

"The southeast attack worked better than expected," Bocheng said. "We caught them with their pants down. The next round will be even more devastating due to cascading failures of the first. We will hit the grid in both northern and southern California. It will stretch their resources and capacity to the breaking point."

"It must not be traced to us," Jeng said. "It could easily lead to war."

"Let it," Bocheng said. "We can beat the Americans."

"Do not let your arrogance override common sense," Jeng said. "We may be able to, but it is not a certainty. Putting them back into the dark ages will be punishment enough."

"The last administration was a joke," Bocheng said. "While they were playing politics with the pandemic, we made great strides in our military technology and attack strategy. We are ahead of them strategically at every turn."

"I agree," Jeng said. "Especially here. But this new president is an unknown. So far, he has refused to speak with Beijing."

"Why?"

"Unknown. Possibly because he wants to make certain of his foothold with the spineless congress he inherited. We have offered our assistance for this blackout, but they said they could handle it and would get back to us if they couldn't, thanking us for the offer."

"That's not good," Bocheng said.

"Why?" Jeng asked, leaning forward, eagerly awaiting the response.

"Because it means that they feel they know who carried out the attack," Bocheng replied. "By now they know it was deliberate and it will have been narrowed to three potential scenarios. First, terrorists; second, Russians; third, Chinese. I'd be willing to bet before they even investigated, we were first on the list. Eventually, the terrorists and Russian theories will go out the window."

"How long before that happens?" Jeng asked.

"I would give them a week," Bocheng said.

"And if the next attack is successful?" Jeng asked.

"It won't matter by then what they think," Bocheng said. "We will have the upper hand. A house in turmoil can usually not mount an effective defense."

"Regardless," Jeng said. "It would be wise for us to keep our strategies unknown for the moment."

"Agreed," Bocheng said. "I will focus on the task at hand. If the time comes for war, we are ready."

"Yes," Jeng said. "We have been for a long time. Their weak spined government will only serve as a help to us."

"It's ironic," Bocheng said. "We've been working under their noses for decades and now openly. Because of the criminal nature of the last administration, we have almost all of them on our payroll. I think the politicians will invite us in with open arms. Then, we can stage a coup without firing a shot."

"Let's not get too far ahead of ourselves," Jeng grinned.

"Would you like to stay the night?" Bocheng said. "It's getting late. You can return to the garrison in the morning."

"Yes, that would be great," Jeng said. "We can continue our conversation over dinner."

"Outstanding," Bocheng said. "My first-class chef will not disappoint."

Colonel Wu quietly knocked on the door to give the general a security update.

"All is in order sir?" Wu said. "Security is as prepared. Do you need anything general?"

"Yes," Bocheng said. "Please have the chef prepare dinner for our esteemed guest, Deputy Director Po. I want you to come too."

"Very well sir," Colonel Wu replied, saluting.

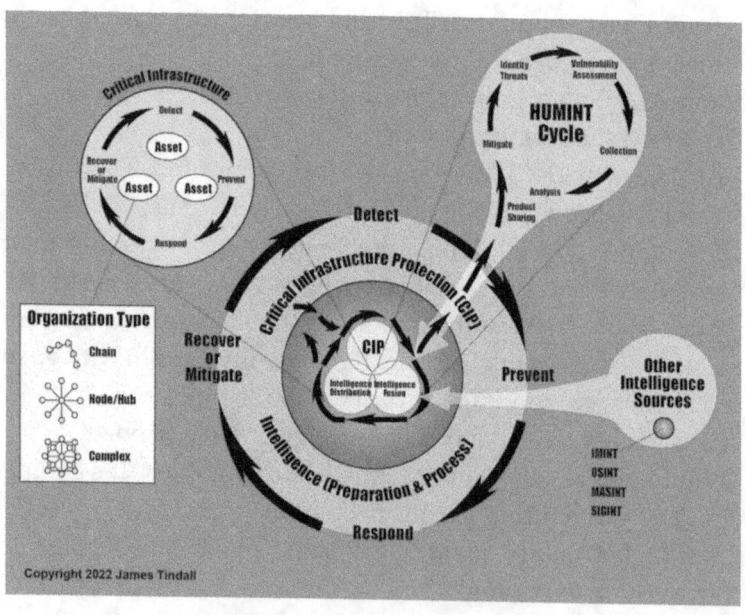

CHAPTER 7

Pamela had been joined in her office by Steve and Al; the directors were on monitor. They were awaiting word from the team on operational status. Suddenly, static came from the phone, which Pamela put on speaker.

"Coyote, Roadrunner. Coyote, Roadrunner."

"Coyote," Steve responded.

"Roadrunner out of the nest in thirty."

"Roger," Steve replied, disconnecting.

"There you have it," Pamela said. "They will launch their assault in thirty minutes."

"How long before we know mission status?" Jonas asked.

"We will know instantly as long as their cameras work. If they don't then, within thirty minutes of assault," Steve said. "Otherwise, we will consider mission failed."

"What about the cruise missile?" Phil asked.

"It is on station as planned," Al replied. "We have an interceptor boat ready to exfil the men on the trawler. It will be scuttled directly after launch."

"I'm not sure this is the best move," Phil said. "If they find out it is us, there will be hell to pay. We'll all end up as cooks in fast-food joints."

"Do not worry sir," Pamela said. "The missile will destroy any evidence of the team and the weapons they'll be using. Everyone is wearing a camera so we will know all that is going on instantly. If they fail, the missile will cover us."

"And assuming they succeed?" Jonas asked. "What then?"

"The missile will still be launched to cover their tracks," Pamela said. "Nothing will be left to chance."

"Alright Pam," Phil said. "You're in control. We will rely on you and your station's expertise. The three of you make a good team by the way."

"Sir," Pamela said. "We don't get the news here as well as we should. What is going on back home?"

"It's nasty," Jonas replied. "The entire southeast is in blackout. We will do what we can but starvation of many is inevitable."

"I'm afraid he is right," Phil said. "I don't know what the president will do but knowing the warrior he is, I'd be praying if I were the Chinese."

"That brings us to the next point," Jonas said. "Once the team is done here, you are to have them board a transport for Los Angeles as we discussed before. The FBI and JTTF think they have narrowed the location of the MSS agents to either Los Angeles or San Francisco. Every intelligence agency has been directed to find them. I would like Steve to accompany the team as our liaison."

"Yes sir," Steve replied.

"We already have the transport waiting for the team when they arrive," Al said. "My instincts tell me the groups back home are bucking you on this."

"You would be correct," Phil said. "But we have it in hand. Their order to accept the team came directly from the president."

"I see," Al grinned.

"How long before they touch down in Los Angeles?" Phil asked.

"The current assault, exfil, and takeoff is estimated to be about three hours," Al replied. "Flight time over the Pacific to LAX, including refuels will be approximately twenty-one hours. Total time will be twenty-four hours from now sir."

"Understood," Phil said. "Get them there with all possible haste."

"Coyote, Roadrunner," the speaker crackled. "Flying the coup."

The group settled in to watch the assault. Technology had long made it possible to monitor special assault teams performing their duties in clandestine operations although the terrain in some areas made for poor reception.

As leader, JB gave last minute instructions to his team while making final preparations.

"Xin Cao," JB said. "Everyone, turn on your cameras. Half of your men will enter here, through the front gate. The rest of us, including Li Na, will enter the compound through the gully you enlarged on the back side."

"Do you want us to split up once inside?" Xin Cao asked.

"No," JB said. "Go straight for the bunker. Make sure to clear the small structures before you do. Eliminate anyone in your way. Two of us will head toward you from the other side of the compound. The others will quickly clear the small barracks, the general's office, and the other two buildings."

"When do we move?" Li Na asked.

"No one moves until you quit hearing the pops from the micro drones," JB said. "Once we take out the roving patrols, we move directly to insertion points. I will send up the micro drones as soon as we eliminate the patrols. Stay on your comms. Let's get the patrols first. Move out."

Xin Cao took three men with him to find the first patrol. They waited until the patrol had exited the compound so they would have the longest amount of time to get in position near the front gate. The nature of the mission was like that of the agency they were surrogates for, clandestine. The fact they needed to succeed at all costs was not lost on any member of the team. The little news they had gotten back was that the U.S. was in a crisis of epic proportions. Xin Cao had to put it out of his mind as his team moved into position. Unlike the large caliber handguns used in most assaults by the military, each of the team had an integrally suppressed .22's. The pistols were whisper quiet compared to a 9 mm. Still sweating from the hot day and high humidity, his team snuck through the undergrowth to a point where the trail turned back left, and the undergrowth began to open a little. They heard the two Chinese soldiers before they saw the red glow of their flashlights. With their night vision goggles, the two soldiers were easy to distinguish between the trees of the forest. They were walking slowly, smoking cigarettes, talking about what they would do back home with women once they were done with this assignment. Like soldiers in all armies, they were just doing their job.

The two soldiers passed the men hidden in the shrubs and trees. About fifteen feet past them, there were four shots that sounded like dull thuds. The sounds of the soldiers' bodies hitting the ground was louder than the bullet strikes. Each had taken two shots to the back of the head. Xin Cao and his men quickly drug them into the undergrowth, covered their bodies with branches, took their radios, and headed swiftly toward the front gate for the aerial attack before they would enter the post.

"One patrol down," Steve said. "Two more to go."

Li Na had taken two men with her to find the second patrol. Based on their schedule, they knew precisely where they would be. This patrol was closer to the shore. The sound of the waves cascading along the beach obscured all other sounds. She had posted her men ahead of her then, circled back and behind the patrol, following them down the trail. The light was low, the moon being obscured behind clouds. The two soldiers were oblivious to her presence as she calmly walked behind them keeping a pace just a little quicker than their own.

"What the hell is she doing?" Phil asked.
"Her job," Steve replied. "Patience sir."

Li Na was upon the men within seconds. She didn't use her pistol as the other team members but the trusty katana in her hand. The guard on the right let out a soft moan as he raised to his tiptoes. The guard on his left pointed his flashlight at him to discover the katana's blade sticking out a foot in front of the man's chest. He started to turn to point his AK-47 at Li Na who swiftly withdrew the blade, grabbling it with both hands, covering to a high-ready position. Without loss of motion, the blade descended on the other guard. The Ak-47 had scarcely begun to move when the blade slashed into his neck, almost severing his head. He fell atop the other guard, a gurgling sound emanating from his throat, his eyes already glazed over in death. Almost before the bodies had hit the ground, Li Na's men were moving them into the undergrowth.

"Good God!" Phil exclaimed. "That's ghastly."
"Death is death," Al sighed. "She's a Master of it with her sword. You wanted stealth; you just witnessed it."
"Don't get any bright ideas," Pamela said, smiling. "She's spoken for."
"I wouldn't dream of it," Phil said, feeling sick to his stomach. The group continued to watch the assault as the teams moved toward their main objective.

Rather than wait for the patrol to reach them, JB and a team member headed directly down the trail toward the approaching patrol. Both had grown up as hunters and moved making little sound. Like the other patrols, they used red lensed flashlights to stay on the path, which made them move slower than during the day. The two soldiers were not twenty feet from JB and his partner when they noticed them. Already aimed in, each shot six rounds into the guards: five to the chest and one to the head. Following the same process as the other team members, the bodies were quicky moved into the undergrowth. JB and his partner then raced for the small clearing to deploy the weather balloon.

"Coyote, Roadrunner. All dispatches made. Now checking weather.

The team members reached their respective positions while JB filled the balloon with helium and attached the closed basket to a rope beneath it. The basket had an electronic latch, which he had tested earlier.

"Give me five minutes," JB said. "Then launch the balloon and run like hell to the insertion point."

His partner nodded in understanding as he took off on a dead run to meet the other part of his team on the backside of the compound. Nearing the rendezvous point, he made contact with Li Na and the other half of his team members.

Peering into the compound, there wasn't much activity. "Perfect," he thought. "We still have the element of surprise." He had brought the Black Hornet with him and launched it straight up to three hundred feet. Using the FLIR camera, he could see the balloon when it was released and steered it via the small console toward the compound. The wind was blowing in precisely the direction he needed it.

"Here," JB said. "Steer the balloon to this point; depress this button when I tell you."

Li Na steered the balloon as directed, while JB tracked overhead with the Black Hornet.

"Now," JB said.

Li Na depressed the button on the console and the basket opened, releasing death from above upon the unsuspecting soldiers.

"Keep your heads down everyone until the pops stop."

When the basket opened, the micro drones fell a few feet and came to life, seeking their targets, the olive-green hue of Chinese military uniforms. Within seconds there was gunfire. The soldiers shot at the drones to no avail and began running in panic-stricken fear. Soldiers within and outside of the compound were running for their lives, seeking shelter and protection from the palm sized killers. General Bocheng, Jeng Po, and Colonel Wu raced from their dinner table to the small deck outside.

"What the hell is this?" Wu asked.

Without warning, a small drone hit his forehead and he fell dead at their feet.

"Why aren't they attacking us?" Jeng asked.

"I don't know," Bocheng said, as they watched in horror.

Many of the soldiers had already been killed by the drones. The two watched helplessly as they heard the high-pitched sound of the drones that seemed to get louder as each homed in on a target, the remnants falling to the ground once it made a kill.

"It's the uniforms," Bocheng screamed. "They're going after those dressed in uniforms."

General Bocheng started screaming orders and got about two words out of his mouth when JB, Li Na, and members of the team surrounded the two men, guns pointing directly at them. Li Na's eyes were red from years of pent-up anger. She flew into a rage. Before anyone could stop her, she had put six bullets in the general's chest. His eyes widened in terror; she immediately drew her katana and lopped off his head, blood spewing over all of them, he was dead before he hit the decking. Her rage consumed her as she continued hacking the general into pieces. Two of her men grabbed her to calm her down. Breathing like a racehorse, she collapsed to her knees.

"Damn it," JB said. "It would have been nice to keep him alive for interrogation."

"I couldn't help myself," Li Na gasped. "It is finished."

"What the hell did she do that for?" Phil asked.

"He is the man that killed her family and parents," Pamela said quietly. "The only reason she was on this mission was to kill him."

"She succeeded alright," Phil said tersely. "That man could have given us critical information. Now, we have lost it."

"Not necessarily," Al interjected. "Isn't that Jeng Po, the Deputy Minister of Operations for the MSS?"

"You're right," Pamela replied. "Roadrunner, Coyote. Bring that man to the nest. Make sure he remains safe."

"Roger Coyote," JB replied.

One of the team had gone into the general's office and searched his desk and surrounding rooms. Finding what had been described to him, he exited.

"Is this what you wanted sir?" the team member asked.

"Coyote, Roadrunner," JB said. "Are you seeing this? Is this what you wanted?"

"It is," Jonas replied. "Bring it to the nest. Make sure you keep it secured."

Xin Cao and his team had come in the front gate and cleared the small buildings around the compound. Looking carefully in and around each, they next made their way to the bunker where the computers were housed. The humming of the drones could no longer be heard; they had done their job. The soldiers who had been guarding the entrance lay dead at the top of the stairs. Xin Cao and his men worked their way down the lit hallway and found several other guards lying in the walkway. They rounded the corner to find a locked steel door with a keypad. There was no camera or peephole. He presumed the computer hackers were behind it, appearing to be the only way in.

"Stay here," Xin Cao said to his men. "Let no one out."

He ran up the stairs and across the compound to find Li Na

and JB.

"All the guards to the computer bunker are dead," Xin Cao said, catching his breath. "The men are guarding the entrance."

"Ask him if he knows the code to get in" JB said.

Li Na questioned Jeng.

"This is not my post," Jeng said. "General Bocheng was in charge."

"He doesn't know," Li Na said. "Even if he did, he wouldn't tell us."

"Very well," JB said. "Take the other men and search the entire compound; we will blow the bunker door and take care of the computers."

Li Na led her team away, searching every building carefully, including the ones that had already been searched. Xin Cao and JB walked down into the bunker and examined the door. It was solid steel. The only way in was to blast it. One of Xin Cao's men placed C-4 explosives at each corner and over the two hinges on the left side. Linking them with DET cord, they moved back around the corner. He looked up at JB.

"Let's keep as many as we can inside alive," JB said. "They can give us valuable information. Blow it!"

With the press of a button, the door catapulted into the computer room filling most of the hall and room with dust. The team rushed in; guns ready. They could hear moans coming from all around the room. The men moved quickly to each man in turn. Two had been unharmed, which included the leader of the group. Three other men were dead and dying from the concrete shrapnel that had been propelled across the room from the door blast.

"Let's get these men topside," JB said. "The rest of you set charges. Use M-15 grenades on all the equipment; plant C-4 around the room. We need this place obliterated. Make sure you collapse the roof. Set timers for thirty minutes."

The team busied themselves setting charges. The M-15's would be set off first. The white phosphorous would melt the equipment, continuing to burn even when the concrete and earth above collapsed on top of it. As soon as the M-15's went off, the C-4 would explode.

JB got the two technicians topside and sat them down next to the general.

"Zip tie their hands behind their backs," JB said. "Also, gag all of them. We don't want them talking and corroborating a story. Leave one guard. The rest of you set charges to the generators, satellite dishes, helicopters, and other equipment. Set them for twenty-five minutes. Move quickly."

Every team member darted to their assigned areas and planted explosive charges on each piece of equipment. When the explosives went off, everything would be destroyed beyond repair.

"Coyote, Roadrunner" JB said. "Task complete. Retrieved three packages including a white rabbit. Heading to cliffs."

The directors and Pamela were all smiles. The team had pulled off the mission. A successful exfiltration would make them all happy. Pamela picked up her cell.

"Colonel Diets," Pamela said. "Arrange pickup in twenty."

"Looks like we may get more information than we anticipated," Al said.

"Agreed," Steve replied. "Those two in the lab coats know the complete hacking process. One of them is the leader of the hackers."

"How do you know that?" Jonas asked.

"That's what JB referred to when he said white rabbit," Steve replied.

"It would be nice if you spoke in plain English," Jonas said smiling. "I know it's required but I've been out of the field too long."

"Yes, you have," Pamela replied. "We have an opening if you're interested?"

The group laughed.

The team had rounded up the hostages and quickly made it to the shoreline. Scanning with night vision, they were able to pick up the silhouettes of the two interceptor boats, that had moved closer to shore when the patrol boat moved away. Moving the boats in as close as they could, the team climbed aboard each of the interceptors. Within five minutes they were racing across the small waves at 75 miles per hour.

"When does the party start?" the captain asked.

"In about two minutes," JB said, looking at his watch.

The team members and crew on each boat kept looking back. Already over two miles from shore they witnessed a giant fireball reach toward the sky as the plastic explosives detonated, joined by multiple small explosions. After a couple of minutes, the sky went dark again. The men smiled, knowing they had accomplished the mission on time and without casualties.

Alarms began blaring at Hong Kong Garrison. Lieutenant General Shing Teng slammed down the phone.

"Get me three Z-8 helicopters; land them in the park across the street," the General screamed at his aide. Next, he dialed the number of the garrison barracks.

"I need seventy-five men fully equipped and in the yard within ten minutes."

Unlike most militaries who ran drills and practiced being ready, the Chinese troops at Hong Kong Garrison were able to be dispatched within minutes. They were like many Americans who used go bags. Everything needed for an emergency was in it and all one had to do was grab it and go. It was so with the troops under Lieutenant General Shing Teng. Ten minutes after his order, seventy-five troops came pouring out of Amethyst and Blake Barracks Blocks and lined up in the yard across the street.

"Men," the General said. "We have trouble at one of our posts. Consider it a hot zone. Your commanders will brief you on the way."

He had barely gotten the word out of his mouth when three Z-8 transport helicopters landed behind him. The troops rushed toward them, twenty-five in each. They were eager to go being thoroughly bored with the placid life in Hong Kong and the inactivity that all warriors generally suffered when absent from war.

"Pamela," Al gasped, rushing into her office. "Satellite is picking up three helicopters heading to the post. Look like Z-8's."

"How long before they arrive?" Pamela asked.

"About an hour," Al replied.

"Hmmmm," Pamela mused as she thought.

"Al," Pamela said. "Launch the Chinese cruise missile in forty minutes."

"But that will kill all the response troops," Al replied.

"Yes," Pamela said. "And with all the extra bodies, they won't be able to sort out which soldier is from what outfit. It will cover our tracks better than anticipated."

"That's a lot of deaths for the price," Al interjected.

"Maybe," Pamela said. "Compared to the deaths that will occur because of the blackout they created, they should consider it a gift."

Al picked up his sat phone and gave the order. He wondered what the Chinese general and the politicians up the line would think when they discovered the strike was one of their own missiles?

"What do you want to do with the hostages?" Al asked.

"Take all three to the safe house for interrogation," Pamela said. "We can use them for barter after that. Start them off with stress analysis."

"You think that will be enough?" Al asked.

"Probably enough for the two computer techs," Pamela replied. "For the deputy minister, I'm guessing you'll need to do a full-court press. Whatever it takes. I want every iota of information from each of them that they can give."

"Understood," Al said.

"Where is the team now?" Pamela asked.

"They were picked up twenty-five miles offshore by helicopter," Al responded. "They will be aboard the transport in about thirty minutes."

"So far, so good," Pamela said. "Do you know who they will be working with once they reach stateside?"

"Jack Donovan," Al said. "He's not a field person now but was a good one in his day in the Middle East. He's now head of the FBI counterterrorism division."

"I hope he is on board with the team," Pamela said. "We don't need any foul ups at this point."

"They are directed from the President," Al said. "Besides, he and JB go back for some years. I'm more worried about finding these guys than a jurisdictional pissing contest between agencies."

"Quite right," Pamela said. "If we don't find them, nothing else will matter."

The men on the trawler had locked the cruise missile onto the target coordinates while the interceptor boat pulled alongside; they jumped aboard. The countdown timer decreased second by second while they glided slowly across the water and stopped about two hundred yards away. A bright flash erupted from the rear of the missile when the engine roared to life. Streaking into the blackened night sky it quickly picked up speed. A few seconds after the launch, the mission leader pulled a DT remote firing device from his jacket pocket and pressed the on button arming it, and then, button number one, which lit up following arming. The boat had now moved about a quarter mile away when he depressed the first button followed by the fourth button.

The men had set small charges in the bow and stern areas along with two more amidship. The first two buttons blew holes in the wooden hull of the trawler fore and aft. Most compartments at once flooded causing the ship to sink to deck level within thirty seconds. It was then that the team leader pressed the remaining two buttons. There was a large dull thud, flame erupting on deck; the sound of detonation had been deadened by the water. The entire trawler disintegrated, leaving only a small amount of debris floating on the surface, which would be quickly dissipated by the waves and wind over a wide area. What was left of the ship settled to the bottom twelve hundred feet below. No one would ever find it. The mission successfully completed, the interceptor boat went to full throttle, speeding back to base.

Seventy-five, fully armed Chinese troops landed in the compound next to the still burning hulks of the helicopters that had been destroyed by Roadrunner. The commanding officer, a colonel, deployed his men immediately. They found body after body that appeared to have been shot in the head. The area where the computer bunker had been, was a gaping hole in the middle of the compound. The colonel only knew that it was a communications facility.

"Sir," the captain said. "We did as you commanded. General Bocheng is dead, over by the steps to his office, along with his aide Colonel Wu. It looks like the general was hacked up by a machete or sword. We haven't found anyone alive. All the equipment was destroyed along with the satellite array. We're still searching the area. So far, it looks like a complete loss. We will know more at daylight."

"Thank you, captain," the Colonel said. "Keep searching."

The colonel was trying to piece together what could have happened. It looked like the post had been the target of a raid, but by who. He immediately guessed it was Americans, but that seemed rather farfetched, especially in Chinese territory. He picked up his sat phone to contact General Shing Teng.

"Sir," the colonel said. "The post is a complete loss. We found no one alive and the general is dead. It appears . . ."

"Hello, hello," the general shouted.

The colonels' words stopped, followed by a slight crackling sound and then, nothing. The line was completely dead.

A thousand pounds of high explosives had detonated when the missile, traveling at 500 miles per hour, struck the compound. The bodies within were turned to mush by the concussion and strewn over a quarter mile radius by the force of the blast. No-one remained alive. The explosion was so forceful that it was heard on the outskirts of Shantou. People watched the fireball in the night sky. Emergency crews were already racing toward the scene. Above the post, a Chengdu Pterodactyl was sending General Shing Teng aerial views of the carnage below.

"There's nothing left," Shing Teng whispered to himself. "How could this be? Captain, get me Lioh Hintao, Chairman of the Central Military Commission at once. Tell him it's a matter of national security; an emergency."

It was better to get the higher ranks involved now. "I don't want this coming back on me like it was my responsibility," he thought. No one would be pleased with what happened and they would want answers immediately, as well as a scape goat. The general dispatched another fifty troops to keep order and keep out those who had no need to know. There was no use letting locals fan the flames by hearsay and gossip.

Jack Donovan was sitting in the conference room sifting through the latest data he had received from several intelligence agencies. There was nothing out of the ordinary, which is what he expected. He had called in an agent that spoke fluent Mandarin and was familiar with clandestine ops. Together they were examining various pieces of phone chatter that the Defense Intelligence Agency has sent over, which had been picked up at Ft. Huachuca by their ground radar station, still very active in the never-ending drug war.

"What are they saying?" Jack asked.

"They're talking about a sweet and sour chicken recipe," Ling said. "But it doesn't make sense. First, they say the ingredients then, say the recipe will be made in two days."

"It sounds like a code," Jack said. "Anything else?"

"Only that they will begin cooking it once it is made," Ling replied. "Then, they'll meet at the predetermined restaurant. Sir, this is a code for what you're looking for."

"What's your best estimate?" Jack asked.

"I would speculate that the recipe is the mission equipment and related items," Ling said. "The predetermined restaurant is their rendezvous point."

"Hmmmm," Jack said. "That could be anywhere; we need to narrow the location."

"Do we have the location of the phones where these messages were intercepted?" Ling asked.

"How would that help us?"

"Well sir, they will probably be in the broad area where they are operating," Ling replied. "What I mean is that if they are in southern California, the operation will likely be in that area. They're likely not going to be hundreds of miles away."

"Makes sense," Jack replied, depressing a button on the conference phone. "Dorothy, get me General Dawson. It's urgent."

The DHS Intelligence and Analysis group had already made a list of potential targets throughout the state. Jack was hoping they would get lucky. The phone began buzzing.

"General Dawson on line one sir," Dorothy said.

"Thank you, Dorothy," Jack replied. "General, I need a favor. I'm not asking for your intelligence source just to relieve your fears."

"What do you need?" Dawson asked.

"Could you tell me the general area where the phone transmissions came from?" Jack asked.

"You're referring to the transcripts we sent you?" Dawson asked.

"Yes."

"That won't be a problem. Hold one moment please."

Only a few seconds, that seemed like an eternity, had passed when the general's voice came back online.

"The transmissions came from the San Jose and San Francisco areas," Dawson said. "We also just picked up another from the Sacramento area. I hope that helps in your hunt."

"It should help immensely general," Jack said. "I owe you one."

"What do you think?" Jack asked.

"I think we need to concentrate our efforts in the northern California area," Ling responded. "More importantly, we need information out of Chinatown in San Francisco."

"Why there?"

"Because these MSS agents are Chinese and they will feel safer among their own," Ling replied. "I hope your team speaks Mandarin well."

"They are all fluent," Jack replied. "We had better notify our departments and cooperating agencies. I'll notify the transport to divert to San Francisco International."

"I wouldn't do that sir," Ling said. "The Chinese have eyes and ears everywhere in the San Francisco area. If they see a military transport plane land, they'll report it immediately."

"Where would you suggest?" Jack asked.

"Beale sir," Ling replied. "It's just over a hundred miles away from downtown. Plus, any necessary equipment they need will be on hand."

"Good idea," Jack said.

The C-17A Globemaster III transport had just finished its midair refueling when the intercom crackled to life.

"Sir," the co-pilot said. "You have an incoming call. It's urgent."

"This is JB."

"This is Jack Donovan. How are you JB?"

"You old rascal," JB said, a smile coming to his face. "What have you been up to? I assume this isn't a social call?"

"I'm afraid not," Jack replied. "I'd like to catch up soon, but I'm diverting you to Beale Air Force Base."

"But we were supposed to land at LAX," JB said.

"Understood," Jack responded. "But the President has ordered us to help you locate the MSS agents."

"You must believe you have if you're diverting us," JB said soberly.

"We believe so," Jack replied. "We have every intelligence agency working on this. Right now, we feel that based on DHS and FEMA reports of the most potential targets, as well as phone transmissions, that they are in northern California. Likely in Chinatown in San Francisco. At least one of my field agents suspects so."

"Is your agent there now?"

"Yes. His name is Ling Thomas. His mother was Chinese, and father is American. They met in Hong Kong while his dad was stationed at the embassy."

"I'd like him to speak to Li Na."

"Very well," Jack replied.

"This is Li Na," she said then, at once began rapidly speaking Mandarin. The two talked for a few minutes and Li Na explained to JB all that she had said. He had understood the gist of it.

"I asked him how he learned Mandarin so well," Li Na said. "He grew up until about ten in Hong Kong and his mother taught him. It was the only way he could understand his Chinese relatives. He's very fluent. They moved to the states after his father's embassy tour ended. He went to Stanford and then, into the FBI and has been with them for about ten years.

He seems trustworthy."

"That's good to know," JB said.

Jack was asking Ling what they had discussed.

"She asked how I knew Mandarin so well," Ling said. "Mostly questioned me about my upbringing and role here. She was just testing my speaking skills."

"I assumed you passed," Jack replied.

"Oh yes," Ling smiled.

"And how are her speaking skills?" Jack asked.

"Impeccable sir," Ling replied. "Impeccable."

"JB," Jack spoke again. "It seems the team cooperation is off to a good start."

"I need to ask you a question," JB said. "I assume letting my team run this is ruffling some feathers. Is that the correct assumption?"

"You always were a quick study," Jack said. "Yes, it has. However, they are all in line as long as they have a liaison with you."

"Who?"

"Well, me of course," Jack replied. "I can tie us into the FBI and other groups for rapid support. Whatever you need."

"That's great," JB said. "We also have a liaison from the CIA; to observe and give us any high-tech support we may need in a hurry. Are you okay with that?"

"No worries my friend," Jack said. "After seeing what has happened with the southern blackout, everyone here is open to all the help they can get. For the first time in a long time, all the kids on the playground are playing well together."

"Great," JB replied. "I'll see you at Beale. We should be there in about six hours. I'll introduce you to Steve then."

During their conversation, the team had felt the aircraft turn slightly to the left. They anxiously awaited news on what JB had been talking about.

"Listen up," JB said. "The feds believe the MSS agents are in the San Francisco area; Chinatown to be exact. We will hit the ground running at Beale Air Force base. Vehicles will be waiting, and they'll fill us in once enroute to San Francisco. Get some rest while you can. I have a feeling we are in for a long haul."

"You think we can catch these guys?" Li Na asked.

"I think our chances just got a big boost," JB replied. "The crises they created in the south has everyone on alert; they're paranoid. You have experience with the PLA, what do you think these agents will do since the post is no longer sending them communications?"

"They will likely assume that something is wrong with the equipment," Li Na said. "They will proceed with the mission."

"Any chance of them being contacted by other MSS leaders?"

"Not likely. That post was the only one communicating with them. Its highly classified nature makes it unlikely that anyone else has the communications procedure, excepting perhaps MSS headquarters. There is the possibility the agents may attempt to contact Xiyuan. They don't know it yet, but they are now on their own."

"I agree," JB said. "However, we must not underestimate them."

"No," Li Na said. "We should not."

Leaning back in her seat, she grasped his hand and squeezed it slightly resting her head on his shoulder. Everyone was thinking about the mission ahead. Tired from the one just accomplished, they drifted into an uneasy sleep, rough weather making for a bumpy ride. They were awakened by the tires of the transport striking the tarmac on runway 33 at Beale Air Force base. The plane taxied to the far end then, onto a large tarmac area north, northeast of the runway close to the hangers. It pulled into a 45° position about two hundred feet from wingtip to the tail of another transport plane on their right. The team members had collected their gear and were standing on the ramp as it lowered. Jack Donovan and Ling, along with several other agents had pulled four vans near the rear of the aircraft.

"Welcome JB," Jack said, extending his hand. "It's been a long time. Come with me. We have a two-hour ride to the hotel. I'll fill you in on the way."

"First, let me introduce you to Steve Watson, our CIA liaison, and Li Na. You've read their dossier's no doubt; you can talk to them more later. Team, put on your comms. I don't want to have to repeat anything. If you don't hear something, you weren't meant to."

Li Na, JB, Donovan, and Ling climbed into the first van. The remainder of the team loaded into the other three. Within minutes, they were on CA-113 headed to I-80 West. There was little time for chit chat as Jack and Ling filled them in on what they had discovered. Ling had pulled out a map rather than hover over the glare of a monitor.

"We picked up transmissions here and here," Ling said. "According to DIA, these are precise locations. Then, DIA picked up another transmission from this location."

"Have they heard anything else?" JB asked.

"No," Jack replied. "The last ping was from a tower near the western most end of the East Bay Bridge. The other two pinged in the heart of Chinatown. We have not detected them again."

"Burner phones," Li Na said. "That's what they are trained to use. You'll need to filter traffic and see if you can pick up their transmissions again."

"We hoped we were wrong," Jack said. "But you're confirming what we suspected. I hear you have worked with the PLA. Any suggestions for us?"

"Yes," Li Na responded. "Keep searching phone communications. Even though we knocked out their post, they are trained to continue unless told otherwise. Above all, do not underestimate them."

"She is right," Steve said, looking at the map from the behind their seat. "I'm head of counterintelligence for Taiwan Station.

The Chinese counterintelligence group, MSS, go back to the days of the Flying Tigers that protected them from the Japanese during World War II. They also have received clandestine training from the CIA and other U.S. military operatives since. They have vastly improved. Li Na is correct. And these agents are every bit as good as ours."

"That's not the best news," Jack said. "But it's what we suspected. There is one thing we could use from you and that is a good aerial surveillance platform. Can you get us one?"

"I anticipated that and have one on the way to Beale," Steve said. "It will here before dark. A maintenance team is coming with it. We can feed the surveillance to several locations, including the operators."

"How long can it stay up?" Jack asked.

"It's a Global Hawk," Steve said. "It can maintain station for thirty-two hours plus and has a range of 14,000 miles. It also has a cruise speed of about 350 miles per hour. It is observation only with aerial photos, FLIR, and radar."

"That will work just fine," Jack said. "What if we need a major strike?"

"I have a Predator standing by with hellfire missiles," Steve said. "We will launch it, but if we need to fire the missiles, your agency will give the command."

"Certainly," Jack said. "Our command center is in a hotel down by Fisherman's Wharf. All of you are booked under a general FBI cover. A suite will serve as our makeshift command unless we need to move."

"What about counterintelligence?" JB asked.

"That will be covered with some additional agents we have assigned here and from our main counterintelligence office in Los Angeles."

"How difficult is hotel access?" JB asked.

"Easy access at the junction of North Point Street and Columbus Avenue," Jack replied. "The parking lot sits a little below the main street level and is obscured by shrubs along the property border. Directly behind is a pizza joint and a Korean restaurant. Here we are now."

The vans pulled into the hotel parking lot. As soon as they got out, they could smell the salt air. A lingering smell that was stronger than that along a typical beach. There was the smell of fish, as well as baking breads and other odors that mingled to give the air a peculiar smell all its own. Each of them lugged their gear to their rooms without talking. They were tired from the long trip.

"Look," Jack said. "We are still gathering intelligence. Let me sort through it and let's meet at 0600 in the ops room. Get some sleep and be ready to hit the ground running in the morning. All of us will be much better for it. These guys are going to be slippery; it won't be easy to get a bead on them."

"Sounds good," JB said as he and Li Na walked away.

The team members were double bunked per room, except Li Na and JB who had their own rooms. The room JB occupied was on the back side of the hotel. He was on the top floor and had a small view across Fisherman's Wharf into San Francisco Bay, Alcatraz standing like a lone sentinel just over a mile away. He partially opened the window to take advantage of a nice breeze blowing in from the bay. Pulling a chair closer to it he sat down, taking in the view, the sounds, and the smells of the wharf. It wasn't like the swamp back home, but like the swamp, had its own unique smells and sounds which took him back to his childhood when he used to poll a small dugout through the swamps, gigging for frogs and fishing. It seemed so long ago, but he could remember it like it was yesterday. He could still see the Medicine Man's face close to his while being instructed in the fine art of tracking. Although he showed compassion, the Medicine Man was stern and an absolute task master. Until you mastered the skill he was teaching, you were not allowed to learn another. But, like most of his friends, JB had caught on quickly and was like a sponge when it came to learning new skill sets. He just soaked them in. He couldn't remember the last time he had reflected on his youth. More importantly, the memories seemed to refresh his mind and take him away from what was happening. It was a wonderful stress relief. He was jolted out of his reflections by a soft knock on the door. At first, he didn't know where he was, but quickly opened the door.

"How are you?" Li Na asked.

"I'm good," JB replied. "Come on in. I was just reflecting on some childhood memories on the reservation."

Li Na closed the door behind her, giving JB a kiss on the cheek. Walking to the window, she sat down watching the seagulls float in the air above Fisherman's Wharf. They were like tiny gray specs, but she knew them well. It seemed that no matter where there was a beach or shore, they could be found with their shrill calls, gliding aloft, waiting for someone to throw them a small morsel of food.

"What are you thinking?" JB asked.

"I was just looking at the seagulls thinking what a carefree life they have."

"Yeah, I know what you mean. I wouldn't mind having a carefree life myself."

He had drug another chair across from hers. She stood and walked to him, sitting in his lap.

"Well, just maybe I can help for a little bit today."

She kissed him passionately on his mouth, arousing the sexual desire in each. He picked her up in his arms and playfully tossed her onto the bed. She sighed realizing her feelings for him; they were unlike any she had before. He was willing to help her hunt down the man who had killed her family. And this evening, she would have him all to herself. The mission was put on hold for a few hours as the two enjoyed moments of bliss. Li Na had learned much about him already. Despite his ability to deal death, he had a surprising amount of compassion toward others. He jumped on top of her, kissing her lips and neck, bringing her slowly to arousal.

He could smell her fragrant perfume and breathed it in as he bent down, kissing the nape of her neck while he slowly moved his hands up and cupped them over her firm breasts. Li Na was lithe and athletic. He unpinned her hair, letting is cascade across the sheets. He had forgotten how long it was and so black there was an almost blue sheen to it. Her skin was pale and soft and felt like velvet as he caressed her cheeks and let his fingers drift up under her blouse, undoing her bra. A soft moan escaped her lips as she looked him in the eyes, so dark and deep that he found himself lost in them. He melted because he could sense her love for him. A love, like his, not easily given. He wondered what would happen once the mission was over. He hadn't realized she had undone his belt and was swiftly pulling off his trousers. Within a few seconds, they had stripped each other, and he straddled her, looking down into her face. She pulled upward and kissed him, her tongue exploring the depth of his mouth and his exploring hers. She could feel his manhood begin to throb against her thigh as she pulled away, then, using her legs, rolled him to the side so that she now straddled him.

"I see you like to be a woman in control." He smiled at her. A small tear was running down her cheek.

"What is it?" he asked.

"I fear for our future, and I want to know what you think of our relationship?"

"You want complete honesty?" She nodded.

"You know more than anyone what I was trained for. Since we have been on this mission, I have breathed and lived it; it is how I am. But at the same time, I find myself emersed in thoughts about us and admire your beauty. It is like we think alike. And I admit that I am taken by your intelligence and most of all, your feistiness. No matter what I'm doing I find myself thinking about you. I promised myself I would not let my guard down again after the death of my fiancé but for you, it has been very difficult. I feel an attraction that I have never felt before for a woman."

"I feel the same," Li Na whispered, another tear rolling down her cheek. "You give me butterflies in my stomach every time I think of you and of us. All day, I long to be with you and too often I find myself daydreaming about you."

He pulled her to him, kissing her deeply. She began to writhe atop him and return the kiss with an unbelievable passion, her hair cascading around his head like drawn curtains. Daylight was quickly fading as the sun set far across the Pacific out past the Golden Gate Bridge. An orange orb emitting a faint aura around it as it hung, for a last brief moment, above an orange strip of light basking the top of the water, waves glistening as it disappeared.

Both were filled with lust as JB pulled her to him harder, kissing her more deeply as he felt her firm breasts against his chest. She bounced and writhed atop him, kissing with a passion he had never known. She raised up a little as he pulled her white thong off and tossed it to the floor. No sooner had he done so than she pushed him hard against the bed, delivering a wet passionate kiss as she scratched his back with her nails. Slowly, ever so gently, she began to kiss his neck and down his chest to his groin, as he began to moan. He rolled her over, kissing her nipples, tracing circles around them. She began to squirm as he continued kissing and lightly licking her heavenly mound. Laying in naked splendor, her nipples standing erect in her excitement.

"My turn mister," she said as she rolled him over and regained her position back on top.

She eagerly pulled off his jockey's then, pushed him back on the bed as she began licking his nipples; he lay naked before her. He was well built, and in good physical shape. It always surprised her to look at his body. Her lust made her ache; she tingled with a desperate need as she stared at his bulging manhood, veins distended, his erection so hard it arched above his lean abdomen, pointing at his navel. Moisture beading on the dark, plum-colored head. She grasped hold of it, tugging gently toward her, unconsciously licking her lips as she slid down and licked the plum-colored head, arousing him immensely. She climbed swiftly back on top and grabbing his manhood, guided it to its target. He had been softly massaging her flower box, occasionally letting one and two fingers insert themselves inside. Once she guided the projectile to its target, he couldn't help thrusting hard, going deep inside. She began to squirm almost uncontrollably as she bounced up and down, in control of the moment. He caressed her nipples as he got into the rhythm she had created. Lest he reach a climax too quickly, he rolled over and slid down so that his tongue gently licked her nipples as he firmly ran his fingers through her pubic hair, then slowly began kissing her inner thighs, her legs spread wide. As he kissed, he slowly let his tongue drift to the skin surrounding her flower box. He began kissing it, little succulent smacks, lips pursed, no tongue. His first kisses were below her raspberry as he began to softly breathe hot air gently across and onto her vulva then, ever so slowly, began to blow it across her raspberry as he inserted two fingers to rub and gently caress her sensitive insides. Li Na was writhing, her body undulating as waves of lust and pleasure washed over her, surrendering to ecstasy and spasms of satisfaction as she lost herself in the moment.

He was savoring every second; there was no rush, they had all the time they needed. At this moment, there were no other cares. While he continued softly kissing and lightly blowing, he ever so gently began caressing her raspberry with his tongue, his fingers still inserted. Her scent was provocative and her taste powerful as he next plunged his tongue deep inside her box. She began to moan, louder and louder. She was in pure ecstasy. His tongue mightier than the sword, it was like his kisses and licks were perfectly alluring, never knowing what would happen next as her excitement built. He backed off the kisses and began flirting with the inner lips of her vulva, tracing the edges with his fingertips as he squeezed and pinched them gently. He was making love to her as subtly and lightly as a feather. He could tell she was getting too excited and began to pull back, to prolong the pleasure. He started to gently stimulate the smooth area just above the hood then, softly began to tap the region just below it and above the main entrance. He began to tease her again with his tongue, this time at the bottom of the lower entrance and slowly began to gently lick the area, stimulating the raspberry with his right thumb. He was wandering now with both fingers and tongue as he brought her excitement to a crescendo and then backed off again and again. She began to moan loudly; she was near exploding. He worked his way up again to her nipples as she suddenly grabbed his manhood and thrust it inside her again. This time she would not let him roll and take it out.

Oh my god she thought as he began a slow rhythm. She was enjoying every stroke enormously as he slowly pumped in and out, probing deep. Wrapping her legs around and behind his waist, she began forcing him harder and harder into her, getting into a rhythmic motion. She was about to climax but didn't want to. Suddenly, she twisted to the side, throwing him on his back in the cowgirl position so she could control the pace. She began with a slow tempo at first and began to increase the pace as she grew more excited. Both were moaning, getting louder with each passing moment as their ecstasy shifted to pure pleasure. She slowed just enough to change position into the reverse and began a frenzied pace, as fast as she could. They were both screaming like one long moan as they came together. He thought his brain was going to explode; it was on fire. Li Na fell beside him, quivering with an occasional spasm as both, breathing hard, stared at each other in surprise, not believing they could have such joy. They fell asleep, exhausted. Coupled with the recent mission where their adrenaline had flowed for hours, their sleep was so deep that they didn't move until their alarm went off the next morning. He wrapped his arms around her and held her tight as they kissed and enjoyed the feel of each other's warmth. Feeling aroused again, they fell into the thrill of the moment and enjoyed each other once more. It was 0500; they would be meeting Jack and the rest of the team at 0630. Li Na returned to her room. After a quick shower and dress, they met downstairs for a continental breakfast.

"I trust you had a good rest," Jack said as he poured a cup of coffee.

"Yes, I did," JB replied. "It was much needed and from the looks of the men, they did too."

"That's great," Jack replied. "It's likely the last good sleep you will get for a couple of days."

"I gathered that," JB grinned.

"Seriously," Jack said. "The director had a conference meeting with the President, DCIA, and DDOE this morning. They want this mission executed successfully, at once."

"Can't say as I blame them," JB said. "We may have gotten the hackers offline, but if I know these guys, they have backups for that too. Especially now that they have lost communications with the post."

"What do you think they will do?" Jack asked.

"Initially they'll pass it off as bad communications due to equipment," JB replied. "After that, they will assume the hackers were eliminated and will execute their Plan B."

"How long do you think we have?" Jack asked. "What will Plan B look like?"

"We took out their primary," JB said. "I'd say we have twenty-four hours before they go to their secondary plan. They will need access to a large computer array to couple with their field assignment to make it work. Any ideas?"

"The biggest computer network around is what is referred to as the telecom hotel," Jack said. "I don't think that would be the target because security is exceptional. You're not getting in without the proper ID and even if you killed the security guards, you still wouldn't get in without some serious explosives. Before you could make it far enough the FBI and local police would be on top of you."

"What other options do they have?" JB asked.

"Hmmmm," Jack Mused. "Ling, come here for a moment."

"What do you need?" Ling asked.

"The MSS agents may need a large computer bank or array to complete their mission," Jack said. "We have ruled out the telecom hotel due to security. What options would they have?"

"The next best option would be Globe-Com Headquarters in Mountain View," Ling said.

"That's about forty miles away," Jack said. "Why there?"

"They have massive banks of computers," Ling said. "Also, they are open to the public during the day. Anyone can visit and wander around the campus for a few hours."

"But you cannot just walk into a building can you?" JB asked.

"Certainly not," Ling said. "The majority of the buildings are only open to employees, but there is a problem we have been concerned with. Shall I tell him?"

"Yes," Jack replied.

"We have been worried about computer issues there before," Ling said. "You may know that there is a large Asian population in the bay area. We have picked up chatter that points to Globe-Com headquarters and that appears to be friendly to China and the MSS. We have not nailed it down yet. A big problem in this case is that if you know someone who works there, you may be able to arrange a tour of some of the office's and see the inner workings of the company."

"What you're telling me is that if I were an MSS agent and knew someone there, that I could likely gain access." JB said.

"Exactly," Ling replied.

"Not only that," Jack interrupted. "It is possible that the MSS has an agent or several agents that work in the facility. We do not know for certain but have speculated for some time now that at least one person has access to the kind of equipment they need."

"That makes our mission two-fold," JB said. "We need to find what they have been doing in the field and we need to find the potential agents at Globe-Com."

"That's right," Jack said. "We have no time to lose; let's adjourn to the operation's center upstairs. Our strategy needs revision."

The team and agents ate quickly then, walked upstairs to the suite that served as the operations center. Additional FBI agents and DoD personnel were manning various computers and control consoles. Several large, dry-erase boards had been set up to fine tune activities for each group and to serve as a map hanger. Using a large map, Jack began explaining the most recent intelligence they had been able to gather.

"Working with DIA at Fort Huachuca, the last voice transmission we detected was here, near the corner of Powell and Jackson Streets."

"What's at that location?" JB asked.

"The San Francisco Public Library," Ling replied. "It's on the edge of Chinatown and has free Internet access and a wealth of information on infrastructure and other key resources around the area."

"Do you believe they are in Chinatown?" Li Na asked.

"Yes," Jack replied. "It seems since most people speak Mandarin fluently, they would be able to somewhat control their surroundings."

"And don't forget that the triads and MSS have worked together before," Ling said. "My guess is they are providing a safe house for these men during their mission."

"They won't be easy to find, but this is probably the place to start," Jack said. "After all, wouldn't they need to finish their field operations before gaining access to an array of computers to make their plan work."

"Yes," Ling said. "They will complete that part of their mission first."

"How large is Chinatown?" JB asked.

"It is twenty-four blocks for the major part," Ling said. "It spans from Kearney Street on the east to Powell Street on the west. Then, from Broadway in the North to Bush Street in the south. It's quite large."

"We have a lot of work to do," JB said. "I assume most of the Asians in this area speak Mandarin?"

"A poor assumption," Ling said. "I made it myself and was surprised. Chinatown in San Francisco is the oldest Chinatown in North America. I walked through the area a few days ago. Most of the people speak Cantonese, the language of Southern China. I spoke to some shopkeepers who know some Mandarin, mostly due to tourists from China. It turns out that around 1986 about 70 percent of the residents spoke Cantonese compared to about 20 percent Mandarin. Gradually that has shifted and while there are no statistics I could find, it appears that Mandarin speakers now number about fifty percent of the population. But Cantonese is still the primary language of the shopkeepers at least."

"Any other surprises?" Li Na asked.

"A small history lesson may suffice," Jack said. "According to Ling, written Chinese is the same for both languages, but various characters are pronounced differently, and some have different meanings."

"A lot of them," Ling interjected.

"It was established in 1848," Jack continued. "And has been influential in politics, customs, languages, social clubs, places of worship and overall identity through its history. New immigrants move in daily, mostly older. And perhaps most fortunate for your team, it draws more tourists annually than the Golden Gate Bridge."

"That should help us blend in," JB retorted.

"Most of my team speak Cantonese equally as well as Mandarin," Li Na said. "It is a must among the triads."

"This will not be easy," JB said.

"How are you going to approach it?" Jack asked.

"Head on," Li Na said. "We will seek out promising prospects in the area saying that the See On Yun triad mentioned the possibility of obtaining work here. We'll see who bites."

"What triad is that?" Jack asked.

"One that we know well," JB replied. "The least said the better. We will need some of your agents scattered about for backup and surveillance."

"No problem," Jack said. "We have twenty agents at your command. Gather around men, he yelled. What do you need them to do?"

"Assuming they are all trained in surveillance, I want them to observe. Trail anyone they believe is suspicious, particularly after we speak with them. We will split our team into pairs. With that many agents, place one with each team and then the remainder throughout Chinatown on overwatch."

"I'd like to say something," Li Na said. "The criminals you usually encounter are bank robbers or worse. These men are cold blooded killers who are trained much like CIA agents; they are extremely brutal. They will kill a woman or child as easily as you do an armed felon, and they will enjoy it. If you draw down on them and they make the slightest move, shoot them or you will be dead."

The FBI agents around the room glanced at each other and then at Jack, wondering what he would say.

"She is correct," Jack said. "Do not hesitate or as my friend JB learned from his karate master, those who hesitate will be meditating permanently in a horizontal position. These men are deadly; treat them as such."

The words created a soberness. The agents were accustomed to common criminals on America's streets but working against those who would shoot you for the fun of it was going to be a new, if not deadly experience.

"Gather around and I will assign areas to each team," Jack said.

Following the strategy that JB had laid out, Jack assigned

agents to each of the two-man teams that had been chosen for each quadrant of Chinatown. Each team was labeled Alpha through Delta and would cover a six-block area beginning at Broadway. The plan was to inconspicuously infiltrate the entire area as they meticulously blended into the crowds and people on the street.

"Everyone," Jack yelled above the din. "Every agent will wear one of these, as well as your team JB. I'm an old hand at surveillance. You will always keep your comm on to be as covert as possible. You will note they are not the traditional coiled earpiece that most tactical units or even the secret service use. These earpieces are designed by an audiologist. The speakers are so small they will not block the ear canal, which will give you the ability to talk on a phone or to a person in front of you, as well as hear sounds coming from all around, without removing it. These are virtually undetectable and will allow each of you total situational awareness. If ever you needed it, now is that time. Put them on and test them with all other teams."

"Men," JB said. "Make sure you use your teams call sign when you speak. Also, assign a number to each member of the team. As an example, when you speak, say Alpha two, potential bogey at three o'clock. For those on overwatch, it is important that you maintain contact with all teams you are covering. Move if you need to. We have zero room for error. If the MSS agents are successful, life as you know it in the U.S. will be over. Potentially, millions could perish."

"What you're telling us is that this is not a typical FBI assignment," an agent said.

"It is not," Jack replied. "This assignment is a matter of life and death for the country and for yourselves. Show no mercy to the enemy for none will be afforded you. Men, you have entered the wild west where the only law is in your pistol. Turn on your comms and prep your equipment. Also, chamber a round; you won't have time to do it later with these agents.

Blend in as nonchalantly as you can. We disperse in twenty. Get to your locations via walking, train, or trolley. No taxis."

"Why no taxis?" an agent asked

"Because most of them are Chinese and often serve as lookouts for the triads," Li Na said. "The goal is to keep our eyes open, and mouths shut as much as we can. Too much talk will make you a target."

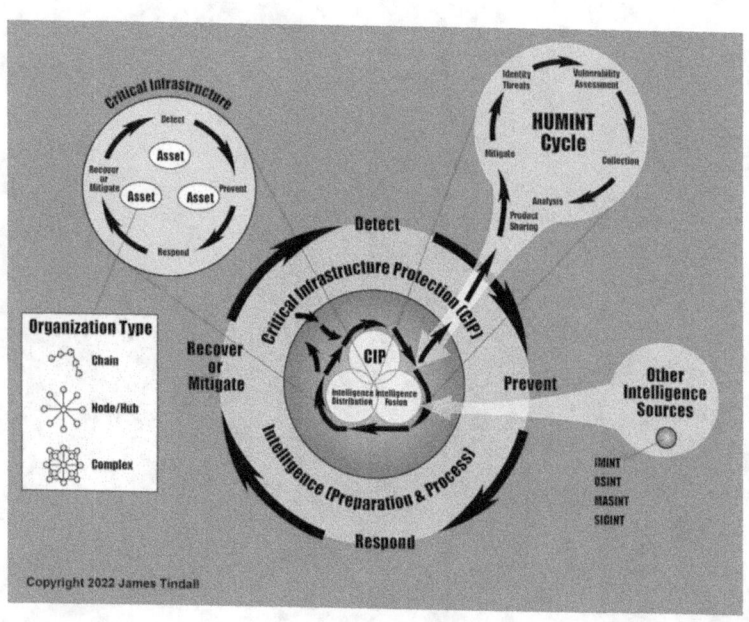

CHAPTER 8

Lieutenant General Shing Teng, for once in his life, had made a very excellent decision. Kicking the problem up to the Chairman of the Central Military Commission had put him in a key position of reliance to them, which may in the future result in a promotion. More importantly, he was now the go-to person to dig into the operation. He had just entered a small conference room when the large monitor on the wall turned a bright white and revealed the entire military commission. Lioh Hintao was seated in the middle of the table, clearly the leader of the group.

"General Teng," Hintao said. "What can you tell us about the incident?"

"Gentlemen," Teng said. "I have been on scene myself. The underground bunker is destroyed; collapsed from the explosion. There are close to one hundred bodies around the compound, most of them unrecognizable. A few were identified. General Bocheng among them, as well as Colonel Wu."

"Do you think this was the Americans?" a member asked.

"We have considered it sir," Teng said. "But so far, we have no evidence. I am having the explosives analyzed to determine, which force they belong to."

"Was this a missile strike?" Hintao asked.

"It looks like it sir," Teng replied. "If I'm not mistaken, having been on scene myself, I would say it was a cruise missile with cluster munitions."

There was a soft knock at the door. A colonel entered handing the general a paper folder with classified analysis inside.

"Please hold a moment," Teng said to the commission.

He quickly perused the analysis the colonel had given him, his eyes opening wide in surprise. His right hand began to quiver, which didn't go unnoticed by Hintao and the remainder of the commission. They were experts at reading people. They had to be if they wanted to be effective in their jobs.

"What's wrong?" Hintao asked impatiently.

General Teng looked up. Thoughtfully eyeing the commission. "Do you remember the development of our cruise missile, the DF-16B?" Teng asked.

"Yes, of course," Hintao replied, the rest of the commission nodding affirmatively.

"If you recall, we didn't know if the design would work," Teng said.

"You mean a combination of a high explosives combined with cluster munitions?" Hintao asked.

"Correct," Teng replied. "To determine and gather data, we adopted several of our land-based cruise missiles to test the theory. They worked, which is how we completed the design."

"What of it?" Hintao asked.

"This analysis," Teng said, holding up the papers and folder, confirm that the missile that struck the compound was one of ours."

"That's impossible," Hintao said.

"It should have been," Teng replied. "But I heard a rumor that one of the three prototypes for testing malfunctioned. Somehow, it must have ended up in an enemy's hands."

"So, you're telling us the missile that struck the post was one of ours?" a commission member asked.

"The analysis doesn't lie, sir," Teng replied.

"Hold a moment," Hintao said.

The sound went dead although General Teng could see the commission in deep discussion. Apparently, an argument was going on. Teng watched, amused, while they talked. He could imagine they were each thinking about their tenure long term as they discussed this bewildering act. A post struck by one of their own cruise missiles. Not only a post, but the hub of cyber-attacks against the U.S. and Europe for the last decade. They had probed, initiated viruses into the American infrastructure and banking systems, and delved into the systems as much as they could until they realized it would take a dual approach of both computers and men in the field to achieve the results they desired. Now that they had accomplished such a goal in the southern states, they were intent to continue. The problem was that now, they could not effect an attack from China. The result was more risks, more exposure, and potentially, war.

"Do you have any suspicions of how this happened?" Hintao asked, the sound restored.

"You know as well as I do Chairman, that our policies are not popular with the people," Teng said. "Just last year, a Uyghur man was sentenced to death for keeping history books of WWII resistance against the Japanese and how our people accomplished their defeat. Further, those history books demonstrated how the Party is aiming to control and reshape the Uyghur community. The Party, in the name of ethnic unity continues to push a more assimilationist policy on the Uyghur, Mongolians, Tibetans, and other ethnic groups. The entire policy scales back bilingual education. In all, there is more intense policing of Uyghur history and other ethnic historic narratives. This has resulted in the Party treating all this as separatist propaganda."

"What are you inferring?" Hintao asked, his eyes narrowing.

"As you know, I'm pro-China," Teng replied. "However, it appears that there must be a formal resistance now against the Party. I say this because I do not believe that the Americans could have pulled this off. It seems to me that it would have to be done by someone among us."

"A traitor in our midst?" a member asked.

"Respectfully sir, more than one," Teng replied. "Are you aware that the men affectionately refer to the post as the camp of death?" Teng asked.

"Why?" Hintao asked, surprised.

"Because every man or woman who has served there ended up dead before they got home," Teng replied.

"What?" a member asked. "How?"

"From what I know of the rumors it's true," Teng responded. "Apparently, General Bocheng would have the soldier followed and put to death before they could reach the outside world to potentially talk about what their job was. Brutality in its most evil form if you pardon the pun."

"We did not condone such actions," Hintao said. "You're telling us that everyone who has worked there has been killed after leaving?"

"Exactly," Teng replied. "But not all. At least three escaped death and disappeared. Two were computer technicians and one soldier."

"If this gets out, there will be massive demonstrations," Hintao said. "Any suggestions on how to handle it?"

"You are the politicians sir," Teng replied. "However, I would suggest two things. First, do not say it was sabotage. That will only give the resistance, assuming there is one, more fuel for the flames."

"And the second?" Hintao asked.

"Don't blame it on the Americans," Teng said. "They could probably prove it was not them. This leaves a final explanation and one that I would put forth."

"Well, what is it?" Hintao asked impatiently.

"I would say that the aviation fuel tanks for the helicopters on base exploded due to a faulty electrical pump, caught fire, and the flames engulfed the entire post."

"That may be difficult to pull off," Hintao said.

"No sir," Teng replied. "I control the scene. No one other than my troops have access. I will dress some of the men up to be interviewed with a well-rehearsed response. They will be dressed in disheveled uniforms that appear they barely survived. They will confirm the news you distribute. Further, it will save face with the Party and others. After all, such accidents happen around the world all the time do they not?"

"That's brilliant," a commission member joined in. "We will rebuild the site and double your command."

"I appreciate that sir," Teng replied. "I need to mention one other thing."

"More bad news?" Hintao queried.

"I'm not sure yet," Teng said. "We have not accounted for everyone at the post, but it appears that Jeng Po, Deputy Minister of Operations for MSS is missing. My aide tells me he took a chopper to the post and was likely there when the explosion occurred."

"That is not good news," Hintao said. "Find him or his body at once. Keep us informed."

The monitor went blank. Teng knew that he was now in the good graces of the commission, their man on the ground. Soon, he would be promoted. If they needed anything, they would come to him first. And, if Jeng Po could not be found, his promotion might be to DMO for MSS. Things were looking up, but it was time to put his shoulder into the work. It would not be easy identifying a single body among all the dead in the compound.

Pamela was at the safe house along with Al, who had decided to watch the interrogation. They were waiting when a small white van pulled through the roll-up garage door, which closed as soon as they were in. Several agents walked toward the van's sliding door to retrieve the prisoners, each wearing a black hood so that they could never reveal the location of the safe house.

"Put each in a separate room," Pamela said. "Aaron, you take the deputy minister. Al and I will each take one of the computer techs. We need to crack them quickly. The deputy minister will be harder to squeeze information from."

Within a few minutes each of them was standing in front of one of the hostages who had been seated in a chair with no restraints. A small bowl of sweet and sour pork and a can of soda sat before them on the table, an agent stationed outside each door. It took a moment for them to adjust their eyes to the light when the hoods were removed. This was going to be a good old-fashioned interrogation. First, the hostages would be befriended and then, the fun would begin. It is believed among many that if you torture a prisoner, they will say anything to make the torture stop. However, in this case, they would allow each prisoner to choose their fate. It all depended on if they cooperated and if the information conveyed could be verified. Each of the interrogators would initially make identical statements, using fake names to identify themselves.

"Good morning," Pamela said. "There is some food for you if you wish to eat. Would you like some coffee? Tea perhaps."

"Where am I and who are you?" the technician asked.

"You may call me Susan if you wish," Pamela said. "I'll be back in a moment with some tea."

Pamela knew that even though coffee was a growing beverage in China, tea was the primary drink, especially for these men. They were from a remote post and only tea would generally be served. She had been associated with China and Taiwan for most of her life and knew how to brew perfect tea. In the small kitchen, she took some green tea leaves and steeped them in hot water, adding jasmine flowers, which added a pleasant floral taste, overpowering the earthy green tea vibe. She was careful not to over-brew it. She made three trays, placing a traditional Chinese tea pot on each, along with two cups, small spoons, and several different sweeteners. With everything prepared, she called to an agent.

"Take one of these to each room," she said. "Tell the interrogator to place it in the middle of the table within easy reach of the hostage. Then, tell them to pour two cups and to drink it first so that the hostage will know it is not poisoned."

"Yes ma'am," the agent said.

He summoned another to help and instructed him on what to tell the interrogator. Soon, Pamela entered the room and sat down in front of the hostage who had eaten his food and drank the soda. She knew as all professionally trained men and women in the spook business, that you had to eat when occasion allowed because the next meal might be long in coming.

"I thought you may like some tea," Pamela said, speaking Mandarin. "I wasn't sure if you preferred sugar or not, so I brought several sweeteners for you."

Pamela poured tea into the cups and sat the tea pot down. She was about to put honey in her cup when the technician took it and slid it to his side, forcing her to take the other cup. He was calmly looking at her to judge her reaction. Pamela looked at him softly, realizing he was well trained. He had assumed that the cup she was using was clean and that his may have been doped. The small gesture told her a lot about this man. They both sweetened their tea and he watched and waited until she had taken the first sip, a small bridge of trust being built. He smelled the tea, the pleasant aroma of the jasmine wafting up his nostrils as he sipped.

"Very good," he said. "Who made this?"

"I did," Pamela said. "My mother taught me."

"You learned well," he said. "I appreciate it."

"Thank you," Pamela said. "We may as well get down to business. It is obvious we know where you worked and the purpose of the facility. I'm sure you know that your recent operation did a lot of damage to our country and our national security."

"I did only what I was ordered to do," the man said. "My name is Sing. I also will get directly to the point. I'm a Chinese national and work for the PLA as a civilian. But I'm sure you already know that. I know from the length of transport time that I am in Taiwan. What options do I have if I cooperate with you Susan?"

"You have multiple options," Pamela responded. "We can send you to Gitmo, let you stay in Taiwan with a new identity as our asset, send you back to the mainland as a trade, or throw your body into the ocean. It's up to you. You choose your fate by your degree of cooperation."

"If I'm sent back as a trade, I'll be shot," Sing said. "You know that. They will assume I am your asset or that I was captured because I didn't fight back hard enough."

"Yes," Pamela said. "I understand. It's just the Chinese way of avoiding risk."

"Precisely," Sing said. "If I choose to be an asset, will I be kept in a stockade or will I have my own apartment with freedom to roam."

"You will have the latter," Pamela responded. "And I would much rather you show us how you hacked our systems than have you in confinement."

"Then, I will choose the asset option," Sing replied. "I have never agreed with our government in this venture, but it was obey or die. I will answer your questions as much as I can."

"Very well," Pamela said. She must be careful not to slip up with this man. He was very intelligent. "How long have you been at the post?"

"Since its construction," Sing responded. "About ten years."

"We looked for it for a long time," Pamela said. "How did you avoid our satellite detection?"

"General Bocheng and his advisors chose a spot that had thick undergrowth to cover everything," Sing said. "The road from the river to the compound was carefully constructed to meander through the undergrowth so that it would not be visible from above. As they cut it out, they would throw leaves and small branches onto the bare road so it would not be visible to satellites unless you knew where it was. We even tested it with our own satellites to make sure it remained unseen."

"What about the bunker?"

"It took a year to dig it out by hand and distribute the soil around the area, which was quickly overgrown by the jungle around it. The satellite array was put in by hand as well and then, camouflaged perfectly with the surrounding jungle. We took satellite pictures of the space and hand painted each dish to match the picture. When we put in the dishes, our best trained engineers were unable to identify where they were."

"That explains why we could not find the post," Pamela said. "Some other questions I'd ask are now moot from your response. Explain to me how the satellite dish array was used to hack into our systems."

"I will try not to get too technical," Sing said.

"I appreciate that," Pamela responded.

"Essentially, we would piggyback onto an IP address we knew was coming from your infrastructure," Sing said. "Once we had that, it was a matter of hacking in."

"But you couldn't know that without field agents?" Pamela responded.

"Correct," Sing replied. "We have agents everywhere in your country. You must know that. They filter through the information and relay it via secure communications. Then, we would go through your telecom hotels in New York and San Francisco where all data across the Atlantic and the Pacific passes, thousands of megabytes each minute — our signals are lost in the shuffle."

"You think that is why we never found you?" Pamela asked.

"That, and the fact that you Americans want everything so easy," Sing replied. "I watched a presentation by a PhD turned student at the U.S. military school in Monterey. During that presentation and from his book on water security, he urged your leaders and private enterprise owners to 'air gap' the data for infrastructures."

"You mean put the codes on a CD and only use it when needed then, take it out?" Pamela queried.

"Yes," Sing replied. "That is the air gap. Except when needed, operational codes for equipment are kept on the CD in a safe place. You did not listen to that man. We did. Failing to air gap such needed control data made it much easier for us to hack you."

"But you needed to also adjust some system components in the field as well, correct?"

"Absolutely. But that is easy," Sing replied. "Because much of your systems remain legacy type using SCADA controls, our agents can hook a keypad to your datalogger controls and upload new commands."

"Is it that easy?"

"It is," Sing said. "Did you know that a few years ago there were almost 200 natural gas pipeline explosions in your country? Most were minor. They were trial runs. According to your infrastructure experts they could only prove that about twenty were accidental or intentional. What if I told you that 135 of them were intentional?"

"My God," Pamela mused. "You've been working against us right under our nose."

"Not me or others like me," Sing replied. "Our MSS agents have been embedded in your systems for several decades. We simply needed a facility that could make everything happen, which you finally found."

"Is there another facility?" Pamela asked.

"We have a secondary site," Sing said. "It is fully operational except for computers. I will show you where on a map if you wish."

While the two were talking, Pamela and Al could hear each other through their comms. They wanted to be able to verify the information of each by asking the same or very similar questions. It turned out that both men had relatives in Taiwan who had escaped mainland China years ago and they were eager to live the capitalist lifestyle, rich or poor, compared to the brutal regime they had lived under all their lives.

A few minutes passed then, a map was brought and placed before both men to determine if they were telling the truth. From the information divulged so far, most of which Taiwan Station would be able to quickly verify, the technician's stories matched. They didn't have anything to lose and knew fully that what they said could be verified.

"Show me on the map where the other facility is," Pamela demanded.

"It is here," Sing said, placing his finger on the spot. "Three miles south of this small village. I know because I was required to inspect the bunker and the satellite array to ensure a swift transition if needed."

"Thank you," Pamela said. She walked to the door and whispered to the agent to bring in satellite views of the area at once.

While they waited each sipped tea, talking about where Sing grew up and how he had gotten involved with the PLA.

"It's simple," Sing was saying. "There are not a lot of good paying jobs in China, and I knew early, from an uncle in the army, that technology was the key to the future. So, I became a computer equipment and software expert. By the time I was fifteen, I could hack into almost any system. The PLA caught me hacking into their system in Beijing and hauled me in. They told me I would work for them or be shot. It wasn't much of a choice, so they sent me to college at Tsinghua University in Beijing. I finished on a Friday, Saturday morning a sedan with two MSS agents showed up at my door, helped me pack, and

I was sent directly to the post. I supervised the entire build and software system. We have hacked into the Pentagon, large companies, as well as defense contractors, and others. Often, we were never discovered."

Pamela realized that he was giving her a wealth of information. More than they had ever dreamed. With the cooperation of these two technicians, years of damage could be corrected, and they would be able to protect their Internet assets and communications more adequately. The door opened and an agent placed a large satellite image on the small table.

"Here it is," Sing pointed. "With this amount of detail, you can see the outlines of the satellite array, the generators, the helicopter landing pad, and structures. The pad where the helicopters land is camouflaged as you can see. There is the entrance to the computer bunker."

"It looks unoccupied," Pamela said.

"It is," Sing replied. "It's a backup for what just happened to us. Within three weeks they will have this location operational."

"They can do it that soon?" Pamela asked.

"Perhaps sooner," Sing replied. "Unlike Americans, we plan tactics and strategies years in advance. All they need is a person like me to hook up the computers and they're ready to begin again."

"We would be prepared to offer you and your friend a handsome deal if you will help us identify such facilities and how to prevent the hacking that these facilities are capable of. Also, can you identify this?" She pulled a technical device from a box on the floor.

"Ah, the countermand device," Sing said. "It is a mechanism to countermand controls in a nuclear power plant. That's the original we got from some of our people cooperating with Mexican cartels. It was apparently used by the mafia on a nuclear plant in mid Florida and works quite well."

"What do you mean original device?" Pamela asked.

"We used that one to make a dozen more for use on western nuclear plants. It's not needed for substations or grid attacks."

"I see," Pamela replied. "Think about what you want. I'll get us some more tea. Would you like anything else?"

"Would it be possible to get a cheeseburger?" Sing asked. "I've always wanted to try one."

"I think that can be arranged," Pamela said, closing the door gently behind her.

She was elated, but also concerned. It was rare to get such cooperation. Pamela made a quick call to Taiwan Station to her assistant and divulged most of the information Sing had given her. The team at the station would verify as much as they could within the hour. Al approached from the room down the small hallway.

"From what I can tell," Al said. "Both men have given the same information. We know they were unable to talk on the way here from the post. So, they are either telling the truth or they concocted this charade far ahead of time."

"I believe they are speaking the truth," Pamela said. "The satellite view of the other post is almost exactly like the one we destroyed. That alone demonstrates they are likely telling the truth. But not to worry; station personnel are verifying everything they can within the next hour. The rest of the information will be placed on priority verification."

"How is Aaron doing with the deputy minister?" Al asked.

"He is not as cooperative," Pamela said. "He may come around and give us some information."

"I believe it is imperative to know how they intend to carry out the planned attack in California from the field," Al said.

"Exactly," Pamela said. "Let's verify as much as we can and strategize about additional questions, we need to ask for the next run at them. I'll head back to the office. Keep me apprised of Aaron's progress with the deputy minister."

Aaron Smythe was the deputy head of counterintelligence at Taiwan Station. He was aggressive and sharp of wit, one who understood what made others tick.

"Sir," Aaron said. "I'm going to ask you a few questions, which I hope you'll give me truthful answers to."

"My English is likely better than your Mandarin," Jeng Po responded. "Why don't we speak in your language."

"Very well sir," Aaron said. "What is your name?"

"Jeng Po, Deputy Minister of Operations for MSS. But you already know that."

"Yes. I do. I just want us to be on at least a basic trust level."

"You mean you want a foundation for voice stress analysis to determine if I'm telling the truth. Isn't that correct?"

Aaron at once realized that Jeng was both resourceful and intelligent. Care must be taken not to offend so that he could extract as much useful information from him as he could.

"Yes sir," Aaron said. "I won't lie to you. That is correct. We are being monitored via microphone."

"You can ask me whatever you wish," Jeng replied. "If I deem the question too classified. I will not answer it. So, first, let me ask you a question. What do you intend to do with me?"

"That is out of my control," Steve replied. "However, I will tell you the offer made to the computer techs. If you cooperate fully you can remain in Taiwan or maybe elsewhere as an asset, we can send you to Gitmo, or dump your body in the ocean. The last choice would be to return you home in exchange for one of ours or for promises of compliance in a variety of strategic issues."

"I know your tactics well," Jeng said. "If you return me to my country, you know what will happen to me. Let us begin and we will decide my fate."

"As you wish," Aaron replied. "What are your primary duties?"

"I'm a manager," Jeng said. "I manage the entire MSS group and monitor field operations."

"How many agents are in the MSS?"

"I will not tell you that. But we are comparable to your CIA."

"He is telling the truth," A voice spoke into Aaron's comm.

"What were you doing at the post?"

"Visiting my old friend General Bocheng whom your female agent butchered with a sword."

"I regret that," Aaron said. "It was apparently a long, on-going feud between them."

"He was my friend."

"We all lose friends in this business," Aaron said softly.

"Yes. A tragedy of the spy trade. Getting personal is wasted energy."

"Were you aware of the activities the post carried out?"

"Certainly. They were hackers whose main purpose was to gather ELINT and hack into American systems."

"Oh, they did much more than gather electronic intelligence. Did you know that they hacked into the southern U.S. power grid and the lives of ninety million people are in jeopardy?"

"I was aware. I have MSS agents in the field in the U.S. just like your CIA has operatives in Hong Kong. Their goal as you know was to determine how to cripple your power grid."

"He speaks the truth," A voice said again.

"So, you were aware of this planned attack?"

"Of course. It required field and computer personnel. However, unlike you Americans, very few know a target and a planned attack on it."

"Explain please," Aaron responded.

"The operation you speak of is an example," Jeng replied. "The general would have known, the head computer tech, myself, and the field agents since they are under my control. But the general was in complete control. Other than that small group, the commander of the general and perhaps two others would know."

"You refer to Lioh Hintao, Chairman of the Central Military Commission?"

221

"Yes," Jeng replied. "You've done your homework. Him and maybe one or two of the other commissioners. We cannot afford to involve more than is necessary to those who need not know otherwise, secrets won't remain secret."

"A wise policy," Aaron replied. "We could learn a lesson from you."

"For decades we have learned that lesson," Jeng responded pensively. "You see, in our country, the price of failure is great. In your country, politicians let secrets out of the bag on national television."

"But isn't that because they work for you?"

"Ah, the light shines in the dark. Yes. More of them than you realize, which I am unable to divulge because I do not know who they are."

"He is speaking the truth," The voice whispered into the comm.

Aaron looked at the man in front of him. He was astute and as honest as he could be given the circumstances. The way he spoke led Aaron to believe that he was as cooperative as he would be, without betraying his country. It was almost a certainty that specific facts and figures would not be forthcoming. If he could just get some basic information, it would perhaps be enough.

"Do you know where your MSS field operatives are in the U.S.? Aaron asked.

The minister looked at him for a moment before he spoke.

"I can tell you they are somewhere in San Francisco and Los Angeles. That is all I know. Without being at my desk, I do not have the information to contact them."

"He speaks the truth," the voice said in his comm.

"Would you like some more tea sir?" Aaron asked.

"Yes. That would be nice. The tea before was exceptional."

Aaron walked to the door and made the request in whispered tones.

"What is your name young man?" Jeng asked. "I know that

you usually give fake ones."

Aaron looked at him calmy and weighed his options. Sitting before him was the head of MSS operations. Likely he already knew his name and all those at the station. Telling him the truth may help build trust.

"My name is Aaron, sir. I am not allowed to divulge my last name."

"I understand Mr. Aaron Smythe, Deputy Head of Counterintelligence for Taiwan Station."

"Now who has done their homework?" Aaron asked, without exhibiting concern. This man knew much more than he was saying and had likely said all that he would say.

"Touché," Jeng replied.

"Tell me," Aaron said. "Since the post has been destroyed, how will your field operatives complete their mission?"

"Let me answer with a story," Jeng replied. "It begins during WWII with the Flying Tigers, which history lists as the First American Volunteer Group. It consisted of American pilots who fought in the Chinese Air Force to help us against the Japanese. Their shark's-mouth design is the only thing most people remember about them because it terrified the enemy. Their famous unit insignia of the winged Bengal tiger was designed by the Walt Disney company. My grandfather told me their commanding officer, Claire L. Chennault was a retired captain from the Army Air Corps who had been working in China as an advisor to the Chinese Air Force when the second Sino-Japanese War broke out in 1937. It's a long time ago, neh? Anyway, Chinese General Chiang Kai-Shek quickly hired the man to head up the training of our fighter pilots. With his help, we were able to resist Japanese attacks for two years with planes donated from the Soviet Union. It took two years before the Japanese were able to destroy our air force advised by Chennault. The man was a person of great character and honor. He knew the ramifications of China being defeated by the Japanese. So, he flew to Washington to buy us more aircraft and recruit more pilots. Your President Roosevelt was more of a strategist than we realized and agreed to allow American pilots to resign from the military to serve in the Chinese Air Force. It worked because at this point the U.S. had not entered the war and, by doing this one act, it let the U.S. appear to maintain a position of neutrality. We lured them to China with the reward of better pay. Almost one hundred pilots came, along with two hundred support troops. My grandfather worked alongside these brave men. When they arrived in Burma, it was the middle of the monsoon season.

Doggedly, they assembled their own aircraft before they could begin training. During the next few months, Chennault trained his men in realistic dogfights and combat training. They lost a few planes and men, but that was the price of the war, and the pilots were as prepared as they could be. Chennault was shrewd; according to my grandfather who was also trained as one of the pilots, he trained them to avoid one-on-one dogfights and to plan their attack in pairs. After all, during the two years before the Japanese destroyed most of our air force and how they did it, he had gained a wealth of experience. He divided the group into three squadrons who received a lot of help from our people to house them, construct and store planes, rescue downed pilots, and serve as lookouts for Japanese attacks. The hills were full of eyes as my grandfather portrayed it. When the U.S. finally entered the war due to the Pearl Harbor attack, the Japanese attempted to seize control of the only land route providing goods to China. So, Japan invaded Burma, attacking the city of Rangoon. With help from the Hell's Angel squadron of the Flying Tigers who fought with the British Royal Air Force, the fighting went on for months. The Hell's Angel squadron was finally relieved by the Panda Bears squadron. The former, along with the Adam and Eve squadron retreated into China and continued to launch attacks against the Japanese. I have often wondered if the Hell's Angel motorcycle group in your country took their name from these brave men. Thanks to the Flying Tigers, the Japanese were stopped. They were ferocious and admired by our people. For each plane lost, the Flying Tigers downed about twenty-five Japanese planes. Quite an accomplishment. Your country finally defeated the Japanese and liberated the region. That was more than eighty years ago."

"What's your point?" Aaron asked.

"Your country helped us in a time of great need," Jeng said. "We saw your honor, delved into your strategies, and were taught by some of your very best. We have copied your technology and improved on it in every area. Our intelligence apparatus is modeled after yours. Every weakness we saw we converted into a strength. So, I will answer your question with a question. What would a group of your special operatives or agents do if they were confronted with the same problem as the agents from the MSS that are in your country?"

Aaron realized two things when Jeng had finished. First, that his agents were trained much the same as the CIA. Second, that he would not give a specific answer that he felt would betray his country. And he realized that he had learned the same honor from his parents and grandfather that had been so greatly displayed by the Flying Tigers. It was ironic that the people of both countries could honor and respect each other but the governments always destroyed any built trust, causing one crisis after another. He also realized that unless he and his group could gain the trust and cooperation of Jeng as a potential asset to learn more about the MSS, that nothing more would be forthcoming, at least nothing of value. As much as he tried not to, Aaron couldn't help having great respect for this man.

"Thank you for the lesson," Aaron replied softly. "Excuse me for a moment."

He walked out the door and down the short hallway.

"Pamela," Aaron said. "I'm sending you the transcripts of the interrogation. I do not believe we'll get more out of the minister that will help us. It boils down to the fact that we need to ask Jack and JB what they would do if they were in the shoes of the MSS operatives they are hunting. Those agents need a communications facility. That's my best guess."

"Alright," Pamela replied. "Let us know if you need anything and we'll get right on it. By the way, the information from the two technicians has all been verified."

"At least we have a good handle on some of the intelligence we needed," Aaron said.

"Yes, a good start," Pamela replied.

"We need to find these agents," Aaron said.

"We will."

Phillip Ross and Jonas Rothman had just gotten out of a meeting with the president. Damage assessments, outages, logistical reports, and the status of grid operations, along with many other survival issues had been discussed. Everyone knew they were in a pickle and every agency and able-bodied person was doing all they could to reduce vulnerabilities to the people and systems within the affected area. The crowdsourcing and public announcements had calmed everyone it appeared and there was overwhelming support from people throughout the country to give assistance to those in the southeast. The strategy of the staging areas was working well. The National Guard had been deployed into major cities and around critical infrastructure for safety and, overall, their proposed solutions were functioning about as good as they could expect. If the next attack could be stopped, the two directors felt confident that the country could be back to normal in most areas within a couple of months and the rest within the year.

"That was quite the butt chewing," Phil said, as they walked toward their mobile command post near the Capitol Building.

"Agreed," Jonas replied. "But look at the stress he is under. Major crises like these tend to bring down presidents and eliminate the possibility of a second term."

"True," Phil said. "I wonder, must all things reduce to politics?"

"Perhaps not," Jonas grinned. "But in DC, that's the given."

"How well are the staging areas working?" Phil asked. "I mean I know what you told him."

"They're working great so far," Jonas replied. "The crowdsourcing has worked great for people who want to help and who are bringing food and other supplies directly to the affected area. It is helping to free up federal manpower for other logistical operations."

"Do you have a handle on the number of deaths so far?" Phil asked. "That will be the tell-tale sign of how the people will feel about the current administration."

"Originally, we estimated a twenty percent death rate," Jonas replied. "The staging areas are working so well that we may end up with a five percent death rate, mostly among the elderly."

"Hmmmm," Phil mused.

"What are you thinking?" Jonas asked

"Five percent is not bad," Phil said. "The figures should be less than half that, about two million people. If we can convey to the media this was a terrorist act and that they got caught and that we prevented another attack of similar nature in California, the president would be hailed as a hero."

"We could state the facts of the millions of lives potentially saved by thwarting the second attack," Jonas responded. Also, we could add that by preventing the attack, we saved the economy of the country. I will begin working on a media campaign talking about the first power outage."

"Good," Phil responded. "We need to say it looks like a sabotage of a number of power plants by a terrorist group."

"That will give us some breathing room for now," Jonas replied.

"Yes," Phil said. "And while you're doing that, I will be

developing a strategy to say that we caught them and prevented another attack in the west, along with the potential number of the affected and the dire consequences that would have happened. The only fly in the ointment is whether JB and his team can catch the MSS agents before they succeed."

"Who's the FBI contact with them?" Phil asked.

"Jack Donovan," Jonas replied. "He's head of FBI counterintelligence. Not only that, but he and JB served together in the Middle East."

"Ah, I remember now," Phil said. "That's good news. Maybe for once in our tenure the agencies will put the good of the country first and not step on each other's toes."

"They better," Jonas said. "If they don't, they won't have a job for long."

Li Na and the team had split up and arrived at their assigned areas in Chinatown. It was early in the morning. Many of the shops had opened and there were already crowds of people walking along the sidewalks to work. Unlike the outside world, work in Chinatown never stopped. To make a living required getting up long before dawn and going to bed late at night. Young or old, work beckoned one out of their warm beds into the damp chill of the bay area. Looking down the street, JB couldn't help noticing that the colors of the clothing worn by Asians and others alike was subdued, mostly dark grays and black. Occasionally, there was a blue or red jacket with a multicolored scarf as if the wearer was making a statement against the dull colors worn by others. Their clothing, mostly black with gray and dark brown pants that they wore, blended in well with the crowd. He and Li Na had been assigned the area stretching along Broadway down to Kearny Street and back along Jackson Street to Powell Street. Several of his agents began visiting various establishments using the See On Yun ploy but no one was biting, which demonstrated that the MSS agents were totally secretive.

"Team Alpha," JB said. "Is overwatch in place?"

"Roger that," a voice said. "Overwatch Alpha atop building, Pacific and Powell."

"Overwatch Bravo atop Internet building; Kearny and Jackson. Eighty percent coverage."

"Overwatch Charlie atop Mandarin Tower; Washington and Stockton.

"Overwatch Delta atop building; 555 California Street, Pine and Kearny. Eight hundred feet plus elevation, ninety-five percent coverage."

"Understood," JB said. "Everyone stay on their comms. Report anything suspicious."

"We're ready to go," Li Na said. "All teams proceed."

The four small teams began to slowly move along the streets in their assigned areas. It wasn't people in the crowds along the streets they were most interested in but those who quietly waited or congregated in small numbers — from an individual to perhaps three. They would be nonchalant, maybe hanging out at the edge of a building, near a street vendor, or quietly smoking a cigarette, but overly observant. The overwatch teams were scanning every street and building for the right signs. Their ten power binoculars could detect a dime on the sidewalk from such short distances. Each overwatch team had a sniper with them, just in case; the goal was to find, observe, then, follow their targets.

"Keep your eyes peeled," JB said. "This is going to be like finding a needle in a haystack."

"True," Li Na responded. "But I know they're here. They'll move out about sundown is my guess. We just need to find them before they do."

"Yeah, that's the hard part," JB said.

The four teams moved at a slow, fixed pace, stopping occasionally as they walked. The area for each team wasn't large so they would be able to surveil it several times before darkness fell. It was about noon when found a small, local sidewalk vendor to buy lunch. There were no seats to sit down so most of the teams leaned against the closest building to the vendor, slowly eating with their chop sticks as they continued to observe their surroundings. The lucky team was Bravo who was able to relax on a bench in Portsmouth Square Park. They had been sitting for about thirty minutes, chatting as they ate, when they became aware of two men on the north side of the park. They did not quite blend in with the rest of the people walking through, nor those sitting on other benches. The two seemed agitated and were talking in hushed tones. Bravo team discreetly watched them for several minutes. Their clothes suddenly catching their attention. They were like those worn by others in Chinatown but had a definite other country appearance.

"I recognize that style of clothes," a team member said.

"Me too," the other man said. "They are like those my uncle in Beijing wears. We may have caught a break."

"Alpha this is Bravo," the man said. "Potential target, northeast corner of park between Clay and Washington, bordered east by Kearny. Two men on bench, olive drab jackets, light green pants; both wearing baseball caps, black."

"Roger Bravo," JB said. "Overwatch Bravo, do you have them?"

"Roger, Alpha. We see them, will observe, and advise."

The two men continued to talk to each other as they looked about, like they were expecting someone to pounce on them at any moment. It became clear that these two must be some of the MSS agents the team was seeking. Judging by the boxes next to them, they had come to eat lunch. Bravo team casually ate while they continued their vigil. The Chow Mein noodles they were eating helped them look like a typical Asian in the community. A few minutes later the two MSS agents stood and walked toward the south end of the park within a hundred feet of the team. Bravo team, unobserved, followed a couple hundred feet behind. The targets strolled along Kearny Street and then ambled east on Sacramento Street, away from Chinatown.

"Alpha, Bravo. Targets headed east on Sacramento."

"That seems odd," JB said. "I wouldn't expect that."

"Patience," Li Na interrupted. "They will likely double back. This is what they are trained to do to identify tails. Bravo, be careful. Fall further back."

"Can you see them Overwatch Bravo?" JB asked.

"They just turned north on Montgomery; we lost visual line of sight."

"Roger that," Li Na said. "Bravo team, move up. Maintain at least a three-hundred-foot distance."

"Understood."

A few moments later the targets turned south along the east side of Battery Street.

"This is Overwatch Delta. We can see them moving south on Battery. We are catching them at intersections only."

"Roger," JB said. "Charlie team, reposition to the corner of Battery and California. Delta team, move to Bush and Battery. One man on each side of the street. Overwatch Delta and Bravo, advise of route."

"You're taking a risk pulling the other two teams off their assigned areas," Li Na said.

"I know," JB replied. "But I think these are our guys. They've already changed direction several times and our team say they seem to be paranoid. We should know soon. If this isn't them, the men can return to assigned areas."

"Alpha, Bravo; the two men turned west along Pine Street. They seemed to have picked up their pace. Wait, one of them is turning north on Sansome. The other is continuing down Pine."

"We have the one on Pine," Overwatch Delta said. "Lost sight of the other."

"Bravo Team," JB said. "Follow the man on Sansome. Charlie Team, follow the other on Pine. Delta Team, parallel the target on Pine along Bush."

"Use care," Li Na said. "They are making sure they are not followed. Drop back far enough to make sure they don't see you."

"Roger that."

"Alpha, Bravo. The target turned west onto California. Will advise."

"The man on Pine is jogging," Overwatch Delta said. "West on Pine."

"Charlie Team," JB said. "Do not follow. Overwatch Delta will help direct you. Delta Team, jog quickly along Bush heading west. Stay parallel to target. We cannot afford to lose these men."

"Alpha, Bravo. Our man just broke into a jog. Advise."

"Do not follow suit," JB replied. "Overwatch Delta, call it out."

"We have one target on east side of California, heading west, jogging. The second target is headed west on Pine, jogging as well. He crossed the street. He may be headed south on Stockton."

"This is Overwatch Charlie. Roger, target headed south on Stockton."

"The second target slowed to a walk," Overwatch Delta said. "He's standing at corner of Pine and Stockton, looking north on Pine. Wait, the second target just appeared. He crossed Pine and they are together again."

"What are they doing?" JB asked. "Standing and looking back in from directions they came."

"Bravo and Charlie Teams; proceed carefully," JB said. "Overwatch Delta, maintain visual and advise. Delta Team, move to corner of Bush and Powell."

"The two agents began moving again," Overwatch Delta said. "They are walking along Pine casually. Wait. They stopped at a building, looks like a small business and apartment building on the corner of Pine and Powell. They just entered. Lost visual."

"Understood," JB said. "All teams converge on Powell and Pine. Spread out."

"It looks like we may have found them," Li Na said.

"I believe so," JB replied. "But we need to catch them sabotaging our power grid, or at the computer array they are going to use. The problem is we do not have information on either."

"Alpha Team, Control" Jack said. "Standby for building information and layout."

"Roger," JB said. "It's time to get that drone up in the air."

"They've been giving me a hard time about that," Jack replied. "I'll stay on it."

Steve was in the tactical operations suite talking to Phil about the needed drones.

"I'm Steve Watson. Head of counterintelligence, Taiwan Station."

"How are things going?" Phil asked.

"The air force and DoD are giving us problems with the drones sir," Steve replied. "They told me they need your authorization to commit."

"Hold on one moment," Phil replied.

A couple of minutes later he came back online.

"They have the authorization," Phil said. "You and Jack Donovan now have control. Let me know if you have any more problems with them. Let me speak with Jack."

"Hello sir," Jack said.

"What's the status so far?" Phil asked.

"We think we found them," Jack replied.

"Anything I can help you with?"

"Yes," Jack replied tersely. "Your group is being difficult about launching the drone. They're telling me I don't have authority even though we supposedly had an agreement."

"I've just dealt with that," Phil said. "Both of you have control now. Keep me apprised, out."

Looking through his small journal, Steve found the number of the CIA group controlling the drone at Beale Air Force Base. "This is Steve Watson, ID #CI2525793AD1. Launch the drone immediately. Head to coordinates. . . Jack, what are the coordinates?"

Jack pointed to the building that had been pulled up on satellite.

"The coordinates are 37°47'27.44" N; 122°24'31.26" W. How long until it can get there?"

"We just launched it sir," the agent replied. "It should be on station within twenty minutes."

"Good," Steve said. "I'll hand you over to a tech. They'll explain how to pipe us the live feed."

"Roger sir."

"You there, tell my man how to pipe the live feed here," Steve said, handing the tech the phone. "I want it done immediately."

"Yes sir," the tech responded.

Li Na, JB, and the rest of the team had closed in on the apartment building the targets entered. Two of them were outside, watching. Slight bulges in their clothing indicated they were armed. Their mannerisms depicted the two men were well trained. Suddenly, a third man, younger than the others, emerged from the building. They spoke for a few moments appearing to argue about something. Finally, the younger man walked across the street to a small convenience store. He had been inside for a few minutes when they noticed a police officer walk in. Li Na and JB got a sinking feeling in the pit of their stomachs. A patron entered the store, and they could hear yelling coming through the door.

"Is that drone on station?" JB asked. "We're going to need it quickly."

"JB, this is Jack. It is directly overhead."

Gun shots erupted inside the store; the police officer stumbled out the door where he collapsed on the sidewalk. His partner, in a squad car fifty yards away, began running toward the store when the MSS agent stepped out and shot him, wounding him in the lower abdomen."

"What the hell is going on?" Jack screamed in the comm.

"One of the agents just shot two cops," JB said as people ran out the store; everyone on the sidewalk ducking behind cars and any cover they could find, afraid to raise their heads. Eight MSS agents ran out of the apartment building across the street and scattered.

"The agents are leaving," JB said. "There is one heading south on Powell, wearing a light gray jacket and baseball cap. Target him with the drone. All teams and overwatch, follow whichever individual you can. They'll be headed to a safe house or rendezvous point somewhere."

"We are on him with the drone," Jack said. "What happened?"

"The police officer asked him for his ID," Li Na said. "He seemed young. I guess he panicked."

The two were standing on the edge of the sidewalk, looking in four different directions. The MSS agents had disappeared. Sirens were growing louder as they neared the scene. Li Na and JB calmly walked away and were halfway up the block when a half dozen squad cars pulled up and blocked off the streets, several ambulances hot on their tail.

"Do you think they'll live?" Li Na asked.

"The officer in the door had a wound to his lower back around the kidney area and the other to his lower abdomen," JB replied. "I think they'll pull through. Jack will keep us up to date. Right now, we need to find these men. We know they were going to finish up in the field and then, likely head to the computer banks."

"Unfortunately," Li Na said. "We do not know where for either scenario."

"We better find out fast," JB said. "Let's head back and see what Ling and the rest of the teams have dug up."

The tactical operations center was buzzing with activity when the team walked in.

"What's all the excitement?" JB asked.

"The drone followed the target," Jack replied. "All of the agents converged at the same point. Here, at 5th and Harrison. He got into a van. The remaining agents were there in a few minutes."

"They just merged onto I-80 East sir," the tech said.

"What are you thinking?" Jack asked.

"Do you remember the mission we did in Afghanistan?" JB asked.

"Sure," Jack replied. "The goal was to sabotage the fuel depot in the north and then head south about a hundred miles and sabotage another, explode them at the same time."

"And we were successful," JB said. "I think these guys may be using the same principle. Did your energy expert arrive?"

"He's waiting in the other room," Jack said. "Keep us up to speed on these guys Susan."

"Roger sir."

The team walked into a small room, along with Steve and Jack.

"This is Dr. Altman," Jack said. "Dr. Altman, this is our team. Please fill them in on what we discussed."

"Alright," Dr. Altman said. "Agent Donovan has informed me that you may be on the trail of someone attempting to seriously damage our power grid."

"That's correct," JB said. "Can they do so?"

"More easily than you think," Dr. Altman said. "By the way, call me Dean. Most people believe that you need to damage a major power station like a nuclear power plant or large 40 megawatt generating plant. But there is an easier way."

"How?" Li Na asked.

"By giving electricity nowhere to go," Dean replied. "The major power plants generate the electricity; it is the transmission lines and power substations that regulate it."

"Would you explain that to us Dean?" JB asked. "We are pressed for time."

"Certainly," Dean replied. "A substation is essentially part of an electrical distribution system. They transform voltage from high to low or vice versa so it can be used by recreational, commercial, and residential clients. Each has unique requirements. Between the main power generation station and the client, electric power can flow between one or several substations at different voltage levels. The typical substation includes transformers, some of them very large. For example, one just outside of Los Angeles has five 220 kV transformers. That's 220,000 volts; each with a capacity of 150-million-volt amps or MVA. Destroying or disabling even one of its transformers would disable the entire substation. That's what happened in the NYC blackout in 2003. The substations couldn't handle the load rerouted through them and the transformers blew."

"Are you telling us we could target a couple of these substations and take out the power?" Jack asked.

"That's correct," Dean responded. "If you had the knowledge of which ones were most important and crippled them, you could take out the entire western grid. Even more so if you coupled it with a computer hacking event. And I should remind you that the primary weakness of a substation in my opinion is that generally, they are unattended and rely on SCADA for control."

"What is SCADA," JB asked.

"Supervisory Control and Data Acquisition," Dean replied. "It is how we control and manage the substations remotely."

"My God," Jack said. "They're going to take out substations along the entire state."

"If they do that, it will create a back surge that will take out power from southern California, north to Idaho, parts of Oregon and east to Nevada and Utah," Dean said. "The entire western grid would be offline. Depending on transformer damage, we could be dark for several years in many areas."

"Sir," Susan interrupted. "They are taking a plane out of Hayward. It's heading south."

"Get the tail number with the Global Hawk and find out where?"

"I could suggest an answer," Dean said. "Based on maximum damage they're headed to Los Angeles. I forgot to tell you there are different types of substations, which include, distribution, transmission, converter, switching, collector, and mobile. The best targets for them would be transmission, distribution, and converter substations."

"If you were them, where would you attack?" Steve asked.

"A good question," Dean replied. "The most damage could result by attacking substations away from the generating source. The three largest in the Los Angeles area are the Diablo Canyon nuclear plant, the Topaz solar farm that provides 550 megawatts of AC power, and the Solar Star that provides 579 megawatts of AC power. All three are north of Los Angeles. But there are multiple others as well that are a little further south and east. Disabling some of those would achieve the same results. It would be difficult to pinpoint a specific one as their attack point."

"Before, you mentioned SCADA controls," Jack said. "Aren't those what are called legacy systems where you can enter codes by plugging in a keypad."

"Yes," Dean said. "If you enter the code and disable the Bluetooth, the controls react to the last input commands."

"In other words, they could have already input new commands," Jack stated.

"Yes,' Dean responded. "And there would be no way to know without manually checking each against the last inputs. They could also simply leave the Bluetooth on and hack via computer to lock out all other incoming instructions. Assuming they want to create maximum damage, I would use the hack to manipulate the control switching. They can blow all the transformers."

"But we could just replace them, right?" Jack queried.

"No," Dean said. "Like everything else in the U.S., their manufacturing has shifted overseas. Some of them are so expensive that there are only a couple of spares in the country. Those we could get quickly would be in the range of three months; that is just to procure them. Like everything else, since the move of manufacturing to China, everything has changed to ship on demand. I'm afraid it would be quite devastating."

"This just keeps getting better," Steve murmured.

"Sir," Susan interrupted again. "The flight plan shows the plane is headed to LAX."

"Thanks Susan," Jack replied.

"Team," JB shouted. "Back to Beale, quickly. We're going to LA."

"I'll get a transport helicopter here ASAP," Jack said. "Pack your gear and wait in the parking lot."

Twenty minutes later a Coast Guard CH-53 Sea Stallion landed. They loaded their gear aboard and were on the ground at Beale Air Force Base within forty minutes. All FBI and JB's teams rushed from the helicopter to the transport plane, it's engines already purring. Five minutes after boarding, they were airborne, heading south to LAX.

Lieutenant General Shing Teng had spent quite some time at the post sifting through the remains of buildings and bodies. The Deputy Minister of Operations for MSS's helicopter had been identified, but there was no sign of the minister. He had just finished putting his report together when the conference room monitor sprang to life, again revealing the members of the central military commission.

"Ah, Chairman Hintao," Teng said. "I was just finishing my report and about to call you."

"We have serious concerns about what happened at the post,"

Hintao said. "How far along are you in the investigation and what can you tell us?"

"I'll brief you now and forward the complete report after we finish our discussion," Teng said. "This is what we know for sure. It was one of our cruise missiles that destroyed the post. We discovered eighty-seven bodies in and around the area. The deputy ministers' helicopter was on the post, but we have not found his body. My guess is that he was taken prisoner."

"Why do you say that?" a committee member asked.

"Because we found five bodies with bullets in the back of their head and another hacked to pieces," Teng responded.

"What is so odd about that?" the member asked.

"They were away from the compound and hidden in shrubs. The bodies were close to a trail that surrounded the post perimeter. Judging by their uniforms they were soldiers assigned to patrol," Teng said. "One of our men is a hunter; he traced drag marks and at least ten sets of footprints from the post to the shore."

"Could you tell what type of weapon was used to kill them?" Hintao asked.

"My experts say it was a .22," Teng replied. "Although some bullet wounds at the post match to our firearms, including AK-47 cartridge cases we found, other evidence points us in a different direction, especially the .22 head shots."

"Explain please," Hintao said.

"Well sir, the missile was ours," Teng said. "Some of the bullets in the bodies we found appear to be ours, but the explosives used to destroy the bunker were not. We found traces of white phosphorous and C-4 plastic explosives."

"Americans?" a committee member asked.

"I believe so," Teng replied. "And, we found these, extending his hand so the committee could clearly see two micro-killer drones."

"Those seem too small to do any damage," a committee member said. "What are they?"

"They are micro-killer drones with a 0.33-gram shaped charge," Teng replied. "They land on the head of a combatant and the shaped charge goes off, penetrating the skull and killing the target. We could not determine if all the men had been killed this way, but at least forty were found with wounds consistent with the capability of these drones. None of the bodies without uniforms had such wounds, which means they were programmed to attack only soldiers."

"This was definitely the Americans," Hintao said. "Don't you agree?"

"Agreed sir," Teng said. "However, there is no way we can conclusively prove it."

"Hmmmm," Hintao mused. "What else do you have for us?"

"According to records for the post, two computer technicians are missing sir," Teng replied. "From the ID's we found on the bodies in the bunker, they are the head computer technician in charge of hacking into systems and his direct subordinate. And, since the minister's helicopter was on post and destroyed, I would suggest that they have him as well."

"This is dreadful news," Hintao said. "He could greatly damage our security if he talks."

"He will not sir," Teng said. "I know him; he will not betray the country."

"We cannot afford to take that risk," Hintao said. "Excuse us for a moment."

The members remained visible to Teng on the monitor. Turning off the sound, they were in earnest conversation as they leaned toward each other. Teng knew they were very concerned about a potential breach of national security and understood the dilemma they were in although he found amusement in the fact that for once, it was the committee rather than the generals they commanded that were in a squeeze. There was a loud thump as the speakers were turned on.

"Lieutenant General Teng," Hintao began. "The committee

members and I have already spoken with the President and Standing Committee of the National People's Congress. Because of what has happened, you are appointed acting Deputy Minister of Operations for MSS. This will likely become a permanent appointment. You will assume Jeng Po's duties immediately."

"What about my command?" Teng asked.

"You will assign it to General Liu," Hintao replied. "He will take over for you and you will use first through sixth bureaus to find out what happened to minister Jeng Po and the technicians."

"What if they have been captured?" Teng asked.

"You will eliminate all of them," Hintao said. "In addition to controlling MSS, you will work directly with the Director, Military Intelligence Department. Find out who took the minister, what they plan to do with him, and eliminate all who have come in contact with him."

"When do you want me to begin?" Teng asked.

"Yesterday!" Hintao exclaimed. "You will have the necessary paperwork within the hour. Run operations from your current office until you have completed your task. The President, Council, and I am counting on you."

The general sat down the moment the monitor went dark. He was more exhilarated than he had ever been. It was as though he had won an Olympic Gold Medal. His pay would greatly increase, and he would have more clout and control than he had ever imagined. More often than he could fathom, he would be giving the President a brief of intelligence operations and breakdown of what they meant, much like the President of the United States and the DNI's daily brief. Often, he had dreamed of being in such a position, but in China, dreams rarely came true. He called his aide.

"Colonel," Teng shouting, almost in glee. "Get me General Liu. Have him report immediately. Then, get me the committee secretary."

"Which one sir?" the Colonel asked.
"Political and Legislative Affairs."
"Yes sir."

Phil and Jonas were still working from their command van. So far things were working out, despite their race against the clock. The call they had been waiting for finally came through.
"What's your status?" Jonas asked.
"Sir, we have hit a small snag," JB said.
"How small?" Phil asked.
"The targets have headed to Los Angeles," JB said. "We are about one hour behind them."
"You cannot afford to lose them," Phil said.
"We won't sir," JB replied. "The Global Hawk is keeping them in sight and agent Donovan is moving FBI teams into place for surveillance."
"Are they still in route to Los Angeles?" Jonas asked.
"Yes sir," JB replied.
"Why don't we just blast them out of the sky?" Phil asked.
"We do not have the authority sir," JB said. "Besides, it's not that simple."
"What do you mean?" Jonas asked.
"According to our grid expert, they appear to be running a dual attack," JB said. "They have been sabotaging substations, by-passing SCADA controls and then, will likely perform a joint systems hack."
"I suppose that's a worst-case scenario," Phil queried.
"Exactly," JB replied. "They can both take a substation offline, as well as cripple the ability to control it via the Internet. If we do not catch them, this will be worse than the southeast."
"What are you talking to us for then?" Jonas asked. "Catch them at all costs. Deadly force is authorized."
"Yes sir," JB responded.
"The CIA is not allowed to use force inside U.S. territory," Phil

said. "I'm not sure what I can do to help you."

"No worries my friend," Jonas replied. "I can temporarily deputize some of your agents in my Federal Protective Force and as for JB, he is listed as an officer in the FPF. Can you get another Global Hawk out there?"

"Certainly," Phil said. "I have several at Miramar. Where do you want it?"

"Coordinate with the team," Jonas said. "We need overlap. With only one bird, we cannot afford to lose contact."

"Quite right," Phil said. "I'll get on it."

The plane touched down on the tarmac onto runway 7L and taxied as quickly as it could to the east end of the runway, crossing the service road and pulling up on the corner of an apron where multiple FBI vans were waiting for them.

"Sir," Susan said. "The target plane landed at Daugherty Field."

"Isn't that Long Beach Airport?" Jack asked.

"Roger sir," Susan replied. "They landed about forty minutes ago and climbed into two silver vans. They are on the 405 headed north."

"Where are they now?" Jack asked.

"They just crossed the 110-freeway sir," Susan replied.

"That means they'll pass by us if they continue the same route," JB said. "Are you thinking what I'm thinking?"

"Yes," Jack said. "The expert may be correct; they'll head for the Diablo Substation."

"Or the solar farm northwest of Maricopa," JB said. "You don't think they're going to hit both places, do you?"

"I would if I were them," Jack replied. "Isn't that what we did in Afghanistan?"

"Hmmmm," JB mused. "Susan, let us know if they head north on I-5 or turn onto the 101."

"Roger that."

"You know, they could strike several locations before dawn

and then get to wherever their computer array is for the final blow to the system," Jack said.

"That's what worries me," JB said. "What if they have more men than we have seen? They could contact them easily enough to accomplish whatever they're planning."

"I've thought about that too," Jack responded. "They don't need to sabotage all of their targets; they could simply blow the controls."

"Yes," JB replied. "That would be the best option for the solar farms. According to our grid expert, that would simply halt production of power from them."

"It will still leave us more vulnerable," Jack said. "We better get moving. I'm thinking they'll complete their mission tonight and cripple us just after dawn."

Given what was happening, this wasn't expected to be a cordial phone call. Apprehensive, he dialed the number.

"Mr. President," Phil said. "The western operation is getting critical."

"I assume you need authorization of some kind," the President said. "I'm guessing it's a mess."

"Well sir," Phil said. "The MSS agents have been embedded for some time from what we can tell. Their most devastating attack would be to combine field sabotage of SCADA with computer hacking. Our field ops feel certain they can interrupt the field operations to an extent that potential damage could be lessened."

"Jonas," the President said. "What do you think?"

"I agree Mr. President," Jonas replied. "We do not know how many agents may be involved. And, if they get to a computer array of any kind, the west will end up like the southeast."

"Understood," the President said. "I'm guessing you may need a missile strike?"

"Yes sir," Phil said. "It would be on a civilian complex. It may be the only way to make certain they cannot gain control."

"What about collateral damage?" the President asked.

"It's something we will need to live with sir," Phil said.

"It's better that a few perish rather than millions," Jonas joined in.

"I do not see a way out of the predicament," the President responded. "Let me think about how to make that happen with the least political and legal ramifications. We're probably going to need to make it a black operation. I'll get back to you in an hour."

"Thank you, sir," Phil said.

"There's only one small problem with that scenario," Jonas said.

"What's that?" Phil asked.

"We need to find the array before we can order a strike," Jonas replied. "Let's contact JB and Jack."

"Jack. Jonas Rothman here along with Phil Ross. We need a question answered. Do you know where these agents may be able to gain access to a computer and data array?"

"Let me pass you to Ling," Jack said. "He's the expert on this."

"This is Ling. How can I help you sirs?"

"We need to know where the agents can potentially access a data array in the LA area."

"I've been looking into that," Ling replied. "We believe they have inside people; at least one or two may be in the Globe-Com offices near San Francisco. Globe-Com recently purchased and renovated the old Spruce Goose hangar in the Playa Vista neighborhood at the corner of Bluff Creek Drive and S. Campus Center Drive. It's barely two miles north of LAX."

"Would that facility serve the needs for hacking into the grid?" Phil asked.

"Certainly," Ling replied. "It is a main data storage center for Internet based cloud operations, massive banks of servers, and computers in almost every room."

"How fast could they hack and upload into the grid?" Jonas

asked, dreading the answer.

"They have cable broadband, fiber optics cable connections, ISDN, T1 and T3 lines and who knows what else."

"And?" Phil queried, exasperated.

"I'll spare you the techno babble," Ling said. "Suffice it to say their connections are faster than yours; much faster. Once inside, twenty minutes is all they would likely need."

"Thank you," Jonas replied.

"Pull up a satellite view of Playa Vista, California for this address," Phil said, passing a piece of paper to the technician.

"I have it sir," the technician said. "It's 1.8 miles north of LAX. The area is populated south, but east, west, and north is an industrial park. I overheard your conversation sir and was formerly in ordinance in Afghanistan. May I?"

"Proceed," Phil said.

"To kill all the Internet connections, you need to take out the entire building unless the trunk lines for the Internet come into one area," the technician said.

"How?" Jonas asked.

"The best method is multiple Hellfire missiles. The version I would suggest is the Hellfire II, blast fragmentation. I'd say four would do the trick. These are specifically designed for soft urban targets such as buildings, bunkers, caves and so forth. The warhead is both blast fragmentation and incendiary."

"You're saying it will take out the building, the Internet connections, and burn it to the ground," Phil queried.

"Yes," the technician replied. "It is geared for soft and urban targets, not armor. Also, I was recently reading an article on the building renovation. The inner wall structure along the entire sides of that facility is wood. It is unlikely given the location that there would be any collateral damage sir."

"Thank you for the information," Phil said.

"What do you think?" Jonas asked.

"It was recommended by both JB and Jonas to have this on standby," Phil said. "We will do as they suggested. It will be our deadly-force option of last resort."

"Agreed," Jonas replied. "Make it happen."

"I'll call Miramar," Phil said.

Phil walked away, carrying a secure sat phone. He was just out of earshot of the rest of the men. The conversation was straightforward and intense.

"Alright," Phil said. "If we need to use it, everything is a go. I arranged for an MQ-9 Reaper to be armed with eight Hellfire missiles as discussed and we also have the Predator, although I would prefer not to use it. The Reaper will be on standby within two hours at March Air Reserve Base. We moved a lot of the drones there from George Air Force Base in Victorville about a decade ago. They are going over strike plans as we speak."

"God help us if we muck this up," Jonas said, raising his eyebrows.

"We won't," Phil replied.

"I'll notify Jack and JB," Jonas said. "They'll tell us when to get it airborne."

General Teng, the new deputy minister of operations for GMSS had met with General Liu who had taken over the investigation at the base and assumed leadership for Hong Kong Garrison. It was time to spring his idea on the committee secretary.

"Secretary Li," Teng said. "I presume you know of my position change."

"Yes," Li replied. "How can I help you?"

"As you know sir," Teng said. "I believe and General Liu and others concur, that Jeng Po was taken by the Americans, as well as two technicians."

"I am aware," Li replied. "Are you contemplating getting them back?"

"Yes sir," Teng replied. "You are aware that Jeng Po and the head technician has knowledge and information vital to our operations and national security. We cannot afford that information to fall into the hands of the Americans."

"I concur," Li said.

"I would like your permission to raid the safe house where they are kept and retrieve them."

"Do you know where it is located?"

"Not yet, but we have a pretty good idea. The last I spoke with Po, he indicated he narrowed it to one of three places. I am talking to those agents now and should have the exact location soon."

"Proceed with the operation minister," Li said. "If you are unable to retrieve the packages, eliminate them. Is that understood?"

"Yes sir. I understand."

The team was using the cargo bay of the plane as a base of operations for equipment and personnel. Time was running short as the field operatives jumped into the FBI vans and headed to the 405. They were minutes behind the MSS team. The Global Hawk overhead continued a steady stream of communications on the location of the MSS vans. The team had been following them for about two hours.

"They are getting off the 101 onto Avila Beach Drive," Susan said.

"That's only five miles up," Jack said. "Looks like they're headed to Diablo Canyon Power Plant as we suspected."

Team members looked at each other; like a SWAT team, they made last minute checks on their equipment. They had turned off freeway at the same exit as their targets.

"Jack," Susan said. "They stopped a couple of minutes from you."

"Where are they?" Jack asked.

"They pulled into the parking lot on the west side of the post office," Susan said. "They are at the south end, next to San Francisco Street that passes through the lot. The entrance to the post office is on San Miguel Street. If you traverse that street, you should be able to see them. They are the only vehicles present."

"I know where that is," the driver said. "I've brought my family up to the beach several times. It's a huge lot. If you want, I can pull in front of the post office without them seeing us."

"Do so," Jack said. "Susan, send us the current satellite view."

The vans parked in front of the post office, lights off. Team members exited and gathered in front of the building. Looking through his binoculars, Jack could easily see the vans, which were dark inside.

"They are just setting there," Jack said. "Let's have Alpha team backtrack and go around to the west side of the lot. They can pass through this grass section and approach the rear of the vehicles. Bravo team can pull up beside this building at the intersection of 1st Street and we can approach them from the front."

"That's sounds good," JB said. "Let's get in position."

The teams moved quickly to reposition themselves. There was enough traffic on the roads that they appeared to be just another vehicle. Alpha and Bravo teams, reaching their new locations, waited, and watched for over an hour. The drivers of the target vehicles had gotten out and were smoking cigarettes, laughing and joking. It was like they had nowhere to be.

"I don't like this," JB spoke into his comm.

"Something's up," Jack said. "Not only that, shouldn't these guys be Chinese?"

"Yes," JB said. "Why?"

"They look Caucasian to me," Jack replied.

"We can't see their faces," JB said. "Let's get a closer look."

Xin Cao and JB moved closer to the two drivers, using the cover of trees and grass on the southwest corner of the lot. They weren't more than fifty yards away when they trained their binoculars on them. Streetlights behind the vans lit up the windows just enough to see that they were both empty.

"Something is wrong," JB whispered. "Move in, now!"

All teams moved from their position toward the drivers without hesitation. Within ten seconds the teams had surrounded the vehicles and drivers, guns at the ready, flashlights pointed to the inside of each van. The vehicles were indeed empty. The driver's jaws were open wide in surprise, their eyes fearful.

"Where are the men that were in these vans earlier?" Jack asked.

"We let them out at the first underpass on the 405," a driver stuttered. "They got into three sedans and told us they would meet us here after they were done sightseeing."

"Damn!" JB said. "We've been played."

"When were you supposed to meet them?" Jack asked.

"They told us about 10:00 pm," the driver said, his hands shaking. "About thirty minutes from now."

"Lower your weapons men," JB said. "We were never here. Got that?"

The two men nodded affirmatively.

"Men, retreat to overwatch," JB said.

The teams waited for another hour. They realized the agents were not coming. This was a decoy; they had been suckered.

"Load up," JB said. "These guys are very slick. Back to base."

The safe house was not far from the airbase where JB and his crew had come and gone after a successful mission. They had decided to use it instead of the one in Taipei because it was closer. Only a few men were present. Mostly on guard duty. Four MSS agents crept forward, along a small fence to the back, adjacent to the airfield. There were lights here and there as they furtively moved around the edges of the structure. It was surprisingly dark for a small house in the city; it looked deserted. All four agents positioned themselves along the side, studying it. Lurking in the shadows, they examined every inch of the building with night vision and thermal optics. There was no sign of anyone.

"This doesn't feel right," Bohai said. "There is no activity. Are you sure you heard the commander correctly?"

"Yes," a team member responded. "This is the correct address; the satellite photo also shows the correct position as well."

"Let's wait for a while, "the leader said.

About 0200 the team noticed someone open the back door and look across the airfield as he smoked. He was dressed in casual civilian clothes. It appeared that he was somewhere else as he gazed at the runway lights. The leader pointed to two of his men, made a circling motion for them to go around the house and take the smoker out. It was barely more than a minute when the two men reached the opposite corner. A team member with the leader threw a small rock that landed against the fence, the sound drawing the smoker's gaze. Within seconds one of the team members was on him, cupping his left hand over the man's face while stabbing him in the back between the sixth and seventh ribs, directly to the heart. He collapsed dead in his arms; he and his partner drug the body around the corner. No one would find it until daylight.

The door had been left open a few inches. The team slowly moved through it and along the wall that led toward a dim light at the end. Their adrenaline had started pumping as they became more excited, moving in for the kill. Creeping down the hallway, they realized they were moving along interrogation rooms on the right. Passing a small kitchen on the left, they crept through the opening where a door had once hung.

"Those rooms are interrogation rooms," the leader said. Near the end of the hall there are several with lights on. Our targets are probably in those. Let's get the job done and get out quickly. I'll take the far room; you take up watch at the end of the hall; the rest of you take the other two rooms."

Moving slowly down the hallway again, their suppressed, Type 92 pistols at the ready, they reached their respective rooms and peered through the bottom of the glass window. Inside each were their targets, the minister and the two computer technicians. The man directly in front of the leader crept to the end of the hall and took up position to thwart a possible attack. The leader, in a kneeling position, held up his hand raising one finger, then a second, and a third at which time the operatives flung open the doors and shot each of their targets center mass three times, blood flying from the wounds. Suddenly, gunfire erupted to their left. The team member guarding them was propelled against the wall, shot in the shoulder. He quickly recovered as the team retreated to the door where they had entered. Two men were firing at them from the corner. Returning fire, they were able to back out into the night and race around the corner of the safe house and back the direction they had come. The team member who had been shot was dragged a hundred yards to their vehicle. Climbing into the small sedan, they drove several blocks before turning the headlights on.

"That seemed too easy," a team member said.

"It always does when a mission goes as planned," the leader said. "But we were lucky to get out with only one of us wounded. Besides, remember the foreign operative whose moves we imitated. We owe the success of the mission to him."

"I suppose," the team member said.

"Get me Dragon," Bohai spoke into his sat phone. "Yes, Tiger here, the packages were wrapped. Out."

General Teng was pleased. A wry smile crossed his lips. He never had any intention of rescuing Jeng Po. It was always easiest to eliminate. Killing him made his new position completely secure.

"Chairman Hintao please. This is General Teng."

"How is the mission?" Hintao asked.

"It is complete sir," Teng replied. "Unfortunately, we were unable to effect a rescue. We were forced to eliminate the minister and technicians. I'm sorry sir."

"That's how it works sometimes," Hintao said. "What about your men and our secrecy."

"One was wounded sir," Teng replied. "Our secrecy remains intact. They won't know it was us."

"Excellent," Hintao said. "Your command is starting with a good track record. Prepare your teams for another potential mission."

General Teng was pleased. He was already in the good graces of the Central Military Commission and the Standing Committee of the Communist Party of China. He was quite certain that Po had never gotten this far. By the time all of this was over he would have cemented his position as permanent and would become a key player in the CPC.

CHAPTER 9

Darkness of night had a knack for bringing out the worst people, especially spies.

"Here they come," Al said through the comm. "Don't attack until I give the command. Wound one or two, don't kill them." Pamela watched the video feeds as the MSS team approached the safe house, killing the guard, a Taiwan national, and crept down the hall to the interrogation rooms.

"I have to hand it to you Al," Pamela said. "You called this one right on."

"You know this business as well as I do," Al replied. "There is no way they would let a minister fall into our hands."

"Neither would we let ours fall into theirs without an extraction or prejudice mission," Pamela said.

"Now!" Al shouted.

Two of Al's agents moved down the hall, engaging the MSS agent at the corner. Once the agents fought their way out the door, personnel at the safe house attended the men in the interrogation rooms. The gun squib charges they had placed on them worked perfectly. The bullet proof vests each wore had prevented the 9 mm bullets from penetrating the body, though they would be sore for a week or so. The decoys were of Asian descent and in the dim light, the agents would report back that they had killed the prisoners. The real prisoners were safe at Taiwan Station.

"Good work everyone," Al spoke into the comms. "Clean up and get back to work."

"Pretty shrewd setup Al," Pamela said. "We let the MSS agents get away and they'll report they completed the mission."

"It was the only way," Al said. "Wounding one of them made them think they got out lucky. They killed one of our guards, a tragedy. The Chinese will remain in the dark and we will extract more secrets. The death of one man is a small price to pay to save millions."

"I agree," Pamela said. "We need to find a safe place for our new friends. Any suggestions?"

"Yes," Al said. "Send them to Langley and let them become their headache. We'll get the credit without the hassle."

"Good idea," Pamela responded. "Let's call the directors."

B ack at the tactical operations center, Jack and JB were laying out a new strategy that would hopefully narrow the location of the MSS agents.

"Susan," Jack said. "Try to get some satellite feeds of the time and area we lost them. According to the van drivers, they let them out here, under this overpass. Here's a description of the vehicles. Let me know what you find."

"Yes sir," Susan replied.

"Dr. Altman," JB said. "I thought you said Diablo would be a good location for them to sabotage. They baited us into following them; now time is more critical than ever."

"I told you it would be because it is," Dean said. "Take a look at the board behind you. I've placed pins on the map of every potential substation that will yield the results they seek. There are 55,000 such substations spread across the U.S. power grid." When JB turned to look at the map he was appalled. There were more than thirty locations.

"Are there that many?" JB asked.

"Those are only the major ones," Dean replied. "I'm sorry to say that if they sabotage multiple secondary locations, they can achieve the same effect as they could with a couple of primary substations. Some experts will tell you that if you sabotage only a dozen substations in the country that it will knock out the entire grid. They are wrong; the grid is much more resilient than that, despite its weakness. Can I ask you men a question?"

"Certainly," Jack replied.

"How do you know they haven't already sabotaged the locations you are looking for?"

"We don't," JB said. "How could we tell?"

"You cannot," Dean said. "If they used keypads to implant new codes, you would never know. I'm not an expert in your area, but I'd probably look for where they will access the computer array they need to complete their task."

"Doc," JB said. "We cannot afford to lose time searching out each of those stations. If we chose two or three probable locations, could the grid experts at those locations determine if the operation codes on the legacy systems have been changed."

"Yes," Dean said. "Why would you want to do that?"

"If they have been changed as you suggest," JB replied. "We can narrow our search to computer arrays they can use within the surrounding area."

"Can you contact the correct people?" Jack asked. "Tell them you're working for us and to do it quickly. Select the top four or five substations and let us know."

"Alright," Dean replied, picking up his cell. "I'm on it."

"Ling," Jack yelled over the din of people. "Come help us."

"What do you need?" Ling asked.

"You told us before these agents needed a computer or Internet connection on a grand scale to complete their mission," Jack said. "You narrowed down one building for us. What about others they can use?"

"We're in Los Angeles," Ling said. "There are more than two

dozen."

"That's still too many," JB joined in. "Reason it out for us."

"I chose the first location because we know they have contacts with Globe-Com," Ling said. "It seems most logical to pursue that path."

"But?" Jack queried.

"This is an assumption on my part," Ling said. "Theoretically, they can use any location that has fast Internet connections, from an Internet service provider to a cell-phone communications company, a television station, critical infrastructure security company, or others."

"Make a list of as many as you can and quickly. Put the pins on the map the Doc made of the substations. Maybe we can correlate them somehow so there's some logical sense to this."

"Yes sir," Ling replied. He walked over to several agents to begin comprising a potential list from locations he had already scouted.

"What are you thinking?" JB asked.

"That these agents have already completed their field work," Jack replied. "At least most of it and they'll be getting close to the data array they will use."

"I'm thinking you're right," JB said. "This is like a military operation. They would have already planned far ahead."

"And we're playing catch up," Jack replied. "Not the best situation to be in."

"No, it's not," JB responded. "But we have home field advantage."

"Gentlemen," Dean yelled. "I have some results for you."

"Let us have it," Jack said.

"I made the calls, and it turns our commercial electricians were already onsite at all four locations," Dean said, excitedly."

"Tell us you have good news," Jack said.

"Not for them," Dean said. "But perhaps for you. Three of the four locations had the operations codes changed. The electricians have input the original codes and taken the system offline from further communications."

"So, we were right," JB said. "Tell me Doc, how long does it take to input such codes?"

"A few minutes if you know what you're doing," Dean replied.

"A penny for your thoughts," Jack blurted out.

"If it only takes a few minutes, they could have sabotaged many more substations than we thought."

"True," Jack replied. "Since we don't know how long they have been here we would only be guessing."

"Let's assume they sabotaged three each night," JB said. "We know they typically have eight-man teams. Two-man teams would go to each substation. If it is the same team that sabotaged the southern grid, they could have sabotaged at least a dozen substations minimum."

"I see your point," Dean interrupted. "Most of these substations in the metro area are not very far apart. I think you have underestimated the number. They only have chain link fences around them, no physical security. All they need to do is jump the fence, find the specific location in the station, and input the new code."

"That's scary," Jack replied.

"Li Na," JB called. "We need your opinion."

"How can I help?" Li Na said, panting, running over.

"We are presuming two things," Jack said. "First, these agents have completed their field work. Second, they need a computer/communications array. You know them better than us. What would you do if you were in the team leader's shoes?"

"If they have finished everything, they will find a safe place to lay low," Li Na responded. "They will not be getting communications from the base we destroyed so they will do one of two things, perhaps both. They will attempt to contact someone in China, which may take hours. Or they will wait a set period and proceed with their mission."

"What's your experience on their wait time?" Jack asked.

"Six to twelve hours," Li Na responded. "They will not wait twenty-four. You have both been in the field. What comes first?"

"The mission," Jack and JB said in unison, looking at each other.

"I would suggest that we have until about noon," Li Na said. "It's already 0400."

"Is there a possibility they will wait longer?" JB asked.

"Not likely," Li Na responded.

"Hmmmm," JB mused. "I see your point."

"Sir," Ling said, walking over. "We've found the best locations they would likely use for Internet access. Check out the yellow pins on the map."

Jack, JB, and Li Na walked to the map. The substations were marked with red pins. They began comparing distances between the red and yellow pins.

"What's this pin way down here below the last substation?" Jack asked.

"That's the office of the largest communications provider in the metro area," Ling replied.

Li Na was looking north on the map, tracing the MSS agent's movements from San Francisco to Los Angeles.

"You know," she said. "We assumed that the team traveled from San Francisco to Los Angeles to finish their mission. What if they did everything here and then, sabotaged stations in San Francisco and returned."

"That seems out of the way," Jack said. "Why wouldn't they do the field ops here before San Francisco?"

"Look at the size of the Los Angeles metro area," Li Na said. "It has over 17 million people, not to mention a wealth of locations for both substations and communications networks, as well as many suitable escape routes. Imagine trying to escape San Francisco. There is a major route north across the Golden Gate Bridge, another across the East Bay Bridge, and the several south and of course via boat. Compared to LA, successful escape out of San Francisco would be much more difficult, especially if local law enforcement, homeland security, and the FBI were onto you."

"She has a point," Jack said.

"It makes sense," JB replied. "And it's like what we did in the Middle East. But we need to answer one question first."

"What's that?" Li Na asked.

"Given what has happened, do you think they are suspicious that we are on to them?"

"They are trained to be ultra-suspicious to the point of paranoia," Li Na said. "The incident in San Francisco likely tipped them over the edge. I mean, if some cop out of the blue asked you for your identity among all the other customers around, wouldn't that make you suspicious?"

"I would wonder why he picked me from the rest," Jack said.

"Not only that incident," JB interjected. "The decoy at Diablo Canyon was well planned. The fact that their base is not in contact with them is also making them suspicious, at least I would think so."

"So," Jack began, "they are now on the loose and planning the last phase of their operation. It will be like looking for a specific grain of sand on the playground. I agree with Li Na. That's why they came back here. The likelihood of finding them will be slim."

"Perhaps not," JB said. "We are assuming everything is in place and they are just waiting for the right moment. Either word from their bosses in China or a preset time."

"What are you implying?" Jack asked.

"Let's ask Li Na," JB responded. "If you had everything ready and had been on edge for at least a couple of days or longer, what would you do?"

"I'd try to relax some," Li Na said. "When I worked with them, we would go to a Chinese restaurant, unwind a little, eat some food and have a drink. After a couple of hours, we would get right back at it."

"Put yourself in their shoes," Jack said. "If they did this right now, where would you go?"

"Chinatown!" Li Na said emphatically. "It would be easy to ask around and find restaurants not frequented by long noses."

"Long noses?" Jack queried.

"Americans," Li Na responded.

"I couldn't help overhear," Ling said. "Chinatown is east of the 101/110 freeway exchange. There are lots of restaurants that don't look like restaurants from the outside. Unless you speak Mandarin or Cantonese you won't find them welcoming."

"Understood," Jack said. "Ling, could you print photos of the men we saw in San Francisco? It may help us find them."

"I've already done that," Ling said. "They're on the table by the map."

"Good," JB said. "Now all we need is a strategy to locate them."

"I've been thinking of the best way," Li Na said. "We need to locate them then, follow them to their end location to make sure we have all the agents. That won't be easy. Perhaps the best way is to post individuals in as many overwatch positions throughout Chinatown as we can and then JB and I along with Ling and Jack can start surveilling the restaurants. Hopefully, we will get lucky."

"Sounds like a shot in the dark," Jack replied. "Unfortunately, I don't see another way. I hope you're right about this. I'll post men on the ground as well and get as many eyes in place as we can."

"Men and ladies," Jack said. "Gather round. We are going to Chinatown, Los Angeles. Our mission is to find these MSS agents. We have clear pictures of three of them on the table by the map. You can ill afford to be spotted. Take a picture of each of the men on your cell phones, that way you won't be holding a photo in your hand, which would be a dead giveaway. Pardon the pun. Anything else you can think of JB, Li Na?"

"Use extreme caution with these agents," Li Na said. "As you Americans are fond of saying they are armed and dangerous. Like I told you before, they are trained like spies because they are spies. Laws are of no concern to them. If they suspect you or anyone else, they will shoot to kill. If you see them, call through your comms for backup."

Training at the academy in Quantico and studies in homeland security had suddenly become much more valuable to these men and women about to lay their lives on the line. Everyone in the room was overcome by the fact that this would be no picnic. The next few hours passed quickly as Ling and Dr. Altman correlated all the numbers they had for the best places to cause failure in the grid and respective locations to communications facilities. Bringing a new map and easel, the two men made constant calls and began placing pins on the map.

"Is your new map derived from a target centric approach," JB asked.

"How do you know about that?" Ling asked in surprise.

"My mentor Lunadi taught it to me in Colorado," JB responded.

"Most people who know of it do not understand how it works," Ling said. "I can see my efforts are not wasted on you. As you are aware, the collaborative team concept for intelligence has the potential for addressing two important pressures that we face with this opposing network. First is the information glut. We're going to get lots of information coming in from all our men. A problem with it will also be the number of restaurants that could become suspect."

"So, you will use compartmentalization to deal with that?" JB queried.

"Absolutely,' Ling said. "Otherwise, we cannot constrain it. The second problem will be your teams demand, along with Jack, for more details. That's going to become somewhat of a problem."

"How can we help?" Jack asked.

"All team members from all groups need to have firm mutual trust and understanding between them," Ling said. "This generally requires team building and extended social interaction, which we don't have time for. Thus, we may have a big problem in our intelligence network."

"I can solve part of that quickly," JB said. "Men, let me have your attention. As you are aware we are not part of the FBI. We are helping you at the request of the President. So, when all of this goes down, we were never here. Your groups and agency will get full credit for the operation. We need to do this as a matter of trust. If we don't trust each other completely, the mission will fail, millions of people will die, and the U.S. will be forced into the dark ages overnight. So, watch our back and each other's and we may get through this successfully."

"We will succeed," an agent shouted, to which everyone applauded.

"Does that help?" JB asked.

"It's as good as we will get given the time we have," Ling said. "I appreciate it. This may be lost on some of the others, but each of these targets, even though men and women, are complex systems and more especially so when coupled with the substations and communications facilities. All of you need to look at them as dynamic and evolving. And not only that, they are also nonlinear because they cannot adequately be described by a simple structure such as a fault tree or, that of a traditional intelligence model."

"Very interesting," Li Na said. "This brings up some thought-provoking concepts. What you're saying is that we are a network and so is the opposition."

"Correct," Ling responded. "In our network we have analysts, like the Doc and I, customers, which is you, and collectors, which is you and your team, as well as local resources. The opposing network can be thought of as a collection of people, organizations, places, and things."

"It's like a complex puzzle," JB said. "We can use the main concepts of intelligence such as communications and social networks to work against them."

"Partly," Ling replied. "But our short time frame will center on the communications focus initially. Their network, like any network is comprised of nodes with links between nodes. In this case the nodes are the individual agents. You have severed contact from the hub, the base you destroyed. Now, they are trying to repair that."

"I understand what you're saying," Li Na said. "They will hit a restaurant and it is there that they will discuss the time and communications problems. I was wrong, they won't strike by noon, but sometime tonight. I'm certain of it."

"How can you be so certain?" Jack asked.

"Because this is exactly like one of the training scenarios we went through as intelligence officers in the Chinese army. Both the army and MSS take much of the same training. How would you suggest we attack our problem?"

"You need to think network centric," Ling said. "You're looking at substations, agents, and communications. Shift in focus from the single node target, the agent, to the network they are part of. Think about how you would develop a strategy for that. Next, shift your view of the agents, not as independent, but as a system that continuously adapts. Finally, develop your strategy to account for the dynamic adaptation."

"That is asking a lot," JB said.

"I realize that," Ling replied. "But it is the only way."

"He is right," Li Na responded. "Besides, we only know about the few agents we have seen."

"What do you mean," JB asked.

"I know how these groups think and develop strategies," Li Na responded. "It is unlikely they would attempt such a significant endeavor with only six to eight men over such a large area. The team we saw and are attempting to find may be one of two or three."

"Are you saying they may have twenty or thirty men here?" Jack asked.

"Precisely," Li Na replied. "Think about it. Look at the number of communications facilities on the map and an almost corresponding number of substations that are relevant."

"There is no way we can cover that many targets," Jack replied.

"All the more reason to develop our strategy as Ling suggests."

"Let's get on it then," JB said.

Hong Kong was hot and humid. Typical for a summer day. "General Teng," Colonel Han called out, rushing into his office. "We have an MSS agent call in on a secure frequency sir."

"Have you verified it?" Teng asked.

"The frequency is valid sir," Han said. "It is an embedded team in Los Angeles. They're still calling sir."

"Do you have the code in information?"

"Yes General," Han said.

"Put them on speaker," Teng replied. "Have them code in."

"Xiezhi calling Qilin, over," Bingwan Luan said, repeating the call three times."

"That is the correct call-in sir," Han replied. "They use the mythical creatures Xiezhi, the high intelligence unicorn and dragon and Qilin, the fire breather. It is authentic according to our logs."

"Who was their handler?" Teng asked.

"General Bocheng sir."

"Have them code in," Teng responded.

"This is Qilin, code in please," Han responded. "Again, code in please."

"Alpha one six Charlie papa tango two zero bravo," the voice said. "Again, Alpha one six Charlie papa tango two zero bravo."

"Hold one," Han responded as he looked up the agent codes.

"Sir," Han said. "The code is valid. It is agent Bingwan Luan. He is one of the best I'm told."

Luan was ecstatic they had finally gotten through. But this was an emergency contact not his primary handler. He immediately wondered what had happened.

"What is your status?" Han asked.

"We have all contractors in place," Luan responded. "Contact issue with Qilin for past two days."

"There was an accident," Han said. "Non-repairable equipment failure."

"Understood," Luan said, realizing the post had been destroyed, as well as his handler.

"General," Han said. "His code means that they are ready for our computer hackers to initiate the final sequence for catastrophic failure."

"Xiezhi, Qilin," Teng said. "Equipment repair will take six months. Do you have alternate plan?"

"Yes Qilin," Luan responded. "I need comm facilities for continuance."

"Have you selected one?" Teng asked.

"Several," Luan replied.

"Do you have enough contractors for the work?" Teng asked.

"Yes," Luan said. "I have contracted with a group of twenty-eight and will choose one from them. However, we may have a problem?"

"Details?" Teng commanded.

"I believe we are being considered for a job," Luan said.

"Very well," Teng replied. "Consider accepting it."

General Teng knew the code meant, that there were twenty-eight agents in the field and that Luan would split them into three teams then, choose three communications facilities thus, greatly increasing the chances of success for the operation. Because they believed they were being hunted and watched, they would engage evasive protocols.

"Colonel," Teng asked. "Are you familiar with this type of

operation?"

"Yes, General," Han said. "The teams will carry out the mission on their own."

"Do they have the needed computer skills?" Teng asked.

"Yes," Han replied. "The operations plan indicates they have five computer specialists with them. All they need is access to an adequate communications facility, which as you heard, they have already chosen."

"Xiezhi, Qilin," Teng spoke. "Proceed with repair. Call with estimated schedule."

"Understood Qilin," Luan replied.

"Colonel," Teng said. "You worked for MSS until coming into military intelligence. How long to do you think it will take them to complete the mission?"

"I looked over the mission report while you were talking," Han said. "They were supposed to sabotage various electrical facilities and when finished, contact General Bocheng who would initiate an immediate hack. They have completed that; all they need is access to a facility and the computer specialists will complete General Bocheng's task. My presumption is they will move at dark. Once inside the facilities they will have uploaded the necessary codes within twenty minutes. Working from three facilities, the first to initiate the codes will complete the operation."

"What trouble could they run into?"

"The worst would be if they are followed," Han said. "If so, it is a certainty they are American CIA and or the FBI. They will need to be very cautious. Splitting into three teams will give them an edge. They need to avoid detection until one of them has uploaded the necessary codes."

"You make it sound so simple," Teng replied.

"It is both simple and pragmatic," Han said, grinning. "The complexity arises when as the Americans say, a fly is in the ointment."

"What is the time difference," Teng asked, looking at his

watch.

"They are sixteen hours behind us sir," Han replied.

"So, if we assume a midnight access to a facility, we should know mission success in about fourteen hours give or take."

"Yes sir."

"Alright, Colonel," Teng said. "Dig into all the mission parameters and update me as soon as you can. I need to inform Chairman Hintao. Also, if Luan needs more resources, especially men, check if we can provide them given his established timeline."

Jonas and Phil continued operating out of their command van that had relocated it to the Farm. It was uncertain who they could trust and until they knew, they would remain mobile. The power was still out from major substation failure on the outskirts of DC. Currently, Langley was running on backup generators, which had kicked on a couple of minutes after the blackout happened.

"What's the news?" Phil asked.

"We have two of the large generators moving into place," Jonas said. "It's much sooner than I anticipated. They will bring the power back to DC."

"The people in the south aren't going to be so happy with that while they remain in the dark," Phil said.

"True," Jonas replied. "But it's about continuity of government. They do understand that."

"How long can we pacify them?" Phil asked.

"I'm not sure," Jonas said. "We need them to keep thinking America and not parties. If we can do that, they will work for the overall good."

"I'll take your word for it," Phil said. "By the way, you know due to my position that I'm paranoid. So, I need a sounding board. It is my conviction that this blackout had help from the inside. How else could they have known. I mean I know there is a lot of open-source information out there, but the operational keys for grid operations are tightly held."

"You're not paranoid or maybe we both are," Jonas replied. "I was thinking along the same lines. I know the energy sector well. My hunch is there are a couple of insiders, an expert in the grid, a civilian who is likely coupled to at least one legislator on the Hill."

"That's a relief," Phil said. "I thought I was going crazy."

"No," Jonas said. "There has to be at least one insider and as we both know, many in congress and the senate are on the Chinese payroll."

"How many people are we looking at?" Phil asked.

"There is the House Committee on Energy and Commerce," Jonas replied. "I do not believe the main committee members are involved, but those in the Subcommittee of Energy and Power. It has thirty-two members. There is also the Senate Appropriations Subcommittee on Energy and Water Development with eighteen members."

"Are there any others we need to look at?" Phil asked.

"One more group," Jonas replied. "The Senate Armed Services Committee on Cybersecurity with eight members. That's a total of fifty-eight."

"That's a lot of investigation," Phil said.

"Yes, it is," Jonas replied. "But you have the resources. Don't forget to look for overlap."

"What do you mean?" Phil asked.

"It is entirely possible someone from the cybersecurity group is cooperating with the House Subcommittee on Energy and Power. I would concentrate on those first."

Phil walked away, his aide trailing. They could be seen in earnest conversation, their tones muffled as they began making notes and calling intelligence officers. If there was complicity in this attack with American legislators, there would be hell to pay. Somehow, Jonas had an inkling that JB would be involved. He felt certain the U.S. Government would not be able to handle a scandal after all that had happened and what could soon happen. Deep down, he knew the personnel in the CIA would find anyone else that would be involved. While technically not allowed to operate in the U.S., they did so more often than people supposed, usually in the form of cooperation with the NSA who could easily access, with authority, any data on any U.S. citizen or visiting foreign national. Phil, along with the NSA would cast a broad net that would tighten quickly. There would be no place for the traitor to hide. God help him or them when caught.

Activity in the TOC was high. Every agent had received instructions on what they would be doing and how they would carry out their assignment. Jack assumed the lead role since the FBI was the domestic intelligence agency inside the U.S. to conduct such operations.

"Li Na," Jack said. "Do you really believe they have additional operatives?"

"Yes. They would need to for such a critical mission."

"JB, do you have access to additional small drones?" Jack asked.

"Let me call Jonas and see if they have anything in this area," JB said. "In Florida we used what we called Dragon. They would be of help here since they have a twenty-mile range and can remain aloft three hours at time."

"Good," Jack replied. "We need all the help we can get. These guys gave us the slip before. With multiple teams they will have a huge advantage. We need to find them fast."

Whipping his cell out, JB made several quick calls and was directed to a field office in Simi Valley. He explained what he needed.

"Hold a moment please," JB said, placing his hand over the microphone. "Jack, the field office in Simi Valley has four of them. Where do we want them?"

Jack was scrutinizing the map and pointed to two locations. "Place them here and here so they overlap the suspect area,"

Jack said. "Do so immediately. I'll contact local law enforcement and have a couple of officers meet them at each location so that no one interferes with the operation."

"Roger," JB said. "Okay, I need two at the corner of the following intersections, two police officers will meet you at each to ensure your security."

While JB was issuing instructions to the technicians who would be operating the drones, Jack made his way over to Ling, Li Na, and Xin Cao.

"Any thoughts on how we cage the prey?" Jack asked.

"I've been digging more into the communications facilities," Ling replied. "Theoretically, many could serve their purposes. Check out those blue pins on the map."

"I see three of them," Jack said. "So what?"

"Remember we thought the agents would go for the one in San Francisco or the one on Campus Center Drive."

"Sure."

"Those three belong to Globe-Com as well," Ling said. "My guess is they will go for the smaller, less visible, and isolated facilities. I'm guessing they have less security than the larger one north of LAX."

"Makes sense," Jack said. "Perhaps we should concentrate our efforts near those locations."

"I would not be so hasty," Xin Cao said. "Those are the obvious targets. They may have wanted to bait us to the larger facility just like they did for Diablo Canyon, but you can bet their leader knows all those facilities are under the same ownership umbrella."

"What are you saying?" Ling asked.

"It's too obvious," Xin Cao replied. "We have four targets they could infiltrate. However, assume they are on to us. What would you do if you have three teams or maybe four? I would randomly pick two of those four facilities and then, choose another that is more remote and not linked to Globe-Com."

"What he's saying makes a hell of a lot of sense," Jack said.

"What facility would you choose?"

"Based on what Ling has told us, I would choose one of these three?" Li Na said. "They are close to several of the more prominent substations and not owned by Globe-Com."

"Of course, this is just a shot in the dark," Xin Cao said. "But it would fit with their strategy and general operations procedure."

"That's a lot of locations to cover when you combine it with Chinatown," Jack said. "I'll need to get LE backup from the local area."

"I suggest the LA County Sheriff's Department," Ling said. "They have a long history of successful surveillance with their plain clothes deputies."

"Good idea," Jack said. "I'll get on the horn and tell them we have a potential terrorist attack on our hands. We can cover Chinatown and I'll get them to cover this area. If they see anything suspicious, we'll have the drones examine the facility with their FLIR cameras."

"These men won't be as visible as you think," Li Na said. "They are all trained in infiltration and counterintelligence. You likely won't see them until they're at the door."

"I'm open to suggestions," Jack said.

"I suggest putting the drones on a polygon track over the suspect area," Xin Cao said. "If the FLIR camera picks up anything, pass the information to the deputies and have them take a closer look. They'll have night vision and can get more detail."

"That doesn't sound too bad," Jack said.

"Just remember one thing," Li Na said. "Once inside, they only need a few minutes to connect and upload the codes. We may not be able to get to them in time."

"You're proposing a missile strike, aren't you?" Jack asked.

"It's the only way to make sure these men are neutralized," Li Na said. "You're already authorized for the major facility. It would be easier to take out smaller facilities. The areas are less populated and would draw less awareness from the public."

"That's shrewd," Jack said. "Ling, contact the sheriff's department, I'll get JB to talk to the directors. Also, have our media representative begin working on a cover story to give the press for the two different scenarios. I don't need to tell you the one used must be convincing."

"I'm on it."

The Capital South Metro Station was idle when the congressman stepped onto the platform. Due to the blackout, only a few people were around. He guessed it was because of habit although emergency electrical power was operating; perhaps they were taking advantage of the emergency lighting. He made his way to a pair of pay phones near the Addfare machines hoping they still worked, he cautiously looked about. Sure no one was watching, he dialed. To his amazement, the phone worked. They worked because of a dedicated copper pair of copper wires. Such were always buried; neither hurricane, ice storms, nor tornados would cut them because the power needed for them is minimal. The phone company had extensive backup battery systems for them, as well as backup power from generators. Fortunately for him, such stable systems made it easier to commit treason. "Have you noticed anything suspicious?" Clint asked. "I thought I saw someone following me on my way to work this morning."

"No," Blaine replied. "Look, this is no time to get paranoid. We gave them the information they wanted; they paid us for it. Come to my place tomorrow night. Did you make the necessary arrangements?"

"Yes. I'm packed."

"Good," Blaine said. "We leave on a private plane at midnight. Be cautious and keep your eyes open. There's nothing to worry about. Our part is done."

Near the end of the platform, a man was leaning against the wall, reading a gossip tabloid. His partner next to him held a bionic ear, a parabolic sound amplifying device attached to a set of headphones. The tabloid obscured it from view of the congressman and casual passersby. The audio tape would be in the director's possession within the hour.

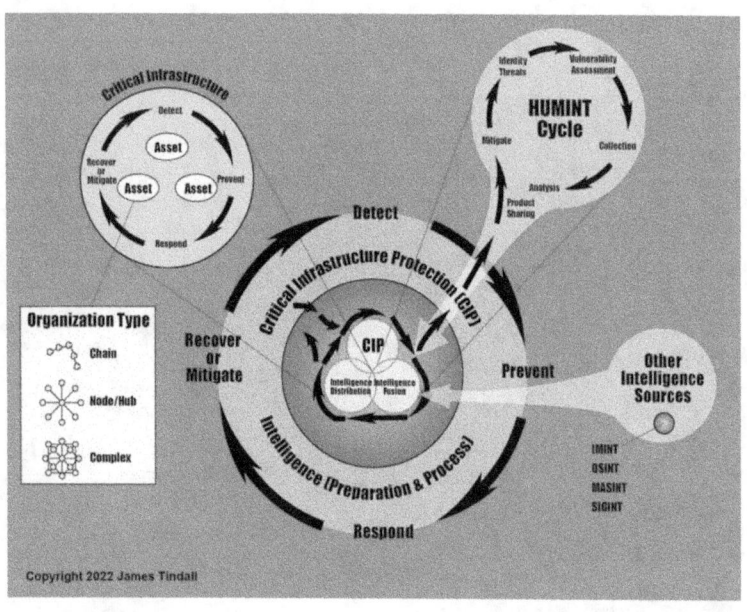

CHAPTER 10

A dark colored sedan raced up the road, screeching to a halt close to the command van. Agents had raised their hands and drawn automatic weapons at its approach. Recognizing the driver, they lowered their guns. Phil and Jonas were standing outside, enjoying the weather before it started raining. The driver, carrying a manilla envelope, raced to the director. Stopping in front of him, he handed it over, panting from lack of breath and excitement.

"We have them sir," the driver said. "Listen to the tape. There's also a late report that came through. It was slow due to what's been happening. It turns out we have been following them for some time."

Phil pulled a small digital recorder from the envelope and pressed the play button. The recording was the earlier discussion in the subway.

"Did you identify them?" Phil asked.

"Yes sir," the driver said. "It's all in the enclosed written report. It is congressman Blaine Childress from New Mexico and Clint Spicer, a power grid expert out of California. I hate to say it sir, but they sold critical information to the Chinese about the grid. So far, we know they were involved in the southern grid attack, at least they sold the grid information to the Chinese."

"What about the California operation?" Jonas asked.

"Yes sir," the driver said. "They are involved in that too. We have contacted the NSA and will have transcripts of every conversation. They were slick in their communications. Mr. Spicer appears to have always contacted the congressman from his cell to pay phones within the Metro subway system and others around the capital. One other thing. The congressman was using a dead drop near the Lincoln Memorial. We are currently following his handler."

"Excellent work," Phil said. "Get the information to me as soon as you can."

"What do you make of this?" Phil asked.

"We have two rats in the house," Jonas replied. "They have sold out their country. Hundreds if not thousands, maybe more, will die because of them. Will you get enough information to put them in prison?"

"Certainly," Phil said. "I'm not sure the president would want to go that route with it. Such trials are always too public. The NSA will have a recording of every conversation. It's as simple as tracing what numbers Mr. Spicer's cell phone called. They will have an entire social network completed within minutes from their Salt Lake City facility. We will look over the transcripts and divulge any information that may be useful to JB and Jack and then, turn it over directly to the president. It will be his decision."

"You mean to put the culprits on trial?" Jonas asked.

"Yes," Phil replied. "If he opts for a trial given our current circumstances."

"I understand," Jonas said, a distant gaze on his face. Trying times required severe penalties to traitors whose thought was only of money.

Pamela had move the prisoners from the safe house and had kept questioning them. So far, they continued to cooperate. Sitting at her desk she was sifting through the information they had volunteered. The minister had given little but was being as helpful as he could without betraying his country. She wished that the politicians on the Hill were as loyal to America as Jeng Po was to China. That was a laugh. They were the most crooked of all, a bunch of criminals. It always amazed her and saddened her that those elected to such powerful positions were so easy to sway with money and would sell out their country the power and control they were addicted to. One would think they would be satisfied with the millions they stole from taxpayers. After all, they loved continuing resolutions which hid where government funds were disbursed. Unlike a passed budget that showed line-item expenditures and accounted for all funds, a continuing resolution veiled all money spent and where it was spent. They got away with stealing billions without anyone being aware except the thieves among them.

"You have a call Pamela," her assistant said. "It's JB."

"Put him through."

"How are you JB?" Pamela asked.

"Fine," JB said. "I need some information if you can find it."

"What do you need?" Pamela asked.

"I need to know if the two techs have any information on what parts of the grid their agents are going for?"

"They're under guard in the conference room with Al as we speak. Let me connect you. Hold on."

She pressed a button on her phone and walked past the guard into the conference room, nodding to Al, who depressed the conference call button on the table.

"This is Al."

"Al, this is JB. What can the technicians tell us about the potential targets in Los Angeles? I'm sending you a map of what we are working on."

In a few seconds, the map that Ling and his group had developed was on the monitor in front of them. The colored pins stood out clearly from the geography of the aerial photo of the entire metro basin.

"Ask your questions," Al said.

"Do the blue colored pins indicate the communications facilities for your backup plan?"

"We had nothing to do with that," Sing said. "The yellow pins are some of the locations?"

"Can you point out the exact ones?" JB asked.

"Not from the map," Sing said. "We could with IP addresses if we had access to a computer."

"Al, can you help them?"

"I'll get our computer experts in here with a laptop right away," Pamela called out as she left the room.

A couple of minutes later, two IT and data analysis experts entered and set up a laptop, flanking Sing on either side. Sing immediately found an IP address and logged in. It was in Chinese. Pamela stood behind them to make sure Sing didn't attempt to contact his Chinese colleagues. She really had nothing to worry about since Sing would give anything to stay out of mainland China.

"Okay," Sing said. "I can press enter. When I do the page with the IP addresses will come up and I can do a print screen, so you have them."

"Sounds like there's a catch," Pamela said.

"There is," Sing replied.

"When I press enter, it will show someone is accessing the system."

"Will someone be watching?" Al asked.

"Most likely," Sing replied.

"We can mask it with our alternate IP address," the other technician said.

"What does that mean?"

"That it will look like the request came from their backup

system," Brad said. "They may just think it is a glitch or they may assume it is the field team verifying the locations."

"Hmmmm," Al mused. "We cannot let them know we are on to these locations. Is there a way to ensure that?"

"We will discuss it," Sing said. "Perhaps we can come up with a better solution."

While the two men discussed potential options, Pamela listened in to make sure they were not going to sabotage the operation. Too much was at risk to make another mistake. The two talked back and forth, while Pamela translated additional questions from Brad.

"Do you have an IP address for the MSS?" Brad asked.

"Yes, several," Sing replied.

"Do you have one in Beijing?" Brad asked.

"Of course," Sing replied. "It is the main headquarters."

"You mean with the Ministry of Public Security near Tiananmen Square?"

"No," Sing replied. "That is just a front. The main headquarters of the MSS is in Xiyuan next to the Summer Palace about three and one-half miles west. You can find it on the map. Route 332 of the Beijing public bus service runs between the Summer Palace and the Beijing Zoo and has a stop at Xiyuan. About 550 yards to the south of the bus stop is a road junction. To the east of that junction is the Beijing Chinese Medicine Hospital and directly west is the MSS. The stop after Xiyuan is the Summer Palace. Anyway, I have that IP address through a back door."

"Good," Brad said. "We can run your communication through a special software program we have. It will direct the ping through an overlay network with more than six thousand relays and will conceal our location and usage. I can plug in their IP address so even if they could trace it back, it will look like it's from MSS headquarters."

"Do it," Pamela commanded. "How long will it take Sing?"

"Just a few minutes."

"Get that information and let's relay it to JB and Jack," Al said.

"Do it now!"

The Oval Office was quiet. It seemed far away from the turmoil and power failure in the southeast, which was beginning to claim its first lives from starvation in less accessible areas. The four men present spoke in hushed tones, leaning toward each other from the opposing sofa's they sat on, a small walnut coffee table between them, devoid of the bouquet of flowers that usually adorned it. The President and Vice President were sitting across from the Directors looking over the report that Phil had delivered.

"This is despicable," President Bill Armstrong said.

"Worse," Vice President Vince Reisner touted. "It's treason in its highest form. You're sure about this information?"

"Absolutely," Phil said. "I helped vet it myself. Only the four of us in this room, two agents and the NSA director know."

"We need to keep it that way," Bill said. "If this is leaked to the public, we will have a nation-wide lynch mob on our hands; it won't stop with these two. They will want the head of every politician."

"Agreed," Vince replied. "It's all we can do now to keep a lid on the emotions and anger. Already the people are beginning to say we were lax in our duties."

"What a nightmare," Jonas blurted out. "What are our options?"

"We cannot have a trial," President Armstrong said. "Does everyone agree?"

The men nodded their heads in unison, knowing there were only two choices.

"So, either Gitmo or death," President Armstrong said. "If death, raise your right hand; if Gitmo, raise your left hand."

The men raised their hands; the vote was unanimous.

"It is settled then," Vince whispered, grimacing. "This information never leaves this room. Phil, take these transcripts and dispose of them. They and we were never here. When JB has completed his current mission, schedule a meeting. We will meet with him privately."

"God help us if we fail," Bill said. "The country will fall and succumb to armed civil war. What is going on in California?"

"We are working with a grid expert," Jonas replied. "He is identifying the most likely targets. One of Jack's men has been a big help identifying potential communications facilities."

"Not only that sir," Phil said. "Taiwan Station is getting the two technicians we captured to help identify the original backup facilities if the MSS team lost contact with the mainland."

"I don't want this tracing back to us," Bill said.

"We have made arrangements for it not to," Phil replied.

"Do we have enough agents on scene?" Vince asked.

"Yes sir," Jonas said. "With help from local law enforcement and the DOE, we have sufficient for surveillance. It would be nice to have more."

"We can give you whatever you need," Vince replied.

"Jonas and I discussed that," Phil said. "While it would be nice to have more men, the more we have the more likely this operation will leak. We do not believe the risk is warranted sir."

"Hmmmm," Bill said. "I agree. If you need anything, more, Global Hawks, whatever, let us know immediately."

"Will do sir," Phil replied. "But time is running short. We will either catch them tonight or."

"Or what?" Vince asked.

"They will achieve success in their mission and the U.S. becomes just another lesser developed, third world country," Phil responded.

"Vince and I will hold the fort down here," Bill said soberly. "Keep us up to date."

The long rays of the sun shortened as the sun sank beyond the horizon far past the Pacific Ocean. On any other day,

Li Na and JB would be looking forward to a wonderful evening. But on this day, the future of the U.S. hung in the balance.

"This is the most critical mission I have ever served on," Li Na said. "The fate of the world hangs in the balance."

"Correct," JB said. "I find it odd that China and other countries want the U.S. to fail when they are keenly aware that economic disaster will be global, and they will themselves be pulled down."

"How true," Li Na replied. "But never underestimate the power of envy and hatred. Singly or coupled together, they fill the soul with a lust more powerful than any addiction."

"That is true," JB said. "Tragic, but true."

"It seems like the odds are against us," Li Na said, clasping her hands. "Do you believe we can succeed?"

"Definitely," JB said. "We have some of the finest men and intelligence gathering network in the world. Together, we have succeeded in desperate challenges. More importantly, the Medicine Man and Lunadi have often told me that it will not be from without, but from within that our great country will fall. That time is not yet."

"You really believe that don't you?" Li Na asked.

"Of course," JB said. "The Great Spirit does not lie."

"But you have killed many men," Li Na said. "Don't you fear for your soul?"

"No," JB said. "All those gone the way of the earth have earned that which they received. Have you not read in the good book how the Great Spirit killed entire cities that would not follow his word? I am but a servant to help keep the innocent free. In this case, the American people. Their time of probation will be extended so that they have longer to repent."

"I never took you for a religious man," Li Na said.

"I am not," JB said. "Religion, like politics has almost eight billion different sects. I have a simple job. For those who would betray or attack our country, my role is to set an early appointment for them with Jesus."

"You do not blindly follow those you work for do you?" Li Na asked.

"I do not," JB replied. "I serve at the request of Jonas, Phil, and the President. All are honorable men. You see, often there are tasks we do not wish to carry out. But for the good of most of the people, some tasks, however unpleasant, must be carried out. It is like the old movie said. The needs of the many outweigh the needs of the few, or the one."

"You really believe that don't you?" Li Na queried.

"Yes," JB said. "It keeps me on the right path."

"If that is true, then how can you love me?" Li Na asked. "After all I have done, am I not at the bottom rung of the ladder?"

"I don't believe so," JB said. "You are a warrior at heart like me. You have not killed the innocent, but those who do harm to others. Perhaps they should have been brought to legal justice, but that system is for profit. Ironically, to protect and serve does not refer to the people but to the leaders and facilities of those they serve. They care not for the people. Let me ask you a question. If you consider yourself evil, who is eviler, those that commit murder of the innocent or those that kill the murderers of the innocent?"

"I never thought of it that way," Li Na said. "I would say those who kill the murders are less evil."

"Precisely," JB said. "We learned on the reservation that the best way to make the law work is to execute it yourself. Never call a police officer to do a job that everyone knows needs to be done."

"Have you ever done that?" Li Na asked.

His face turned cold. She noticed a single tear roll down his cheek. When he turned to look at her, his glare penetrated her to the core. She felt fearful at first then, open before him.

"When I was a young boy," JB said. "A sixteen-year-old girl was raped by two white men and a black man on the reservation. The reservation police and those in Ft. Lauderdale were notified immediately. Several in the community knew who committed the vile act, including the young girl. The police were unable to make a case; the three had alibis. And after all, the word of a white man was more valuable than that of an Indian girl. The men worked for a farmer on the edge of the reservation, clearing his land. When the police failed to do anything about it, the Medicine Man called a council of a few good men, warriors who had no one to war against. The Medicine Man reminded them of their duty to the people and admonished them to fulfill it so the spirit of the young girl could go free. The next day, the warriors found the three men. They took the girl to identify them. After she did, they took her home and returned to deal out the agreed-on punishment for the crime.

One of the men was skinned alive. He managed to crawl out on the road, looking like an anatomy chart, just as a Florida State Patrol passed. He died the instant the trooper stopped. The second man was forced to wade through jagged grass, sawgrass to the uninitiated. While trying to get away, his clothes were completely shredded and bleeding from all parts of his body, he emerged into a large pond, collapsing into the water from the ordeal of his struggle, bleeding from the many cuts where his clothes had once been. He let out a loud yell when a fifteen-foot alligator pulled him beneath the surface of the coffee-colored water. The third man, the leader of the pack, was led into the woods onto a large pine and palmetto flat. They made him get on his knees and forced a rag into his mouth to muffle his screams while they drove a nail through his penis deep into a lighter wood stump; a pine stump that was full of pitch from being cut down long ago and hard as a rock. They laid a dull butterknife atop the stump and walked away. The man eventually freed himself but bled to death before reaching the highway. My sister never knew what the warriors did. She died three months later from the physical and emotional trauma the men had inflicted on her."

"That's grisly," Li Na said.

"To some," JB stated. The cold look remaining on his brooding face. "I never really got to know my sister because of those three men. But, on a hot, humid day in the swamps, justice was served. By the people, not the police with an agenda to follow. No matter who carried it out, my sister rests now. I no longer involve the police in my problems. Being a for-profit business, they rarely serve us. I prefer Indian Law because it always provides justice."

Li Na put her arm around JB's shoulder attempting to comfort him. Tears quietly poured down her cheeks. Despite the horrific details of the event, she knew the warriors had done the right thing. Their law was not the white man's law. She now understood more than ever why the two of them were like peas in a pod. He would never kill someone without reason. It was clear a death must be warranted.

"What's up with those two?" Ling asked.

"He probably told her about how his sister died," Jack responded.

"How?" Ling asked

"The short version is that she was raped by three men," Jack said. "You don't want to know what happened to the men. However, I will tell you that justice was served."

"He's different, isn't he?" Ling asked.

"Yes," Jack said. "He doesn't think like us if that is what you mean. When the chips are on the line it is about right and wrong with him. He will go through hell to protect his teammates. Let me tell you a story.

Five of us were assigned to destroy a small power plant in Afghanistan. The Taliban knew it was a priority target and had it well guarded. It was positioned in a way that aircraft could not take it out. We climbed up a hill overlooking our objective hidden in the overhang of rocks with a steep walled canyon on three sides. We thought with a couple of shoulder-fired rockets we would complete the mission and be out of the place quickly. What we crawled into was an ambush. There was no way out. Somehow, we were able to slink behind the cover of some large rocks, under fire from all directions. We estimated about twenty men surrounding us. Before we knew it, JB said, "Wait here, I'll be right back," and he was gone. We kept our heads low and tried to pick off the Taliban one by one. It was a no go. A vehicle mounted machine gun began firing at us from the closest perimeter of the power plant. The four of us decided to conserve ammunition and only fire if one of the enemies was in clear view close to us. The gunfire slowed to occasional shots. A group of three Taliban made it to within about twenty yards. I thought one of the men threw a grenade, but later found out it was JB. The machine gun pinning us down suddenly stopped. We thought they were reloading. A couple of minutes later JB was standing in front of us looking down. "You gonna stay behind those rocks all day?" he asked. "We have a job to do; move it."

When we emerged from the rocks, we saw the enemy laying here and there, blood all over their front from a slice to the throat or bullet hole to the head from his 9 mm pistol. The men couldn't believe it. He had killed over twenty Taliban with a knife, a pistol, and a couple of hand grenades. He saved our ass. Every time I think about it, I thank God for JB. Be glad he is on our side."

B rad and Sing had made the necessary computer tweaks. Al found it amusing two well versed computer experts from different countries, enemies, could cooperate so quickly. He didn't find it amusing that the Chinese were better skilled than he anticipated.

"Pamela," Al said. "You better get in here; they're ready."

She rushed through the door to find all the men looking at her. The looks on their faces made it clear they were ready to go. All they needed was her permission.

"Are you completely ready?" Pamela asked.

"Yes," Brad said. "All Sing needs to do is depress the return key."

"Do it!" she commanded.

Sing gently depressed the key. As soon as he did, lines of code began racing across the screen.

"I hope this works," Pamela said. "Are you sure it won't come back on us?"

"I'm sure," Sing replied.

"I concur," Brad said. "It should not draw undue suspicion.

A couple of minutes later, a red background highlight on a computer screen at MSS headquarters in Xiyuan instantly caught a computer technicians' attention. He carefully examined the notification. It was an access request for the targets for Operation Guillotine. The man was well trained in computer operations involving intelligence and data collection and analysis. As he watched the screen in front of him, he realized it must be the field operations team leader because the request appeared to be coming from an internal IP address. At the same time, if something were potentially amiss, it was his head on the chopping block. He wouldn't take that chance and without hesitation, picked up the receiver and called.

"Sir," he said. "I have a request within Operation Guillotine. Your number recently was listed as the communication point."

"Hold one moment," Colonel Han replied.

The colonel rushed to the general's office who was in conference with General Liu.

"I apologize for interrupting," Colonel Han said. "But something has come up with Operation Guillotine. I have an MSS technician on line, one from Xiyuan."

"Stay Colonel," General Teng said. "We need to know if this is important."

"This is General Liu. You're on with General Teng and Colonel Han. What is your situation?"

"Sir. I am Tang Pi. Officer in charge of communications for

operations. We just received a request for target information. It appears to come from the team leader. I wanted to make you aware sirs."

"What information specifically," General Teng asked.

"It was for GPS coordinates of communication facilities in the metro Los Angeles area."

"Where did the request initiate?" General Liu asked.

"It came from within headquarters, sir," Pi replied.

"Is that unusual?" Teng asked.

"No sir," Pi replied. "The exception is that such requests are typically sent to control at the field operatives base of operations. In this case, it should have been at the base northeast of Shantou."

"Hold one moment," General Teng said, muting their conversation.

"You're more familiar with this than I am," Teng said. "What do you think?"

"Pi is correct," General Liu replied. "The field operatives would normally check with base to verify target and or communications coordinates. In this case, because they could no longer communicate with base, they contacted headquarters via networked systems."

"So, you're saying this is standard protocol when communications are a problem?" General Teng asked.

"Yes," General Liu said. "The reason for it is that sometimes targets change or are updated before the final mission sequence."

"It seems to me that nothing is out of the ordinary," General Teng said.

"I agree," General Liu replied, depressing the talk button again. "Pi, carry on with operations. Thank you for bringing this to our attention. It appears to be standard protocol. However, to be sure, trace down the IP address from the sender and investigate verification of the requesting agent. Let us know if anything appears out of place."

"I will look into it sir."

Sebastian Franks was sitting in the conference room with Jeff McClinton. He was in session with Pamela, COS Taiwan, Jack, JB, and Li Na.

"I have everyone online," Sebastian said. "President Armstrong just contacted me; the conversation was terse. I don't need to tell you Pamela how critical this is becoming. What do you have that can help us in our search?"

"We are looking at potential targets from the map you sent us," Pamela responded.

"We have the map on the monitor here as well," Sebastian said. "Are we close?"

"Two of the targets match the GPS coordinates we obtained," Pamela said. "Al has just sent them to you. There is a problem with the third set."

"What kind of problem," Jeff asked.

"It is team leader selectable," Al replied.

"What the hell does that mean?" Sebastian asked.

"Because the team lost communication with their base, the leader selects the third target," Al responded. "It's a failsafe for just such a scenario. Potentially, he could select two."

"In other words, we need to pinpoint the last facility?" Jack said.

"I'm afraid so," Pamela replied. "According to the technician, the third target could be anywhere."

"Oh, there's one other thing," Al said. "Their mission is called Operation Guillotine, perhaps most notable is the fact they have a full team of twenty-eight men."

"Damn!" JB exclaimed. "That is many more than we suspected. They can split into many smaller teams; finding that many is almost impossible."

"I'm sorry, JB," Al said. "We've been online with the Directors, just as Sebastian has been online with the President. We are prepared to offer you whatever assistance you need. We have added another MQ-9 Reaper, armed as the first, for your assistance. The FBI will give the operational order. We also have added two more Global Hawks for surveillance. If you need anything else, have Jack request it through Sebastian."

"The number of men they have is the problem," JB said. "We need more men."

"Not only men," Jack joined in, "but men who can be trusted."

"I thought you might say that," Sebastian replied. "Al and Pamela convinced the President to order fifty U.S. Army Special Forces and a half-dozen Task Force 160 pilots, the Night Stalkers. The latter are on their way from Fort Campbell Kentucky. Half of the Special Forces are from the 10Th Group out of Fort Carson, the other half, all Spanish speaking are coming out of Elgin Air Force Base. If the Green Berets aren't trustworthy, we're in serious trouble. I might also mention that there are a dozen Mandarin speaking individuals in the groups. Utilize them as you see fit. To avoid Posse Comitatus, they'll be directly assigned to the FBI under Jack and JB's direction. Make sure they all wear plain clothes. By the way, they're touching down on the tarmac as we speak. All of them."

"How did you know we would need them?" Jack asked.

"The mission is too critical to fail," Sebastian responded. "Pamela and Al convinced us of the potential need. We felt better safe than sorry. I don't know about you, but I'm not yet ready to begin a second career at a fast-food taco joint."

"This will be a huge help," JB said. "Thank you, sir. Hold the taco's for now."

Everyone laughed.

"No need to thank me," Sebastian said. "If this doesn't work, we're all in the soup."

"Very well," Al said. "Keep us posted. We will send any additional intel your way if we get some."

Pamela and Al had signed off leaving the rest of the group. "The Green Berets will be at your location momentarily,"

Sebastian said. "If you need anything else, get on the horn."

"What are these special forces groups he referred to?" Li Na asked. "I am only familiar with some in Asia."

"These are the Green Berets," JB whispered. "In war they usually infiltrate behind enemy lines and collect intelligence without being detected. In other situations, they are typically assigned secondary missions that include vehicle and soft-target interdictions, combat search and rescue, manhunts, and other-directed activities, even humanitarian. In this instance, they are under direct authority of the President and thus, us. The Night Stalkers are helicopter pilots that support them in such activities. They are very, very good. If we cannot find them with these men, we aren't going to."

"A good thing I suppose," Li Na mused.

"Absolutely," JB said.

As he spoke, six Apache Longbow helicopters landed directly outside, drowning his words. The entire group, as well as all the agents focused their attention on the helicopters, a dark green in color with no markings. When the blades stopped turning, two men climbed down from each, walking directly toward them. Approaching, the lead pilot recognized Jack Donovan from their brief and strode directly up to him, his men following on his heels.

"Sir," he said, saluting. "I am Captain John Privy of Task Force 160. We are the Night Stalker's. I have been ordered to report to you."

"Thank you, captain," Jack said. "This is JB, Li Na, Susan, Xin Cao, and many of our agents."

"What are you armed with?" JB asked.

"This is the Apache 64-D," Captain Privy said. "We are capable of operating in any weather condition. Each chopper carries a full complement of 30 mm rounds, as well as eight Hellfire missiles with thermobaric, enhanced blast warheads for use against ground forces and soft urban targets. If a snake crawls on the ground, we will see it. The pilots are all chief warrant officers. For your operations planning, we can remain aloft two and one-half hours. One more thing sir. Each craft has an integrated radio modem with a sensor suite that allows the data to be automatically shared with all other Apache's and allows all birds to fire on any target or targets detected from a single Apache."

"We have a serious problem captain," Jack said. "We have up to four targets, it could be more, that we may need to fire on at the same time. Can you do that?"

"Easily sir," Captain Privy said. "Each of my birds can track up to 128 targets and fire on 16 of those at one time."

"Perfect," Jack replied. "Relax and get your men situated. Once the Green Berets arrive, we will begin our briefing."

"Yes sir," Captain Privy said. "Follow me men."

They had scarcely made their way toward the planning board when two transport planes taxied onto the tarmac directly behind the Apache's. The ramps lowered, fifty men walking down; they headed directly toward Jack and JB, saluting and shaking hands.

"I'm Colonel Joseph Roberts, 10th Special Forces Group. This is my counterpart, Colonel Brian Stout of 7th Special Forces Group."

"How do you do sirs?" Colonel Stout asked.

"We're in a serious bind," Jack said. "We're hunting a team of twenty-eight MSS agents who intend on taking down the power grid within a few hours."

"We need to find them ASAP," JB said. "The fate of our entire country depends on it. We need good manhunting skills."

"Our men are trained very well for that," Colonel Roberts replied.

"Absolutely," Colonel Stout joined in. "We are expert at that as well as vehicle interdiction, urban situations, surveillance, and more. Just tell us what you need."

By this time, the Green Berets under the Colonel's command had surrounded them in a semi-circle. All were dressed in plain clothes for the weather, carrying side arms, communications, binoculars, and M4's. They were listening intently to the discussion; it was apparent they were eager to get started.

"Susan," Jack said. "Please have a few men bring the planning board and maps to the end of the plane. Set it up in the middle so we can get the briefing underway.

"Colonel's," Jack said. "Have your men spread out a little and get comfortable for the briefing. We need to be out of here and in the field as quickly as possible."

"Understood," Colonel Roberts replied, turning to direct his men.

For a few minutes there was a flurry of activity. Out on the tarmac, more than a dozen vans pulled up and opened their side doors, the drivers remaining by each vehicle. Their arrival didn't go unnoticed.

"Are those for us?" Colonel Stout asked.

"For all of us," Jack replied. "We'll be leaving immediately after the briefing."

"Alright," JB yelled. "Can I have your attention please? I'll first give you a rundown of what we've done so far. Save your questions for after the brief. Then, Jack Donovan, Head of the Counterterrorism Division for the FBI will fill you in on the protocol we'll be following. I'm guessing most of you may have heard, but I'll repeat it anyway. The southeast U.S. power grid was sabotaged by the same group we're working against here. We were sent to capture or kill these agents. The trail was picked up in San Francisco. One of the MSS agents was approached in a store by a police officer who he then shot and made his getaway, shooting a second officer in the process. The rest of the group, eight in total, fled with him. We have a Global Hawk up that tracked them here. During this time, we have mapped potential electrical substations they may attack and communications facilities they could use to hack the system. It's the same process they used to bring down the southeast grid. With help from the CIA in Taiwan, we have been able to narrow the communications facilities to two, but we know there is a third, perhaps a fourth. They gave us the slip. Now, we need to find them before they reach the two facilities. The crucial one is the third facility. We don't know where it is and if we don't find it. Well, you know what the result will be."

"What makes you think they won't just blow the substations?" Colonel Roberts asked.

"We believe they will follow the same procedure they did for the southeast," JB said. "First, they sabotage the substations then, they hack the grid to initiate system failure. We are certain all the facilities are already sabotaged. So, they need a computer facility to complete the mission, which they call Operation Guillotine."

"But can't they hack the facility from someplace else?" Colonel Roberts asked.

"Absolutely," JB said. "But to do so they need the right equipment. The location where they would have launched the attack from was destroyed and three hostages taken."

"Do you know that for sure?" Captain Privy asked.

"Yes," JB said, pride entering his voice. "My team and I, waving his hand behind him, destroyed the facility north of Hong Kong and extracted as much information as we could to get to this point."

Stories had already been circulating through these clandestine groups who suddenly realized they were looking at a formidable agent whose reputation had preceded him and the lady of death as she was known among them, who had ice water flowing through her veins. It was easy for all the men to identify the team behind JB. All wore black; all were Asian, and all were watching them with penetrating stares. It was a sobering moment to meet true masters of death. Without noticing it, the men had quietly exhaled as they clearly comprehended who stood before them. Jack sensed what they were thinking and began to brief them, so their attention was elsewhere.

"Thanks, JB," Jack said. "I'll take it from here. Men, what JB didn't say was that the agents you are up against are trained MSS agents equivalent to our CIA field operatives that you are familiar with. They are as well if not better trained. Further, there are twenty-eight of them. If they follow our Special Operatives procedures, they may split into eight-man teams or, they may split into four or even two-man teams. Because we are in a densely populated area, all men will use suppressors on their weapons. We need to be as discreet as possible.

This map denotes the two communications facilities they may access. The third one, as has been mentioned, is up in the air, which is why we need your help. Li Na, who has Chinese Army intelligence expertise believes they will link up in Chinatown. She is familiar with their operating structure and strategies. They've been on the move for a while and the last couple of days, since the southeast grid attack, has likely heavily taxed their endurance. So, we believe they will go to Chinatown and have some much-needed hot food and drink. They will most likely discuss their final strategy and split up to complete their mission."

"What makes you think they'll show up there?" Colonel Roberts asked.

"As Jack explained, they are likely stressed," Li Na said. "I know their habits well. However, the men that will meet are only the team leaders. The rest of their teams will be in other locations."

"You are assuming they'll blend in," Colonel Stout said.

"Absolutely," Li Na said, speaking in Spanish.

"What did she say?" a Green Beret asked. All around him others were explaining what she said.

"You see, Colonel," Li Na explained. "Just as your men are trained in Spanish, these men are trained in English. They may have an accent, but the average American will not be suspicious of them. And they will likely frequent a restaurant that caters more to Chinese culture."

"Thank you, Li Na," Jack said. "Are there any questions?"

"What call signs should we use to communicate?" Colonel Roberts asked.

"Excellent question," Jack replied. "JB and his team are Fox Bravo One. Sequential FBI teams will be Fox Bravo and their assigned number. The colonels can assign each of you to teams. Your call sign will be Golf Bravo for Green Beret followed by respective number of the team. Captain Privy and his Apache's will be called November Sierra for Night Stalkers followed by their respective number. I should mention that JB and I will be in charge. He will issue orders in the field, and I will be relaying orders for the Night Stalkers, Global Hawk, MQ-9 Reaper, and other needs."

"That sounds good to me," Colonel Roberts said. "Colonel Stout and I will assign teams to each of the locations you illustrated on the map. We will do that now."

"Men," JB said. "As much as I would like to put a bullet in the head of each of these agents the minute I see them, remember that the first part of the mission is to identify and track. We need them to lead us back to the rest of their men."

"Can we kill them once we know for sure?" Colonel Stout asked.

"With prejudice," JB responded.

The men laughed at the comment. This was not a humanitarian mission. There was a bustle of activity as they prepared for the night.

"Colonel Stout," Captain Privy yelled over the din, quickly walking over, shaking hands. "It is so nice to see you again sir."

"Likewise, John," Colonel Stout said. "I hope this works out better than the mess we encountered last month in Venezuela."

"Got that right sir," Captain Privy replied. "We will be covering your men tonight sir. Let me know whatever you need."

"How are you going to run the operation?" Colonel Stout asked.

"You know our airtime. Since we can remain aloft for two and one-half hours, I'll always have two birds up. When you give us the go that you have found these MSS agents, I'll put up all birds operating in pairs. We've got your back sir."

"Good," Colonel Stout responded. "Make sure to go over this with Jack."

"I will sir," John said. "But I have one concern,"

"What is that?" Colonel Stout asked.

"This is a densely populated area," John replied. "I'm hesitant to shoot Hellfire missiles into a facility you may identify."

"I'm with you on that," Colonel Stout said. "All of us are. But there is too much at stake for the country to hesitate if that's needed. The grid expert informed us that if we do not stop this enemy group, the entire western power grid will go down. Coupled with the southeast, our country will erupt into tribalism with no continuity of government for the foreseeable future. There's also the potential for the loss of millions of lives. From what they said, most of these facilities are far enough away from neighborhoods that there will be minimal collateral damage. Don't hesitate my friend."

"Understood sir," John replied, saluting before walking away.

The colonel watched him as he wound his way through the rest of the men to talk with Jack. Like John, he was also hoping that they would not need to engage the MSS agents with missiles. But it would be what it would be. He turned to address his men who had been sobered by the conversation.

"We have work to do men," Colonel Stout said. "What happens tonight will cast the future path of this country, especially if we are unsuccessful."

Green Berets from 7th and 10th Groups began rehearsing their assignments and testing equipment to ensure all was in order. This was not a time for mistakes. Nothing would be left to chance. The maps that had been provided were put to good use as they went over their assigned areas.

"They are a welcome sight," Jack commented.

"Yes," JB responded. "I think we now have enough men to get the job done."

"These men will leave nothing to luck," Jack said. "You remember when we worked with some of them in Afghanistan?"

"I do," JB said. "They were as precise as a luxury watch. There was no wasted energy or time in their operations. When we pin these agents down, they will be the calvary."

"Absolutely," Jack said. "The MSS agents will surrender immediately or die."

"It would be nice to capture a couple of them alive," JB said.

"Ummmm Hmmmm," Jack grunted.

Phil and Jonas were on edge as they followed the progress of the operation. They were interrupted by a soft knock on the command vehicle door. Turning, Phil saw it was his agent who had been tracking the congressman and grid expert.

"I have an update for you sirs," the agent said.

The two men climbed out of the vehicle and walked a short distance from curious ears.

"What's the skinny?" Phil asked.

"We followed the congressman around the Lincoln Memorial," the agent replied. "We watched the dead drop; a Chinese agent we suspected put a note beneath it. The congressman picked it up."

"And?" Jonas asked, excitement in his voice.

"The note was the payoff drop location," the agent replied. "We were able to maintain surveillance on the congressman. He was given two black leather duffle bags, the kind you would travel with on a plane, but larger."

"What did he do with them?" Phil asked.

"He returned to his townhome in Alexandria and went in with

them but didn't come back out."

"Can you estimate how much?" Jonas asked.

"No need sir," the agent replied. "We intercepted a call with him and the grid expert. The figure discussed was ten million dollars. They will be meeting at 2200 tomorrow night at the congressman's place to split the money and get out of country. They have a plane leaving at midnight. We have all the necessary locations covered sir."

"Very good," Phil said. "Keep us informed immediately of any changes."

"Yes sir," the agent said as he climbed back into his vehicle and sped off.

"Isn't it amazing what people do for money?" Phil asked. "Ten million to sell out the country and kill countless thousands if not millions with no remorse."

"The lust for money is an addiction," Jonas replied. "As much as that for power. Worse than a drug addict."

"The question is what do we do about it?" Phil asked. "It would be easy to put a bomb on the plane and destroy it over the water."

"That would be too easy," Jonas said. "But remember, the President wanted to see JB immediately upon completion of the mission in California. And remember our vote."

"You think he is going to assign him to take care of this?" Phil asked.

"You're the spook," Jonas responded. "I think it's a good guess, but you tell me."

"Hmmmm," Phil mused, staring off into the darkness.

General Teng was drawing out communications diagrams along with complex models of potential scenarios. Before he had worked in the field as an intelligence operative, Beijing had trained him as an intelligence analyst. Like any top-tier analyst, he was calm, logical, reasoned, and unemotional. His goal was discovery of the truth, and he was determined, especially in this case, to uncover it. Regardless of how he felt about Jeng Po and the base, he was inquisitive and skeptical. He was questioning the data that had been collected so far, asking himself questions. Why do I believe this? Is the source credible? Is there an alternative explanation? He was approaching the problem from varied and many perspectives, using the evidence to visualize what had happened and what was happening on the west coast of the U.S. The more he poured over the reports and asked questions, the more solid the mental picture that he developed. He was in a deep trance when his phone rang.

"General Teng."

"This is Tang Pi in Xiyuan general. You asked me to contact you if I received additional information."

"Have you found something?"

"Sir. The protocol for the access we discussed before was not accurate."

"What do you mean?"

"The access should have identified the agent by code number sir. It was not given."

"So, you think someone other than Liu Wei accessed the servers?"

"I do," Pi said. "The agents are too well trained to make such an obvious error."

"Contact Bingwan at once," General Teng said. "Tell him to alter facilities. They have backup plans, correct?"

"Yes sir," Pi responded. "They will implement them immediately upon direction. I have tried contacting them but per operation schedule, they are in communication blackout for the next two hours."

"Very well," General Teng said. "Contact them as soon as you can. Tell them to go to alternate plan and keep me informed."

"It shall be as you request sir."

The general stared at the papers before him realizing that he would need to alter the diagrams for the new problem that had developed. He began turning over the pages that he had organized chronology, wondering who could have accessed the servers. Looking out the window at the afternoon sun, a thought suddenly struck him; he turned in his chair and stacked all the papers atop each other. The first one began with destruction of the base. His eyes darted back and forth, continuing down the page then, the next page. Their; at the end; three men were missing. The MSS team had reported success in Taiwan. Had they succeeded or was it a set up to make it look like they had? The name Sing stood out from the rest. He was the head computer technician that did the hacking for the southeast power grid. He, more than the others would know what to do; how to get in.

There were multiple file folders on the corner of his desk. Sifting through them, he found the one that contained all the information the military had on Sing. He had served honorably but had not wanted to go to the post. His desire was to remain in Beijing or Hong Kong. Why? It was as if the words screamed at the general from the page. Sing had grandparents and other relatives in Taiwan. The general knew that if the CIA promised him a new life and the opportunity to be with his relatives, he would undoubtedly take it. Sing was the one who had used his knowledge to get into the servers. What was he seeking? He wasn't aware of field operations so it couldn't be that. He dialed the number; he had to get to the bottom of this.

"Tang Pi, General Teng. What is the most important item in the code?"

"I would say it was the GPS coordinates of the communication facilities sir. There would be no way for the team to complete Operation Guillotine without access to those facilities since the base was destroyed."

"Three people are missing from the base. They include Jeng Po the deputy minister, Sing the head computer technician and another technician. Would any of those have access to the servers there?"

"Only Sing sir," Pi said. "My records indicate he oversaw all computer operations. I might also add that he is the only one that probably had the necessary skills to get in."

"Thank you, Pi," General Teng said. "Lock everyone out of the operation communications for now except the two of us. Keep up the good work. There's a promotion in this for you. I could use a good computer technician."

"Thank you, sir."

The general realized that the success of the operation in California was in jeopardy. Further, the operation to eliminate the three men in Taiwan was a set up to look like they had. They needed to get word to Bingwan to execute the secondary plan. The communications blackout could prove disastrous. He made up his mind to change that policy for future missions. Inability to communicate was always disastrous in intelligence operations. Only luck could pull them through. He didn't believe in luck. He must get a message through.

Chinatown appeared calm. Long shadows from a setting sun drifted across the buildings, casting silhouettes onto the grass of Alpine Park where Jack had a small command vehicle parked to help guide his teams. Golf Bravo teams one through five had dispersed along North Spring Street which marked the east boundary from south to northeast. They would slowly move west. Two-man teams from the FBI were converging toward the center from North Figueroa Street. Additional teams headed by JB and Golf Bravo six and seven were slowly moving from the north, converging down North Hill Street and North Broadway where there was an abundance of traditional Chinese restaurants. They would eventually reach West College Street and spread out more.

"Eyes up everyone," Jack spoke into the comm. "You'll need to explore each restaurant. All of you have a team member from JB and Li Na's group who speaks fluent Mandarin. Use them to advantage."

"It would be nice if we could have some overwatch," Golf Bravo One said.

"Unfortunately, the area is too large for coverage due to the sporadic building height," Jack said. "We have two Global Hawks aloft. When you spot something, we have several Dragons circling about a thousand feet up for better tactical use. Identify possible targets and the small drones can be overhead in seconds to help us ID the person."

"Golf Bravo three, roger that."

The teams began moving toward selected restaurants that Xin Cao had identified during mission planning. The Global Hawks steadily broadcast intelligence of people in the area all afternoon. It was believed that the operatives had not yet met. Jack and Susan's eyes were glued to the monitors in front of them. Each team leader had been issued a GPS location device to delineate them from the MSS agents. Jack could see where all teams were at-a-glance.

"Golf Bravo four. Be advised we see three individuals exiting a parked van along Bamboo Lane. They are heading toward North Broadway. The Dragon video has identified one of the men."

"This is Golf Bravo four. Acknowledged."

"Just turned south on North Broadway."

"Roger."

"Fox Bravo two. We have another group of three exiting a vehicle in a parking lot on Lei Min Way. Also heading toward North Broadway."

"We have them."

"Dragon 2 has also identified one of those men," Jack said. "It's going down teams; stay sharp."

"This is Fox Bravo one. There is a Pho type restaurant on the east side of North Broadway between those two locations. Advise if they converge on it."

"Roger that," Jack said. "Group one is walking south along North Broadway. They are crossing street to that restaurant.

Group two also crossed street and walking north. It appears they may also be going to the restaurant as well."

"All groups be advised," Ling said. "A third group of two exiting vehicle on north side of restaurant. Hold one minute. They are entering. Second group also entering. Dragon 1 identified the last of the three men we have photos for in the last group."

"All groups. Fox Bravo one. Be advised targets now in Pho restaurant. Fox Bravo two, take up overwatch position on northeast corner. Golf Bravo teams converge from east and south. Assume surveillance positions along adjacent streets."

Xin Cao had assigned one of his team members to enter the location beforehand. He was sitting at a corner table, almost unnoticeable to most in the restaurant. Casually eating a bowl of soup and wontons, pretending to read a Chinese newspaper as he ate. He watched the groups enter, all meeting at the same table about thirty feet away. His listening device picked up bits of their conversation; all were Chinese. He began describing the dress of each man, which matched the overhead views before they reached the restaurant. The conversation confirmed these were the agents.

"This is Fox Bravo one. All teams be advised these are those we seek. Get into position to trail vehicles. Command, zero in on vehicles with Global Hawks. The Dragons will not be able to keep pace with the vehicles."

While he spoke, several agents approached each of the MSS vehicles and attached a magnetic-based, GPS locator onto the frame beneath the rear bumper. Unnoticed in the darkness, they hastily walked away.

"We are under communications blackout for just over another hour," Bingwan said. "I'm concerned we have not been able to contact base. But we have been given the go ahead. Are your teams ready?"

"Yes," said a member, the others nodding in the affirmative.

"Good," Bingwan replied. "We will finish what we came here to do."

He grew silent when the waitress came. Acting the charming gentleman, he joked with her as they ordered. She smiled politely before scurrying off to get their meals to the kitchen. She returned a couple of minutes later with drinks. Their conversation turned to banter as they ate, feeling the stress leave their bodies after the harrowing last few days. It was good to sit among friends and have a hot meal. Soon they would be back in China preparing for another mission. They were a disciplined group, familiar with the rigors of the spy business and what it meant for their country. They were prepared to pay the ultimate price for the mainland to accomplish their goals.

"I'll be contacting Xiyuan in about thirty minutes," Bingwan said. "Finalize status and maintain constant contact."

The men nodded as they stood and slowly exited the restaurant.

"All teams. Be advised targets are exiting. Assume your assignments," Jack said.

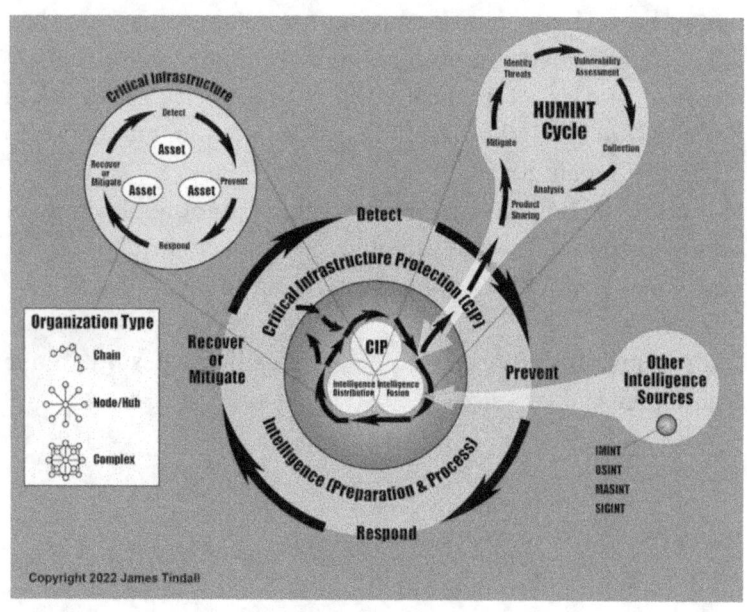

CHAPTER 11

B uilt up stress and anxiety began to disappear. The hunt was on and within a few hours, the fate of a nation would be determined. The Chinese agents were as intent on destroying the U.S. as the Green Berets and federal agents were at protecting it.

"We're on everyone," JB spoke into the comm. "Stay on your toes."

When the Chinese agents walked out of the restaurant, they retraced their steps back to the vehicles they had arrived in. Golf and Fox teams had hastily made it back to their vehicles and remained far enough behind each of the MSS to avoid detection. They took turns changing lead and passing each MSS vehicle a couple of times to make sure they remained undetected.

"Xin," JB spoke into his comm. "Are you sure this is the leader of the group?"

"Yes," Xin Cao replied. "He was the one giving orders. Why do you ask?"

"Because he is not going to any of the areas, we thought he might," JB said. "He's going northeast. Is there a communication facility in that area?"

"There is a small one on the map," Xin Cao replied. "But wouldn't he need to get to his team first?"

"Perhaps they will meet at a pre-arranged location."

"Hadn't thought of that," Xin Cao said.

"All teams. Fox Bravo one. Be advised agents may be meeting others at preassigned location. Stay sharp."

One of the MSS agents answered the ringing sat phone.

"Xiezhi, Qilin," Tang said, repeating the call several times.

"Qilin, Xiezhi," Bingwan replied."

"Tell them they have been discovered and go to alternate plan immediately," General Teng said.

"Xiezhi," Tang Pi said. "You have been identified. Change plan to alternate immediately."

"Submit authorization," Bingwan replied.

"Authorization Sierra one five niner Tango Zulu zero seven Alpha zero one," Tang Pi said. "I repeat, authorization is Sierra one five niner Tango Zulu zero seven Alpha zero one."

"Authorization confirmed," Bingwan replied. "Changing to alternate. All agents, change plan to alternate. Take evasive measures immediately; meet at scheduled coordinates. I repeat, all agents, change plan to alternate. Take evasive measures immediately; meet at scheduled coordinates."

The vehicles the MSS agents were in suddenly did a complete reversal in direction, going back the way they had come.

"This is Fox Bravo one. Back off everyone. Something is up. I think they are onto us. Back out of visual range and follow the GPS locator of your assigned target. Command, we need visuals from Global Hawks. November Sierra one, divide birds to follow each vehicle."

"November Sierra one, roger that."

Changing direction had thrown off the pursuit momentarily as JB's teams immediately regrouped. The MSS vehicles reversed direction then, began evasive maneuvers to make sure they were not being followed. They were all over Los Angeles. One headed west on I-10 and merged onto the 405 ending up in a parking lot in Westgate Century City. Another headed east on 60 and north on the 605 ending up in a hospital parking lot in Duarte. The third vehicle drove south on the I-5 to a parking structure in Anaheim.

"All teams, November Sierra two. Men are changing from suspect vehicle to dark colored sedan."

"All teams, November Sierra one. Be advised targets also switching vehicle in Century City."

The same report came in for each vehicle. They no longer had the luxury of GPS; surveillance had become much more difficult.

"Command, Fox Bravo one. Can you send us visuals of new vehicles?"

"All teams, Command. Visuals on the way."

Despite the change in vehicles, the MSS agents were tracked to their targets. One of the facilities had remained the same. Eight Green Berets were waiting, performing overwatch.

"Fox Bravo one, Golf Bravo nine. Hostiles on site. They are getting in position to enter facility. Shall we terminate?"

"Golf Bravo nine, Fox Bravo one. Attempt to corner and prevent entry."

Golf Bravo nine deployed its men surrounding the small facility; two-man teams splitting up to cover the corners of the facility and access door. They had no sooner gotten into position than hell erupted. Bullets struck all around them. Returning fire, they sought cover. They managed to kill one of the agents defending the access door. The remaining agents shot a shoulder fired missile at them before retreating inside.

"Fox Bravo one, Golf Bravo nine. One hostile down, the others entered the facility. They are well defended."

"Golf Bravo nine, Command," Jack said. "We cannot give them have time to enter the codes. Retreat to safe distance immediately. November Sierra two, start the music."

"Command, November Sierra two. Twins coming down; mark, shoot."

Two Hellfire missiles flamed into the night sky, streaking toward the facility a mile away. The Green Beret teams dove for cover. A large fireball burst into the night air when the missiles exploded. Nothing was left of the facility. Golf Bravo nine moved in to check for survivors and exfil the dead so no evidence was left behind.

"Fox Bravo Command, Golf Bravo nine. No packages remained intact. We are wrapping residues and headed for command."

"Roger," JB said.

He knew the team was cleaning the target and removing bodies. He was hopeful Jack would be able to get some intelligence from the bodies.

The second team of MSS agents were meeting a half-dozen men at another suspected site. This time, the Green Berets were waiting for them. The facility was larger than the last with several doors for access. Two teams had stationed themselves in hidden positions and lay in wait for their prey, like a leopard in the jungle. The MSS agents split into two groups, each taking an access door. The moment they reached the door and attempted to enter, a command was yelled in Chinese.

"Stop where you are. Lay down your weapons."

Without hesitation, they aimed their AK-47's in direction of the voices and opened fire. Green Berets returned fire attempting to wound rather than kill. The MSS agents were too exposed, falling to the ground quickly as bullets penetrated their bodies. Two remained who threw up their hands and surrendered.

"Fox Bravo one, Golf Bravo six. Two packages wrapped; others scattered. Cleaning up, heading to command."

"This is great so far," JB thought. "Twelve dead and two captured alive. But that's only half the number Pamela and Al said there was. What were the agents planning? Would they pick one large target or split in two and choose two or more

312

smaller ones?"

His question was quickly answered.

"Fox Bravo one, November Sierra one. Be advised target vehicle has reached destination. There are at least a dozen hostiles. Located in large parking lot south of building northwest corner of Bluff Creek Drive and South Campus Center Drive."

"Roger November Sierra one. This is the main strike. All teams converge. Golf Bravo teams, provide overwatch from hills three hundred yards southeast of main building. Fox Bravo two, provide overwatch from top of apartment buildings two-hundred fifty yards north-northwest of facility. All other teams converge on corners.

It had not been an accident choosing this building. There were multiple entrances, and it had the fastest communications network of all the facilities. Even though they had been correct, if the MSS teams got inside, it would be impossible to take them out before they could upload the codes. It was imperative they bring them down. Fox and Golf teams arrived mere moments after the MSS agents who had already penetrated the facility.

"Fox Bravo two, holding at one-two corner."

"Golf Bravo three, holding at three-four corner."

"Fox Bravo four, holding at five-six corner."

"Golf Bravo overwatch in position."

"Fox Bravo overwatch in position."

"Fox Bravo one, holding at seven-eight corner. All teams, move in."

In one instant the FBI agents and Green Berets entered the building under a hail of gunfire. Recently retrofitted, the upper floors had excellent positions for standoff defense. The MSS had the high ground; the best position to hold in tactical or strategic defense. Fox Bravo one had worked its way along the corridor on the northeast side of the building. The heaviest gunfire was coming from ahead of them about two-thirds the length of the building.

"Fox Bravo Command, Fox Bravo one. Where are the main servers located?"

"Fox Bravo one. Location is near east end on northeast side."

The response confirmed his estimation. The teams were closing in on the server area when the MSS agents began firing into the team's positions opposite them on the southeast side of the building. His comrades began falling quickly.

"Damn," JB said. "They have ZH-05 combat weapons"

"What's that?" Command asked.

"It fires smart explosives, similar to grenades that can kill the enemy behind cover."

"Golf and Fox teams on southeast corner, fall back to southwest corner and regroup."

Several Golf team members had brought fragmentation grenades and threw them toward the MSS agents to provide cover. The grenades fell short, though they allowed the agents to retreat, leaving them unharmed. While the teams had been retreating opposite the agents, Fox Bravo one had crept forward to within a few yards of them. Bingwan had just rounded the corner when he came face to face with JB who stepped forward gaining control of Bingwan's weapon, knocking it to the floor. Fox Bravo was firing into the MSS positions. Bingwan and JB were oblivious to the bullets flying around them as they began a physical free for all.

Bingwan threw a low right kick to JB's shin, which he avoided, returning with a shin kick to Bingwan's inner thigh, stepping forward to spread his legs and throw him off balance. Turning slightly, JB struck with a right upper forearm. Just as it made contact, Bingwan grabbed the jacket front on both sides of JB's chest and fell backward to nullify the strike.

"I know you," Bingwan said. "We studied you at school in Xiyuan. You're supposed to be dead."

He punched JB in the jaw knocking him back against the wall then charged him. Pinning Bingwan's right arm, JB struck him with a right inward elbow to the head.

"Hardly," JB grunted, throwing a right knee to Bingwan's stomach, which he thwarted by twisting so the two were leaning against the wall.

"You're good, but not good enough," Bingwan said. "You're too late."

The two maintained their grabs as they threw each other against the wall several times, by pivoting position. During pivoting, JB had gotten hold of Bingwan's left ear. Just when it appeared he had the upper hand, one of the MSS agents drew down on him, the bullet grazing his head. He ripped off Bingwan's ear; the MSS agent holding the side of his head, seized the opportunity to retreat and dove for cover near his men, forcing JB to retreat while bullets ripped the wall next to him.

"That wasn't too smart," Xin Cao said. "Getting into a brawl in the middle of a gunfight."

"No, it wasn't," JB replied. "But it was fun. That was their leader."

"Command, Fox Bravo one. They are dug in like ticks here. How long do they need to upload the files?"

"How long do you think?" Jack asked.

"About twenty minutes or less," Ling replied. "Getting the connection will take the longest portion of the time. Once they have it, the files can be uploaded almost at once."

"Fox Bravo one, Command. About twenty minutes at most. Assume that's on the long side."

Glancing at his watch, JB instinctively knew they would be unable to fight their way in within the given time. There were no other options.

"Command, Fox Bravo one," JB said, "We're out of time."

"November Sierra one, Command. How many birds do you have up?"

"Three."

"Lock on target. Full count. Command, give go to MQ-9 full

count. The facility is much larger than we estimated. Countdown three minutes on my mark. Mark. All teams pull back. Overwatch teams fire through windows to keep them occupied."

The FBI and Green Beret teams pulled back. High above, the MQ-9 Reaper circled like a bird of prey. The three Apache's locked on target. Command coordinated fire.

"Control MQ-9, Command. Start the music."

"Command, MQ-9 control. Four blast frags headed your way."

"November Sierra one, Command. Standby to fire." Jack counted down ten seconds. "Fire!"

"Command, November Sierra one. Twenty-four Thermobaric's on the way."

The Apache had locked on target and when November Sierra one fired, all three Apache helicopters launched eight Hellfire missiles with the press of one button. The teams had pulled back around the corners of other buildings. The facility erupted into a giant fireball. There would be no survivors. The impact of the missiles felt like a small tremor. Most of the fire died out in minutes. The teams converged to sift through what was left of the building.

"I don't think we will find anyone alive," Colonel Roberts said.

"Doubtful," JB replied. "Take your teams back to base for a quick debrief. It was a pleasure doing business with you Colonel."

"Likewise."

"Xin Cao," JB said. "Where is Li Na?"

"She said she had a hunch to follow," Xin Cao said. "She commandeered a sedan before we entered."

"What would she do that for?" JB asked.

"She said something about this was probably not all of the agents."

"Command, Fox Bravo one. Play back the video feed and count the number of agents that entered the building."

"Hold one moment. We count twelve, triple checked."

"That's means there are two MSS agents unaccounted for," JB said. "We need to find Li Na. Turn over scene to FBI so we can control it long enough to clean it up before the fire departments take over."

Darkness had become their best friend as the two MSS agents crept up to the door of the small facility. The connections here were not as fast as at the other targets but would be sufficient to upload the files and then, join with their fellow agents at Long Beach Port for a slow trip home. They were feeling good about the mission. So far there had been no mishaps, except being unable to reach Bingwan. They had shot the two lights out with their suppressed pistols that lighted the building. The closest homes to the site were over two hundred yards away. They were ecstatic about the lack of people. The access door was not far from the gate they had entered.

"Watch the gate area," the agent said. "I'll pick the lock. If it doesn't open, we'll blast our way in."

The second agent grunted, turning to face the gate. He realized too late they were not alone.

"Can I help you gentlemen?" Li Na asked in Mandarin.

The agent watching the gate turned rapidly, swinging his AK-47. It was too late. Using a one-hand grab, Li Na sliced outwardly to her right, the tip of the blade severing the man's right carotid artery. He dropped his gun as he fell backward, grasping his neck while blood spurted in rhythm to his heartbeat, spraying against the building. The man picking the lock had a look of horror on his face. He attempted to turn and stand, putting his hands in front of his face for protection. Li Na had instantly gripped the sword with two hands. Without loss of motion, it descended from above, severing both wrists, the hands dropping to the ground, while the blade continued to slice through the agent's neck, severing the head from the body. He crumpled against the door. She slung the blood from the blade and then, wiped the rest off on the man's clothing.

"Fox Bravo one, I am at facility six," Li Na said calmly. "I have two distorted packages.

"Fox Bravo one, Command. I am sending two Fox Bravo teams to location. An LA Sheriffs team is close by; they will be there in three. That gives full count of hostiles. Well done all. Return to base."

It was 0200 when the teams had returned and been debriefed. Everyone was tired and grabbed whatever spot they could to get some much-needed sleep, although it would be restless for many of them. They had done an admiral job; they had been lucky. But sometimes luck was the only avenue to success. After all everyone gets a break occasionally.

"Sirs," JB said. "Mission successful. All agents accounted for. Threat eliminated."

"The President is on with us JB," Phil said.

"We need you back here today," President Armstrong interrupted. "There remains an imminent threat. Bring Li Na"

"Understood sir," JB said.

A Gulfstream 400 pulled up nearby beginning to drown out his voice.

"That's your ride," Jonas said. "Get on immediately and bring your gear. Both of you."

"Yes sir," JB said. "Li Na, we need to go. Bring your gear."

"What's up?" she asked.

"I'll tell you on the way. Hurry."

Both trotted to the plane, the door was closed, and they taxied to the runway, receiving immediate clearance for takeoff. They were headed to a small airport outside of DC for a clandestine meeting with the President.

"Relax and enjoy the trip," the pilot said. "We will arrive at our destination in three and one-half hours.

"Where are we going?" Li Na asked.

"To a meeting for some unfinished business," JB replied.

"What unfinished business?" she asked.

"We will find out when we get there," JB said.

"Is this how you used to work?" Li Na asked.

"Yes," JB said. "Like a doctor on call, just not to the hospital."

She laughed at his comment.

"I love you," she said, as she kissed him and leaned her head against his shoulder, clasping his hand.

"I love you too," JB whispered, smelling her hair. "My love."

She smiled as she drifted to sleep. He sat wondering why he needed to meet with the president, his eyes growing heavy.

The two were awakened when the plane touched down onto a small rural airport. The runway lights were only on long enough to land and taxi to a small hangar. Li Na and JB disembarked to find a small army of no less than a dozen secret service agents surrounding it. Off the right, JB noticed Marine One. Further out on each side, there were multiple Suburban's with several secret service agents around each. There to greet them were Phil and Jonas.

"Hello; I'm pleased to meet you again Li Na," Phil said. "We would like to express our thanks to both of you for an excellent job. Thanks to you and your teams, the country is safe again."

"Why all the secrecy?" Li Na asked.

"Come this way," Jonas said. "We want you to meet someone."

Secret Service agents allowed them to pass. They were led through a small door into the hangar and toward the back where several more secret service agents stood around a table surrounded by six chairs, occupants in two of them, backs toward the group. Both men stood, turning to face them. Li Na recognized them instantly, gasping.

"You may leave us," President Armstrong said, the agents exiting the door the group had come through.

"JB my old friend," Bill said. "So nice to see you again and this must be your companion Li Na, shaking her hand. Please sit, all of you."

"It is an honor to meet you both," Vince said. "I am a great admirer of your work. Congratulations."

The President and Vice President looked at the two of them, staring into their face and eyes. Li Na could tell they were assessing her. She decided to break the silence.

"You are wondering if you can trust me Mr. President, Mr. Vice President," she said.

"Can we?" the President asked.

"I believe my record over the past few days speaks for itself, as well as the mission prior to that."

"My sentiments exactly," President Armstrong replied. "Please, we're on a first name basis. Call me Bill."

"If JB trusts you, the rest of us do," Vice President Reisner said. "Let me ask you a question," Bill said. "What punishment would you recommend as a judge to a traitor of the country that had caused thousands to die?"

"Death," JB and Li Na blurted in unison.

"Traitors cannot be allowed to live," JB said.

"Where I grew up," Li Na said. "We had a saying. Traitor to one, traitor to all."

"We have surmised the same," Phil said. "But we have a problem. A trial in the courts would bring undue attention to the country and given their liberal nature, justice would remain unserved."

"A surer way is needed," Jonas interrupted. "One that is swift and certain."

"I think I see where you are going," JB replied. "You have discovered the one or one's who started this fiasco and they need to be brought to justice to tie up loose ends as it were — physical excision."

"That is correct," Bill said. "I have people that can perform the task, but at the same time, I am unsure if we can trust them. We know we can trust you. We need you to implement and fulfill the mission."

"How much were they paid?" JB asked.

"Ten million dollars," Phil replied. "As of yesterday, 43,000 have died due to failure of the southeast grid. More will die and many more would have died if we had not prepared as we did."

"JB, we've known each other a long time," Jonas said. "The four of us took a vote and are asking for your help. We cannot let this loss of life go unanswered."

Li Na leaned over and whispered in her companion's ear. "This is our chance to make things right," she said. "No one else will do it. I'm in if you are?"

"Very well," JB said, looking the president and vice president. "We will perform the task. What do you need us to do?"

"Show them the folder," President Armstrong said.

Phil opened the folder and pushed it across to table. Inside were pictures of Congressman Blaine Childress and Clint Spicer. The congressman was well known; JB recognized him at once.

"Who is this other man?" JB asked.

"He is Clint Spicer," Phil said.

"An expert on the grid," Jonas replied. "From the intelligence we were able to gather, he identified the locations to sabotage, not only in the southeast, but also for the operation you just thwarted."

"Does it bother you that a congressman is involved?" Bill asked.

"I would be surprised if one wasn't," Li Na stated. "The entire world knows many of them are on the Chinese payroll."

"Not to worry," JB said. "We will remove him from office with permanency. It's the most efficient way."

"When do you want this done?" Li Na asked.

"Tonight," Bill said. "They are meeting at the Congressman's townhouse in Alexandria at 2200 to split the money and skip the country."

"The address is on the last page," Phil said. "We have a sedan waiting for you. It's been scrubbed with no vin numbers. Burn it when you're finished."

"Use your FPF credentials if you need for access," Jonas replied. "Notify us when you have completed the task."

"We're done here," Bill said. "Thank you again for saving the country. You and your teams deserve to be recognized. I'll make sure they are rewarded in some way; it just cannot be public."

You're welcome Mr. President," JB replied. "We understand sir."

"I would like to offer my congratulations again, as well," Vice President Reisner said. "I followed your operation with great nervousness and interest. Your reputation is well deserved. I hope you don't mind that we call on you again."

"Thank you, Mr. Vice President," JB replied. "Not at all."

The directors, Vice President and the President exited the front door. The sounds echoing from Marine One and the vehicles subsided within a couple of minutes. Walking out, the jet had also disappeared. Nearby was a small champagne-colored sedan; their gear sitting atop the trunk. The glow from the rising sun was just peaking the eastern horizon. Daylight quickly approaching, they needed to get away from the airport before anyone saw them. They donned Fedora hats; the brims would be used to hide their faces from cameras at intersections. Each time they passed through one they would tilt their heads slightly downward to obscure facial features. Crisscrossing a few rural roads, they soon made it to I-66 east, heading toward DC. About an hour later they merged onto the beltway heading south, passing through West Falls Church, Annandale, and North Springfield, and onto I-95 south. Exiting on Franconia Road, they bought some sandwiches and soda from a convenience store, surprised to find one open, and pulled into a parking lot at a park not far away.

"It's not the most scrumptious meal," JB said. "I promise to buy you a good one when we're done."

"Where should we go?" Li Na asked.

"I think Miami," JB replied. "We had a good time there before.

It won't be long before they'll call on us again."

Li Na pulled a blanket out of her gear bag and put it on the ground. They had some time, and she was in the mood. The day was pleasant, the warmth of the sunbathing their bodies. Having eaten, they lay close to each other, hugging and kissing like they were newlyweds. He knew his love for her would never die as he wrapped his arms around her, enjoying the feel of her body next to his. The two drifted off to sleep, awakened in late afternoon by a beeping car horn from a mother who was trying to round up her kids. Sitting up, they smiled at each other.

"I guess we better finish preparation," JB said.

"Yes, we better."

A video of the missile strike of the old Spruce Goose facility appeared on the Internet on a social media site. The NSA had been suspecting such a video was inevitable. Before anyone could access it, the video was scrubbed. Tracking down the IP address, NSA continued to block further uploads.

"Damn government," the man proclaimed. I'll find a way to upload this no matter what."

In a remote location near eastern Los Angeles, two CIA agents surveilled an RV trailer hooked to a pickup at the crest of a small hill. There was only one person inside. Confirming the location was where attempted uploads were coming from, the agents walked casually to the door. Knocking, the door swung open.

"What do you want," the man said, a cigarette in his mouth.

"We need your files," an agent responded. "It's a matter of national security."

"Oh, I see," the man replied. "You're with the government. Well, you can have them, over my dead body."

The second agent shot the man with a triple tap; twice in the chest twice and once in the head. The agents stepped inside;

on the table was laptop. Putting gloves on, one agent accessed and reformatted the hard drive.

"Looks like that is the only computer," the other agent said. "I'll check the pickup."

Satisfied there were no other devices, the agents set the trailer and pickup truck on fire leaving the scene, the flames growing larger behind them.

"It's taken care of sir," the agent spoke into his phone.

The morning news was chattering about the old Spruce Goose hangar going up in flames, citing a massive gas leak that caught the timbers on fire and burned it to the ground, the flame so hot it melted the metal sides and roof.

The two, two-man teams of CIA agents had been sitting in their cars for over twenty-four hours watching the congressman's townhome who had arrived about four hours earlier with his secret service agent remaining just inside the gate. A cell phone on the dash vibrated.

"Yes," agent Jones said.

"Is the congressman on site?" the voice asked.

"Yes," Jones replied. "He arrived a few hours ago."

"Very well," the voice said. "Pull off assignment. The operation is on hold until a later date.

"Yes sir," Jones replied, his comm broadcasting the call to the other team. "We're off sir."

President William Armstrong sat at his desk, staring at the phone.

"It's time," he said.

"Yes," Vince replied. "They cannot be allowed to get away with this.

President Hu Zemin," President Armstrong said. "You are fully aware of what you have done to my country. Did you receive the interrogation videos I sent you?

"Yes," Hu Zemin replied. "They are lies."

"You know full well they are not," the President said. "To date, we have over 100,000 dead thanks to your orders. For years criminal despots in this office have kissed China's ass. I will not."

"China is not intimidated by your empty words with no action," Hu Zemin replied. "If you act on us, you will start a war."

"Not true," President Armstrong replied. "Your entire economy will collapse. It is your country that will bear the brunt of the burden. Do you have the two locations I sent you?"

"Yes," Hu Zemin replied. "One is Beijing, the other is outside a small village in southeast China."

"Quite right," President Armstrong said. "Which do you choose?"

"For what?" Hu Zemin responded.

"To be destroyed," President Armstrong replied.

"You wouldn't dare," Hu Zemin blurted. "You don't have the guts."

"I won't do to you what you did to us," President Armstrong said. "I will not snuff out the lives of millions among the twenty-two million in Beijing. However, I will take out the second post that you will move into within a few months for further hacking of our country and our allies. Please watch your satellite feed of the post."

"General Burton," Vice President Reisner said. "Send down Blue."

About a minute later, the post exploded. A BLU-113 bunker buster missile, with a two-thousand-pound warhead was launched from an F-35 out of Taiwan. Twenty seconds later, a dozen Tomahawk cruise missiles struck the post to ensure complete destruction.

"You are asking for war," Hu Zemin blurted, red faced. "We are not going to stand for this."

"You knowingly crippled our grid!" President Armstrong

stated emphatically. "You're lucky this the milder action we have decided to pursue. If we find another hacking facility, it will meet the same fate."

An aide to President Hu Zemin whispered into his ear.

"I presume he is telling you about the three naval fleets off your coast in the South and East China Seas," President Armstrong said. "If you flinch, every cruise missile and ordinance they have, along with their jets will be launched into China against specific military targets. Along with the seven ballistic missile submarines that accompany these fleets, your country will lay in ruins. I suggest we have a serious discussion soon."

"Very well," Hu Zemin said. He knew he had little choice because he was facing an unpredictable enemy who was a warrior at heart. Armstrong would not go along to get along. "I will plan to visit the Whitehouse next week. Will that be satisfactory?"

"Yes," President Armstrong said. "Quite satisfactory. I look forward to meeting you."

"Do you think he will test your bluff?" Vince asked.

"I'm not bluffing," President Armstrong replied. "He knows that."

Finishing preparations, JB and Li Na studied satellite views of the address. It was a row of townhomes that looked much like the Brownstone type in Chicago. Certain that they knew the plan well they drove past the congressman's brick fenced townhome once. The car of the grid expert was in front on the street, almost adjacent to the next townhome. When they drove past, they noticed a secret service agent near the front gate. No doubt a pawn of the congressman. It was 2200; traffic in the neighborhood was sparse. Li Na parked the car just down from the gate, so it was not visible from the inside of the townhome. Affixing the silencer to the end of his 9 mm pistol was a conditioned habit along with putting on gloves; JB exited the vehicle and walked calmly past the gate. The agent was not at his post. He looked left and right before picking the lock and running to the shrubs surrounding the front door. Just as he reached them, the agent came out. His heart pounded while he squatted in the bushes, the agent walking by without noticing him. Back at his post, he peered out the gate. Seeing the car and a person in it, he stepped onto the sidewalk. Not realizing it, the agent had left the front door unlocked; JB strode with purpose through the doorway, greeted by waving shadows cast from candles sitting on tables throughout the foyer and living areas. Creeping down the short hallway, he found the congressman and Spicer sitting in two chairs, a duffle bag near each of them. They hadn't noticed him; he watched them for a moment, looking around the room.

"What are you going to do with your money?" Blaine asked.

"Buy some land in Belize and take it easy," Spicer replied. "I won't be coming back here. What about you?"

"I'll retire citing health reasons then head to southern Brazil where I have a few friends."

The deliberate scuff of his heel alerted them to his presence. They immediately wondered how much he had heard.

"Gentlemen," JB said. "I have been sent to collect you."

"Who are you?" Spicer asked.

"How did you get in?" Blaine asked.

"Neither question matters," JB said, turning the gun on Spicer shooting him with a rapid triple tap. He next turned the gun on the congressman.

"I know you," Blaine said. "You're a government spy; you're supposed to be dead."

"I keep hearing that today," JB replied.

Li Na was sitting behind the wheel when the agent stepped through the gate. Seeing her, he calmly walked toward the car, motioning to roll the window down so he could speak with her.

"You cannot park here Miss," the agent said.

"I'm just waiting for a friend," she replied. "She shouldn't be long."

He bent down so they would be face to face.

"I'm sorry but, . . ."

She thrust a tanto into the base of his throat, the ten-inch blade penetrating his entire neck. He grasped his throat with both hands, releasing one of them, struggling to draw his pistol before collapsing onto the asphalt. Li Na stepped out of the car, looked both ways, and drug the agent behind the gate close to the fence then, closed it and sat behind the wheel again. She looked cautiously around. The streetlights didn't cast their light far; the mature red maple trees bordering the sidewalk absorbing their beams. Panting from excitement of the kill, she patiently waited.

"You know, the director doesn't mind you making money on the side, he just prefers you didn't make it by selling secrets to the Chinese."

"Money makes the world go round," Blaine said. "I remember you now. You're the infamous Jackson Black. You wouldn't shoot a sitting congressman."

"That's right. I'm Jackson Black. Consider this a recall vote!"

Two bullets ripped into the congressman's chest followed by a bullet into each eye, the force knocking the chair onto its back. Jackson picked up his cartridge casings, making sure he had all seven then dialed the pre-assigned number.

"Excision complete."

Stuffing his pistol into his belt, he collected the two duffle bags, and closed and locked the door. Pulling the gate shut, he threw the bags into the back seat and climbed in on the passenger side. When he looked into Li Na's eyes, she put the sedan in gear. It slipped quietly and smoothly through the night, merging onto I-95 south, heading toward Miami. Jackson Black had returned.

ABOUT THE AUTHOR

James Tindall is the author of Jagged Grass, The Transparency, Sun God's Treasure, Alas Omega, and other books, including two best-in-field textbooks. He grew up on a Florida reservation wrestling alligators and training horses to earn money. He is a U.S. Army veteran who served in intelligence and is an expert in sharpshooting and hand-to-hand combat. He has five martial-arts black belts of advanced rank including a 9th degree in Kenpo, as well as four college degrees. As a federal scientist, he specialized in water, energy, and food security, engaging him in the areas of homeland and international security and counterterrorism. His assignments have taken him from Latin America to Brazil, Mexico to Alaska, Turkey to China, and many points between. When not writing, he consults and helps solve tactical and strategic problems for international governments and SOGs.